"A riveting, pulse-pounding story about family, love, and what happens when the end of the world turns out to be the beginning. I loved the fierce, funny, and fantastic Juniper sisters."

—Kathleen Glasgow, *New York Times* bestselling author of *Girl in Pieces*

"Tense and compulsively readable ... I won't be forgetting the Juniper sisters any time soon."

—Kara Thomas, author of *The Cheerleaders*

"ABAO: All bets are off in this intense, action-packed thriller. *Last Girls* is both a sister story with heart and a deep dive into doomsday prepper culture that will keep you up all night turning pages."

—Kelly deVos, author of *Day Zero*

"*Last Girls* is a harrowing view into a world where sisterly bonds are sealed in blood and doomsday is only a breath away. Demetra Brodsky's portrayal of three girls living on the fringes of society, learning to question authority, identity, and the definition of family, kept me riveted until the final page."

—Gillian French, Edgar Award–nominated author of *The Missing Season* and *The Lies They Tell*

"An impressive, immersive, addictive tale of a world that never ends—the beating heart of sisters, breathtaking and unstoppable."

—Emily Murdoch, author of *If You Find Me*

"The moment I picked up *Last Girls* I fell in love with the Juniper sisters. Full of twists, turns, and adventure, this action-packed tale of love, loyalty, and betrayal kept me on the edge of my seat until the very end, then left me wanting more."

—Suzanne Lazear, author of the Aether Chronicles

"This gripping thriller laced with dark family secrets had me tearing through the pages. . . . Prepare to stay up late reading this one!"   —Emmy Laybourne, internationally bestselling author of the Monument 14 trilogy

"Brodsky weaves a suspenseful tale reflective of the current political landscape, interwoven with Shakespearean subtext. . . . This is a story of survival and figuring out who to trust in a world where the characters have been taught to trust no one."
—*School Library Journal*

"[This] effective mix of mystery, romance, and strong, capable young women is a real page-turner and will send fans back to Brodsky's first novel, *Dive Smack*."   —*Booklist*

"A twisting, suspenseful YA thriller about sisterhood, survival, and family secrets set in the world of doomsday prepping."
—The Children's Book Council

Also by Demetra Brodsky

Dive Smack

LAST GIRLS

GIRLS

DEMETRA BRODSKY

A TOM DOHERTY ASSOCIATES BOOK

New York

LAST GIRLS

A Tor Teen Book
Published by Tom Doherty Associates
120 Broadway
New York, NY 10271

www.tor-forge.com

Tor® is a registered trademark of Macmillan Publishing Group, LLC.

The Library of Congress Cataloging-in-Publication Data is available upon request.

ISBN 978-1-250-25658-4 (trade paperback)
ISBN 978-1-250-76066-1 (ebook)

Our books may be purchased in bulk for promotional, educational, or business use. Please contact your local bookseller or the Macmillan Corporate and Premium Sales Department at 1-800-221-7945, extension 5442, or by email at MacmillanSpecialMarkets@macmillan.com.

First Edition: May 2020
First Trade Paperback Edition: May 2021

Printed in the United States of America

D 0 9 8 7 6 5 4 3 2

For Zoe and Ava.
Always stick together. No matter what.

Mother do you think they'll drop the bomb?

—PINK FLOYD

Dear Bucky,

We're moving again. To Washington State, where the average rainfall is forty-nine inches per year. It's strange, considering how much Mother hates the rain. During downpours or when it rains for days, even if it's just off and on, her mood is so melancholy she'll mope and keep us close until it lets up. You'd think we were made of something dissolvable in water. Not sugar, but maybe salt. I looked it up on the internet at school and I think she has something called SAD. Seasonal Affective Disorder. It doesn't need its long diagnosis because sad is exactly right. But this makes our fifth move in ten years. Not that I need to tell you that. You know. We'll be the new girls again. Yay! That was sarcastic, if you didn't figure it out. I hate being the new girls. I hate thinking maybe we'll fit in this time, even though I know we won't. I used to hope. But hope can't be trusted. Hope contradicts reality. That's why we prep. And since we've never met anyone else with fifty cans of soup or beans stored at their house, not to mention gallons upon gallons of water, I think this move might be the closest thing to hope we'll ever have. Do you think Mother wants us to take all the food we have in storage? Probably. Maybe we'll eat some of it straight from the cans on the road trip to the prepper compound. Did I mention that? That's why we're moving this time. Mother found a group who were looking to add a family with a nurse at their helm. She thinks being around like-minded people will help give us a sense of community. They call the group we're joining The Nest. That sounds cozy enough, I guess. They grow their own food and have farm animals, which Blue will love.

It'll be different than just stockpiling water and food. We'll learn how to hunt and defend ourselves against enemy invasion in the event of war, EMP, a viral pandemic . . . whatever. I don't know if you've been watching the news, but our president has his finger on the button of some scary stuff. I don't trust him. See, there's no hope. Anyway, Mother says it will be like camp. We'll learn how to survive in the woods, bake bread, can our own vegetables. She's trying to make it sound like this amazing adventure that will change our lives, but Birdie isn't buying into it. I think it's because she doesn't want to leave the boy she has a crush on in her geometry class. You know Birdie. There's always a boy du jour. Not me, though. None of the boys at this school seemed to like me. Not in a girlfriend way. I didn't see anybody worth liking, either, to be honest. And I'm not sure Blue even thinks about boys, so that's no worry. It doesn't matter. Birdie will come around.

We have each other, and that's what matters in the end. And we have you. You get to come with us. I have to go. Mother is calling for me to help clean out the garage. Stay tuned.

Love,

Honey

EVENTUALLY, WE ALL HAVE TO
LEAVE THE NEST.

⁎ ATL ⁎

ATTEMPT TO LOCATE

THE END IS DRAWING NEAR. Either my sister Birdie pulls her act together and finds her Every Day Carry, or we're leaving without it. She can deal with the consequences if today is the day the shit hits the fan. I shouldn't joke. You never know. But it's stupid, really, since Birdie is usually the one who's most prepared, at least physically. The prize for most prepared emotionally goes to our youngest sister, Blue. She's the one least likely to get flustered. A calm blue sea with hair to match, which is why it's unusual to see her in a flurry, tossing saggy, beige couch cushions aside and sliding heavy wooden furniture around to help Birdie search. Not me. I'm waiting with my arms crossed. If Birdie wants to fly out at night to meet Daniel Dobbs from The Burrow, she should have prepped her EDC before squeezing her bedraggled butt through the window and down the cucumber trellis last night.

It's funny how Blue is the most unflappable. When you think about it, logically, that trait should belong to Birdie based on her name. Are names logical? I don't know. Maybe Blue's, but not mine. Women spend their whole lives cringing whenever someone calls them *honey*. Not me. *No sirree.* Mother named me Honey at the outset, so I don't get to be offended. As the oldest, I don't get to be anything except Responsible,

Reactive, and Ready. The three big Rs. Even if that only means having a good comeback ready when necessary, which is more often than you'd think.

"Today will be the day she needs it," Blue says. She's prone to matter-of-fact statements. There isn't an aggressive bone in her body. She's just self-assured and has clear . . . opinions. Sure. Let's call them that.

I flick my eyes to them and sigh. "We have to go, Birdie. Blue and I have our bags. Just stick to the evacuation plan if needed. We got you."

Birdie blows a curtain of thick bangs away from eyes dark as a storm, deepened more at the moment by her annoyance with me. "*Seriously*, Honey? You're not even gonna attempt to help me attempt to locate my EDC? You heard Blue."

I heard her. And it's not that Blue's proclamations don't often come true. They do. Out of all us *weirds*, she's at the top. It's just the world as we know it hasn't ended in the ten years we've been preppers. Not when it was just us stockpiling food and water. And not in the year we've lived in The Nest.

I roll my own, less contemptuous brown eyes at Birdie and walk out. Blue is right in a way, and so is Birdie. Preparedness is the root of prepping. But I'll bet my favorite Gerber folding knife, dollars to doughnuts, my sister left her EDC outside last night. Love makes you do stupid things. Not that I'd know. God forbid I have time for a boyfriend. Even if I did, none of the Burrow Boys appeals to me, and Outsiders are off-limits. For me, it's a zero-sum game.

I hear Birdie grumble, "Typical," as I walk to the kitchen and it puts a hitch in my step. As long as they're following me, it doesn't matter. I wait one second, two . . . expecting them to walk through the doorway and grab their lunches from the table.

Guess not.

Mother glances up from the self-inflicted palm wound she's treating with homemade antibiotics, concocted in our kitchen from bread mold left to grow in the large bay window. The plants filling the same space provide necessary humidity for the process, turning that windowsill into Mother's makeshift laboratory. Complete with microscope and glass beakers. A mix of aluminum and copper pots hang above her head from an oval rack, and bundles of drying herbs are hanging from the wooden rafters. Some of the pots in this kitchen are used for cooking, others for her medicinal experiments. We've had to learn which is which.

Typical.

Sure, Birdie. That's us Junipers in a nutshell.

"You could be more patient." Mother's expression is serious, despite the youthful brown freckles covering her face, including her thinning lips. "You remember when you were a junior, all the things you had to worry about: SATs, driving, piled on top of threats of global warming, economic collapse, a possible viral flu pandemic. You never know how long you girls will have with each other. None of us do. You could be the last girls on this compound. All we can do is prepare, not predict."

Prom and nuclear war, final exams and EMPs, college ideations and bug-outs: Mother loves to throw prepper worries into the mix of things that *are* typical to most high schoolers. Most, but not all. There are other kids like us in The Nest and The Burrow. Girls to the left. Boys to the right. That setup is another story.

"I was hoping we'd get to school early enough for me to work on my self . . . by myself, on a lab assignment for chemistry," I correct my mistake mid-telling. "No worries, though. I have an idea where Birdie's EDC might be."

I turn to head outside and she calls me back. Her voice a butter knife scraping burnt toast until she clears her throat.

"I wasn't aware you had an added interest in chemistry."

Mother takes a glass dropper and lets three fat blobs of a yellow tincture fall onto a petri dish.

I didn't say that. Not exactly. Mother hears what she wants.

Through a filter of her own interests, which are not always the same as mine.

"The chemical reactions are cool," I offer, watching her work at the heavy kitchen farm table.

Chemistry is great. Don't get me wrong. I'm good at it. One of the best in my class, but I wouldn't call my interest *added*. It was just the first thing that popped into my head when I stopped myself from saying I was working on a *self-portrait*. Prepping comes first. Always. The rest—art, literature, music—is extra. Frivolity. According to Mother. The work of dilettantes. On that viewpoint, we'll have to agree to disagree. I'll prep. I'll plan. Hell, I'll show every Nest Girl and Burrow Boy on this compound I can be ready in a flash, just as quick as any one of them if not quicker, on any given day. But if the world does end tomorrow and we have to rebuild society, wouldn't we want the arts to be part of that again? I would. I think there's room for both.

That's my real added interest. Society without culture might as well be dead. An extreme position, I know. What can I say? I'm a doomsday-prepping enigma.

Thankfully, I'm not alone.

A knock on the screen door's wooden frame grabs our attention. Mother stands and waves Ansel Ackerman inside.

Most of the guys in The Burrow wear some version of the same uniform, so to speak. Cargos, crewnecks, button-down flannels. Ansel is wearing a monochromatic version today. A human licorice stick in black cargos, black bomber jacket, black boots. I don't mean that in a tasty way.

"Hey, Honey. Guess I'm not the only one running late today."

"We should blame traffic," I tell him.

Ansel blinks his extra-long lashes before realizing that's a joke. There's no traffic on these rural roads. Being late would be entirely our fault. Birdie's fault, in my case.

"I have everything ready for you," Mother says, handing

Ansel jars of homemade tinctures and the sack of veggies she pulled from the garden.

"Thanks," he says, but won't look at her.

The leader of the compound's son has been sheepish around her lately. I understand why, but haven't had the nerve to say anything to her or him yet. I hold the screen door open for him and he says, "See you among the sheeple."

"Different day, same herd. Baa!"

He grins again, only that's not a joke. Most Outsiders do live like herded sheep. Grossly unprepared for any number of impending threats that could cause The End Of The World As We Know It.

We're preparing for TEOTWAWKI by homesteading. Ansel comes to our house every third Wednesday to pick up medicine, eggs, vegetables, or goat's milk, alternating pickups from the other all-female households that make up The Nest. The Burrow, where he lives, is in charge of all things tactical. Artillery, weapons, ammunition, explosives. Things to ensure operational security in the event of an EMP that wipes out all power or a nuclear attack. We all train together in weapons usage, hand-to-hand combat, and survival skills under the radar of our casual acquaintances. On a day-to-day basis, I think The Nest is the more important garrison. We all have to eat and take medicine whether the world is ending or not.

I head outside while Mother's back is turned and walk around the side of our cedar-shingled house before she regroups and prods me again about my chemistry project at school.

Birdie's Every Day Carry is exactly where I suspected. Perched on the low-shingled roof outside our bedroom, where we sit to stargaze whenever we need a few minutes to chill and pretend we're just like everyone else. Well, I do most of that kind of daydreaming with Blue, really. Birdie embraces being different, most of the time. But in those off instances when she doesn't, when she's tired and had enough, I have to watch her or she'll get into it with Mother, and we'll all pay for Birdie mouthing off. Prevention is the best safeguard for conflict. I guess that's a form of prepping, too.

I whistle long and low with a sharp uptick at the end, so my sisters know to come find me. The flash of Blue's cobalt hair enters my peripheral vision as they round the corner and I point at the roof.

"Oh." That's all Birdie says. Her version of *sorry I acted like a crazy person.*

Blue laughs in her husky-voiced way. She's sounded like an old woman that smokes three packs a day since she could first speak. The voice of someone who's seen more than her years.

"You snuck out *again* and left *that,* of all things, *there?*"

"Shhhh." The hush comes from Birdie and me simultaneously.

"Do you want to spend a night in the bunker?" I ask.

Blue shakes her head. She hates being down there the most.

"Well," I tell Birdie. "Go get it. Hurry up."

Fly, Birdie.

She ties her buffalo-plaid shirt around her waist and climbs the same trellis she used to get herself into this predicament. The red-and-black cuffs on her shirt are fraying, the seat of her black jeans wearing thin. Not that Birdie cares. She'll slap a patch on them and move on. I love that about her, annoying as she is at the moment. I've always been the one who cares too much what the mall rats at school say about my sisters' clothes.

Blue is just starting to notice. It doesn't matter as much because she's sophomore-cute in everything. A genius with needle and thread who embroiders most of her clothes by hand when she's not working on elaborately stitched portraits of the three of us. She only uses floss in every shade of blue imaginable. True to her name. Today, along the collar of her plain white T-shirt, she stitched the words YOU DON'T GET TO TELL ME WHAT TO DO in bright cerulean thread. Blue's a passive but funny badass who literally wears her heart on her sleeve, or collar, or the back of her coat. Wherever the needle fits.

Five minutes later, Birdie lands with a soft thud in the grass, oiled canvas bag secure on her back, and a sly grin replacing her scowl.

"We're good. Let's roll."

She's good. Her lack of forethought means I missed the opportunity to give my self-portrait necessary eyes. They're always the hardest for me to paint. You can read a ton in a person's eyes and having to say something about my own has been tripping me up. Some days, when I look in the mirror, I see my fears written all over my face. Like someone took my normal expression and turned it into a crumpled bag full of fear that something will happen to my sisters if I'm not watching. Fear that one day we'll be separated. Fear that the world will end without warning and all the prepping and training we've done won't matter. My eyes are haunted, accented with shadowy crescents. On other days, I'll gaze at myself in the mirror and see none of those things. Staring back at me is the girl I believe I am. Strong. Capable. Protective. One of a kind.

Blue calls shotgun before we slide into the ancient station wagon Mother argues is vintage. It's the only car we've ever had. I'm glad Birdie is sitting in the back today. Lately, when I've gotten mad at her for not being considerate of anyone's time but her own, I've let my mouth say things I don't mean before my brain catches up. I hate myself when that happens, because any day could be the one that changes everything. Today is as good a day as any.

A musky smell wafts over to me when I start the engine. The vanilla, tree-shaped air freshener hanging from the rearview mirror isn't covering the stench of goat fur rising off Blue's clothes.

"Did you lay down with the goats when you milked them this morning?"

She shrugs one shoulder. "If I don't, who will?"

"They're not pets, Blue. Especially the buck. Someday we may have to eat them."

"Goat jerky for everyone," Birdie chirps from the back.

I flick hawkish eyes to the rearview. It would be a last resort, but she's not helping.

"They're pets to me," Blue says. "I'd rather die than eat them."

"Don't say that."

"Well, if Mother would let us have a dog, maybe I wouldn't need to play with the goats as much."

"You have Achilles. He's better than any dog."

"I still want one. Golden with a black muzzle. I'd name him Banjo."

Mother claims she's allergic to cats and dogs. She can't be near the rabbits, either, even though we breed them for meat. But Achilles is a peregrine falcon. Birdie found him in the woods while she and Mother were hunting, his foot all tangled up in fishing line one of the Burrow Boys left near the lake. She brought him home, even though he was scared and bit Birdie's hand so deep she needed five stitches. Blue offered to take over his care while her stitches healed, and once Blue and Achilles bonded it was bye-bye Birdie.

He has one lame claw, but that doesn't stop him from doing anything. He just favors his left talons. Everyone else in our coalition is cautious of Achilles, just because of the one time he scared Tashi Garcia's little brother Tito so bad he peed his pants. If you ask me, Tito had it coming. That's what he gets for trying to take the pheasant Achy caught himself for dinner. Believe me, there are days after training where I'm hungry enough to make any boy dumb enough to try and take my supper pee his pants too. Fair is fair.

The best thing about Achilles, though, is he'll do the killing Blue won't. That and the little leather hood he wears. You have to see it to believe it. The goats are cool, and the does are ridiculously cute, but my sister really does have the most kick-ass pet in The Nest. Maybe the state.

It's too late to have her change, so I toss her the hand sanitizer we keep in the wagon's ashtray. "Open your window and air yourself out."

I look at Birdie one more time and see her rummaging through her EDC. I hope she's making sure she has everything she needs because there's no way I'm turning around.

I charge down the dirt road to the main, kicking up dust like the riffraff everybody at school imagines we are. In a couple of miles we pass Tashi Garcia's house, followed by Camilla Clarke's, then Annalise Ackerman's, and all the other Nest households. We turn left, away from the road that leads to The Burrow. I spy Birdie staring longingly in hopes of seeing Daniel Dobbs. The lovestruck subordinate dressed in thrift store fatigues from the local AMVETS that's become my sister's *soul* focus. That's not a misnomer.

At school we'll go our separate ways, to classes in different parts of the building, passing each other in the hallways here and there. But I know where my sisters are at all times. I know every exit, entrance, and access point to the school. And so do they. Sometimes, one or more Nesters or Burrowers pull out ahead or behind us and we'll drive to school like a caravan of outcasts. Ripe for being ostracized by people who think the brands of makeup or clothing they wear are their biggest obstacle to survival. For them, they probably are. Surviving high school is as far and wide into the future as they can think. Not that it matters. Today is a good mirror day.

We can handle them. My sisters and I can handle anything.

✦ EDC ✦

EVERY DAY CARRY

THE CHEMISTRY EXPERIMENT in Mr. Whitlock's class today is simple. Fill three balloons. One with hydrogen, one with oxygen, and one with seventy-five percent hydrogen and twenty-five percent oxygen, to see which will cause the biggest explosion when lit with an extra-long torch.

I already know the answer. We have hydrogen and oxygen tanks stored at home for bunker air quality and fuel cells. I have an A in this class, but it'll still be fun to end the experiment with a bang.

Mother would be so pleased.

Our teacher always has us work with a lab partner, and this time Mr. Whitlock stuck me with Shawna Mooney, effervescent president and founder of Elkwood High School's Baking Club. I do a threat assessment of her in fifteen seconds.

THREAT ASSESSMENT:

SHAWNA APRIL MOONEY | 5′6″ **WEAK TO AVERAGE BUILD** | **OPEN SOCIAL GROUP** | **TRUSTING**

MOST LIKELY TO: cry in nurse's office over unworthy boy who didn't like her cupcakes.

LEAST LIKELY TO: hit that popularity status she's striving for with the same said cupcakes.

9/10 WOULD IMPEDE GROUP SURVIVAL IN EMERGENCY
SITUATION.

CASUALTY POTENTIAL: high

"Can you light them?" Shawna asks. "The only thing I've
ever torched is crème brûlée. This seems more like *your* thing."

My *thing*.

I guess Shawna's made an assessment of her own.

"Sure. I do like to blow things up, shoot them, nail them
to a tree trunk with an arrow, then field dress them for dinner over an open fire. Maybe I can bring you some goat's milk
from our mini farm. You can show me how to make crème
brûlée from fresh goat's cream, and I can teach you how to
stop acting like lighting a balloon on fire with a three-foot-long
torch is an assault on your feminine sensibilities."

"Geez, Honey, you could try being as sweet as your name
once in a while."

Shawna pulls her copper-red hair to the front on both sides,
like having it close is a comfort to her.

Hair pulled up and away from an open flame in a chem lab
is what's a comfort to me.

"Shawna, did you know bees make honey for survival?
They store it in their honey bellies for the winter. When we
try to steal it from them, they see us as marauders and sting
us. People discovered honey was sweet and disrupted the social order of bees for personal gain, using smoke like a drug to
calm them down. There's nothing sweet about that."

Shawna's jaw drops, just enough to make it clear she's out
of comebacks.

"'If I be waspish, best beware my sting,'" I whisper softly.

A random snicker makes me turn my head to see who was
listening. Rémy Lamar. Of course. He's working at the lab
table behind us, clearly eating up this exchange. He smirks
when our eyes meet and the misplaced dimple in his brown
upper cheek throws me off my game for a second.

Ignore the obvious threat.

Disengage.

I roll my eyes at him right as Mr. Whitlock shows up to light the torch I'm holding like a javelin.

You have no idea how many times in the last few weeks I've written a letter to Bucky, asking what to do about the attention I've been getting from Rémy Lamar. But Bucky Beaverman is just our imaginary friend from childhood, so the answers actually come from inside me. Still, it's good to get it out on paper. *Dear Bucky* is a lot less odd than *Dear Diary*. We all have our separate ways of coping. Birdie uses him in the comic strip she draws. Blue turned him into a furry creature she stitches into her needlework like a signature. The only one who doesn't remember our obsession with him is Mother. She insists he didn't exist, even as a figment of our imaginations. We all think that's a strange and unnecessary stance. I mean, what's the harm?

"Is it true, Mr. Whitlock?" Shawna asks. Whines, actually. "What Honey said about the bees?"

He blinks blue eyes twice, three times, four, like he's flipping through index cards in his brain for facts. "I teach chemistry and biology, Miss Mooney. And although I have no doubt Miss Juniper knows a thing or two about bees, the fact is after the female honey bee stings it dies. They have to be careful who they choose as a viable threat if they want to survive long-term."

He lights my torch with a quick nod before moving to the next table.

"Ouch. Roasted by Mr. Whitlock?" Rémy says. "That had to—*sting*—a little."

Shawna giggles, of course. And it *is* funny, if I'm being honest. But when I glance Rémy's way, I make sure my eyes and thoughts are aflame to dissuade him.

THREAT ASSESSMENT:

RÉMY LAMAR | 5'11" AVERAGE–STRONG BUILD |

CLOSED SOCIAL GROUP | TRUSTING

MOST LIKELY TO: marry a ridiculous trophy wife.
LEAST LIKELY TO: seduce me with his charms during art class.
7/10 WOULD IMPEDE GROUP SURVIVAL IN EMERGENCY SITUATION.
CASUALTY POTENTIAL: medium

Mr. Whitlock interrupts my mental evaluation by announcing we'll need to use ear protection for the experiment. I like Mr. Whitlock and I think he likes having me as a student. Was he roasting me? I don't know. He's young and new this year. I know a lot about what it's like to be new at a school. I doubt the initial feeling of uncertainty changes whether you're a student or a teacher. I think he was just making a point.

I pick up the rigid earmuffs while Mr. Whitlock instructs us to proceed balloon by balloon, starting with oxygen and making notes along the way.

"I wish I could just use my Beats," Rémy says. I don't know what that means, but I think he's talking to his lab partner, so I ignore him again.

"You're on notes, then," I tell Shawna.

She nods and we secure our earmuffs. Shawna probably wasn't trying to be a jerk before. I just read her comment that way. I do that sometimes. Maybe too much, like it's part of my ingrained survival instincts. The *Reaction* part of the three Rs.

I can't get the earmuffs to rest flat on my head because my messy bun is getting in the way. I have to push the big topknot out of position to get the earmuffs fully secure.

Messy bun. My big effort for fitting in with the Outsiders today. That and a gray lace-trimmed tank top, fully exposed. We can't wear loose clothing during labs, so I had to ditch my oversized burgundy cardigan. Let it be known that just because I wear loose clothes and Doc Martens doesn't mean I sport underwear made for grannies.

I *can* make an entire dinner start to finish from what's

growing or living in our backyard. I think that's something grandmothers used to do. Maybe they still do. I wouldn't know. I don't have any.

I hear Mr. Whitlock say, "Fire when ready."

These earmuffs are NRR 26 dB, meaning I can hear seventy-four percent of all sound.

"You ready?" I ask Shawna.

She nods again and fiddles with her gold, heart-shaped pendant as I inch the lighted torch toward the droopy red oxygen-filled balloon. When the flame makes contact with the latex, it pops like a tiny pistol firing. Easy. And oddly satisfying.

Balloons are popping all around us, followed by gasps and *ahhs*. Shawna and I remove our earmuffs at the same time as Mr. Whitlock, following his lead. He explains oxygen is denser than hydrogen and asks if we think the hydrogen-filled balloon will make a bigger or smaller explosion.

I know the answer, but I'm much more inclined to pop the fully erect hydrogen-filled balloon and let it speak for itself. Everybody puts their earmuffs back in place before giving the next balloon a go. I wait for Shawna to finish jotting down notes before bringing the torch into contact with the swaying white balloon. It pops at least twenty times louder than the oxygen-filled balloon. Flames burst into the air with a whoosh above our heads and dissipate quickly, making Shawna's green eyes pop in shock. I, on the other hand, love it.

This time, when Mr. Whitlock asks about the chemical reaction, I decide to answer. "The hydrogen in the balloons is reacting with the air we breathe. When we add heat into the mix, it makes water, only the reaction is happening so fast it causes a small explosion."

A+ assessment if I do say so myself. My lab partner is going to freak when we get to the combo hydrogen-and-oxygen-filled balloon.

"Correct," Mr. Whitlock says. "Now let's see what happens when you combine oxygen and hydrogen."

Yes. Let's. I start to put my earmuffs on but hesitate when Mr. Whitlock pumps his hand like he's dribbling an invisible ball. A similar explosion reaches us from another class. Then pop, pop, pop. I wasn't aware there was another chemistry class doing this experiment at the same time. It sounds like the Fourth of July. What I don't get is why our teacher looks so stricken.

My answer comes from an unexpected buzz blasted over the loudspeaker that startles everyone in the room.

Principal Weaver's strident voice. "This is not a drill. I repeat, this is not a drill. Follow full lockdown protocols. Authorities are on the way."

Mr. Whitlock rushes to the classroom door and locks it. He peeks out the rectangular window before pulling the shade and moving to the bigger windows on the opposite side of the classroom, doing the same.

Reactive.

In under ten seconds, everything clicks into place. Those pops weren't balloons. This is the real deal. I get my own butt in gear.

"What's going on?" someone asks.

"Were those *gunshots?*" another student inquires.

Fireworks and popping gas-filled balloons can both sound like gunfire. I don't have time to wonder who's asking questions because I'm already digging through my EDC for my flashlight and multi-tool. Calmly. Steadily. Reactive *and* Ready. Following my training, even though my head is playing out active-shooter scenarios.

I remind myself I have one objective. Meet Birdie and Blue in the room most equidistant for fifth period. I can't let my fear slow me down. I tune out the classroom panic and chatter to think. Birdie will be in PE and Blue is in geometry, which means our meet-up point is in the northeast stairwell that connects the academic buildings to the gymnasium. Getting there will take me ten minutes tops overhead.

I slide into my bulletproof vest, sling my EDC onto one shoulder, and place a metal stool on the lab table before climbing up beside it. The expression dotting the faces of my classmates is one of abject horror.

In a split second, I understand they're afraid of me. They think I'm part of whatever is happening outside of this room, like it was planned. People are ducking under lab tables, cowering, hiding behind each other. Even Mr. Whitlock is holding up his hands like I might reach for a gun and start shooting.

"Whatever you're thinking, Honey, don't do it." Mr. Whitlock's tone is pleading. "You can talk to me. Let me be your confidant."

What in the ever-loving hell?

I read his thoughts about me all wrong. The shitty thing is, I've never been anything but cooperative in this class, in any class. I'm on merit roll, for god's sake.

I climb onto the aluminum stool and start unscrewing the chipped and peeling ventilation shaft cover halfway up the wall with my multi-tool.

"Honey!"

I glance at Mr. Whitlock over my shoulder and keep turning out screws. He makes a motion to grab me but thinks better of it and reaches for his cellphone. He knows it's against school rules to touch students, which gives me a necessary advantage.

"I'm sorry, Mr. Whitlock. This isn't about me, or you, or anyone. I just have to find my sisters. I know what I'm doing." I hesitate for a second and offer my best advice. "I don't care what protocol is for this school. Don't stay in this room. It's harder for someone to hit a moving target. Get everyone out of here and make sure they run and weave."

I keep my eyes trained on our teacher as I sling my EDC into the air shaft. My gaze shifts ever so slightly, and I see my lab partner go completely cross-eyed behind him a split second before she stone-cold passes out and crumbles to the floor.

THREAT ASSESSMENT CORRECTION:
SHAWNA MOONEY
10/10 WOULD IMPEDE GROUP SURVIVAL IN EMERGENCY
SITUATION.

Mr. Whitlock mutters, "Christ," under his breath and goes
to see if she's okay.

And then, I do the dumbest thing. I hesitate and look for
Rémy Lamar. I don't know why. I don't care what he thinks.
But I do care that he's watching me through the lens of his
camera like I'm a sight to be recorded, for personal entertain-
ment not posterity. Photos are forever once they make it on-
line and I'm not allowed that level of exposure. Thank god
Mr. Whitlock collects cellphones at the start of every class or
I'd already be all over the internet.

I hold a hand up in front of his lens. "Don't. This isn't what
they think."

He lowers the camera and I pull myself into the ventilation
shaft, sliding onto my belly.

"Honey, stop! Miss Juniper. It's not safe," Mr. Whitlock
calls after me, his unvarnished voice dulled by the building
material separating us. As if his usual politeness can keep me
from following my own protocol.

A few seconds later I hear him say, "Mr. Lamar, get down.
Don't even think about following her," and he isn't as nice
about it with Rémy.

Rémy trying to come after me is shocking. Mostly because
I didn't think he had it in him to go against the rules. But
there's no time to contemplate his reasoning now. Rémy Lamar
is not one of us.

I cough and try not to inhale too deeply. The square, aluminum shaft is clothes-dryer hot and stuffy and filled with clots
of gray dust and insects both dead and alive. Spiders. Flies.
There's only six inches of space around me for wiggle room
as I push my EDC forward and army-crawl toward the first

visible opening. Students in the classrooms below me lift terrified eyes to the ceiling as I pass. I know they can't see me— Honey Juniper, *that weird chick with the Sarah Connor vibe*—and I can't stop to assuage the sobbing and assure them I'm not the threat. That I'm not any threat during daily life as we know it to anyone but myself. A few more pops and minor explosions reach me. I scooch fast as possible over more and more classrooms, trying to avoid banging the metal shaft like a drum. I don't want to draw more attention to myself.

Thick gray clots of accumulated dust are tucked against the sides of the passage, along with the black pellet droppings left by clever mice that figured out a way to remain out of sight. I'd rather be a mouse than a rat. Different connotation.

The air shaft turns sharp right. I have to wriggle my body so I'm three-quarters sideways to make the turn before I can roll onto my stomach. I reach forward to break a spider's web spun corner to corner, artfully woven to catch anything that flies unwittingly into its path, including me. My left knee snags on an uneven seam where two sections of sheet metal meet and the razor sharp edge tears through the fabric of my thin, stretchy jeans. A searing sting zips from my nerve endings to my brain without delay and I bite down hard on my bottom lip to avoid letting profanities fly. You can tell just by the pain sometimes what's gone too deep and will bleed. Add this gash to the list of scars and scrapes I've gotten while training for doomsday over the past year.

I remind myself this isn't an exercise and to get moving. It doesn't feel like an extinction-level event on a global scale, either, but that doesn't mean lives aren't on the line, including Birdie's or Blue's.

TOBYISMS FOR ACTION
1
CHANGE YOUR LIFE

MY CANISTER OF spray paint is mocking me tonight. Hissing and hushing like it's trying to silence my thoughts and actions all the way up until the last particles discharge from the nozzle with my signature. I step backward and let the sharp smell of acetone and liquefied petroleum gas dissipate, but the chemical cloud hangs tight in the air around me. I snap a quick photo with my phone. One and done. There's no extra time to admire my work. I have to flee the scene or risk getting caught. I'll drive by tomorrow to inspect it in daylight. Jonesy says most criminals return to the scene of their crime. It's one of the reasons we've never moved. That said, will my return make me an artist, a criminal, or just someone interested in pointing out the truth?

Maybe all of the above.

I sneak into our house around two A.M. and find my mom asleep in front of the late-night news with our dog at her feet. The television is sending flickering rays across her face, illuminating the open spaces between her thick swatches of dark wavy hair. I catch the glint of her tiny nose ring. Here she is, ladies and gentlemen, the most hip and tragic forty-five-year-old woman you'll ever meet. Strangely, she looks more like me when her hair is wild like this, a little dirty and in need of washing, or maybe I look more like her. She once held my face between her hands, scrutinizing me, before calling it raw grunge meets feminine. The description wasn't meant as an insult. My mom sees everyone and everything through an artistic eye. That's the one intangible thing she'll never lose.

I leave my backpack on a kitchen chair and glance around for hints of what she's been up to while I was gone. There's no sign of Special Agent Blake Jones having made his presence known tonight, just page after page of charcoal drawings laid side by side. The gigantic rectangular bowels of whatever dystopian creature inhabited the world inside her head. Her three-point perspective is masterful. I couldn't do it. I'm a street artist and don't have her chops or her training, but that's not the point. The point is the walls in her art studio are covered with obsessive drawings. There's not an inch of bare wall space left in the room. For a while I was worried she might paper over the windows and block out all signs of life in there. Not unlike the post-apocalyptic subject matter she's been drawing for the past year.

That's the one room in our house Jonesy hasn't seen in the five years they've been dating. Mom calls her studio off-limits, but it's more like off the wall. I wonder what he'd make of her overlapping scenes of military personnel, mass destruction, and strange, eradicated landscapes. Maybe nothing at all, since they're in alignment with the threat of nuclear attacks being spewed on television for all to see by the current POTUS *that struts and frets his hour upon the stage.* The fact that he's actually in office is often harder to accept than the potential nightmares we can all see brewing, *told by an idiot full of sound and fury. Signifying nothing.*

Thank you, Macbeth. I couldn't have said it better myself.

Mom's artwork these days is nothing like the colorful, Shakespeare-inspired paintings that once paid our bills and got her into galleries in New York, Los Angeles, London, scor-

ing her interviews with prestigious art reviewers. I doubt it
ever will again. That work was inspired by how she imagined
her children might look when grown, playing out Shakespearean scenes in today's modern but equally tragic and laughable
world. At least, that's what she said during old interviews when
she was Evie Ellis, rising artist. She hasn't made a sale in years
yet still persists like a woman possessed. Searching for the
same truth through her art as me.

The aluminum take-out tray I brought home from Nikko's, where I work double shifts to help pay the monthly bills,
sits untouched on the TV tray next to the couch. Moussaka
is her favorite. She must have been in a hard trance tonight if
she didn't touch a bite. One of her arms hangs over the edge
of the couch. Smudged like a coal miner's, her fingers are covered to the second knuckle with charcoal dust, like she went
digging for something that will explain how her life became
upended, but failed and was too tired to wash away the effort.
Today must have been a bad-memory day.

I study my own spray-paint-saturated forefinger and puff
out a breath of awareness through my nose. We're not so different on the inside, either, she and I.

"I should have stayed home," she murmurs in her sleep.

That's true.

"Toby should have stayed home, too."

Also true. I'm no doctor to Lady Macbeth, but he nailed
it when he said, *Infected minds to their deaf pillow will discharge
their secrets.*

I let her sleep, let her admit our guilty truth in her dreams,
while I head to the kitchen. I pull out my phone and review
my photo of the message I threw up on a wall across from the
police station. Location is everything. Call it vandalism if you
like. I don't care. You deal with your shit your way and I'll deal
with mine.

The message is loud and clear for all parties involved.
YOU NEED TO CHANGE YOUR LIFE. I use stencils that

I make at home with an X-Acto knife. Occasionally, I'll echo something my mom drew and cut that into the mix, especially when she draws badass teenage girls. I tag everything with the nickname I had as a kid and put it up using this extended Pig-pen cipher my best friend Sebastian and I learned when we were seven. If Jonesy isn't a good enough detective to figure out who's tagging the buildings around the police station, I can't help him any more than he's been able to help us.

My phone pings with a text from Bash, giving me props on the work I did tonight—a girl in a bulletproof vest pointing a rifle at the viewer with the message coming through the barrel. He must have seen it on his way home from his job at The Chicken Coop. This piece is definitely one of my favorites. I appreciate his praise. But whenever I return from tagging a building, deep-rooted feelings churn my gut for a few hours, and I don't want to talk to anyone. Not even Bash. My mom is the same way, switching between wanting complete solitude and needing company, depending on her mood. Bash accepts this about me and doesn't take offense. Good thing, because otherwise I wouldn't have any friends. I grab a soda from the fridge, take the moussaka Mom didn't eat for myself, and open my laptop. It's not the first time I've poached her uneaten dinner and I'm sure it won't be the last.

My phone pings again.

Are you working the dinner shift tomorrow night? Wanna meet up and trade?

Bash means trade dinners. Free food is a perk of working at a restaurant. Sometimes we trade, my Greek for his gourmet fried chicken. This might be hard to believe, but you *can* get sick of eating either one of those things if you eat it often enough. Bash gets sick of his faster than me because Nikko's has a broader menu selection. Right now, I have a different choice to make. I can keep ignoring him and get aggravated by the next series of pings, or answer quickly. A therapist once told me childhood amnesia stops at age seven. Every memory prior is blank. Everything after is up for total recall. Lucky me. Bash has been my best friend since third grade. He's been through everything with me that matters. I don't know what I'd do without him.

I type, *Yeah. OK,* on the food trading thing and wait for his response.

Cool. Cool. Get me the deluxe gyro plate if your douchey manager with the signet ring doesn't object.

That makes me laugh. Stavros isn't a douche. He just keeps a close eye on profit margins and doesn't allow our friends to loiter. He likes me because I'm Greek and pronounce the menu items correctly. Like *year-oh* with a rolled R, the way it's supposed to sound. Not *gyro*, like *gyroscope*, or *hero*, even though the pita-wrapped sandwich is our bestseller and worthy of a gold medal.

The animated dots tell me Bash is typing. I turn off my phone and do the same thing I do most nights, contemplate whether or not to look for my sisters. I always come to the same conclusion, and within seconds I'm searching for pictures of Cassandra online. Because not only do I like to spray-paint graffiti on brick walls, I like to bang my head against them, too.

✠ ASAP ✠

AS SOON AS POSSIBLE

I STOP DEAD in the air shaft when I pick up a metallic thump-thump-thump heading straight for me. For a second, I think it's my own echo, only it keeps clanging. There's no way it's the scurry of a rodent or anything smaller than me because the steady movement is too loud. My heart matches the beat as I wait for who or whatever is responsible for the noise to materialize. Someone escaping the situation just like me, preferably from my own coalition. But if it's not, I have a simple you-got-busted plan ready. Play dumb and fearful of whatever situation is taking place.

I just got scared, Principal Weaver.

I wanted to be with my sisters. We're very close and my mother told me watching out for them has to be my top priority.

I suppose that's more of a plea than a plan.

Truthfully, I *am* scared for my sisters' safety, because that *did* sound like gunfire. And we are very close.

The thumping grows quieter, moving away from me. I keep crawling forward. I've lost thirty seconds or more. Less than a full minute, but that amount of time moves like pond water when you're on your belly in a steamy air shaft waiting to find out what's going on.

I exhale when I spot Ansel thirty feet ahead of me, ready to drop into a classroom.

"Ansel," I whisper-yell his name, but he doesn't flinch.

He must not have heard me. It's not like I can shout, *Hey! What's going on out there?* I can't risk giving up my position, not even for someone I consider a friend. *Just* a friend, despite what Birdie says about him.

The second he drops from the shaft, I crawl faster to see where he's headed, ignoring the sharp pain in my knee. It's a supply closet. As good a meet-up point as any, maybe better than mine. I'm surprised he didn't screw the vent cover back in place. That's sloppy work and not like him, at least from what I've seen during training modules. Then again, those have all taken place on the compound.

I poke my head through the opening like an upside-down gopher and say his name louder. This time he glances up, eyes shadowed by spidery lashes. His normally readable expression is completely blank. He shakes his head, telling me *no*, and splits.

I hear the door to the closet open and close as I whisper-shout his name again. Was he holding bolt cutters? He didn't raise one caterpillar-thick brow or bat a green eye before taking off. We all have our own protocols to follow. Maybe he heard someone coming and couldn't stop. I can't waste any more time guessing and risk getting caught.

I'm above the vestibule that connects the academic building to the gymnasium within a hundred feet, the vent cover left open for me. My sisters are probably waiting, wondering why I'm late. I can see it now, Birdie with her arms crossed and Blue chewing the end of her hair. I crawl past the opening and lower myself into the void, feet first. Once I'm dangling and supported by my forearms, I stretch one arm out for my EDC, resettle, and throw it down. I take a nice deep breath before dropping lower, hanging five feet above the floor by my hands before

I let go and land less than gracefully next to Blue. She's wearing her Kevlar vest. Seeing it makes my thoughts fly to Birdie's *typical* comment this morning.

"You're bleeding," Blue says, staring at my knee.

I pull on my matching Kevlar vest. "I'm fine. It's a surface wound."

"That's more than surface."

I shrug it off. My knee is the least of our problems. "Those sounded a lot like gunshots. Where the hell is Birdie? Her classroom is the closest one to this meet-up point."

"She's hiding," Blue says matter-of-factly.

"What? Why? What makes you say that?"

"I just know. If Birdie's not here, she's hiding."

My youngest sister is weird. Let me just put that out there. There's no denying that fact. I don't particularly like when people refer to us as *those weird Juniper sisters,* but when Blue spouts her *opinion,* it's always absolute. There's never a maybe or perhaps or possibly. I used to think she was a know-it-all when we were younger, but I've learned to trust her. She has a stronger gut response to situations than anyone I've ever met. If Blue thinks Birdie is hiding, she's probably right. It still sends a sinker into the pit of my stomach. But dreadful thoughts of Birdie being hurt or worse will only incapacitate us.

We need to change our plan, but not the goal. Meet up, confirm everyone's intel, assess, and move out. Fast.

"We can't wait around," I tell Blue. "We have to find Birdie ASAP."

This is one of many situations where having more than one cellphone among the three of us would be helpful, but we have to share. It's for us to call home only, and it was Birdie's turn to carry it. In the event of an EMP, the electromagnetic pulse would render cellphones useless anyway, so we train to get by without the conveniences most people take for granted. That's why we prepare plans for different situations.

"Come on," I tell Blue. "Let's cut through the gymnasium. Maybe her teacher made it too hard for her to leave. You know how Ms. Pennick can be."

Pen-cap, as everyone calls her, is the worst pseudo drill sergeant in the history of physical education. I bet she's never run a mile for time in her life. That doesn't stop her from loving two things above all else: her stopwatch and calling out kids with a crappy mile time. We aren't those kids. Ever. We're the well-under-ten-minute milers. The ones coaches are desperate to have on teams we'll never join. Team Survival. The Nest. Those are our only affiliations.

"Did Birdie mention what they were doing in her PE class today?" I ask Blue. "Maybe they were outside on the field."

"She was too focused on finding her EDC to talk about anything else."

"True. Come on, then." I grab Blue's arm and she steps into a jog beside me.

The gymnasium is completely empty when we get there, save for the sweaty stench lingering like a million scent ghosts. We're halfway across the basketball court when we hear, "Go in! I'll flank you."

Blue stops short beside me and one of her Converse squeaks on the high-gloss basketball court, making us cringe. We duck under the bleachers right as the wide double doors open. A portly town cop with gray hair and a mustache enters, followed closely by a younger, slender version of himself. It's our luck that two out of the six cops we have in this tiny town walked into the gym at the same moment as us.

Blue and I lie as flat as possible under the center bleachers. Tucked deep enough we're out of sight if we don't move. I've had my fill of cramped, smelly spaces, but there was nowhere else to hide. It stinks under here like chewed gum and sweaty socks. I hold my breath to get a few seconds' break.

"All clear," the younger cops yells, his bowstring-tight voice ringing louder than necessary, tainted with the fear of inexperience. "I think the incident was contained to the roof and the west parking lot."

"Stupid fucking kids," the older one replies. "Let's check out a few hallways."

The walkie clipped to one of their shoulders crackles, allowing an authoritative woman to enter their conversation. "Circle around to the front. We caught one of them and have the point of origin."

My immediate thought is it could be any number of *stupid fucking kids* in this Podunk town. As long as it's not anyone from our group, we're good. Blue's eyes widen, but she remains motionless. If she lifts her head, her shock of cobalt hair will give away our position. She knows better than to move, but the spacey look in her eyes tells me one of her Blue-isms is bubbling in her brain.

"Roger that." Cop One tsks at his partner. "If these kids think this kind of thing is a joke, they're in for a rude awakening."

I spread my fingers to indicate five minutes. The approximate amount of time I think we should wait before going to find Birdie. The cops should, if protocol is followed, be checking all the classrooms. And when they survey ours, each class will be short one student with the last name Juniper. Not to mention if one of these cops realizes it's faster to circle back and cut to the front the way they came in, we're screwed. Backpacks, cargos, and Kevlar usually make a statement that begs people to assume the worst and ask questions later.

Waiting the full five minutes in silence, though, is another story. I can literally hear my eyelids click when I blink. Have you ever watched water boil? It takes forever. I stare at my watch and try not to get hypnotized by the second hand. When it finally ticks the last second, I'm the first one up and ready.

"Where do you think she is? I saw your face when those cops said they caught someone."

"In the locker room," Blue says.

Locker room it is.

Of course, she's right. We find Birdie pacing in front of a row of porcelain sinks that have been cracked and stained from years of abuse and clandestine smoking. She's chewing her nails, looking like she could use a smoke herself. Not that any of us smokes, even though we stockpile tobacco in case we need to use it in trade when money becomes useless. Birdie's thick bangs are sticking straight up like she's been running her fingers through them, her wavy, jaw-length bob frizzy from the misty weather.

When she sees it's just us walking in she sighs, "Oh Jesus," like we scared her. "You found me."

"Of course we did," Blue says. She glances around the floor and under the benches. "Where's your EDC?"

I was about to ask the same thing. Birdie is never without her bag. She was frantic for it this morning, which might account for her disheveled state.

Birdie shakes her head. "I . . . I don't know."

"What do you mean you don't *know?*" I snip. "We always have them with us at school, so where the fuck is it, Birdie? You know you had our cellphone, right?"

"Swearing won't help," Blue says to me. "There's something *wrong* with her."

"Yeah. She's been acting like a selfish jerk since she took up with Daniel Dobbs."

There is something else off about our middle sister, if I'm being honest. I'm just too short on patience at the moment to care.

Birdie slumps down a tiled wall until she's sitting knees up to her chin on the grimy floor. The flyer for the school musical she scraped off the wall sails to her feet. *The Taming of the Shrew.*

Blue crouches next to her. "What happened? Why didn't you meet us at our spot?"

Birdie grabs small fistfuls of hair on both sides of her head and repeats herself, staring straight into our younger sister's eyes. "I seriously don't know. I think I panicked and blocked it all out. Like right before a car accident. They say people can black out before impact."

I suppress a groan. Keeping my exasperation in check is becoming harder knowing Birdie misplaced her EDC. We carry things most people would find strange if not suspicious. A LifeStraw, Swiss Army knife, compass, glow stick, pepper spray, a lighter, carabineers and paracord, cash, along with the normal stuff for school like notebooks, pens, pencils. And yes, Kevlar. There's been twenty-three school shootings in America this year with no sign of slowing since our POTUS doesn't seem capable of thinking logically about anyone's safety but his own.

"I went to help Daniel," Birdie says, peering at me this time. "He told me they were going to create a distraction so Ansel could sneak into a chemistry supply closet and get something for his dad. They called it a level one civilian interaction training mission."

"What kind of something? I've never heard of Dieter sending anyone on an off-site mission like this before—in broad daylight. What kind of distraction required the whole school getting put on lockdown?"

"I don't know," Birdie answers.

"You don't know?" I explode. "Birdie, you were there." Backing Birdie into a cage never goes well, but my brain might be the next thing to detonate if she keeps lying.

"Stop yelling at her," Blue says, throwing me an exasperated look.

I take a breath in through my nose and wait impatiently for Birdie to explain why on earth she would keep this mission from us.

"I was there, but everything happened so fast. We were on the roof and Annalise got in my face before everything went down. I didn't think—I don't know, exactly. But I remember

Annalise grabbing my chin and blowing on my face, telling me to relax. Next thing I knew, I was at the edge of the roof, Daniel was shaking my arm telling me to run and hide. My adrenaline must have gone haywire, because I did what he told me to do without question. So maybe, in that moment, he grabbed my EDC."

"But you don't know for sure."

Birdie shakes her head and I want to scream, *Bullshit*.

Annalise is always doing stuff that's out of the range of normal, even for someone from The Nest. And I understand how things can happen fast. That's why we train, but—

"Why were you and Annalise there in the first place? And why would Daniel Dobbs take *your* EDC?"

Birdie avoids my eyes. "Maybe because it had some of the flash-bang grenades we made for the distraction inside it."

"What the actual hell, Birdie?" My patience evaporates. "*That's* why you were freaking out over finding your EDC this morning?"

"Oh boy," Blue says. "This could be bad."

"Bad doesn't come close. What were you doing with flash-bang grenades?" My voice pitches higher as my patience wanes again. "You just go along with whatever Daniel Dobbs says to do now without thinking? Is that what you were doing when you snuck out?"

She nods.

"Are you stupid? Blue and I heard the cops say they caught *someone*. If it was Daniel and he has your EDC, there's not much we can do. You didn't involve us from the beginning. What's done is done."

Birdie visibly shudders. "Maybe they caught someone else. Ansel was there. Annalise. Connor."

"That doesn't matter. You don't know what happened after you ran. If *any* of them got caught with *your* EDC then you're implicated in having explosives at school. ABAO."

All Bets Are Off.

"Shit."

Yeah. Shit, Birdie.

She opens her mouth to plead her case again and I hold up a hand to silence her. "Shut up and let me think."

This is one of those moments where I wish Bucky were a real person so I could ask him what he thinks. That's another problem with confiding in an imaginary friend. He's imaginary and I'm jumping to conclusions. But Birdie is real and she's right here, visibly tormented. Even if she is lying through her teeth, she's my middle. She needs me to help her navigate through whatever she got us into. When it comes to my sisters and me there is no *her* or *she*. It's always *us* and *we*.

The whole mission makes zero sense. If Dieter sent the Burrow Boys on an off-site training assignment without telling anyone, why would he send Annalise with them? She's a Nester, like us. If Mother learns Birdie went along, too, a whole different kind of shit will hit the fan at home. To say nothing of the reaction Birdie might get from Dieter. I don't know what kind of trouble any of them will face back at the compound.

I vaguely remember Camilla's brother Connor getting in trouble when we first arrived. I can't recall the circumstances since everything was so new at the time, only that he was made to stay inside a bunker for several weeks. That scared us, considering we hadn't seen the inside of a bunker yet. It's one thing to live and train on the compound and be sent out on assignments. It's another thing to do that when you're Dieter Ackerman's kids or his ward, like Daniel. That alone might get them some leniency. But we've never seen what happens to Nesters that get caught doing something reckless, because my sisters and I never act without thinking. We follow the rules and stick to Nest business. Strike that. Blue and I follow the rules. But Birdie knows better. She's trained for how to react to outside threats, so I don't get what the hell she was doing going along with the Burrow Boys. Not to mention lying to us about being in shock to the point of memory loss.

"You never answered me when I asked if Dieter told you it was okay to go along with them?"

She shakes her head again and I want to wring her neck.

"What about Annalise?"

"I don't know. She showed up later than the rest of us with Connor."

Sticking her nose where it doesn't belong isn't unusual for Annalise, either. But being sent on a mission with the Burrow Boys, if she *was* in fact sent, is off normal protocol.

"Dieter and Mother will be livid if they find out you went without their authority. No matter what happened or happens, we have to deny involvement to the authorities. That's the compound rule. Since we all know Annalise is too slippery a snake to get caught doing anything, it was probably one of the boys."

"Daniel won't snitch," she says. "Even if he's the one that got caught."

"On *you* or the compound?" I'm so mad I don't wait for her to answer. "We have no idea what they found or what disciplinary action they'll take. We have to wait and assess the situation. Stand up and take your vests off, both of you. I'm gonna put my EDC, and Blue's, inside a gym locker so we can get out of here without drawing attention to ourselves. We can come get them in the morning."

Birdie stands without question, conceding to me for once.

"Why can't I put mine in my own locker?" Blue asks.

"Because I want them both in one place for now. I'm not putting them in *my* gym locker. I'm putting them in *a* gym locker. My whole class saw me crawl into an air shaft, so I'm gonna be on everyone's radar no matter what. If they have Birdie's EDC, and put two and two together, they're bound to come up with three as their answer." I point to each of us. "One, two, three."

What I don't say is if the school or cops decide to do a locker search and they end up with all three of our bags, you can imagine what they'll think. The notebooks, pens, and pencils in there won't be enough of what's considered normal school supplies to shake them off the scent.

I pull a combination lock out of my EDC and pick an empty locker. Blue takes off her vest and hands everything over. Birdie does the same, only she doesn't let go when she hands me her vest, to make sure I'll look at her.

"I honestly don't remember everything that happened."

She's chewing her middle fingernail so hard her nose is being pushed up by her other knuckles. If she keeps that up she'll have nothing but bloody nubs by the time we get home. My own gnawing comes from deep inside my stomach. I want to believe her. This is the first time I've had to question why my sister would lie to me, us.

I don't know how to respond, so I turn on one of the sink taps and splash cold water on my face, rinsing away the dust and dirt from the air shaft.

Gone is the good mirror day. Replaced by shadowy worry, seeping into my eyes from the walls of the dim locker room and Birdie's all-consuming, gray uncertainty. Blue hands me a stretch of scratchy, unbleached paper towels to dry my hands like a surgeon before lobbing them into the trash can.

"Let's go find out what's happening," I tell them. "Maybe we'll get lucky and Daniel will be outside with everyone else."

"He's not," Blue says. And her tone is so conclusive neither of us argues.

✛ CYA ✛

COVER YOUR ASSETS

MY SISTERS AND I slip outside and around the building to the front silently and without incident. I size up the situation. There's a news truck across the street, four police cruisers parked at the curb in front, plus a dark sedan with tinted windows that has all the makings of an unmarked vehicle. The news truck troubles me the most. Avoid unnecessary speculation is another rule of our coalition.

We do our best to merge into the background. Hanging close together in a tight triangle while shifting our eyes and ears to the chatter of students milling around, still abuzz with speculation. I pick out relevant pieces of their conversations: the lockdown was lifted but they called parents, the school day is over, everyone can go home. But a lot of people are still milling around, talking, acting like lookie-loos, trying to get the scoop, including us. The more we know, the easier it will be to tell Mother and Dieter what happened.

After a few minutes, our natural defensive vibe relaxes and our shoulders unhunch. If it weren't for the anxious flit of Birdie's eyes I'd almost believe the situation isn't as bad as we thought. But then the all-day drizzle turns to rain, and as the drops prick my cheeks like liquified pine needles, I remember we have to go back home. The rain will add insult to injury with Mother if we're late and she can't reach us.

Blue crosses her arms. "I wish I had the rain poncho in my EDC."

"Me, too. Do you see anyone from The Nest or The Burrow? Ansel, Annalise?" I whisper. "I'd love to talk to one of them before we leave."

Blue is the only one facing the other students. She's also the shortest. I realize I'm blocking her sight line and take a small step to the side.

"No one," she says. "Maybe they all left."

That *is* the second part of our protocol. Return to The Nest.

"Wait. There is someone," Blue says, "standing at two o'clock from my perspective, taking pictures. Of *us*, I think."

"A reporter?"

"No. A student."

I whip around, and sure enough, Rémy Lamar has his camera pointed right at me. He's using a telephoto zoom lens to capture me, us, up close. *What is his fascination with trying to get pictures of me?*

"I've had enough," I tell my sisters. "I'll be right back."

They have no idea what that means, but it doesn't matter. I told him to stop once today, and I'm going to tell him again. Only this time, I won't bother explaining why.

Engage with target.

"Birdie Juniper!" Ms. Pennick's unmistakable shrill tone stops me from taking another step toward Rémy. But when our eyes meet, and he sees the fury in mine, he lowers his camera.

I turn and see Birdie's PE teacher headed straight for her, clipboard firmly grasped in her hand, arms pumping so fast breaking into a run would make her gait seem less precarious. The stopwatch she always wears around her neck on a black lanyard is swinging, bouncing off her ribs in a way that looks downright painful.

THREAT ASSESSMENT:
PAULA PENNICK | 5'8" AVERAGE TO OVERWEIGHT
BUILD | CLOSED SOCIAL GROUP | TRUSTING
MOST LIKELY TO: throw darts at pictures of people she
dislikes in the privacy of her own home.
LEAST LIKELY TO: be nominated for teacher of the year.
7/10 WOULD IMPEDE GROUP SURVIVAL IN AN
EMERGENCY SITUATION.
CASUALTY POTENTIAL: high

Birdie turns her head and gapes at me wide-eyed. It only
lasts a heartbeat before she closes them, pulls herself together,
and swivels to respond to Pen-cap with a sheepish grin.

"Hi, Ms. Pennick. Were you looking for me?"

I'm always amazed by Birdie's ability to play it cool when
the situation is hot, but I'm extra impressed now, given the
unnerved state she was in when we found her in the locker
room.

"Yes, as a matter of fact," Ms. Pennick says. "I'm finding it
oddly curious you requested a bathroom pass minutes before
Daniel Dobbs was caught pulling his little prank. You hang
around with him, don't you?"

My pulse starts ticking like a time bomb when she confirms our fear. I trust for the most part that every Nester
and Burrower will follow the same close-lipped protocol, but
I can't account for how anyone might react under individual-
ized pressure. Especially Daniel. His parents died during one
of Dieter's missions, a year or more before we got here. I don't
know what he was like before, but the Daniel we know vac-
illates between gung-ho, I'll-do-whatever-Dieter-Ackerman-
says, and swoony, let's-hang-out-in-the-barn-until-sunrise with
my sister. That's too unpredictable to bet on at a time like
this.

I hold my breath, waiting for Birdie to panic and crack with
the news. But she doesn't.

"I was hiding in the bathroom," she says. Shoulders squared, maintaining her innocence.

Pen-cap flicks leery gray eyes over us, starting with Birdie and ending with me. The way you might study a pack of stray dogs you aren't sure can be trusted. Trying to decide which one is the ring leader. The alpha.

"I still think we should go speak to Principal Weaver. You too, Honey, since I overheard other students say you weren't in your classroom, either."

"Yes, I was," I flat-out lie.

I search for the classmates who were staring at me in horror less than an hour ago and spot my chemistry teacher watching us. I give him a barely there grin meant as an apology, and he nods once in return. Looking less upset than he should. He starts strolling over, inconspicuously slow, like he's trying to gauge the situation.

"What about me?" Blue asks, returning my thoughts to the fact that we might have to convince Principal Weaver we're not degenerates, despite our reputation as *weirds*. "I mean if you're going to single out *all the Junipers* as dangerous renegades, shouldn't I come along, too?"

"I'm not singling anyone out, yet. The facts merely are as stated. Two out of three Junipers were not where you were expected to be at the time of the incident."

She's wrong. Three out of three Junipers weren't where we were expected, but Blue is the least likely to stand out.

"She has to come regardless," I tell Ms. Pennick. "We're not comfortable being separated in situations like this. It's part of our family creed."

"And what creed it that?" Pen-cap digs the edge of her clipboard into her hip, all official business like she's in charge, which is apparently all she's ever wanted.

"We'd tell you," Birdie chimes in, "but then we'd have to kill you."

"I hardly think this is a time to make jokes," Ms. Pennick

says. "Especially ones of that nature, given the circumstances. If you girls didn't dress so—"

"Whoa!" I cut her off. "How we dress has nothing to do with this."

Pen-cap shrugs one shoulder, looking only slightly shamed.

Her criticism backs up everything I already know people say. I am slightly disheveled by the ordeal. I know that, but it doesn't change the fact that we have to follow her toward the administration building like criminals. I untangle my thick brown hair from its mangled bun instead. I reknot it as neatly as possible on top of my head, smoothing down all the flyaway hairs that came loose in the steamy air shaft. I don't know if that will help, since I'm sweaty and covered in dust, but it can't hurt. Maybe the principal won't notice my blood-soaked knee. Pen-cap hasn't. Yet. Neither has Birdie, which is not a shock considering how the whole day has gone.

Dread settles into my gut as I anticipate the questions that might sail my way during interrogation.

Where were you going when you escaped class through the ventilation shaft?

Why was your sister also missing during the incident?

Do you know who this schoolbag belongs to?

I'm thinking of answers less incriminating than the truth when Mr. Whitlock intercepts us with a block at the pass between buildings. For someone whose car was hit by the flash-bang grenades, he doesn't appear fazed.

"Paula, so glad I saw you," he says. "I can take the Juniper sisters to Principal Weaver's office from here. He asked me to bring Honey to his office if I could find her, and the general consensus is to keep the parties involved to a minimum."

Pen-cap pulls her triangular chin back, regarding Mr. Whitlock's interception like she's put out. "I suppose that makes sense. Daniel targeted your car, after all."

I suck in a breath, loud enough to catch Mr. Whitlock's attention.

"We probably shouldn't name names," he whispers, leaning closer to his colleague. "The powers that be like to keep the identity of those involved under wraps when dealing with minors. But I'm sure we can agree to keep that indiscretion to ourselves. It's not like you gave his last name."

"Of course. I would never. Yes," Pen-cap says, tugging nervously on her lanyard. "Will you let me know how it goes?"

"I will if I can. Again, minors."

Pen-cap zips her Elkwood High windbreaker, and it suddenly seems a size too small to contain her disappointment. I'm not exactly thrilled with my teacher's interception of us, either, considering I went against everything he asked of me in his classroom.

Mr. Whitlock steals multiple glances at my sisters and me as we walk back toward the school. I want to pinch Birdie's arm and ask if they purposely threw the flash-bang grenades at Whitlock's car or if it was an accident, but I can't. Knowing this extra piece of information makes it impossible for me to look at him.

I have to say something, though. I should.

It isn't until we're inside the school again, heading to Principal Weaver's office, that I find the will to speak. "Mr. Whitlock, I wasn't involved with whatever happened. You have to know that. I honestly just had to go find my sisters."

He stops in the dimly lit hallway. "What's your family creed?"

"*What?*" That's a strange thing to ask, given the circumstances.

"Your creed. I heard you mention it to Ms. Pennick."

Mr. Whitlock hasn't accused us of anything without proof, unlike Pen-cap, so I have no reason to keep it a secret. It's not like it's anything incriminating or shocking. In fact, I bet it's the creed of lots of families. Especially when they go on trips and stuff where anything can happen, which is the main point.

I shrug one shoulder. "We stick together no matter what."

He doesn't say anything for a few seconds, just rakes his hand across the top of his head, smoothing down his straight golden hair where he has a cowlick. Against the sky-blue lockers, he reminds me of that highly sensing character in *Fight Club* and all I can think is, *What would Tyler Durden do?*

"I didn't think you were involved," he says. "Not directly. But I think you have an idea who was."

He shifts a suspicious gaze to Birdie and my protective defenses go up.

Don't react. Don't react. Don't react.

Thankfully, my sister keeps her mouth shut.

All three of us need to stay on the same page if we're going to survive this meeting with Principal Weaver.

"Okay then," Mr. Whitlock says. "If you're not involved, and you don't know who is, why am I taking you to Principal Weaver?"

I arch a brow at the trick question, the R in *Ready* kicking into high gear. "Because *he told you to?*"

Trick questions require trick answers.

"Did he?" Whitlock says. "I was so distraught over my car, I guess that request got lost in the confusion of the situation."

He shifts his eyes to the exit. When we don't respond, he tips his head toward the door.

"Are you saying we can leave?"

He moves his head in a suggested *yes,* but I don't trust it. This feels like baiting a trap. Thread something shiny on a hook to tempt the fish before yanking it out of the water by its hungry mouth.

"What's the catch?" I ask.

"No catch. I know more about you three than you might think. If needed, I can come up with something to explain your whereabouts. Where did you stash your EDCs?"

"Our *what?*" Birdie draws out the question, as singsong as her name implies.

Never have I ever seen my sister play dumb so well. Ruffling her bangs with her fingertips like some character in a play about babes in the woods.

Starring Birdie Juniper: Lead Ingénue.

"Your Every Day Carries." Whitlock pats the canvas messenger bag slung across his body twice, as if to say *one of these*. "Where are they? I've never seen any one of you without one."

"He's a prepper," Blue says, cutting straight through the bullshit.

"I'm a *realist*," Whitlock counters. "And from what I've seen since I got here, so are you. I can't fault you for leaving my class the way you did, Honey. I understand following protocol. Believe me, that's my whole life. But you drew the kind of attention to yourself that's hard to recover from without an advocate on your side. That's all I was trying to say."

You can talk to me, he told me. *Let me be your confidant.*

Confidant. My head shakes reflexively. We don't have those outside of our group, unless you count Bucky. The first rule of prep club is you don't talk about prep club. My sisters are my biggest confidantes and right now they look just as perplexed.

Never in a million years did I imagine having to do a surprise threat assessment of Mr. Whitlock, but what choice do I have? We've been taught to exercise caution with preppers who aren't part of our group. Marauders are considered worse than Outsiders, because their interests lie in assessing the stashed assets of other preppers so they can steal them when the SHTF. But Mr. Whitlock, of all people, a prepper? Or worse. A marauder. I don't know.

THREAT ASSESSMENT:
PRYCE WHITLOCK | 5'11" AVERAGE-STRONG BUILD |
OPEN SOCIAL GROUP | UNTRUSTING
MOST LIKELY TO: surprise you without warning.
LEAST LIKELY TO: follow the rules of the establishment.

2/10 WOULD IMPEDE GROUP SURVIVAL IN EMERGENCY
SITUATION.
CASUALTY POTENTIAL: low

"They're in a gym locker," I tell him. "We'll go get them."

I'm mad at myself for not thinking my cautionary plan all
the way through. The school can check lockers because they're
school property. Checking our bags requires probable cause.
Doing so without viable suspicion would be a fourth amendment violation.

"So you're just gonna let us go home?" Blue asks.

I hold my breath, unconvinced, waiting for the shiny thing
dangling in front of us to be yanked away.

"I'll think of something to tell Principal Weaver. And the
authorities. They may decide they want to talk to you at another time, but I'll do what I can for now."

"What about Daniel?" Birdie asks.

I'm leery of how easily she's fallen into trusting my chemistry teacher. I like Mr. Whitlock, like I said, but trusting him
begs me to follow a different set of rules.

"I can only offer the three of you a chance to get out of here
before anyone else comes looking for you. I don't know what
they found on Daniel Dobbs, yet. If that's going to stop you
from leaving, that's fine. I can take you to Principal Weaver's
office now. But if you want me to CYA, you need to collect
your EDCs and get out of here. And I suggest you think long
and hard about what you're going to carry inside those bags
when you return tomorrow."

I nod, knowing, even if we leave, this conversation feels far
from over.

"Tomorrow, then," I say. "We'll go. Thank you." I pull
Birdie by the sleeve because she seems reluctant to move without knowing what's happening to Daniel.

Mr. Whitlock adjusts the strap on his own EDC, completely straight-faced. "Tomorrow it is."

⁑ BSTS ⁑

BETTER SAFE THAN SORRY

WE'RE LATE. MOTHER is standing under the portico with her arms crossed, mouth pulled in a grim frown as we roll up in the station wagon. When she knows we're home, she walks inside without changing her stoic expression. Since coming here, our mother almost always thinks prepping and safety first, feelings second. Right now, she's got that disappointed, we-have-work-to-do vibe draped across her shoulders like a tattered shawl.

I stay behind the wheel an extra second, letting the rain flood the windshield in waves. We didn't do anything wrong. Birdie may have, but that's not the position I'm planning to take.

"Let me do the talking," I tell my sisters. "She's got that look." Ripe for a dustup with Birdie if my sister doesn't keep her mouth shut.

"Maybe I can explain," Birdie offers.

I snap the wagon's gearshift into Park and whip my head to the back seat. *"Can you?"* I know it's snippy, but an hour ago she claimed she couldn't remember what she'd done. "I'll do what I can to keep Mother off the scent of your involvement in whatever the hell you were doing. Don't say a word until she tells us what she knows."

Blue exits the car quietly, but stares longingly at Achilles's mew. He doesn't like to fly in the rain. Falcons need the up-draft of wind, and anything more than light rain makes their wings too heavy. Achilles screeches from inside the mew like he senses her presence, and she smiles, knowing he's safe and sound.

We enter the house rank and file, oldest to youngest, shaking the wet weather onto the ugly brown tiles by the door.

The TV in the living room is tuned to the national news, as always, with the constant chattering of what's happening around the globe. It underscores our daily existence and keeps us informed, or *will* keep us informed until something or someone takes us out. The POTUS has been dropping insti-gating comments about the Supreme Leader of North Korea like they're fighting over who has the biggest toy collection in-stead of focusing on the reality of what a nuclear bomb would do to either country. The wood-burning stove is lit. On any other day, it would take the chill from the house, but it's being replenished by Mother's icy countenance.

"I tried to reach you girls on the cellphone several times. You know how much I worry when you don't answer, espe-cially when the weather is like this. Would one of you care to explain?"

So much for waiting until she gives us her intel.

I swipe away the drops of rain sliding down my forehead. "It's my fault," I tell her. "There was an incident at the school. I was rushing to leave and left the phone in my locker. In my defense, it was out of battery and needs to be charged any-way."

I peel off my wet socks, trying to act as natural as possible.

"That part was my fault," Birdie says, and I wish she'd shut up. "It was my turn to make sure the phone was charged."

"That's not the only complication, though, is it?" Mother says. "Otherwise, I wouldn't have received a call from Principal Weaver saying Honey climbed out of her classroom through the air shaft."

I'm standing in front of her with my back against a prover-bial wall. "I did, but only because it sounded like someone was firing a gun, and we got put on lockdown. I did what I was sup-posed to do. Find Birdie and Blue. Isn't that why we've been training, to be *ready* to *react responsibly* during tense situations? BSTS."

"I can do without the sass," Mother says. "I know very well why we've been training."

She picks up a glass of water from the counter with her bandaged hand, and I see her make the slightest wince.

"Is your antibiotic not working?" I ask. "I can go to the store and buy some Neosporin." I need it for my knee as much as she does.

"The antibiotic is fine. Don't change the subject, Honey." She stares past me to Birdie. "You didn't feel the need to use an air shaft in this situation, did you?"

Birdie shakes her head. "I was on the field for PE."

"I used the air shaft," Blue offers, ever at my defense. "I slipped out of my classroom as soon as everyone started to panic and went up through a vent in the bathroom."

Mother looks down her nose at me, as if to say Blue had the right idea and I messed up.

"My teacher had already locked the door," I explain. "What would you have had me do, leave them to their own fates?"

Mother is silent, thinking.

She knows I'm right. She knows I'm right. She knows I'm right. I try to will her into believing this.

"It's always better to be safe than sorry," she finally con-cedes. "Which is why I told your principal, who for some rea-son knew our family creed, that you had a habit of taking things literally and perhaps too far. That as the oldest you've always felt a larger sense of responsibility to your sisters. I as-sured him it wouldn't happen again."

"It won't," I say. "Unless it does."

Mother's disappointed scowl softens. "The world *is* largely unpredictable, but I had to say something to dissuade him from further questions."

The good thing is there's no mention of Birdie's EDC, so Daniel must have kept his mouth shut. Whitlock probably told Principal Weaver our creed in my defense. I'm grateful we're off the hook with Principal Weaver, but I'm still concerned about the fishbowl I'll be in at school. Speculated upon like some circus freak. The Girl with the Juniper Branch Tattoo. We all have one, actually. I'm not being funny. Mother wanted us to have a distinguishing mark in case we got lost, abducted, or worse. They're dainty, a single sprig on the back of our left arms above the elbow, black ink with three berries positioned in descending order. The one on my arm has the highest berry inked in, Birdie's is the middle berry, and Blue's the lowest. I remember Birdie arguing that she had a mole under her left breast and that was her distinguishing mark. But once I had mine, she wanted one, too.

"Are you gonna tell Dieter?" I ask.

"I haven't yet," she says. "Is there anything else I should know?"

Loads. But I shake my head. It would be so much easier to pass the buck to the Burrow Boys, tell Mother they were up to something for Dieter Ackerman, but I can't. Not until we know more.

I don't have to say another word because the TV switches over to local news, and the royal blue banner at the bottom of the screen spills their version of our story.

SHOTS FIRED AT LOCAL HIGH SCHOOL CALLED AN ELABORATE PRANK.

The flat voice grabs the rest of my family's attention, and we all move closer to the TV without speaking, watching the deadpan news anchor publicize what happened at school earlier. *Publicize* being the operative word.

In local news, what sounded like gunfire this afternoon at Elkwood High School brought authorities racing to the scene in anticipation of what might have been the twenty-fourth school shooting across the nation this year.

Students recall hearing the sound of gunshots before the school's principal issued a mandatory lockdown on what's now being called an elaborate, but dangerous, prank. The student responsible has been identified and could be charged with explosives and fireworks offenses, as well as reckless conduct, as Elkwood Police continue to investigate the incident. According to the school's website, an automated phone call was sent to parents, assuring them all students were safe and able to return to classes as scheduled tomorrow.

They pan the crowd of students outside the school. My sisters and I are huddled in the shot, plain as daylight.

"Why is that camera pointed at you, Honey?"

Not exactly pointed. I shrug and Mother's scowl returns. This isn't good.

Birdie is sitting cross-legged on the floor, staring at the screen like she's hypnotized long after they've moved on to a different story. "What happens when someone is charged with explosives and fireworks offenses? Would they go to jail?"

She twists to look at Mother, gnawing her middle fingernail again.

"Not if they're a minor," Mother says. "Why do you ask? Do you know the student they're talking about?"

I'm primed to kick my sister in her seated bottom. Thankfully, she shakes her head in denial. Mother doesn't know about her and Daniel being a couple, only that they're friends. It's best to keep it that way. The bigger problem we have is if we're watching this air on mainstream media, so is everybody else on the compound.

The CB radio used for compound-wide communication crackles to life in our kitchen with Dieter Ackerman's sharp voice. Piercing the room like the edge of a dull blade being sharpened against a whetstone. None of us has the energy to feign surprise.

"Juniper 4321, this is Ackerman1. Special mandatory meeting called at eighteen-hundred hours in the central training area. Confirm. Over."

Mother gives us a reproachful scowl before walking to the radio in the foyer. "This is Juniper 4321. Confirming receipt of transmission for special mandatory meeting. Over." She turns the radio off and faces us. "Are you sure there isn't anything I need to know?"

I shrug and shake my head before glancing left and right at my sisters, who are, in varying degrees, giving Mother the same nonverbal answer.

"Do I have time to feed the animals?" Blue asks, acting like everything is fine and normal.

Mother checks her field watch. "You should all do it. The other chores will have to wait until tomorrow. Blue, you take care of the chickens, Birdie, the goats. Honey can pull vegetables from the garden for dinner. I'll check our rain barrels before going down there to see what's going on. You have an hour."

"I need dry socks," I tell my sisters. "You want me to get you some?"

They nod and I head for the stairs to our bedroom, ignoring the nagging sensation arising in my mind for why my mother always goes *down there* early or alone.

What I really need is a minute alone to get some bandages and process everything that's happened. I pull three pairs of thick socks from the dresser and change into a heavy sweatshirt. I grab one for Blue, too, because her lips were starting to match her hair in the rain. My knee is throbbing out of sync with my heart like it has a separate sympathetic nervous system. I'm glad Mother didn't spot the jagged tear in my jeans. I leave my pants in a heap on the floor and grab the hydrogen peroxide and first aid kit from the hallway linen closet. The door is slightly askew. Birdie is usually the one to fix things like loose screws on outlet covers or a burned-out lightbulb.

Mostly because her patience gets worn by small stuff faster than mine or Blue's.

I douse the two-inch gash over the tub to save cleanup time. Pink, blood-tinged water runs down the drain before the H2O2 bubbles up white and foamy. I pat it dry and put a couple of butterfly stitches across it to keep it from bleeding. If that doesn't work, I'll glue it shut later. I change into a fresh pair of pants and slip my feet inside the wool hiking socks, covering my damp, shriveled toes, instantly feeling better. I head downstairs, but at the last minute turn and go into our bedroom for the interchangeable screwdriver we keep in the pencil jar. It only takes a minute to fix the crooked door, but it satisfies my itch to have something go right today.

When I get back downstairs, Birdie passes me a pair of knee-high rain boots the color of Spanish olives. "We're gonna need these."

I hand her a pair of wool socks and toss the other pair to Blue with her sweatshirt. Once we're dressed in new layers, we head outside. I grab one of the vegetable-collecting baskets hanging outside our house, thankful Mother didn't assign me the goats. Chickens don't mind the rain, but the goats bray like every drop is acid rain, even though they have a barn that's plenty dry. If you ever wanted to know what stubborn and sensitive looks like, get yourself a goat. Or, better yet, just hang with my sister Birdie. Same-same.

"Do you think Dieter spotted us on the news?" Birdie asks.

"Probably. But if he didn't everyone else did."

"We're hiding in plain sight," Blue says.

That's true, my little. Weird but true. "Maybe that's a good thing. It will make it seem like we weren't involved. That *you* weren't involved," I tell Birdie, "and we were just doing the same thing as everyone else."

Birdie heads for the goats. "I'll see you for sentencing."

"That's not funny."

"I wasn't trying to be."

Blue shrugs. "That's Birdie. Will you throw a few veggies into the chicken pen on your way over?"

"Of course. No problem. Wait for me by the goat pen."

She grins her thanks and jogs to catch up to Birdie, where she'll no doubt perform a subtle temperature check on our middle's mood.

It doesn't take me long to fill my basket with carrots, potatoes, cauliflower, and Swiss chard before heading down the gravel path to meet my sisters. Our gardens are year-round abundant because alongside the vegetables we plant in-ground, we also have two greenhouses installed with grow lights to combat the Pacific Northwest gloom. One of them is locked at all times because it contains plants and trees with seeds that are poisonous in large doses, but useful for making medicine. Wolfsbane, castor, water hemlock, datura. That's Mother's domain. She's mentioned wanting to teach me more of those processes for backup in the event of disaster, which is another reason why my perceived *added interest* in chemistry caught her attention.

Carrying all the makings for a quick and easy soup to a compound meeting reads more *modern-day March sister* than *Sarah Connor*. But here I am, walking toward the training area looking a little like both.

Act natural. Act natural. Act natural.

I spot Mother in the gathered group first, sitting in a lawn chair near the archery targets under an out-of-place, red-and-black-striped golf umbrella. Golf's not a prepper-designated sport. Archery, shooting, running, calisthenics: sure. The closest anyone here has ever gotten to a golf ball is rubbing one under sore feet after a long day. Behind her, someone left three bull's-eye-centered arrows in one of the targets, illustrating the piercing tone all three of us will face if questioned about what happened at school.

Mother's eyes dart between us and Dieter as we approach from the tree-lined dirt path. Everyone is sitting except the Burrower assigned to the lookout tower, Dieter, and

Daniel, who might as well have one of those targets on his back too.

"Oh god," Birdie whispers.

And I know why. Daniel is shouldering an INCH bag. We all know an I'm Never Coming Home bag is used for movement lasting more than seventy-two hours, and his looks stuffed to the hilt. His wet curls are unfurling across his forehead, half covering his hazel eyes, hands tucked deep inside the pockets of his army-green field jacket. The second he spots my sister, his shoulders tense and ride closer to his ears.

I'm not sure what that means outside of his posture saying he's in big trouble, but Birdie is breathing fast and heavy at my side. Ever since she fessed up to her involvement in the locker room, the difference between fear for herself and Daniel has been indistinguishable.

I spy Mother studying me, pulling on the skin of her neck. If she talked to Dieter, and we're about to get handed some kind of compound-issued disciplinary action, Blue won't handle it well and Mother knows this.

"Look who's decided to join us." Dieter Ackerman's heavy-lidded eyes flick to Mother before he checks the time on his mechanical field watch. Silent message: *Get your charges in check.*

Technically, it's only four minutes past the hour.

"We got detained." I load my excuse without giving an explanation, even though I know four minutes can mean the difference between life and death in certain situations.

Dieter scowls and clamps a hand on Daniel's shoulder. "I guess we can get started since you're no longer *detained.*"

THREAT ASSESSMENT:
DIETER ACKERMAN | 6′1″ STRONG BUILD | EXTREME CLOSED SOCIAL GROUP | UNTRUSTING
MOST LIKELY TO: put his life on the line for others.
LEAST LIKELY TO: listen to reason when rules get broken.

o/io WOULD IMPEDE GROUP SURVIVAL IN EMERGENCY
SITUATION.
CASUALTY POTENTIAL: low

He scratches the middle of a thin scar that runs from his right eye to his jaw in the shape of a bent straw. A battle wound he got during combat in the armed forces.

Daniel looks up, straight at my sister. In that moment, I see his fear. And when he lifts one side of his mouth to give Birdie a tentative smile, my eyes dart to my sister. She returns his smile and waits for Dieter's dictate with bated breath, trembling an imperceptible amount. But I see it, as sure as the single tear ready to spring from her left eye.

"Earlier today," Dieter starts, "it was brought to my attention that certain coalition members sent on a level-one civilian interaction training mission were not as discreet as instructed. The OPTEMPO was too fast. Too rash. And unsanctioned distraction methods were used. Because of that, we're going to change the way we do a few things until the scent clinging to our location and operation dies down. Most everyone involved extricated themselves from the situation. Except Daniel, who was left holding the bag. Metaphorically speaking."

Holding Birdie's bag. Holding Birdie's bag. Holding Birdie's bag.

Daniel and Birdie are staring at each other like telepathic cohorts. I elbow my sister to let her know she's drawing attention to herself, and the jabbing movement breaks Daniel's hypnotic gaze.

"First," Dieter says, "I'm issuing a compound-wide curfew. We've run into hiccups that may have put us on the wrong radar. Beginning today, no one under the age of eighteen is to be out after eleven P.M. without the express orders or permission of me and their parent or guardian. Those caught after curfew will be dealt with accordingly. Consider that your only warning. To survive an extinction-level event we must have the ability to gather the essentials without detection at a moment's notice. During an actual ELE, we cannot, and will not, stop to wait for anyone unable to execute protocol."

Dieter is controlling his tone, but the signs of his outrage are visible through the veil of falling rain. The bulging vein in his neck. The reddening of his face.

"This was a failure," he criticizes. "I underestimated our readiness, or perhaps our willingness to follow protocol. The supplies that caused the incident at the high school were intercepted, which means two things. The members involved will most likely be under closer examination, if lucky, or further interrogation if not. We all know obtaining certain necessary supplies can put us on the wrong radar, and we cannot afford detection or speculation from outside officials of any kind." His mouth forms a disappointed square. "Nonetheless, Annalise has reported that news teams and several suits arrived on the scene. It is a rule of this coalition to avoid detection at this level."

Knowing I was right about the unmarked vehicle doesn't bring me comfort, because he's also right. We're not supposed to bring that kind of attention to the compound. At the same time, I'm not the only one whose eyes travel to Annalise, wondering when she started to be included in Burrow business. She peels a wet lock of golden-blond hair off her freckled cheek and holds her cleft chin high. Ever the daddy's girl. Sure. But this is crossing new boundaries. Her mother, Magda, with her wide prominent cheekbones, stands just as proud at her daughter's side.

Magda and Mother have been at slight odds since we got here. Mother's expertise in medicine put her immediately under a proverbial microscope. But it's gotten worse since rumors of Dieter and Mother having an affair started to fly. We've all heard the way some Nesters talk about Mother. How odd it is that she's the only woman here without a husband.

Unless we count Tashi Garcia's *abuela*. Our father died while Mother was pregnant with Blue. Birdie and I were so young we don't remember him, and Mother prefers it that way. She says he wasn't a very good man, and it was always just us girls until we moved here.

I don't know if the rumors are true. I've been too uncomfortable to ask, even though I can't deny the number of times Dieter has shown up at our house as my sisters and I are leaving for school.

"Since authorities were called and the news outlets picked up the story, I'll be handling Daniel's disciplinary action. He's been suspended from school for ten days, pending a risk assessment, and I strongly suggest all of you keep your noses clean and avoid discussing the topic with anyone outside the coalition or during school at all, for that matter. That includes well-intentioned teachers, guidance counselors, et cetera. Since Daniel is my ward, I want any questions about his involvement directed to me. The rest of you are expected to fly below the radar until the attention being directed at us dies down. Any questions?"

When I raise my hand, Birdie elbows me hard in the ribs. I shoot her a quick side-eye glare meant to say *you're the one who got us into this mess.*

"Yes, Honey."

"Did the authorities or whatever name anyone else who they thought was involved?"

"They did not. But I know who I assigned to the mission."

That doesn't tell me what I want to know. I adjust my gaze to Ansel for confirmation that Birdie is off the hook. He's staring at his combat boots like they hold the meaning of life, or at least life within his garrison. He must sense the weight of my stare because he looks up, just a quick cast my way before looking down again. The urge to admonish him for not saying something, anything, in Daniel's defense swells in my throat. Daniel Dobbs is Ansel's best friend. They're like brothers.

But then Ansel lifts his head and looks at me dead-on and I see the black eye. He gives a shallow shake of his head. That's all the explanation I need for now. I'll get confirmation from him about Birdie as soon as I can.

"If there are no more questions," Dieter says. "I have another announcement. In an effort to keep things running smoothly and avoid accusations of nepotism, I've asked Alice Juniper to act as leader of The Nest. She will report to me and we'll make decisions and adjustments to our way of life as deemed necessary."

More than a few gasps fill the air. My head snaps to Mother, but her eyes are locked straight ahead, like she knew this announcement was coming.

"But—" Annalise starts, and her father waves a hand to silence her.

"That's my decision. I believe it's the best one to ensure our survival, and it's final."

Magda's mouth twists like a paper bag being rung. Who can blame her? Dieter is adding torque to the overturned screw on the gossip mill surrounding him and Mother. Magda has always been nice to me and my sisters. She was the first to welcome us on board, making us feel like we belonged, teaching us about hardtack and canning and military-grade survival food.

Annalise glares in my direction. She doesn't hate me, I don't think, but at the same time, she's never been friendly by definition. It's all prepper business or lone wolf with Annalise. Though I think her aloofness has more to do with Birdie, seeing as Annalise is Daniel's ex-girlfriend. We communicate during drills and training as needed, but rarely at school. We've never hung out and talked boys or discussed homework or anything. Not that we have much time for social stuff. Recently, though, she's been hitting me with more and more snarky comments about Mother in passing. Which I usually ignore.

But even Ansel goggled at his father's announcement, so I'm

guessing this new power structure will play out like a barrel of monkeys for my sisters and me. First, Birdie "steals" Annalise's boyfriend, then rumors about Mother and Magda circle, now this. I wonder what this means for me if something dire happens to Mother. I didn't ask for a new, perceived rank-in-waiting, but Annalise will want my head.

TOBYISMS FOR ACTION
2
TAKE YOUR LIFE BACK

THE DINNER SHIFT at Nikko's is slammed. Stavros put his lamb souvlaki plate on special with a wine pairing, and it's been nonstop since five-thirty. Every single table wants to add or sub something: extra side of "sauce"—for the people that can't say *tzatziki*—extra feta, *no* feta, no pita bread. I'll never understand *no feta* people. It's legitimately the food of gods. And the yogurt sauce is pronounced *tsaht-zee-key*, if you didn't know.

Stavros is thrilled with the turnout. The whole place is a symphony of murmured conversation, laughter, and clinking silverware set to a backdrop of Greek music. When a song he likes comes on, he points at me. "Ah, Toby, *opa!*" He raises his arms and snaps his fingers.

"*Opa!*" I tell him and smile at my customers before rushing off to retrieve a third glass of red wine for a woman that only wanted a Greek side salad for dinner no matter how hard I tried to upsell her on some stuffed grape leaves. Value-wise, if you're going to order three glasses of wine at dinner, you're better off getting a bottle.

Just when I think I'm out of the weeds, in walks a single mom with four kids under ten years old. Three girls and a boy who tugs on their hair and runs around them in circles like it's a game of duck-duck-goose. The middle of the three girls wriggles out of her tiny backpack and swings it at him, hard. She misses, but the effort was valiant and reminds me so much of my sister Imogen it stings.

Stavros snaps his fingers in my face. "'Ey? You okay? You look tired. Maybe I give them to Brooke."

I nod. My second shift of the day ends soon, so that's probably better.

Brooke and I went to high school together. The first time my mom met her she took Brooke's chin in her hand and said, "You are a buxom, gorgeous, real thing in a world of fake beauty. Own that."

Brooke Delgado is brunette, broad-faced and freckled-cheeked, with more curves than the roller coaster at Belmont Park in Mission Beach. She breaks every super thin, blond, side-salad-only-for-dinner, Southern California stereotype from top to bottom. And yeah, she owns that. We dated for eight months but broke up because, as she put it, I was too distracted by the past and she wanted to live in the now. We're still friendly, and if I need someone to trade shifts with at work, she's my go-to. I screwed that up, too. They say you earn the things that happen to you. Maybe I deserve to be alone.

I'm bussing a table near the family of five when one of the girls says, "I want the balaclava."

I smile, imagining her in a black ski mask pounding her brother in a sneak attack. When their mom says, "No dessert tonight," it pulls at my heartstrings.

The cooks eighty-six the souvlaki plate and I check the time. One more hour. I put in my personal order for a deluxe gyro plate for Bash and ask them to keep it off the rails for forty minutes so it's not cold by the time I leave.

Brooke comes up behind me to get waters for her new table. You have to ask for water in San Diego because we're usually in a drought. This year has been unseasonably rainy and cold. A realization everyone except our POTUS admits is an effect of global warming, because *false face doth hide what the false heart doth know.* My point is, when you live in a place your whole life and the climate changes drastically over a ten-year period, you notice. Everyone notices.

But thank you, Macbeth. For providing context to another man as duplicitous and phony as they come.

"I saw your masterpiece on my way to work today," Brooke says. "It was eye-catching and thought-provoking. The size and limited color palette made it stand out."

"Thanks. I think it's one of my favorites. But, you know, same subject matter, different piece."

"If it brings you some p-e-a-c-e, I'm all for it. How long do you think this one will run?"

I shrug. "Anyone's guess."

Four days is my record.

My sister Katherina used to spell words out loud like they were all acronyms. It's nice knowing Brooke remembers and still pays attention to my art. When we were dating, I took her to some museums in Balboa Park so we could talk about what to look for when critiquing a piece. She didn't want to meet my mom without knowing how to talk about her art. I think being able to admit you don't know much about something and taking the steps to learn is one of the coolest things a person can do with their time.

Before she walks away, I take a few triangles of baklava from the dessert case and add them to her tray.

"Who are those for?"

"Your table with all the kids." I crouch to get the box full of salt and pepper we use to refill the shakers on the tables. "I heard one of the girls say she wanted it. Just tell them they're on the house because we're closing soon or something."

Brooke smiles like she understands what I gain by making them happy. I stay behind the counter and watch their eyes light up when she offers the dessert. Then I ring up three pieces of baklava and pay for it with my tips.

Once everyone is gone and the door is locked, Stavros pulls me over to the big sink in the kitchen.

"You know," he starts, "my cousin Christos in Greece likes to spray the paint on the buildings, like you." Stavros frowns and shrugs simultaneously. On him, it's more of an acceptance of what is than outright disapproval. "You gonna get caught if you don' wash better. And"—there's the frown again—"it don' look nice when you deliver the plates."

I had no idea Stavros knew I was a street artist. He knows my mom is an artist and that I make art, too, but we never talked about it. I guess the major clue is on the tips of my fingers. I usually clean it up better, using acetone if I have to, but I was exhausted.

"I haven't gotten caught yet," I tell him.

"First times come for everybody. *Próti forá*. First time," he says. Never missing an opportunity to teach me some Greek. "Let me show you something."

He grabs a canister of cooking spray from above the grill, which he proceeds to spray all over my hands. Followed by a liberal application of dish soap and coarse salt. He makes a scrubbing motion in lieu of instruction before walking away, and I'll be goddamned if the paint doesn't come right off.

I head back out on the floor and sit at the counter, waiting for my order and marveling at my hands.

"Why are you staring at your hands like you're on magic mushrooms?" Brooke asks.

"Stavros got all the paint off my skin with dish soap, cooking spray, and salt."

"Wonders never cease."

"Order up!" the cook yells.

"Thanks." As soon as I take the aluminum container from the pickup shelf, my phone vibrates in my pocket. I pull it out and read a text message from Bash.

I'm in front of Tide Pool Coffee. Got you an Americano.

I text, *Be there in ten.*

"Eating or trading?" Brooke asks.

"Trading. You have a ride?"

"I have my car."

She knows I have a thing against people walking anywhere alone.

I say, "Bye," to Brooke and take a left out of Nikko's and start walking the five blocks to The Chicken Coop.

Bash is right where he said. Sipping coffee and stealing my fries, even though his deluxe gyro plate came with some of his own. We swap take-out containers before even saying hello and he hands me a much needed coffee. By ten o'clock at night, most people who work in restaurants are tired and too hungry to talk until they've had a few bites to eat.

"What did you get me?"

"The Mother Clucker."

"Perfect." Best-named sandwich in San Diego.

"I'll never understand mayonnaise," Bash says before taking another bite of his gyro. He proceeds to talk with his mouth full until he swallows the first bite. "I mean, it sounds disgusting in theory, right? Oil and egg yolks whipped together or whatever, but then——" He wiggles his fingers. "Magic."

"There's no mayo on your sandwich."

"I *know*. I'm talking about what I got *you*."

"You want to switch halfway through, don't you?"

"Maybe. This is pretty freaking good, though. They put the *luxe* in *deluxe* over there." He laughs without making a sound, mouth open wide, so I let him have his moment without explaining those words mean the same thing.

"You want to come over and play *Crack of Doom* on Xbox?"

"I can't. I have something I need to do."

"All right, man. Next time." Bash stands and stretches before walking his take-out container to the trash receptacle.

For someone who likes to play survival games, he throws away a ton of recyclable aluminum. "I'm gonna give my fries to the homeless guy that hangs out on the corner outside the bank," I tell him. "Where's your car?"

"Fir Street."

"Same."

When we get to the corner, the homeless man usually sitting on a plaid blanket at the corner of Fir and Kettner isn't there. Aluminum foiled again. I toss my fries into the trash and slip the take-out container into the adjacent recycling bin. Bash and I say our goodbyes when we reach his ancient Honda. He'll go home to his Xbox, and I'll go back to my computer searches.

I didn't tell him about the little kids that came into the restaurant tonight. Bash stopped asking why I couldn't hang out a long time ago. He knows.

Twenty minutes later, I'm jiggling my key in the lock. Jonesy opens the right side of our mustard-yellow double doors and nods his hello.

"Any interesting customers come in tonight?"

"Just a lady with four little kids. Three of them girls under ten. How about you? Catch any bad guys lately?"

"Working on it."

Work fucking harder. I don't say it, but it's screaming in my head.

Jonesy passes me on his way out with a pat on my shoulder. I know it's meant as more paternal than patronizing, but the little kids in the restaurant got under my skin and it makes me bristle. "Leaving so soon?"

He rubs one side of his salt-and-pepper beard with his index finger, gauging my level of sarcasm. "There's work to be done, as you continue to point out."

As I will. Forever. "All right, man. See you next time."

I don't hate Jonesy. I don't even dislike him. He's truly one of the good guys. But I have to blame someone other than myself, or I won't make it to age nineteen.

Mom is parked on the couch with our dog. When she hears me walk into the living room, she shuffles a bunch of loose papers and tucks them into her sketchbook.

"Home an hour before curfew." I can't tell if that statement is applauding me for doing something right or hinting she knows I've been sneaking out.

I'm the only legal adult I know with a midnight curfew. One of the prices I pay for living at home that has nothing to do with the overinflated rent situation in America's Finest City. *If you can afford it* should be part of their slogan.

With the exception of late-breaking stories, news at this time of night repeats the hits from the day. Unless an inflammatory tweet got sent by the current POTUS, from the White House, dressed in his bathrobe, leaving both sides scratching their heads. Visualize that weirdness with me and let it go. Mom rubs her hands over her face and makes her way to the television. Turning it off would be a first, considering she's either watching the news or working on something, but tonight a human interest story catches her attention. She's blocking my view, but I hear them announce the headline as I head to the kitchen for a glass of water.

SHOTS FIRED AT A HIGH SCHOOL IN ELKWOOD, WASHING‹ TON, WERE DETERMINED TO BE AN ELABORATE PRANK.

Mom kneels in front of the screen, watching closely as the camera pans the front lawn where teachers and students are clustered together. The reporter continues, saying authorities raced to the scene in anticipation of what would have been the twenty-fourth school shooting across the nation this year. I suppress a frustrated groan. I honestly can't believe we don't have stricter gun laws. We all know the NRA feeds political campaigns. It's no secret that our country needs to get real about what matters. Namely, people's lives. I'm glad I'm old enough to vote in the next election, because this guy *has not so much brain as ear-wax.* Hats off to Shakespeare's *Troilus and Cressida* for that gem.

The story closes with them saying the student responsible is in deep sheet. More or less. I'm paraphrasing.

Banquo comes into the kitchen when he hears me opening cabinets. He's seventy-seven in people years now, so I let him eat as much people food as he wants. Mom doesn't approve, but he's been through everything with me, just like Bash. He's earned it.

"Hey, Banquo. You want a treat?"

That offer gets his septuagenarian tail wagging. S-e-p-t-u-a-g-e-n-a-r-i-a-n. Banquo is a German shepherd-Lab mix, named for one of the Thanes in *Macbeth*. The one that should have been king. Mom follows him into the kitchen, and I hide my face behind a cabinet door, taking stock of what we have to eat. For some reason, the entire lower shelf is lined with boxes of macaroni and cheese that weren't there yesterday.

"You want me to make you something?" Mom asks.

She's behind me now, sifting through the cabinet over my shoulder. The smell of burning leaves wafts around me, which can only mean one thing. She's smoking again.

Most of the time she's tranced-out working and I bring dinner home. When she pulls the occasional let-me-nurture-you thing, I recognize it as her attempt to make up for lost moments, a poultice against the punishing place her mind takes her when she's working. Not that she was ever a doting parent. Make no mistake. Evie Ellis loves her kids, but she was always a career-driven artist. She left us with our neighbor, friends, anyone that could help, if needed. The sad reality is we both became victims of our selfishness.

"Does it have to be one of the dozens of boxes of mac 'n' cheese?" I throw her a bone, then grab a literal bone-shaped biscuit from the glass jar on the counter for Banquo.

"They were on sale," she says. "Five for a dollar. I thought it was a good idea to stockpile some food in case of emergency.

That way we wouldn't have to go out and fight the people trying to shop. They're meant to be kept as extras."

It rains ten inches a year in San Diego, so unless we're about to get hit by a nuclear bomb, twenty boxes of anything seems excessive for two people. Three if you count Jonesy. But I shouldn't joke. Not when the POTUS keeps insulting world leaders known to have weapons of mass destruction.

I take a visual inventory of everything in the cabinets. Counting the obscene number of canned soup, beans, and pickles until I close the cabinet without choosing anything. She's been stockpiling more and more.

"I'm not actually hungry," I tell her, "but thanks."

"How was work tonight?"

I don't know if she wants to make small talk or if she's asking how much money I made.

"Madness." I dig into my pocket for the tips I made. Then I take thirty percent for myself and leave the rest on the counter. "How'd work go for you?"

I lean against the sink and look into her haunted, oversized brown eyes. I still refer to her drawings and stuff as her *work*, because I don't want to push her over the edge. Especially if she's trying to work for real again.

"I started a new painting that's *also* madness," she tells me, "'*yet there be method in it.*'"

That's the first Shakespeare joke she's made in a long time.

"That's great. I can't wait to see it." And honestly, it is great. A new piece could mean a comeback if she gets back into the swing of painting, but I know better than to get my hopes up.

"Yeah," she says with a shrug, inserting a long pause. "It's just a start. We'll see."

"Every great piece of art had to start with the first stroke. You told me that. Do you want to show it to me now?"

"You want to see it?"

"Of course. You're Evie Ellis. Who wouldn't want to see your new work?"

"Okay," she says. "Yeah."

I follow her and she hesitates before letting me inside her private realm.

Her easel is set up with a big canvas. It's just a sketch covered by a thin underpainting. Three teenage girls that might be a nod to the Weird Sisters from *Macbeth*, but only the one in the center has her features drawn.

"She kind of looks like . . . *me*. And *you*, of course, but younger."

"And infinitely wiser, I'm sure," Mom says. "I can't seem to get her out of my head lately."

Today must have been a good-memory day.

That's also a good thing. Because after the girls vanished, she kind of disappeared. Maybe she's finally ready to paint herself back into the picture.

CLOSE QUARTERS BATTLE

I TOLD MY sisters to head straight to our room when we got home so we could regroup and avoid a close quarters battle, but Birdie isn't having it. She's soaked to the bone, waiting for our mother to get here. I can tell she's ready to get into it by the way she stands taller, arms crossed, despite the pleading look I'm giving her to *not* start something she can't finish.

"What did Dieter mean when he said you were the leader of The Nest?" she asks, before Mother even has a chance to remove her black rain boots.

"It means she's the lady boss of all the women," Blue answers from the couch. She's already stripped out of her wet clothes and picked up her latest needlepoint project. She just keeps her needle going up and down through the fabric without looking at Birdie. I lean closer to see what she's stitching into a shirt, and it says *Only The Strong Survive*. I envy Blue's ability to state facts, but I think we all knew what Dieter meant at face value.

That's not what Birdie's asking, though, and Mother knows it, because she fills a kettle with water for tea instead of validating Blue's answer. She floats lemon balm, motherwort, peppermint, and ginger on the water and places it on the burner. Picking carefully chosen herbs known to induce a calm state while tempering her answer. Have you ever noticed when you're waiting answers, and the other person stalls, how normal sounds become amplified? I swear, the temporary click-whoosh-hah of the blue flame racing around the burner is louder than an ocean wave receding.

"What it means," Mother says finally, "is any decisions pertaining to The Nest will be discussed between me and Dieter Ackerman, making it easier for him to focus on the workings of The Burrow. I'll be performing the same duties with the addition of overseeing tasks decided upon for everyone in The Nest."

"Like a partnership?" Birdie asks.

"In a word."

"So, more than a partnership," Birdie prods. "If it's in a word, what are the other words? Can we get a whole sentence about what your new partnership will mean for us and the rest of the coalition?"

I lean against a wall next and pick underneath my fingernails, where moss-green acrylic paint has made its stubborn home over the last week. I'm waiting for the boom, thanks to Birdie who keeps pushing Mother's buttons. Sure enough, Mother turns away from the stove quicker than usual, her dying patience drawing her mouth into a flat line. But it's the way she lowers the spoon exaggeratedly slow, stopping herself from slamming it down, that gives me pause.

"What exactly are you asking, Birdie? If we're on the subject of words, perhaps you could use yours? I caught the exchange between you and Daniel. Is there anything you'd like to tell me about that?"

I decide to interject before Birdie shoots her mouth off about Daniel and starts singing like a songbird about her own involvement. "I think what Birdie means is—"

"I didn't ask you, Honey. I asked your sister."

I hold up my hands in surrender. Fair enough. I was just trying to divert attention back to what it means for us, my own ranking, hoping to stem the flow of whatever is bound to fly from Birdie's mouth.

"So you're just going to do whatever Dieter wants like you're his—"

Don't say it, Birdie. Don't say it, Birdie. Don't say it, Birdie.

The galled look on Mother's face is enough to stop my sister from blurting what her tone implied.

"She's his second-in-command," I offer. But inside I'm shrinking back, knowing I said something similar to Birdie in the locker room about doing whatever Daniel says.

"I understood," Birdie says. "But why not assign that duty to Magda?"

"You heard him," Mother says with a shrug. "To avoid nepotism. He doesn't want our way of life to be perceived as an inequitable, Ackerman-run compound. He needed someone to act as second-in-command. Someone in The Nest."

"But it is Ackerman-run," I say. "Or it was when we got here, so why the change?"

"Whenever anyone joins or leaves this coalition, The Nest and The Burrow are changed, and hopefully evolve. Such as when we were welcomed because of my nursing background. Duties were shifted. Magda is excellent at gardening and making tinctures with herbs. No one can deny that. But she isn't a trained nurse practitioner with a special interest in pharmacology."

My own feelings about this topic rise to the surface against my better judgement. The tension between the families is rising fast. "But she *is* his wife," I say. "And the other Nesters will think—"

"I know very well what they already think," Mother snaps. "Just because I understand Dieter's larger vision for this compound does not mean I jumped into bed with him the first chance I got."

"Fine. If you say it's not true then I believe you."

"I should hope so," Mother says. "If I don't have the trust

of my own daughters, then I've done something very wrong in raising you."

Birdie stares at me without comment. That doesn't mean I don't know what she's thinking. We all get the same verge-of-an-eye-roll look whenever Mother makes statements steeped in as much guilt as the nurturing tea she's pouring into mugs.

I heard what Mother said. I'm just not as quick to believe it. Especially since her defense was that she didn't jump into bed with him the *first chance* she got. We've been here for a year. That's a lot of chances. I am glad Birdie stopped pouring gas on the inflammatory situation, though. Last time she entered a crossfire with Mother, it was over Birdie's annoyance with the way the genders are divided into separate garrisons. The blowback resulted in us cleaning our assigned bunker and rotating supplies. We still had to spend a couple of hours rushing through our homework when we were done. H-o-m-e-w-o-r-k. Half-of-my-energy-wasted-on-random-knowledge. It was two A.M. before we crawled into our beds.

Mother snaps at Birdie the most, to be honest, because she's annoyed my middle sister doesn't love her the way she craves, with unwavering attachment and unflinching allegiance. We're more loyal to each other than anyone else, and I think it's slowly driving Mother mad. Maybe it was different when we were little and needed her more. I don't remember. But ever since we came to The Nest, Mother has followed Dieter Ackerman's dictate like a loyal dog, no matter what it means for my sisters and me. That's how I knew Birdie was on the verge of saying *like his bitch,* because she's said it before in private. Out of the three of us, Birdie is a perfect example of why we need rules. I enforce them. Blue acts like they don't apply to her. But Birdie will flat-out disregard them if she's got an agenda. A lovestruck liar's agenda.

I say, "I have to hit the books," the same time Mother says, "It's getting late."

The circles blooming beneath her eyes are undoubtedly

from fretting over our whereabouts earlier. We need to get our cellphone back before she tries to call us again.

"Finish your tea so you can head upstairs and try to get some sleep," Mother says.

Fine by me. I've been trying to get my sisters into our shared bedroom since we got home. Our house is a rustic two-story bungalow with wide-plank wooden walls and three bedrooms, built specifically for life in The Nest. There are three rooms on the second floor that we have to ourselves. Mother uses one of the downstairs rooms for her bedroom, a tiny room made for storage that barely fits more than her bed and a small dresser. She claims she likes sleeping close to the front door and keeps a loaded gun behind a painting on the wall next to her bed. For safety and quick access. I was under the impression living here, in and of itself, was about safety. That's the way she sold it to us. But Mother says you can never be too safe.

Luckily for Birdie, Mother's room isn't underneath ours or she'd never get away with sneaking out to meet Daniel. I've only snuck out once, with Blue, and it was to follow Birdie and make sure she was okay. My sisters and I share an upstairs bedroom for sleeping and use the other for doing homework. The extra room is small, more of a walk-in closet that's filled with supplies we've stockpiled. Canned soup and vegetables, dried foods like macaroni and cheese, powdered milk, and medicine. The bedroom and study are separated by a long bathroom with two sinks, accessible by adjoining pocket doors on either end.

I've never minded sharing sleeping quarters with my sisters. We all have our own twin beds. Mine is in a corner since I'm the oldest. Birdie and Blue are in bunk beds. None of our blankets and sheets match like you see in fancy catalogs, but they're warm and we did get to pick them out ourselves. Sometimes I wish I had my own room, and at least a full-sized bed, but I prefer being near my sisters at all times. Rationally accepting a situation is part of the way we live and train. This aboveground setup prepares us for living in close quarters in the bunker in the event of a nuclear attack or natural disaster.

"I have zero interest in going to bed," Birdie says. "Despite Mother and her attempts to baby us into complacency with her dumb herbal tea."

She paces around the room and pulls back the curtain, peering outside like she wants to flee.

"Don't even think about roaming around tonight. Not after that meeting."

"She won't have to," Blue says.

Of all the *weird* shit Blue has said, this one takes the cake for vaguest. Birdie stares at her like she has gamma rays for eyes and can see inside Blue's brain.

Something scrapes against the house and Birdie rushes past me to the window. I follow in close pursuit, and sure enough Daniel is making his way onto the roof. The uneven row of nailhead-sized freckles puckering above his brow.

My sister lifts the sash and wraps her arms around his neck so quickly he nearly loses his balance.

"What happened?" Birdie asks.

"I had to see you before I leave."

"No. I meant that literally," Birdie says, momentarily clueless to his adoration. "What *happened?* What do you mean *leave?* For how long? Where are you going?"

"We did what we were supposed to do," Daniel says, which tells us nothing. "Dieter is sending me out on a solo mission. Somewhere in the woods. He says it's a test of fealty. I'm supposed to lie low and retrieve things on a list using a topographic map and coordinates. He expects me back by the time my suspension is over. I saw the list and distance and think I can be back by Monday."

"But we never go anywhere by ourselves," Birdie says.

"Ansel asked if he could come with me, but his father said no. He wants me to think about how and why I got caught alone."

One corner of his mouth twitches, and anyone can see he knows why he got caught but doesn't want to say.

"Because of me?" Birdie's singsong voice quavers. "I think I panicked and blocked pieces out. They say people can black out from stress."

My sister is staring at him for answers with the big brown eyes of a doe, her long end-lashes curling and blinking in a way that makes Birdie appear innocent, even when she's not.

Daniel shakes his head. "You didn't black out. You threw the first one."

"No, I didn't."

Daniel tips his head like he doesn't understand why Birdie is denying her involvement. To him of all people.

"Yes," Daniel says. "You did. Annalise pushed you into it. Don't you remember?"

Birdie shakes her head. The opposite of Big R *Responsible*.

"Did she hit Whitlock's car?" I ask.

Daniel nods and I throw up my arms in frustration.

"My god, Birdie. He's my *teacher*. What were you thinking?"

"Don't worry," Daniel tells us. "Dieter doesn't know you were there, and never will."

"She *shouldn't* have been there," I snap.

"I know. That's my bad. It got intense. But Birdie's capable of doing more than milking goats and collecting eggs."

"Of course she is, Daniel. We all are. That's not the point."

Daniel's eyes dip because he knows I'm right. Unlike Birdie, who looks like she just hatched from an egg.

"Dieter might not know Birdie was there, but Annalise does," I tell them.

"Ansel is working on that," Daniel says.

Ansel, who couldn't look me in the eye for more than a few seconds.

"I'll come with you," Birdie says. "All I need is my bug-out bag."

"The hell you will," I tell her. "I'm not going to be the one that has to explain why you're gone to Mother, first of all. Second, we stick together, no matter what. If you go, we go, and I'm not about to risk facing some huge punishment so you can follow your heart into the woods." I look at my sister's boyfriend and he hangs his head. "No offense, Daniel, but I'm not down with all this secrecy."

He doesn't meet my eyes when he says, "None taken," because his pained gaze is glued on my sister. "Honey's right. You can't come. It will just stir up more trouble."

"Since you seem to remember what happened, maybe you can explain what the hell you guys were doing in the first place."

"I wish I could tell you, but if I say anything else about the mission or where Dieter's sending me, he said I won't be allowed back into the coalition. Talk to Ansel."

Daniel is quietly confident to a fault. Quick to learn and succeed in all our training. But right now his thin smile is revealing his own apprehension.

"He shouldn't go," Blue says, so quietly I forgot she was in the room. She's breathing heavier than normal. The words barely escaping her lips. She's always been like this, an empath in touch with people's feelings. This time she's picked up on Daniel's reluctance to leave.

"I don't think you should go, either," Birdie says. "I've never heard of Dieter sending anyone out alone."

She glances at me and back to Daniel. Caught in her own struggle with fealty.

"It does seem kind of harsh," I offer.

Daniel looks away and I can't read his expression.

"I'm not the first. He sent this guy named Thane out once. He was a guy Dieter knew in the military. He didn't have a family and wanted to join up with us, but he was aggressive with his opinions on how we should do everything. He thought because they went to Desert Storm together, Dieter would put him in equal control of everything. When he didn't, Thane tried to recruit Burrowers into a new group. My dad said he thought the guy had Gulf War Syndrome. But Dieter is all about loyalty. If you break that trust, he wants you to prove you're worthy of staying."

"What happened to him? Where is he now?"

"Dieter sent him on a solo mission to think about what he wanted. He asked my dad to follow Thane to see if he might fake out and circle back. We all thought Thane would leave and not come back. He never fit into the greater group, and because of that they never trusted him." Daniel shrugs one shoulder.

"So he came back?"

He shakes his head and chews the inside corner of his mouth. Reading body language is an important skill for preppers. We use it to assess people's motivations, based on their energy. I don't know how Daniel's parents died, but his energy is telling me this isn't the right time to press him about it. "Did you bring Birdie's EDC with you?" I ask, changing the subject.

"No. Ansel has it somewhere safe." He peers over his shoulder at the yard like he didn't come here alone.

I rush to the window. "Is he out there?"

Daniel fills up the window with his frame to keep me from looking out, giving me my answer. I turn and grab my flashlight from my nightstand. Before Daniel can even make sense of what's happening, I yank him into the room by his jacket and take his place on the roof. The Burrow Boys don't make the rules here. I do. I shine my tactical flashlight on Ansel, hitting him with twelve-hundred lumens right before his own light fades and he ducks behind a tree.

"Why is he hiding?" I snap.

"Because he brought me out here against his dad's orders. He didn't want anyone to know in case someone followed us, or we got caught again. That's why we didn't bring Birdie's bag."

I crawl back inside. "You better go."

"Don't go," Birdie pleads. "Blue is right. She's always right."

"I know. But this is my only home, Birdie. I have to prove myself so I can come back here. To this. To you."

Her shoulders sag before she wraps her arms around herself. It's hard to tell if the visible chill that runs down Birdie's spine is from the cold air filling the room or Daniel being sent away.

He removes his army-green field coat and drapes it around my sister's shoulders. "Take this. Wear it until I get back. It will be like a hug from me every day."

I roll my eyes hard enough for a full rotation, because Mr. Chivalry is the one who got her into this mess.

"Promise me you'll come back," Birdie says.

"I promise, Birdie. I'm gonna do this fast and be back by Monday. End of day, the latest. If anything else comes up about what happened at school, play dumb and DTA."

Don't Trust Anyone.

"What about Ansel? We have to get our phone and her EDC back."

"He'll get it to you," Daniel says. "I trust Ansel with everything, even my life."

Birdie hugs Daniel tight enough to crack his spine. Normally, I'd look away and give them some privacy, but his gaze is locked on me, making sure I heard him, so I nod without knowing why. My top priority is keeping Birdie from flying out that window. If Daniel thinks something might come up and can't or doesn't want to tell us more, you can be sure I'll do whatever it takes to find out why.

Before he leaves, Daniel turns and gives Birdie the same crooked smile my middle sister fell for in the first place, all mischief and adventure and promises made with kisses in the dark. "I'll see you soon," he says.

Daniel is halfway down the cucumber trellis when I duck back onto the roof, closely followed by Birdie. When he reaches the trees, he turns and waves. The gulp of Birdie choking back a sob hits me and I sling my arm over her shoulder, pulling her into a sideways hug that she only allows for a few seconds before going inside. Not me. I wait until Ansel emerges from the trees, and just as expected he glances up at our roof, at me, before they jog through the trees to The Burrow.

"What is happening?" Birdie fusses when I get back inside. "Dieter is sending Daniel out alone, Mother is the leader of The Nest, Annalise looks like she wants to murder us. The whole coalition is in flux."

"Did it occur to you that you participated in something that's creating that flux, even if you *supposedly* can't remember?"

Birdie's hands jump to her hips. "Don't believe me. I. Don't. Care. I know everything can't stay the same forever. We know that better than anyone. But if Daniel isn't back by Monday, I'm out of here."

"Stop saying irrational shit, Birdie, before I tie you up in a bunker to save you from your own stupidity."

"We'll all see reason," Blue says nonchalantly.

My eyes flick to where she's stitching nothing but eyes onto a ten-inch, stretched hoop, using every shade of blue that comes with a rainy day. All-seeing.

"You are *not* the boss of me, Honey," Birdie gripes, grabbing the comic she's been working on and flopping on her bed. A comic where post-apocalyptic Bucky Beaverman is wearing his cape and saving us from a dark rabbit hole where Alice, our mother, lives deep underground.

"Yes, I am. And if I have to tether us together for the next ten days, I will."

I ignore her passive grumblings and grab my own notebook so I can write a letter to Bucky, the only person who won't turn a deaf ear to me today. How's that for *weird?*

Dear Bucky,

I have been wanting to talk to you since the shit hit the fan. Not in the ultimate prepper way, but still. I knew it would once Blue and I found Birdie hiding in the locker room. I can't believe she tagged along with her boyfriend on a training mission. She helped them make flash-bang grenades to use as a distraction so they could "get something" for the leader of the prepper compound. Steal something is more like it. Yeah. You read that right. How many ways are there to say dumb? Birdie seems genuinely sorry and distraught. Frankly, everything is a mess. The only saving grace is Birdie not getting caught, otherwise Dieter would be sending her away with her boyfriend, who I don't like much, to say the least. The leader, not the boyfriend. I wouldn't go so far as to say I hate Dieter Ackerman, but I've been inching toward it for months. I'm still holding out some hope that he's a decent guy, since he is the one who offered us a place to live where we'll be safe if and when the proverbial shit hits the fan for real. Stability isn't something we've ever had. Daniel, Birdie's boyfriend, that messy-haired rebel with a cause who stares at Birdie like the moon rises and sets in her dark eyes, is kind of sweet, if I'm being honest. But he still put her in harm's way by dragging her along for the ride. And now, he's off proving himself to Dieter, whatever that means. And tomorrow, the three of us have to go back to school, after I crawled through an air shaft in front of my entire class to escape during a lockdown. You read that right, too. I may have to talk to my chemistry teacher again, who we think is a prepper like us, but could be a lone wolf trying to feel out our group. Most of all we have to try to act somewhat normal, if that's even possible, because what's normal? For us, prepared is the new normal. We'll be the odd girls out in a new and improved way. Rémy Lamar is the only one who won't treat me any different. But I wish he'd stop trying to take my picture, or get to know me or whatever. Shit! Birdie just started sobbing in her bunk. She's wearing headphones, which makes me think she might be listening to songs she and Daniel talked about all those times she snuck out. I've run out of things to say to her that might make her feel better. She's not alone. The entire compound got put on curfew. Dieter's personal version of martial law. Birdie told Blue and me she doesn't remember everything that happened, but that seems impossible, right? So why is she lying? What if they were trying to steal something for Dieter that could get them in real trouble? Ansel knows. He must. I don't care if his father said we weren't allowed to talk about it at school. It's happening. Ansel has Birdie's EDC, and a lot of explaining to do. Thanks for listening to me vent. Update soon.

Love,

Honey

∗ FUD ∗

FEAR, UNCERTAINTY, AND DOUBT

I **LEFT MY** EDC in the station wagon, opting to bring a plain black backpack to school. Mr. Whitlock, my prepper-slash—chemistry teacher, is probably right about erring on the side of caution. BSTS. I waited to be summoned to Principal Weaver's office all day, but nothing interrogatory happened by definition. That could mean Mother handled it sufficiently or it's still coming. Either way, I've championed through the unavoidable speculation of five of my classes. Honestly, I deserve a pat on the back for managing to not give my thoughts to my tongue during this class in particular, because I definitely noticed the eyes glancing my way while Mr. Whitlock taught today's lesson. Heard the occasional whispers of *weird sisters, involved, Daniel Dobbs,* and succeeded in keeping my hair-trigger responses on safety. Mr. Whitlock must have heard them, too, because his eyes landed on mine several times. I only noticed because I was watching him like a hawk—no—like Achilles. Anticipating what he might say or do in case I had to swoop in, but he gave away nothing about what happened, and that leaves me waiting for him to yank away the dangling fish he held out for us yesterday.

For now, he's letting us use the last twenty minutes of class to make up work from what he termed as yesterday's interruption.

Let's agree right here and now that *interruption* is an excellent example of putting it mildly.

I try to focus on my own paper, but I'm sharing a lab table with Shawna Mooney, Rémy Lamar, and his lab partner, Brian Sharazi, who's been elbowing Rémy in the ribs for the last twenty minutes like it's an uncontrollable twitch. I don't know much about Brian. He's on the soccer team with Rémy and they hang at the same table during lunch. I saw him there today. Stealing glances at my sisters and me, but mostly Birdie, who was perched on the table with one foot on the bench, legs crossed casually, looking around at, well, everyone, daring them to comment. Other than noticing how often Brian scrolls through social media on his phone to laugh at whatever he's seeing, the frequency with which he copies Rémy's work, and his overall lack of participation in class, I know nothing. I've never gone to a soccer game to see how he performs on the field, but I'd be surprised if his disposition was any different. In fact, I'd wager he's a perpetual wingman. On and off the field. Right or left wing TBD.

THREAT ASSESSMENT:
BRIAN SHARAZI | 5'9" STRONG TO AVERAGE BUILD |
CLOSED SOCIAL GROUP | TRUSTING
MOST LIKELY TO: try and become an internet sensation.
LEAST LIKELY TO: achieve said level of success based on work ethic.
8/10 WOULD IMPEDE GROUP SURVIVAL IN AN
EMERGENCY SITUATION.
CASUALTY POTENTIAL: medium

"Would you *stop* doing that," Shawna snaps at Brian through gritted teeth. "You're only making it weirder."

Yes. Please don't test the oldest *weird sister*.

I'm startled by Shawna's outburst. And thankful for it, truthfully. But when our eyes meet, she shies and dips her eyes to the peanut butter cookies she added to our table on the sly, even though food isn't allowed in the labs. I read her wrong. Shawna Mooney is a rule-breaker. Still, the static tension in the air around us is higher than if we were doing the balloon experiment all over again. I focus my attention on documenting the chemical reactions, hoping their fear, uncertainty, and doubt about my unconventional exit doesn't make things weirder.

Rémy clears his throat.

I stand corrected, and ignore him.

He clears it again. "Hey, can you tell us anything about what happened yesterday?"

I shift my gaze to him without answering and without moving my pen from the page. He's leaning in, eyes two shades darker than his skin, wide and expectant. The same color as the sticky-sweet molasses I rotate monthly in the storage cellar. I stare at him without responding, and out of the blue he adds, "Your eyes have a lot of light and dark variation on the color, like sugar-pine-tree bark. I wasn't expecting that."

"O-kay. *Thanks.*" I give him more what-the-fuck attitude than he warrants. Considering Rémy just unwittingly helped me solve a problem I need to address in art next period. To be fair, I should probably be glad he didn't liken my eyes to juniper bark, which is the boring putty color of a decomposing dog turd.

Brian elbows him again and Shawna makes an annoyed "Tsk."

"Yeah, so, yesterday?" Rémy prods.

"No," I tell him.

He recoils. I don't know why he's taken aback. It's not like we're friends in the truest sense. Rémy has always been nicer to me than most people. And sure, we talk in art class because our easels are side by side. Let me rephrase. Rémy talks to *me* in art class and I usually answer noncommittally. That doesn't mean we're friends, does it?

"No, as in you're not gonna tell us?" he prods. "Or no, you can't talk about it because Principal Weaver said you couldn't?"

I glance at him, full side-eye, letting that serve as my answer.

"Come on. Not even an explanation about climbing into the air shaft?" Brian adds. "I mean, that was badass, don't get me wrong, but definitely outside the scope of normal."

"Whose definition of normal?" I ask. "Yours or mine?"

"I actually wouldn't mind an explanation, either," Shawna says. She rubs the back of her head where she must have hit it during her tragicomic collapse.

I take a deep, audible breath.

"If she says she can't talk about it, maybe we should let it go." Rémy picks up his pen and pretends to study his homework, but really he's just fidget-tapping the end on the table.

I have a twinge of guilt in my gut about Shawna, especially now that I've eaten three of her peanut butter cookies. Rémy, on the other hand, isn't fooling me by coming to my defense. I know he tried to follow me into the air shaft. I just don't know why.

This is one of those times when the Ready part of the three Rs perplexes me. I'm ready for catastrophic events. Hell, I'm ready for normal stuff, too, like having to pick up and move, which can also be disastrous depending on the circumstances. But I'm not, and have never been, ready to explain being a prepper to my peers. Mostly because they're not my peers. What I mean is, they're my peers to a degree when I'm at school and trying to blend, but they're not in the eyes of what everyone at the compound considers pacifist Outsider society. The casualties lying in wait.

Plus, once you're labeled an outcast in high school, it's hard to come back from it. I have nothing to gain by way of explanation. I've been the new kid enough times to understand high school acceptance ranking. I'm not all the way at the bottom, but I'm nowhere near the top with the mall rats. I'm with the poets and band geeks and tabletop-game players. What Blue calls the comfortable middle.

The thing most people get wrong about me is I'm *not* gung-ho for the end of days or excited about taking a harsh stand against Outsiders when the SHTF. I just understand the reasons we're not inclined to let anyone take the provisions we've worked so hard to amass. They've already forgotten the storm last winter, right after we first arrived, where we lost power. They just need to think of that on a massive scale, how people were buying everything they could get their hands on in case power didn't return for days, or weeks, which wouldn't be worst-case scenario. What about if it doesn't come back on for months, a year? Preppers hope for the best, plan for the worst, and have each other's backs.

My eyes flick reflexively to Mr. Whitlock's gunmetal behemoth of a desk where he's grading papers. I'm not surprised to see he's paying attention to this exchange, listening as best he can from four tables away. He gives me that knowing prepper nod again. And there's the rub. Dieter Ackerman told us to act normal, so I should probably give them something simple to chew on.

I sketch a juniper branch in the corner of my notebook while I answer as honestly as I can. "I have this long-standing agreement with my sisters that if anything dangerous goes down while we're at school, we'll meet at one of several predesignated spots. That's it, really. Not much else to tell."

"That's kind of sweet," Shawna says.

"Did you just say Honey was sweet?" Brian jokes. Like I haven't heard *that* one before. Folks, I've got a million of them.

"Oh, shut up, Brian," Shawna chastises. "I meant the closeness of Honey and her sisters."

There was genuine awe in her sugary voice. And sure, for me it's sweet the way air is necessary for breathing, just not sweet enough for them to invite us to any of their parties.

Antifreeze sweet. In opposite world, I guess that makes us Outsiders, too.

I turn to the side and tie my right boot laces, rolling my eyes hard enough to see my own gray matter. Because that's what this is, isn't it, a gray matter? There's nothing black and white about crawling into an air shaft in front of everybody. Questions were inevitable. I don't know why I can't let my sisters too far out of sight, in all honesty. But sticking together has always been the unbreakable rule clicking away in the back of my mind.

Mercifully, the bell rings and saves me from this awkward moment. The sparing is temporary since I have my last class of the day with Rémy, who always insists on talking to me regardless of my answers.

I stop myself from being the first one to rush the door. I don't want to be last one out, either, because I need enough time to find Ansel. Avoiding Mr. Whitlock is futile—I know that—but I might be making mountains out of molehills since he doesn't say my name or ask me to stay after class like I assumed. Instead, he asks Rémy to stay behind, and for some reason that bothers me more. I keep my eyes on Mr. Whitlock as I walk to the door, and he slings his presumed EDC onto his desk like he wants to remind me of my own. I nod my understanding, even though *my* bag isn't the one in question.

I should be paying attention to where I'm walking, instead of ogling Whitlock, because I crash into someone coming through the doorway as part of a larger pack. The way the most popular kids in school always migrate. Safety in numbers. I barely have time to register who I've collided with before a baritone voice snips, "Watch where you're going, *weird*." And someone with a more honeyed voice, ironic as that sounds, says, "Apparently she's using the hallways to get around today."

"Yes," I fire back, "I'm only using vents to get into your houses tonight. Sleep tight." *Don't let the EMP bite.*

I don't bother looking to see who I'm talking to because

they're usually all the same, and the *Ready* and *Responsible* part of me needs to find Ansel. But I've clearly had enough of holding my tongue today. Damn the consequences.

Once I'm in the crowded hallway, I search for Ansel's wavy golden mop. The same tall, athletic build that makes the football and wrestling coaches cry from loss also makes him easy to spot at his locker. Even when he's dressed like a gray man and has his head down to hide his blackened eye. When he sees me walking toward him, he closes the sky-blue metal door, spins the built-in lock, and walks away. Fast. Weaving in and out of people. Ansel is one of the only, if not *the* only, Burrow Boy I consider a friend. We talk in the hallways, when he comes to our house on errands to pick up eggs or tinctures. He even eats lunch with us sometimes because he and Daniel are such good friends. Birdie is convinced he has a crush on me and can't believe I'm not more into the freckle-nosed cutie (as she calls him), because it's obvious he wants to be my End Of The World Buddy For Life. Truth: I'm all for having Ansel as my platonic EOTWBFL. Which is why I don't understand what's gotten into him. Unless I'm right about how he got his black eye.

I call his name and he picks up his pace, turning a corner in a way that's intentionally evasive. I try to catch up without breaking into a jog, but I'm on the wrong side of traffic in this hallway. People are coming at me in waves, bumping my shoulders when we split around each other. By the time I reach the corner, Ansel is nowhere to be seen, leaving me at a loss since Daniel told me I should talk to him about what happened, and Birdie's EDC.

I'm contemplating whether to give up or keep looking when someone yanks me into the ADA elevator by my field jacket. I spin, ready to lash out as the doors pinch behind me, and find Ansel with his index finger pressed against his pursed mouth.

"Don't yell. We can't get caught talking together. Not by anybody at school or from The Nest or The Burrow."

"Why? Because your dad said so?"

It sounds snippy, even to me, but the initial shock of being yanked into the closed box hasn't waned.

"Yes and no."

My pulse slows and I examine Ansel's black eye. That color reference is not what an artist would consider the amalgamation of all colors. His bruise is raw umber and alizarin crimson with yellow ochre bleeding out around the edges. I could mix the shades perfectly without my palette knife ever touching a dab of black paint.

"Did Dieter do that to you?"

I reach for his cleft chin to get a better look at his corporal punishment, and he jerks his face away. That's how I know the wound is more than flesh deep.

"It was a backhand for fucking up and mouthing off in Daniel's defense. It doesn't matter. I pulled you in here to say I have your sister's EDC."

Those are the words I wanted to hear, but—"Ansel, it *does* matter."

He may not have spoken up in Daniel's defense at the meeting, but he did speak up.

"Let it go, Honey. Please. I'm taking a risk just talking to you at school. Can you meet me in the woods after curfew so I can get it to you? Alone."

"Who am I, Birdie? Flying out windows to meet a Burrow Boy in the woods. You sure you don't want to climb up the trellis instead like Daniel and drop it off?"

I'm trying to lighten his dark mood.

Ansel doesn't respond to or acknowledge bringing Daniel to our house, but I notice both his eyes are swollen from lack of sleep.

"Those two act like Romeo and Juliet. It's kind of sickening sometimes," I add, trying.

He runs a hand through his wavy hair, making it stick up in awkward angles. "I don't think you're Birdie, but I'm not allowed to come to The Nest right now. Can you meet me or not?"

"What if we get caught? Won't that be worse?"

"Are *you* gonna get caught, Honey Juniper?"

I stare at his black eye and weigh the consequences, even though I know the answer. "No. Of course not."

The five-minute warning bell trills and Ansel releases the finger pressing the elevator's Closed button. "Exactly. Neither will I. Meet me at the abandoned treehouse at midnight."

The doors glide open and he's gone, hitching his EDC up on his shoulder and heading to class. I wonder if he edited the contents of his bag, too.

I remember too late that I want to ask why he ignored me in the air shaft, and what they were getting for his father that's so secret.

"Ansel, wait."

He doesn't acknowledge me calling his name for the third time in the last two days. There's nothing I can do but wait. I have to get to art class and deal with how I see my own eyes. Not to mention a different boy who very much won't ignore me.

✦ FWIW ✦

FOR WHAT IT'S WORTH

I LOVE THE Band-Aid smell of acrylics and how it blends with the dankness coming from the stack of always-damp plastic tubs next to a sink crusted with dried paint swatches from other people's art. I take comfort in the sighs emitted by people releasing tension from their day before they start working. I'm more relaxed in this room than I've been in days. Thankful for the break, no matter how short-lived. I unroll my paintbrushes from their canvas wrapping and give more thought to what Rémy said about my eye color.

I don't need a fancy cellphone to look up photos of sugarpine bark. Our phone doesn't have those bells and whistles, but even if it did, I wouldn't carry it enough to rely on that rather than my own memory. I've spent enough time among the trees in and around the compound to know sugar-pine bark has deep, irregular threads of dark raw umber running through the burnt sienna. I grab several shades of brown and Payne's gray acrylic paint, and squeeze them onto my palette.

We each have a rectangular mirror clamped to our easels to facilitate our self-portraits, and I'm staring into mine when Ms. Everitt comes by and says, "The eyes. I know they're the windows to the soul, Honey, but you'll have to make an honest decision about yours soon. To know your own eyes is the only way you'll be able to paint another person's realistically. You have it in you to see your truth."

I think it would be amazing to paint Ms. Everitt's portrait. I love her thick champagne-blond hair and translucent green, sea-glass eyes. Her bone structure is delicate and sharp, a living Modigliani painting, where my family features, oversized lips and eyes, would best be served by Dante Gabriel Rossetti, or one of the modern artists Ms. Everitt showed us, like Evie Ellis. I was drawn to her artwork like a moth to a flame during a slide show last month. I couldn't stop wondering what it would be like to paint myself in a dreamlike prepper, worst-case scenario scene, and here I am.

No small feat considering today is another bad mirror day. Thanks to the added stress of meeting Ansel after curfew, worrying that Birdie is too impatient to wait for Daniel to return, and our Mother's new role in The Nest. The only person not currently adding to my tension is Blue. Now, that *is* typical.

I hear the scraping sound before I see Rémy Lamar predictably dragging his wooden easel an inch or two closer to mine.

"How's it going?" He leans forward on his stool and studies the blank mask of creamy Naples yellow taking the place for my eyes, like the shade of hot tea with a splash of milk holds my secrets.

Detach.

The warning goes off in my head, but I ignore it this time. "I finished painting my eyes inside my mind, so really my work here is done. I should call it a day."

"Sarcasm. Wow. That's a new look for you."

The playful jab is so unexpected I can't help throwing him a reply. "Yeah, well, I like to be as unpredictable as possible. Obviously."

He grins and the dimple in his upper cheek gets deeper. Admittedly, this trait makes Rémy Lamar harder to ignore.

"For what it's worth," he says, "I like your choice to have only the middle face exposed. Assuming your eyes will be open once you put them on the canvas. My takeaway so far is there are several sides to you, maybe some faces you're hiding or trying to protect, but at your center, you know who you are. Honestly, it's aces and helped me with mine. But without the eyes, she looks like you but doesn't."

Times where I'm at a loss for words are few and far between, but presently this is one. First of all, I wasn't expecting Rémy Lamar to have that much insight into my work or have it inspire anyone, let alone him. Second, he's wrong. The figures on the right and left are Birdie and Blue, who's shorter than both of us by an inch. I just masked their faces so Ms. Everitt wouldn't be able to tell. It was my way of saying we're so close it feels like we're one person sometimes. I painted Blue's eyes effortlessly, because they say something different than my own. Sympathetic and mystical. Compassionate and dreamy. Peering through the openings in the balaclava. I don't know what my eyes say yet. I'm working on it. My sisters are tucked behind me on either side, the shoulder closest to me slightly hidden. Birdie is to my right in a flowy white jumper over a fitted black T-shirt, ripped black tights, and Docs, her face fully covered by a gas mask. Blue is to my left in a black balaclava, skinny black jeans, Docs, and one of her embroidered white T-shirts that says *We See What We Want To See* stitched in sapphire thread along the collar. In the distance, you can see Achilles soaring in the sky. I'm dead center in black shorts over tights, white tank top under my army-green field jacket, and burgundy Docs. Eyeless and waiting.

Rémy is staring at me like I fell asleep with my eyes open.

"Thank you," I say with some hesitation, afraid anything else will encourage him to ask about yesterday now that Brian and Shawna aren't with us.

"Yeah. And the whole moody post-apocalyptic thing with the security fence and the mushroom cloud off in the distance, leaving you whole and in place like you're untouchable. It's honestly brilliant."

"I agree," Ms. Everitt chimes in. "I think you should rethink your reluctance to enter into the Scholarship for the Arts America. They make a huge deal about the national self-portrait scholarship competition. News crews come and interview the winner. It gives the budding artist a nice buzz for their college applications."

"I appreciate the vote of confidence, but going to art school isn't part of my plan. At least, not right away."

"That's a shame," she says. "You clearly have the talent. Then again, lots of talented, successful artists never attended art school. The trick is to keep painting. But maybe Rémy can change your mind. He's the one who found the scholarship and suggested we make it part of the curriculum for the semester."

Ms. Everitt rests a caring hand on my shoulder before going to help a student who needs a wrench to open a stuck dry tube of acrylic paint.

"Where *do* you want to go?" Rémy asks, settling back toward his own canvas.

Right now, home.

"I don't know," I say. "I'm taking a year or two off first."

"Smart. Like a gap year or two to travel or something and figure it all out. I get that. The rush to college is about as American a construct as you can get. Sometimes it's better to not have a plan and see what happens."

I'm quiet, weighing the risk of telling him anything else about my life, or that the real reason I'm not going anywhere is my sisters. I've lived in six states and travel isn't part of the current equation. But now that he's piqued my interest with his assessment of my art, part of me wants to ask why he tried to follow me into the air shaft. I'm just not sure I'm ready to open that can of worms.

I reciprocate by studying his self-portrait, a simple but

accurate rendition of what Rémy must see in the mirror, what I see when I look at him. Open expression, easygoing, a slight twinkle in his eye that reads optimistic ninety-nine percent of the time. It screams of a person who knows exactly who he is and isn't trying to hide.

That said, in the time it's taken Rémy to complete a painting equivalent in size to a head shot, I've nearly finished painting three figures on a canvas four times the size. The secret, and the trick, is that I've always kept painting. I just don't know which Honey I want to put at the center. Fierce-eyed prepper Honey, worried-about-her-sisters Honey, or tired, please-give-me-a-moment-to-dream Honey. When I reminisce about the pieces of art I've left behind over the years, I get pensive. I could have taken them, but I chose to leave them behind, in places we lived, in art rooms at different schools. Never signed, but as an artistic Honey Was Here trail.

"Are you entering yours in the competition?" I ask Rémy. "Most people struggle with brown, but the way you use all the umbers and sienna with peach and violet highlights is spot on."

"I like this one, but I'm entering a black-and-white self-portrait. I took it from behind myself with a tripod and timer. My face is in the mirror next to this painting, so in that way I'm entering the painting, too."

"Oh!" Surprise escapes my lips. "Seeing yourself through your camera is actually a great idea."

"Thanks." He smiles, and it's the most humble thing I've seen in a long time. Most of the Burrow Boys are so cocky and self-assured. Not that Rémy isn't confident. It's just that he doesn't need to be holding a rifle to prove it. Unless you count his camera as a weapon, and I usually do.

"Maybe I can show you the comps I've taken some time," he says. "It'd be great to have another set of eyes helping me pick the best one."

"Sure. Or you could just bring them to class and put them up for everyone."

Don't ask me out. Don't ask me out. Don't ask me out.

"*Or,* I could *not* bring them to class, and we could exchange numbers and meet somewhere. Do you like coffee?"

Shit.

"I don't have a cellphone."

He's gaping at me like I really am an oddball. "Are you Amish?"

I get it. No one my age outside the coalition can believe anyone, in this day and age, is walking around twenty-four-seven without a cellphone.

"I *have* a cellphone, but I share it with my sisters. It's only for emergencies. Do you want my email address?"

"*Email?* Yeah, sure. Why not? It'll be fun to pretend it's the early nineties."

Rémy pulls up the add-contact screen on his phone and hands it to me so I can type in the email address I've been using since I was twelve: Honeybee123@suremail.com.

Rémy gives me his signature dimpled smile when I hand back his phone. Not just an oddball, but an amusing one. His reaction doesn't tell me anything I don't already know. When it comes to technology, we Junipers are behind the times.

What I should have said when he asked is, *Of course I drink coffee.* Pints. Usually at the crack of dawn while I'm feeding chickens in my rain boots and pajama pants. I avoid responding to his offer for coffee in any way by turning back to my canvas. But in doing that, I bang my wounded knee on my stool and the sting rips through my nerve endings, making me grit my teeth.

"Are you okay?" Rémy asks. "That was kind of a big reaction for a small bump."

"I cut my knee yesterday," I tell him. "It's still in the raw stage."

"You cut it yesterday?" He shifts his eyes around the room before whispering, "When you disappeared through the vent? Do you need to go to the nurse? You might have tetanus."

I stifle a laugh. "I did it at home," I lie. "Tripping over a log while feeding our chickens."

"You have chickens?"

"And goats."

"That explains your youngest sister."

I narrow my eyes, hackles up.

Rémy shakes his head and holds up a conciliatory hand. "It's just, I've seen her picking fur and feathers off her clothes."

"Blue has a pet falcon named Achilles."

"Seriously?" His eyes globe. "Does he come when he's called, like a dog?"

"Yes, but only to her. They're bonded. He comes down if she calls him Achy, which kind of sounds like the Spanish word for *here*, but it's short for Achilles. If she needs to do it more quietly, she just lifts her arm and whistles. Sometimes he goes out on longer flights searching for food, but he always returns to Blue."

"That's incredible. I'd love to see that in action."

That's never gonna happen. I tie a canvas apron around myself so I can get on with painting. Not that I care if I mess up my clothes today. I'm wearing all black, leggings and a sweater, the fastest thing I could find after not getting much sleep. But now that he said it, I pick a few pieces of goat fur off my pants.

"I better sketch these eyes before the end of class," I tell him. Hoping that serves as an exit from further interrogation. I don't have the heart to tell him he'll probably never get to see Achilles and Blue in action. "Thanks for calling my eyes sugar-pine bark in chemistry. That's actually helping me with the colors."

"My pleasure. I mean, if I can't lavish a compliment on a girl by saying her eyes look like tree bark, what good am I?"

I can't help but smile at any self-deprecating humor, but the smug satisfaction on Rémy's face, like he just got a present he's been asking for all year, makes me wipe it away fast. This is why I should have disengaged. I don't know how to do this friendship, or whatever he's getting at, thing, and now I've backed myself into a corner by showing more than minimal interest.

I let the room dissolve and disappear around me and sketch my eyes, making them oversized, like my mouth. Both have always seemed too big for my face, my lips perpetually swollen, like I got them stuck in a narrow jar and tried to suction them out. I study the irregular peppering of darker brown fanning out from my ebony irises, and I see myself reflected there, shiny twins, moving as one in the black dot like a hovering ghost asking who I am.

I loosely sketch myself into the irises, similar to the way Rémy said he's doing a picture of himself in the mirror, only through the tiny cameras of my own eyes, the iris a lens. When I've got something workable down in pencil, I step back. I like what I see, someone protective and resolute. Responsible, Reactive, and Ready. And I know, if we ever move again, this is one painting I won't want to leave behind.

TOBYISMS FOR ACTION

3

THE LIE IS IMPLIED

MY LATEST PIECE had a three-day runtime before it got massacred. Someone covered the entire brick wall with matte-black paint, inadvertently giving me a clean slate and a fresh idea. I took a piece of the neon-yellow chalk we use at Nikko's to write the daily specials on the sandwich board, and on my way I wrote, *Paint Won't Fix The Writing On The Wall*, across the brand-new surface.

Bash is with me tonight, acting as my rook since the person that painted over my last piece went to such great lengths to erase it from existence. I'm going for something different tonight. A boy in black and white with one hand outstretched, releasing three exploding balloons that are floating away from him and transforming into ravens. The message this time reads THE LIE IS IMPLIED. I let the red letters in LIE drip down the wall like blood. Jonesy once told me we have to consider my sisters may have been murdered. I refused to accept that as a possibility because I would know. Somehow, I would be able to sense the complete loss of them, and I don't.

"Someone's coming," Bash says. "I think they're cops."

"Shit."

I shove the paint canisters into my backpack, and we make

a run for the wire-mesh security fence separating the buildings from the train tracks. The openings are tight together, unlike chain-link, so you can't put a toe inside an opening and climb. Bash is already over the top when I make a run at it. I use the cross-brace at the bottom of a line post and jump high, landing my right foot on the pointy ends at the top. But when I jump down to the other side, the strap on my backpack gets caught, pulling me back as my body weight flies forward. I'm no physics expert. I just know the outside of my forearm gets sliced on the spiky metal, and I can't let the string of profanities running through my head fly or I'll risk alerting the cops.

Bash makes an ooph sound with the thumb side of his fist pressed against his mouth like he feels my pain. Then he grabs me by the front of my sweatshirt and pulls me into a run. "I was scared for real," he says when we're far enough away. "You see how fast I bailed out? That doodle was worth it, though."

I hold my arm up. The sleeve of my hoodie is ripped, and blood is running from the gash in my arm.

"Oh shit. You need stitches?" Bash comes closer, shining his flashlight on it.

"I don't think so. Maybe a new sweatshirt, though. You want to come over? I can drive you back to your car later."

"Yeah, all right. You got anything to eat?"

"As much mac 'n' cheese as you want."

"Cool. Cool. You sure you don't need a tetanus shot or something?"

"Nah. I'm good. It will remind me of that piece after they scrub it away."

Half an hour later, I'm cleaning my cut in the bathroom while Bash makes a couple of boxes of macaroni and cheese. Both of us trying to be as quiet as possible because my mom is sleeping, and we don't want her walking out asking why we're up at one A.M. The cut on my arm is bad, but I don't think it needs stitches. Maybe one or two on the end where it snagged, but it's not an emergency. I lay several butterfly stiches from our first aid kit across the gash and wrap it in gauze. Then I head to the kitchen to clean the paint off my fingers with cooking spray, dish soap, and salt like Stavros showed me.

It's getting harder to keep quiet when Bash is doing impersonations of people who came into his workplace. He's been doing this since we were little kids and should seriously consider becoming a voice actor. Currently, he's impersonating an adenoidal Valley girl type. Banquo whines from inside my mom's bedroom. I rush over and crack her door open to let him out so he can also be entertained by Bash.

"And then she was like ... *Do you have any* fried *chicken, but* like, *without the skin*." He puts his index finger and thumb together and pretends to ring a bell. "Like that, man. She mimed throwing away the skin on the chicken. First off, that's criminal in the fried chicken world. Just order a grilled breast or whatever sad piece of chicken you need to eat. Am I right?"

"One hundred percent."

He flops onto the couch holding a cereal bowl full of mac 'n' cheese, but quickly readjusts his position and pulls one of Mom's sketchbooks out from between the cushions. "Oh man, I hope I didn't crease anything important."

"I'm sure it's fine. Give it here."

I flip it open to check and a series of age-progression photos of my sisters fall out. Not the ones they did eleven years ago, or even six years ago. These are dated last week.

"What is it?" Bash asks. "Your mom drawing nudes? Let me see."

I hand them over and watch the color drain from his face. My reaction exactly.

"Oh shit. Did she show these to you?"

I shake my head, breathing deep through my nose to stem a bout of nausea.

"It's crazy," Bash says. "Imogen looks so much more like you in these."

He's right. She was always the most stubborn, too. I don't say any of this to Bash because I'm zoning out. Remembering the way Mom said she couldn't seem to get *her* out of her head. Which *her*?

I make a beeline for Mom's art studio. "Toby," Bash whisper-yells. "You all right? You gonna puke, man?"

It's happened before, but no. I'm not gonna puke. I'm gonna look at the painting she's been working on. The one Mom *can't get out of her head.* I let the solid wood door swing inward slowly, opened by a ghostly hand dealt from the past. I stand in front of her ten-foot easel and stare at the portrait of three girls, huddled so close together only the center figure is facing front. Only one of her eyes is showing because she's partially blocked in front by the others. The iris of the one unfinished eye is practically glowing. A bright white circle giving it the appearance of seeing everything and nothing. The muted colors mimic the rain that's made their dark hair hang in damp wavy tendrils. I knew who they were the other day because they look like me. More feminine, but with all the grunge. Bee-stung lips below noses with a flattened bump on the bridge. I study the progression photos in my hand to see if I'm sure about the one staring back at me.

Katherina.

Cassandra is on her right, shorter than the others and a touch more vividly executed. Imogen, always the darkest in both mood and coloring, looking the most despairing to the left. I cover my mouth, because now I might actually puke.

Behind the easel, taped to the wall, are dozens of drawings of eyes. Every expression imaginable, like she's struggling to pinpoint their feeling after all these years. I look away and catch my own reflection in the gold-framed mirror hanging on the opposite wall. How about the unfocused gaze of disbelief?

She purposely hid these from me when I came home from work the other night. I remember her stuffing them into her sketchbook before offering to make me something to eat. Not like everything was normal. The exact opposite of our normal.

Bash walks in behind me. "You want me to go so you can wrap your head around this? I'm cool to call for a ride."

I nod. It's probably for the best. Bash knows this will send me down a rabbit hole for hours. Maybe days. He claps a hand on my shoulder before he leaves. I wait until the front door clicks. Then I walk out of Mom's studio backward, staring at that one glowing eye until my socks meet the edge of the navy-and-gold Persian rug where we used to wrestle. I won't be able to get her out of my head, either.

I sit at the kitchen table and take snaps of the photos with my phone that I can post on social media. The tab to access the catalog of missing persons is always open and active on my laptop. And tonight, I search for Imogen first. Based on these new progressions. Not the image I've been carrying in my head from eleven years ago when she was as stubborn and toothless as the little girl in Nikko's. Imogen is the reason I have an inch-long scar right below my lip. She wanted to sit on my new skateboard and ride it down the driveway. When I said no, she made a run at me head down like a ram and knocked me off the board. My front teeth sliced clean through my skin. I'll never forget how much she cried afterward, harder than me, and I'm the one who needed seven stitches.

Most nights it's hard not to think I've wasted tons of time looking for them. I could have easily gone over to Bash's tonight and played Xbox, just like we did that fateful night. But I'll tell you a secret. I don't really like video games anymore, and I never rode a skateboard again.

SERE

SURVIVAL, EVASION, RESISTANCE, ESCAPE

DIETER IS CALLING over the CB for mandatory training drills in two hours and cutting off power to both garrisons for the next twelve. Because, as he put it, we're not acting like we'll be able to handle ourselves when the shit hits the fan. By the time he's finished telling us how the rest of the day will go down, I've filled the cast-iron kettle and our three biggest stockpots with the water we'll need later. I'm so behind on everything, I wish I could split myself in two. Maybe that's a concoction Mother can work on in her kitchen lab, because at this rate we'll never get ahead.

We don't have enough time to get our homework and chores done before we have to meet on the training field for our assignments. Dinner will have to be MREs when we get back. Meals, Ready to Eat are never my choice. They should be called Meals, Rarely Edible, but it's one of those things you practice for survival. The military has to eat them all the time when they're deployed, so Mother makes us eat them once a week to get us used to them. I take a visual inventory of our useable stash and pull out three vegetarian Chili Mac meals. They're the least gross of all dehydrated meals and have a seven-year shelf life. That should tell you everything you need to know about the quality of the MRE dining experience.

A series of clicks and dull pops is followed by a second-floor groan from Birdie. There goes the power. I take the stairs to the study two at a time, the skin surrounding the cut on my knee stretching tight in resistance. I was hoping my sisters would be diligently working on our shared computer, but Birdie is working on a comic strip in her sketchbook and sulking, squeezing a pencil across her two middle fingers hard enough to make it snap. When she sees me standing in the doorway, she hops up from the floor and goes to the window, throwing her arms up like the outdoors are all to blame. "*Training? Now?*"

"I get it, Birdie. We have a lot of balls in the air. I'm frustrated, too. There's nothing I'd rather do than pretend none of this happened, get my homework done, and write a letter to Bucky. But we have to go along with our normal protocols. There isn't enough spare time to debate Dieter's motivations. Did you get everything you need off the computer, because without our cellphone—"

"No," Birdie squawks. "I didn't. Because I can't stop feeling annoyed over Daniel being sent packing alone. There's always two people bugging out, at least. Safety in numbers and all that other bullshit we're always spewing. How will I get my EDC from Ansel, or our phone for that matter, before Daniel gets back? What are we gonna say if we don't get the phone back and I have to tell Mother I was involved in something I can't even remember? Sometimes I wish we . . . it would almost be better if . . . Why did we ever come here?"

"To find our way home," Blue says.

A minute ago, Blue was nose deep in a book, but clearly paying attention in her peripheries. My love for my littlest sister is impossibly strong in this moment, even if what she said makes zero sense. Her calm resolve always balances out my paranoia for my sisters' safety and Birdie's tendency toward a hothead.

"We *are* home," Birdie gripes. "*For now.* And I messed it all up. Not that we'd know what a real home looks like long-term."

"We would know," Blue says, "because Bucky will be there with us."

Birdie throws her arms up in defeat and sinks into a desk chair. "Bucky Beaverman?" She picks up her sketchbook and shakes it at Blue. "You think that's who's going to save us in the end? My comic strip figure? The little blue beaver stitched so nicely into all your needlepoint pieces? Or is Honey gonna write him into existence from one of her many composition notebooks?"

"I never said he was going to *save us*," Blue clarifies. "I said he'd be there."

"Save us from what?" I ask Birdie, because that's the thing that keeps sticking me in the ribs. "Ever since you took up with Daniel, you've been secretive and out of control."

"*Took up* with Daniel? This is why you don't have a boy-friend, Honey. You talk like you're from the seventeenth century when it comes to dating. God forbid you let anyone past your brick wall long enough to know anything about *taking up* with somebody firsthand."

That's not entirely true, but Birdie knew it would strike a nerve. Just because I want to wait for someone who sees me for who I am doesn't mean I'm closed off. I'm not interested in dat-ing anyone from The Burrow, and dating anyone else would expose our entire setup, or so we've been told.

"Stop jumping down our throats, Birdie, we're not your en-emies. But since you brought it up, why *would I* let anyone past my brick wall? Look at yourself. Daniel got sent away for ten days less than twenty-four hours ago and you're stewing like you can't function. You've always been the strongest one, Birdie. Not *me*. You!"

She sighs, releasing the pent-up breath keeping her anger afloat. "I'd just feel better if I had my EDC."

"I know. So would I. I'm working on it."

Her stormy eyes brighten. "Really? You talked to Ansel? Did he say anything about what happened? I've been keeping my distance from him and Annalise because . . . Well, I just feel like I should, but also because Daniel probably got caught because of me, even if he didn't say it."

I have the answer Birdie wants, but if I tell her I'm going out after curfew to get her EDC she'll want to come. I'll be faster and stealthier without her. I'll just leave them a note in the cipher we use whenever we don't want Mother to know what we're saying. I don't remember where it originated, but sometimes I dream of Bucky teaching it to me. Wouldn't that be something? Anyway, I taught it to Birdie, and together we taught it to Blue when she was old enough to hold a pencil.

"I have a plan to talk to Ansel," I tell her.

Birdie's shoulders relax, a clear sign that her anger levee is starting to fail. When it breaks, you can guess who'll be here mopping up the mess.

"Do you think he'll be okay? I have a bad feeling about him out there alone."

Birdie bites her bottom lip and looks at Blue. Waiting for her to spew some near-prophetic statement that will reinforce Birdie's hope. Only, Blue doesn't say a word. She doesn't even look at Birdie. Who would blame her after Birdie's outburst? The sad reality is I wish I *could* write Bucky into existence. Having a fourth opinion on all things Juniper would be great.

We're all silently contemplating our own versions of the last two days when I hear Achilles's cry and spot him soaring toward the window. Blue drops her book and rushes onto the roof. She can't call him down because her leather glove is hanging in the mew, but her smile makes it clear she's missed him the last two days.

I crawl onto the roof beside her, watching him coast on

an updraft with an object grasped in his talons. "What's he holding?"

"It's brown. Maybe a squirrel," Blue says, "or a marten."

Achilles swoops past us and drops what he's holding onto the roof, and it's not an animal. It's a Bivy sack. The compact kind we carry in our bug-out bags, only this one doesn't belong to any of us. The Nesters' Bivy sacks are orange and The Burrowers' are ochre brown.

I crouch and pick it up. "Where did he get this?" My brain flies to a potential problem. "You don't think he's stealing from people on the compound, do you?"

"I hope he stole it from Dieter," Birdie says from inside.

"Achilles doesn't think it's stealing," Blue says in his defense. "Achy is a hunter. Everything he finds is free for the taking."

"I understand that, but we don't need Dieter Ackerman mad at Achilles, too. Bring it to the training area later and we'll say we found it on the road near our house and see who claims it. It's getting late. Leave your homework where it is and get changed. We have to feed the animals before the training drills. Maybe the chickens laid some eggs we can cook later."

We change quickly into Carhartt overalls and Bog boots and head outside, walking downhill a short ways to where we keep the animal enclosures. Achilles follows, circling above us, laying moving shadows that decorate our path. I'll never get over how majestic he is, flying up there without worry. It's nothing short of miraculous that Achilles never touches our livestock. Maybe because there's no hunt involved. Maybe out of his deep attachment to Blue. We'll never know.

"I'll take care of the rabbits," Blue offers. "They need to be held."

I reserve my they're-not-pets look for another time, because she's right and already gone, along with her falcon. Off to Blue's personal version of *My Side of the Mountain*. Okay. That's a bit dramatic. She's only going a quarter mile away. I can't fault her for wanting to hold the rabbits. They're the one animal on this farm that does need to be held so they aren't skittish. We want them to be calm enough to breed.

"Goats or chickens?" I ask Birdie. "Sufferer's choice."

She almost smiles. "Chickens, I guess."

Leaving me with goats, and by nature a ton of pellet droppings. Not as much as Blue will have to handle with the rabbits. "Don't forget the eggs," I call to Birdie after we've split up. A soft-cooked egg on top of my Chili Mac MRE will make it much more palatable.

The goats come out of their small barn to greet me, blubbing and hollering when they see me carrying fresh hay. The first to reach me is Buck Rogers, our black-and-tan male with a supercilious look in his eyes. Followed by three sable-and-white females named Maggie, May, and June, and the all-white female we call Milkshake. She does not bring boys to the yard, no matter what the song claims. She actually avoids Buck Rogers like the plague. Not that it stops him from trying. I enter the enclosure and drop the hay into the feeding rack.

When I'm done making sure they have enough food and water, I look over my shoulder for my sisters. When I'm sure they can't see me, I stroke Maggie's ears. They're soft as crushed velvet, even though the rest of her fur is as coarse as the hay she's munching. Maggie has always been my favorite because she has a funny underbite that makes her seem like she's in on some joke. If Blue saw me petting the livestock right now, she'd call me a hypocrite then jump in the pen and hug them all around their brass-belled necks. The bottom line, though, is they *are* for food and provide enough milk for us to make saleable products. Milkshake alone gives up to two gallons a day.

The other Nesters have their own livestock, and we all share our milk and crops with the Burrow households. The Burrowers know how to butcher animals, and how to milk, just like we know how to shoot and trap. We were given lessons in those things, too. But I'd rather live on our doomstead

than their boring properties any day. The Burrow's misogynis-
tic overtone sets my teeth on edge.

I give the goats all quick pats so they don't feel neglected
then head to the training area, kicking small rocks along the
dirt path. My thoughts veer to Bucky Beaverman, how cyni-
cal Birdie was toward Blue's comment. Birdie, who draws him
as the hero of her comics. We all accept Bucky as part of
our family, the long-standing invisible friend who's come with
us from place to place. He's such a fixture that I sometimes
dream about him and his longer-than-the-rest buckteeth, his
place in our lives from the beginning, wrestling with us on the
Persian rug in muted shades of navy and gold, helping us pull
out our loose teeth when they got wiggly. Bucky is made of the
glue that holds us together. Birdie was just being, well, Birdie.

I arrive on time this go-round. There's no way I wouldn't
after yesterday. My sisters show up within five or ten minutes
of me, along with everyone else. Blue is wearing her leather
falconer's glove, holding Achilles's leash and jess in her uncov-
ered hand like she knew she'd need them. Training drills are
common. We have several every month, along with a monthly
meeting to go over how the coalition is running.

There's no sitting this time. We're not here for scolding
or announcement. This is an impromptu drill because of yesterday. A straight-up continuation of Dieter's disappointment.
Ansel and the older Burrow Boys are standing with their feet
apart, hands clasped in front like soldiers awaiting orders of
deployment. Each face a steady mask of readiness to toe the
line. Dieter glances at his watch, always keeping everything to
the precise minute. His cheeks are more drawn than usual,
giving extra haggardness to his weathered face. I study my
own watch, observe the hour hand click into place, and just
like clockwork Dieter speaks.

"I'd like to get this training moving quickly so we don't
waste daylight," he begins without greeting. That part, at least,
is not unusual. "This is a SERE training. Each faction will be

assigned for survival, evasion, resistance, or escape. Those who were already outside the wire have been instructed to leave their vehicles in place and practice Get Home measures without detection. Since we're on our own property, let's make the OPTEMPO a priority this time. You have three hours max."

Mother is outside the wire. In town, picking up bandages to replenish our storage supplies and selling our surplus honey, beeswax, and the extra heirloom seeds and seedlings to local shop owners. The only thing we don't sell to Outsiders is surplus food. Not even our eggs. We don't want anyone to remember we have farm animals when the shit hits the fan. We keep a Get Home bag in the station wagon that she'll use depending on where she was when she got the call.

Something about the urgency of this training feels like it's meant to distract everyone from the fact that Dieter sent Daniel out on a solo mission. We're all aware now that Dieter could do that to any of us if we do something that draws attention to our coalition. Our current POTUS does something similar. He creates diversions to keep everyone focused on one thing while he does something behind the scenes we don't hear about until later. It's off-putting, in a way, that Dieter would initiate this training without his new second-in-command present. Unless Mother knew this was coming and didn't tell us. Secrets piled on top of secrets.

"The following people are tasked with hunting, bow-and-arrow style," Dieter announces, starting assignments. "The Juniper sisters, and Annalise and Magda Ackerman. Work together to bring back a single kill each."

My eyes shift to where my sisters were standing a few minutes ago. Birdie isn't there. My brain goes haywire thinking she may have taken off while nobody was watching. A few nerve-racking beats later, she sidles up to me from behind. I exhale and shift my eyes to Blue. Thankfully, she hasn't moved an inch, despite Magda and Annalise taking Birdie's spot. Blue is oblivious to them because her eyes are swaying in a skyward arc, watching Achilles. He screeches and her focus jerks to Dieter. He glances at her raptor with admiration, even though he avoids talking to Blue. We think it's because her inferences unnerve him.

Blue raises her hand.

"You can use your falcon," Dieter says without hearing her question.

Blue drops her arm. "Yes. Thank you. I intended to, but I also wanted to say we found a Bivy sack on the path on our way over, if anyone lost theirs."

She glances at me to back her up and I remove the bundle from my back pocket and reluctantly walk it over to Dieter. I wasn't ready to bring it out yet because his urgency was pricking at my consciousness, telling me to wait. A Bivy sack isn't an essential everyday supply, but comes in handy when you bug out and need waterproof or insulated cover.

Dieter studies it and hands it to Mateo Garcia, whispering instruction I can't hear.

Magda catches my eye as I return to where I was standing with Birdie, and the civility usually found in the depths of her oceanic eyes is gone. Replaced by arctic ice that chills me. I guess we have Dieter and Mother to thank for the frigid stare.

"Camilla Clarke will join Tashi and Tito Garcia in setting up booby traps to simulate an ambush. There are headlamps on the picnic table for those who want one, as well as compasses and camo. Ansel, Mateo, and Connor are tasked to bug out in the woods until the counteracting task I've assigned them is completed. The rest of us will bug in at home for the remainder of the twelve hours after completing the assigned tasks. The clock starts at eighteen-hundred hours."

Let the training begin.

We have our own bows and tactical quivers at home that attach to our INCH bags. The same kind Daniel had attached to his INCH bag before he left, presumably for nabbing his meals. Birdie is the first to pick up her weapon, choosing recurve over compound. That's why she's not as accurate a shot as me. Recurve bows shoot farther, but you have to account for their curving. Compound bows shoot faster and straighter. Birdie grabs a camouflage jacket from the pile and walks toward me, pulling it on.

"May the odds be ever in their favor."

"I get it, Birdie. You're upset, but don't piss them off. We're supposed to work together and they're mad enough about Mother as it is."

"So am I," she counters. "I'm not that happy with Annalise, either. I'm just saying, accidents happen."

"That's not funny."

Magda may have overheard us. She's pretending like she's not watching, which only makes it more evident. I wait for her and Annalise to pick out their bows. Then I pull on a thermal camouflage shirt, pick a bow of my own, and sling the quiver across my back.

Blue is waiting to call Achilles down, leather glove out with one finger pointing like a branch extending from her heart. She only has to whistle and call his name once before he swoops down, wings open to slow his arrival as he lands on the glove. Blue attaches the leash and jess with the brass bell that tells her where her hunting partner is at all times. Getting Achilles accustomed to the leash and jess after his injury took Blue months upon months of trust building. She waits for Achilles to dip his head and plants a kiss on top. That's their hunting ritual.

I slide the ponytail holder off my wrist and hold it between my teeth while I braid my hair. Wide headband, braid, ready. I have a ritual of my own.

Magda and Annalise were supposed to wait for us, but didn't. I wish it were just my sisters and me heading into these woods, but I'm not surprised they forged ahead. It's probably for the best. I won't find out how Ansel got his sister to stay quiet about Birdie's involvement until I meet him at the tree-house tonight, but my mind keeps spinning back to Daniel saying DTA.

We don't really need their hunting help. I'm the best shot in the party next to Annalise, who's had the advantage of using a bow and arrow since childhood. Usually a hunting party sticks together, venturing no more than a hundred feet from each other, but they're nowhere to be seen. It's obvious they wanted to get far enough away to be a separate party. I was thinking birds, but they must have their sights set on bigger game.

✣ TPTB ✣

THE POWERS THAT BE

THE TREES RISE around us sharp as needles to poke the sky. The woods are always two shades darker beneath their natural canopy, no matter the hour. Darker, since the days are most often Washington State gray. Between the roots and around fallen branches concealed by moss, new slender green stalks branch skyward. Thriving, refusing to be suffocated by the damp, decomposing leaves, bumpy pine cones, and dead, russet-colored needles littering the forest floor. I pull an arrow from my quiver, keeping it ready to nock, and shift my gaze between the trees in search of wild turkeys.

We keep chatter to a minimum while hunting, staying as silent and invisible as any human can when entering the forest home of wild animals. When you remain silent in the woods, they come alive with the chattering of insects, the occasional dropping pine cone, scattering chipmunks, and ominous creaks and groans of old limbs fighting to hang on. When those ancient extremities do finally fall to their death, the thunderous crack and thud are monstrous.

The ground is saturated from today's rain, dampening the sound of our footsteps as we trek deeper and deeper, walking at least a mile before seeing any clearings. We know our way around these woods like we know the layout of the compound, by recognizing and committing to memory different path markers and landmarks. Some made by us, others by nature.

A shriek from Achilles breaks my thoughts, sending my gaze skyward just in time to see him make a two-hundred-mile-per-hour dive. With vision ten times better than ours, Achilles is always first to bag a prize. He soars high above the trees again, presumably scanning the forest floor for Blue. A minute later he drops his gift, twenty feet from where we're clustered together. I'm convinced Achilles is the only falcon in the world that gives over a fresh kill to his handler before capturing one for himself. Blue earned that loyalty.

We jog on light feet and see the dead grouse.

"I'm done," Blue whispers, picking up the plump-bodied game bird by the feet.

"I still say that's cheating," Birdie says.

"It's not cheating. It's an ancient form of hunting. I can have him get something for you, too, if you want."

"No. Let him go after his supper. I'll get my own."

"Shh," I scold. "None of us will get anything if you two keep talking. Let's go."

My sisters know better than to keep chattering, especially as they follow me into a clearing. Black-eyed Susans pepper the perimeter, making for a happy display if it weren't for the killing requirement to come. A bird in hand, in Blue's hand, technically, is worth two in the bush, they say. But that doesn't apply to this assignment. And unfortunately, Birdie and I haven't seen feather or fowl. That could have something to do with Achilles circling overhead. Smaller birds are his meal of choice.

It would be easy to pick an armful of edible plants in these woods. Ferns, jack-in-the-pulpit tubers, dandelions. Things that have nothing to do with taking a life, but that's not our objective. Protein will become scarce when the shit hits the fan. I bet cannibalism as a necessary means for survival is the real fear beneath the myths surrounding a zombie apocalypse.

Dieter Ackerman believes the military and government are responsible for the things we perceive as paranormal. Zombies, super soldiers, mind control, werewolf experimentation, even Bigfoot—a Washington State legend. Extreme but plausible examples of things that may have resulted from neurotoxins, the sleeping sickness of the tsetse fly, necrosis, parasites, gene mutation, and nanobots.

We're preparing for the scary stuff we see coming down the pike every day on TV: financial collapse, the exiting of a nuclear arms treaty, ballistic bomb testing by North Korea, a potential electromagnetic pulse that wipes out the grid. Things that would lead to martial law, because when the government decides they can take what's yours, the shit will definitely hit the fan.

Blue signals she's going into the woods with Birdie to the left of the clearing. I raise my index finger, followed by two zeros—reminding them not to go more than a hundred feet—before pointing straight across the clearing, then at my eyes with peace fingers to say, *I'll go straight but keep your eyes open for me.* I listen for their movements as I walk through the trees, committing the sounds to memory to distinguish them from other activity in the woods.

When I come to a section of sugar-pine trees, I stop, studying the bark and inhaling the sharp smell of pine. A twig snaps nearby, maybe two hundred feet away, give or take, followed by the yelp of a turkey telling his own flock his location. I scan the woods for my sisters and see the movement of Birdie's jacket stop like she picked up the same call. We make eye contact and I motion with two fingers that I'm moving in on the prey. Birdie taps her ear and points to the right like she heard it coming from a different direction. I motion for her to go straight, frustrated that she always fights to do what she wants. I yelp out the sound of a fast squeaking dry hinge. The only turkey call I can make without the use of a manmade tool.

A long whining click followed by two beeps comes in response. It's a sound I recognize as easily as the rustling of trees, because I've grown more conscious of it over the last few months. Self-conscious, if I'm being honest. I walk ten more feet, twenty, thirty, and stop cold, unable to believe my eyes.

Rémy Lamar is in the woods, our woods, camera slung around his neck while he examines a map like he's lost. Not only is he out of his depths, he's ventured onto Burrow property.

Evade the unfortunate intruder.

Save yourself.

That would be the smart thing to do. But then Rémy might venture too far east and walk onto the actual compound, or get spotted by whoever Dieter has stationed in the lookout tower first. He's turning a map clockwise for the third time, making it obvious he has no idea where he is or how to get out of these woods. I exchange the arrow in my hand for a thinner one, nock it on my bow, and pull back until my thumb is under my chin on the right. I aim for the map, praying he doesn't move, and the small scare is enough to discourage him from coming back to these woods.

Without another second of hesitation, I let the lighter arrow fly. When I'm sure it's going to hit my intended target, I spin back against a tree and wait. I hear the unmistakable snap of my arrow piercing the map in Rémy's hands followed by the thud of it being nailed to the pine tree a few feet beyond where he was standing. At least, that's the way it plays out in my head.

"What the hell?"

I step out from behind the thick tree as Rémy spins, ambushed shock replacing his usual easygoing grin. He pushes his headphones back like reclaiming his hearing will help him see his assailant better. One hand goes to his heart when he sees me, checking to see if he's alive, which I find a bit dramatic.

"*Honey?* What are you *doing* out here? You could have hit me with that thing."

"I could ask you the same thing. What are *you* doing out here? It's hunting season and you're on private property, dressed in dark colors."

I scan his black jeans faded to the edge of charcoal gray, his black pullover sweater with the white T-shirt color showing at the top. The only pop of color he's wearing, as the sheeple say, is his scarf. But even that is dark shades of hunter green and navy plaid. He could be one of us if his clothes were more utilitarian.

He does a quick scan of my thermal camouflage shirt and tawny Carhartts. "Mr. Whitlock told me there's an old, abandoned treehouse out here. I came to get some pictures. Do you live around here? Is this your family's property?"

I can't believe he got this far with a map, to be honest, but maybe he was a Boy Scout.

THREAT ASSESSMENT CORRECTION:
RÉMY LAMAR
**5/10 WOULD IMPEDE GROUP SURVIVAL IN EMERGENCY
SITUATION.**

"We live on Overcast Road," I tell him.

As soon as the words leave my mouth I wish I could exchange them for a better lie. Overcast Road is the street address everyone on the compound uses to keep our actual location secret. It's a real place, a private road, but there's just a bunch of prefabricated trailer-style homes out there we use to collect mail and store supplies.

"Isn't that on the other side of Elkwood? I've seen the wooden street sign."

I step closer. "Yes. Would you mind lowering your voice? You're scaring away all the game." I soften my own tone to illustrate my request. "I'm out here hunting with my sisters. We have the owner's permission."

"Hunting?" He glances at my bow again. "I guess that's more humane than a gun, since you're giving the animal a running chance."

Not necessarily. Speed or strike, distance from target, those things all come into consideration. I don't bother explaining the different types of hunting ballistics, but his aversion to our lifestyle makes my feathers ruffle enough to correct him. "You mean a rifle," I tell him. "Nobody hunts with a pistol. I take it you have something against hunting in general?"

"I'm a black person in America. I have something against all firearms used against the undefended. Trust me, some people hunt with a pistol."

I've probably watched more news than most people my age, which is why I look away, ashamed for not thinking about it from his perspective. Even if hunting is different from people being inexcusably shot by a handgun or assault rifle, the fact is that the latter happens all the time, prejudicially, vengefully, and without nearly enough punishment. I just can't tell him why I'm hunting, or for who.

"Sorry," I whisper. "You're right. I hear you, and I get it."

"It's okay. I get it, too. You have this whole Katniss vibe going on. For all I know, you're gonna go eat a raw fish by the river later and sleep in a tree."

"Never. But one of my Primroses referenced that movie right before we came out here."

Rémy smiles wide, showing teeth white enough to blind someone. "Did you just crack a joke on top of my joke?"

I give him a one-arm shrug. "I'm not all backpacks and random, unconventional escapes."

"I never thought you were."

He says that, but he's staring at me like he's trying to figure me out. The way Rémy always studies me, with amused fascination.

The Hunger Games reference is closer to future truth than he realizes. Closer than most people realize as they go about their lives with only a cursory glance at what's happening. I blame the constant barrage of information thrown at us. Everything from celebrity status to nuclear threats, making it all turn to mind-numbing noise. A virtual drug, meant to keep us wide-eyed and glued to what we're being fed unless we force our attention to things that matter.

A stretch of silence builds between us, allowing the music streaming from his headphones to reach my ears. "Would you mind turning your headphones off, too? If I can hear your music, the animals can definitely hear it."

"You mean Beats," he whispers with a grin. "Headphones are only used by people who don't care about music."

Touché.

At least now, I know what he meant by his Beats in chemistry. Not that I'd know the difference. We use headphones at home, but they're a liability in terms of situational awareness, since they can make you an easy target.

"You shouldn't wear headphones in the woods during hunting season. Truthfully, you shouldn't be in the woods at all during hunting season without wearing a neon vest."

"Noted. Next time I'm out here shooting anything but film, I'll wear neon."

"Good." I should tell him to leave. I really should, but I'm curious about something else and unable to let go of his reaction to me hunting. "Can I ask you something, Rémy. If you were in a situation where you *had to* shoot an animal to eat, would you do it?"

He scratches one side of his chin, the same side as his misplaced dimple. "Only if all other options were exhausted."

I don't disagree. In truth, I had a similar thought earlier. There's one school of thought that says nobody in this world gets a pass on causing harm to animals. Deforestation, fossil fuels, pesticides, all result in the death of wildlife. But those are things that can and should be changed. They're choices.

I walk past Rémy to the tree and pull his map off the arrow.

"Sorry about your map." I study the hand-drawn lines pointing Rémy in the opposite direction of the treehouse, but straight toward The Nest if he kept east on the prescribed path.

"Someone must have pulled a prank on Mr. Whitlock. My sisters and I have been over every inch of these woods. There isn't an abandoned treehouse out here."

Rémy scans the woods. "Sucks for me. I was hoping to shoot something interesting for a photo contest."

"Interesting word choice: *shoot*. It implies your camera is a weapon. *Capture* might be better. Though that's a word used for trapping. Anyway, I'm sure you can find a better subject than some rickety treehouse."

He scrunches one side of his mouth, biting back amusement with a slight nod. "The word *snapshot was* derived from a hunting word, meaning a quick shot taken without deliberate aim. That's not really my style, but I do try to hunt down the best prey." He lifts the Nikon hanging around his neck. "Wanna see?"

I *want* to get him out of these woods without making my fear of being caught with him obvious. I glance over my shoulder, looking for sisters at best. Magda and Annalise at worst.

I step forward to look at the viewfinder on Rémy's camera. Just a few and I'll shoo him away. He presses the forward button and shows me a wavy, light orange wild mushroom the size of a football on the base of a dead raccoon tree.

"That's called *chicken of the woods*," I tell him. "It's edible."

His eyes flit to my face. "Have you ever eaten it?"

I nod and he stares at me uncomfortably long. I forgot for a moment that I'm one of the *weirds*. Rémy stops staring to press the button that makes his captured images move forward one by one. He took a beautiful photo of a doe in a clearing, and some interesting insects on foliage.

"I think that's about it," he says, clicking through faster. He's lowering the camera when I catch a photo of myself. Rémy again presses the button through several frames fast, moving the camera away from my view, but it's too late. I put my hand over his and pull the camera back.

"Was that *me*?"

Rémy scratches the side of his neck like a kid who got caught stealing candy and has to fess up. Eyes down, but stealing a glance at me when he says, "Do you want to see it?"

"I think I have a right to, don't I? Considering you never asked my permission."

His cheeks go red. "I was trying to get photos of you for the yearbook. You're not in any clubs, and I was worried there wouldn't be any pictures of you other than the one we all have to submit as thumbnails with our favorite quote. I went to your social media accounts but there aren't any pictures of you, just a lot of coffee cups and book photos and stuff. It read like somebody else posted everything *for* you."

I can't tell him we don't post anything real on social media because the entire group is hiding in plain sight. We have accounts to keep up appearances, but they're all fake. Comic drawings from Birdie, sketches from me, and Blue's needle-point portraits serve as our avatars. The irony is that we use it the same way everyone does, to project a version of our lives we want people to believe, only we do it to protect our safety and identities, not for likes. Mother says social media and internet usage are how the government tracks people. It's another rule for living on the compound. Controlled online presence. We have sites we can and can't visit, a list of words we can't use in search, and even then we run everything through a proxy to hide our IP addresses from The Powers That Be.

"*That's* why you've been taking my picture?"

"Mostly."

That's a nonanswer. I inch closer to Rémy, closer than I've been to a boy who wasn't engaged in hand-to-hand combat training. Our shoulders are touching all the way to the elbow. Neither of us moves until I put my hand in my back pocket, angling out of the way.

"Why the aggressive interest in my yearbook presence?"

"I'd call it *vested*." One side of Rémy's mouth curves before he clicks the photo back into view. "You were in the art room," he explains. "It was pretty early in the morning. I was going to the ASB room to pull up some photos for the yearbook when I spotted you working... the light streaming in behind you was golden, I couldn't help myself. You looked so—"

"The picture, Rémy." I cut him off before he lays another compliment on me.

"Right."

He passes me the camera. I'm dressed in my light denim overalls with the white paint on the thighs and a black tank top, my hair in a long braid across the front of one shoulder. I'm leaning forward on my stool, putting something down on the canvas. Left hand grasping a second paintbrush loaded with moss-green paint and the top edge of the canvas at the same time. I remember this day. I was painting the gas mask on Birdie's face. I look at ease and completely contented. This is the second time Rémy has rendered me speechless. I'm not sure what to say or do about how the photo makes me feel. Mother doesn't ever take family photos. She rejects all nostalgic recordings of our lives like they're a silly luxury. My sisters and I draw each other, or stitch each other, in Blue's case, but it's never as exact as this, with every little blemish or line visible.

He smiles and his cheek dimple sucks in deep. "I thought it captured how you look when you're working in class, only more intense because you were alone. Usually, you're with your sisters. You guys are inseparable. The Three Musketeers."

"There were four Musketeers."

"You're right. My French mother would disapprove of my

oversight. Maybe I can play D'Artagnan to the Juniper sisters?"

I don't confess we already have a fourth Musketeer named Bucky. "Didn't D'Artagnan have to earn his place?"

"Yes. How am I doing so far? Is that photo a good start?"

Detach.

I study the photo again. Golden rays of light are streaming across my back from the early morning sun. My lips are pursed, the way I always hold them when I'm concentrating. I don't look like a girl who's secretly prepping for a potential apocalypse. I don't look weird. I look like an artist, confident in her work. Rémy's camera is as good as any mirror, maybe better, so why the hell are my eyes pricking? I hand the camera back to him and blink away the confusion of my feelings before they spill out and turn me into someone I won't recognize in *any* mirror.

"Oh man. You hate it?"

I don't hate it. Not even a little. "You just caught me unawares. I've never seen myself that way. You're right about the lighting. It's perfect."

"So you'd be okay with me giving it to the yearbook committee?" His brows form double question marks.

I'm on the verge of saying *yes* when my ears pick up the rustling of my sisters moving through the woods. The jump in my heart makes me whip my head in that direction like a hunting dog on point. Shouldn't they be coming from my left?

I've been talking with Rémy for too long, giving up my spatial awareness. It's getting duskier by the minute. What the hell was I thinking? Magda and Annalise are also in these woods. My pulse taps out an urgent directive, inscribable on paper as Morse code.

Get him out of here. Get him out of here. Get him out of here.

"You should go, Rémy. I mean it. It's not safe for you out here."

"How can it not be safe? I have you as tribute to protect me."

As much as I appreciate his rationale, this isn't playtime, and he's an Outsider. In a real emergency that delineation alone could get him hurt or killed.

"Rémy, I'm serious. I'm not talking about things from stories. I'm talking about real people. My sisters and I aren't the only ones hunting in these woods." The turkey yelps again and I use it to my advantage, standing taller to listen while drawing another arrow from my quiver. "Unless you want to watch me hunt that bird."

His eyes widen. "No, but—" I call back to the turkey, and something about my expression alters the playful grin on Rémy's face. "Okay. I guess I'll see you on Monday. Turkey sandwiches for lunch."

I nod quickly, adding a grin to satisfy whatever closed social interaction he's used to, knowing I've made a promise that might cost us more of our privacy.

⚔ IDF ⚔

INDIRECT FIRE

RÉMY IS OUT of sight when a sharp sting zips across the outside of my right arm. I drop to my knees and see an arrow strike the same tree, right below where my own arrow nailed Rémy's map. I suck in my bottom lip so hard to keep from crying out I taste my own coppery blood and can't help letting out a suppressed groan. Warm blood leaks out through the tear in my camouflage shirt sleeve, weeping into a dark sticky blob. I cover the searing flesh wound with my hand and manage to keep from screaming.

What the fuck? What the fuck? What the fuck?

I can't let the words bellowing in my mind fly out through my mouth or Rémy will turn back. I bite back the pain until I'm composed enough to stand, thinking if the SHTF, I'd have to remain silent. Safe and silent. But from who? Five of us came into the woods with bows and arrows. My sisters would never—

And then I spot Annalise. Walking toward me with mocking concern, her bottom lip pouted but her eyes as hard as one of the stones digging into my right knee, and just as flinty.

"I wasn't trying to hit you," she says. "Just wanted you to know I was watching you with that Outsider from school. Did you tell him where we live?"

"No. Of course not."

"He shouldn't be out here." She tries to examine my arm, but I jerk it away. "I had a feeling your family couldn't be trusted. It was only a matter of time."

"So you decided to *maim* me?" I spit through gritted teeth, while my own hypocrisy mocks me. *Only if she had really wanted to.* "Who says we can't be trusted? Where's Magda? I thought you were hunting together."

Fear for my sisters overrides my pain. If this is some kind of warning to know our true place, Magda might do the same to them. Removed from the sight of other members. Their word against ours. I've heard the saying the sins of the father will be visited upon the children, but what about the sins of the mother? Ours, more specifically.

"She went to get help moving the deer she nabbed." Annalise dips to study my arm again with mock concern. "It's just a flesh wound, but who knows how dirty those arrows were that my dad left out? It might cause an infection. Your mother should be able to patch you up with the antibiotics she's making."

Blood is seeping through my fingers. Annalise meant to hit me. Let's put that lie straight to bed. She's an excellent shot and only missed the straight through shot because that was her intention. She's clearly mad about our mother and taking it out on me.

This is my fault. From a training standpoint, I wasn't Ready or Responsible. Therefore I was unable to React to this attack. Dieter didn't tell us to grab our packs for this training, but we could have gone home for them if we were fast enough. If I had thought to employ the three Rs, I could have Reacted to the assignment by making sure we were Ready for anything, which would have been the Responsible thing to do. Three Rs, all strikes against me. I didn't think I'd get hit with indirect fire, and I have no choice now but to think of how to React to this wound.

Something clean. Something clean. Something clean.

I remove the wide headband keeping my flyaway hairs in control and string my arm through the fabric loop, wrapping it twice until it's snug, but loose enough that I can run it up my arm to cover the wound.

"You can't talk to Outsiders about us," Annalise says. "Trying to be sneaky about it won't work. Coalition members with loose lips aren't tolerated."

"I can talk to anyone I want as long as it's not about the compound or the coalition." I whistle long and low tone with a sharp uptick so my sisters will come find me. It doesn't take long. They know that whistle means *now.*

"Honey." Birdie's whisper-yell cuts through the trees.

I turn my head and see my sisters scrabbling over the deadfall separating us.

"I got one." Birdie holds up a turkey weighing at least forty pounds, just heavy enough to impede her mobility. But she's grinning and proud, tongue pressed between her teeth. I haven't seen her smile in days.

When she catches my pained expression, her joy is replaced by a furrowed brow. She tips her head at Blue, making me wonder if our little sister suggested this might happen in her weird way.

"You have something on your face," Annalise says, pulling my attention back.

I brush my cheek, forehead, and chin with my hands. Not that it matters. I'm so pissed at Annalise right now, I want to tackle her in the muck. And I would if I had the use of both arms and thought it wouldn't cause bigger problems in The Nest.

"No, it's here." Annalise rubs the space beneath my nose hard enough to wiggle the septum between my nostrils. Treating me like I'm some mall rat cokehead in a bathroom with my BFF who's trying to clean me up before we hit the dance floor.

"Stop. You've done enough."

I pull my face away and Annalise raises both hands like she didn't mean to offend. I rub my nose hard and take a deep sniff, cleaning up what she started.

Something about her smile, the way her top lip is devoid of any curve, makes Annalise look extra fishy. Or maybe it's her dead, shark-like eyes, despite their being blue.

"Did she *shoot* you?" The clench of Birdie's jaw and fists mirror mine, and I know she'll lash out physically at Annalise if I don't intervene.

"Not intentionally," Annalise says. The lie leaves her fishy-lips again without so much as a twitch. "I didn't mean to, but accidents happen. Tell them it was an accident."

"It was an accident?" It comes out of my mouth unwillingly as a question, and she gives me a satisfied nod.

"That's not exactly an apology," Birdie says without flinching. "But you're right. Accidents *can* happen to anyone at any time. That's the point of all this prepping, isn't it? To keep our group and everyone in it safe."

The implied warning is crystal clear.

I love that Birdie is being protective of me, despite knowing she made the smart-ass comment first while we were picking out bows.

Annalise shrugs one shoulder. "You should ask your boy-friend about that concept next time you see him."

"I will, Annalise. Trust me."

What happened at school wasn't an accident. It was planned. I don't get what Annalise is implying about Daniel, and I won't until I talk to Ansel.

"It's near dark. We better head back," I tell them. I stare at Birdie hard. Stopping her from stoking this into something bigger.

"But your arm?" Blue says. "You don't have a kill yet."

"I need to get this cut washed out. I'll deal with the conse-quences and figure out something to tell Mother."

Annalise rolls her eyes. "If she's back."

"She will be," I say. "She's the leader of The Nest."

"For the moment."

I had a feeling we'd be on Annalise's shit list after Dieter's promotion of Mother, but I can't help throwing her a dig since she shot me in the arm. "Doesn't that make me second-in-command of The Nest?"

"Nobody said *that*, or trust me, I wouldn't have missed. But since Ansel is on the verge of being demoted, I'm happy to take his place, or yours, whichever comes first."

Demoted? Ansel didn't mention that, but I bet what happened at school is the reason he isn't allowed to come to The Nest.

"We need to get a move on," Annalise says. Assuming the position of leader to prove a point. "Walk slowly and be quiet. Invisible quiet."

Nesters aren't supposed to be at odds with one another, truth be told, but things are slipping in that direction. Presently, I'm tired, losing blood, and willing to let her take the lead. *For the moment.* On that, we agree.

"We're being stalked by a snake," Blue says.

Birdie and I are so used to the stuff Blue says, we're unfazed.

The other Nesters and Burrows look at Blue the same way Annalise is right now. Like she's someone they don't understand. If we were living in a different time, she'd be the first of us *weirds* to be tried as a witch. Birdie would be next, for failure to cooperate with the magistrates. And then me, because with my sisters persecuted I would straight up lose my mind.

"Shh," Annalise scolds, and I obey. She points to her ear and I hear some movement in a patch of fiddlehead ferns, a slow-moving animal. Nothing with two to four feet moves like that in the presence of a small human pack.

"Honey, shoot it," Annalise says, pointing.

I nock an arrow and pull it tight, biting back the pain in

my shoulder that's making me light-headed, waiting, waiting, waiting. I blink my eyes several times before I see the tiniest quake in the foliage and release my grip, fingers spread like a ready slap at my cheek. The arrow flies semi-blind and strikes, sticking up at an angle through a patch of ferns, halting the movement within.

Annalise marches forward and lifts my arrow by the shaft, dangling a western rattlesnake at least eighteen inches long. A complete strike-through. I shake my head and look at Blue. "Snakes don't stalk people."

She shrugs. "Snakes aren't always snakes."

"Better him than us," Birdie says. "Snakes are edible in a pinch. I say that counts." Ever the one to compare what's fair.

"It'll make a statement," Annalise says. "Give it to my father when we get back, but be conscious of its head. A dead rattlesnake can still deliver a lethal bite."

"We should give it to Mother," Blue says. "She might want to extract the venom."

"No. To Dieter," I say. "I have to give it to Annalise's father."

My sisters gape at me like I've lost my mind, but that's what I want to do.

My shoulder is pulsing with intermittent stabs of pain, my nerve endings protesting the attack, making it hard to think straight. My thoughts are equally jumbled by the snide comments being exchanged between Annalise and Birdie. But when I hear Annalise say, "Jump," I do. Over a thick branch. I'm not sure if she was speaking to me or Birdie, so I prick my ears up to listen more closely.

"That was kind of an exaggerated move," Blue says.

"Was it? I felt like it was warranted." I take Blue's hand in mine. The lights from the compound make it easier to see the end of this proverbial tunnel, but I still want her close beside me as we traverse the unbeaten path. She's usually okay with this kind of thing, but tonight she stalls with a tug, staring at me in the dark.

"You're acting strange."

"Am I?"

She'd be acting strange, too, if she got shot with an arrow for talking to an Outsider in the woods. Annalise is hot and cold as a rule, but tipping more and more toward frigid lately. There's no way of knowing how she'll continue to play the new intel she has on me.

We're nearing the edge of the woods when I consider the sight we'd make for the mall rats at school. Annalise and Birdie with their turkeys, Blue with her grouse, and me with my snake. If this *were* the Hunger Games and it was only about getting food, we'd be the victors. Injured, tired, completely at odds with each other and ready to form a rebellion to save Daniel. At least, that's what Birdie wants us to do.

"Honey, watch out! The trip wire."

I heed Birdie's warning, but it's too late. I'm ambushed. Bumbling forward and pulling Blue to the ground with me as a screech alarm blares, alerting everyone on the compound of mock intruders. We were so close. I was so glad to be done I forgot about the tasks assigned to Camilla, Tashi, and Tito. I right myself, choking on my usual confidence as a metaphorical cannon booms, signifying the death of these false tributes. Overall, we were successful. As an individual, I failed the group.

I kneel with my hands on my knees. "Sorry," I tell Blue.

"Don't be. This isn't how our world will end."

That's not the weirdest thing she's ever said.

The majority of Burrowers and Nesters are waiting for us, dimly lit by the solar lights we have around the area. Mother *is* back, standing to the right of Dieter. Not directly at his side, but close enough to be in the near front. Magda's deer is hanging by its rear legs behind them, dead-eyed and field dressed. Innards completely gone. It's something we've seen often, and my automatic response is always to look at Blue.

"I hate it," she says quietly, averting her eyes. "I'll never eat red meat. I don't care if I die from starvation."

"Don't say that. You know I won't let that happen."

Blue is fully aware that hunting and trapping big game is part of our survival training, but she always voices her natural law afterthoughts. More than Birdie or me, who are just trying to get through the task. It's not like it doesn't wreck my gut, too, every time I take a life. Any life. But I'll do whatever is necessary to keep my sisters alive when the time comes.

"You would have all been dead," Dieter admonishes. "Killed by a trip wire that will one day be rigged to cause a deadly explosion upon contact. Next time, we'll be using non-lethal, stun-based training. Real dangers continuously threaten our country and our coalition. If we treat these drills like a game, we won't survive more than a week when the shit hits the fan. We must be ready to protect and defend this compound against attack with counterattack measures at a moment's notice."

Tashi catches my eye through a veil of dark curls and mouths, *Sorry*. I give the slightest shake of my head and smile. She caught me fair and square.

"Magda succeeded in bagging the biggest kill long before you four got caught by the trip wire." Dieter's headlamp is shining uncomfortably in our eyes. "Do you know why?"

"Three," Annalise interjects. "I was hunting with Mom."

"You were moving with the Juniper sisters as one hunting party when you showed up. *Four*."

Annalise clamps her mouth tight, looking at me with wide eyes, jerking her head at the snake. "Throw it at him," she whispers through clenched teeth.

Having Dieter shame us for getting smaller prizes doesn't stop me from throwing my kill at his feet. Rigid arrow still piercing the snake's murky-green and brown body.

"Honey!" Mother exclaims at my disrespect, but I don't care.

Dieter puts a hand up to stop Mother from intervening.

He steps toward me with the snake until he's close enough for me to smell the trapped heat and perspiration rising off his skin as the night gets colder. I study the silver hairs poking out of his stubble before raising my brown eyes to meet his icy-blue ones. The depthless pupil is so prominent in blue-eyed people it can look like a solar eclipse reflected on water. Only what I see in his isn't emptiness. It's my own reflection. The second time in as many days that I've found myself mirrored in the pupil of an eye. I don't flinch. As far as I can tell, I don't even blink.

"Pick up the snake," he says, and I do.

"Hand it to me by the tail."

I do that, too.

He stops looking me in the eyes to glare at Annalise. "Was this you?"

"Was what me?" She steps forward and lays her own kill on the picnic table. "I got this. In case you wanted a turkey dinner from your daughter to go with your *deer* wife's venison. That's two good kills, unless Ansel can prove himself by doing us one better."

That sounded personal. Dieter doesn't react, and no one standing around makes a peep. Ostensibly because Annalise is pointing out what Dieter's recent decision implies about him and Mother and the whole upset of the compound's power structure.

Dieter pulls the snake off the arrow like a sausage on a barbecue skewer. "Honey, take this snake and swing it to Annalise by the tail so she catches it by the head."

I take the snake from him, ready to do as instructed.

Annalise shrieks, "Drop it," countermanding her father.

I drop the dead snake.

"That's what I thought," Dieter says.

Annalise presses her lips into a tight line and goes silent.

I keep my mouth shut through all of it because the leader of The Burrow is testing his daughter, and I know nothing about that dynamic. We've always only had Mother, but learned early on that if Dieter asks us to do something during any survivalist or prepper training, we do it. We do it, because we want to survive.

Survival isn't supposed to be a deadly competition among us.

"I'll take her home," Mother says.

"Good idea. We can wrap things up here, but you and I should meet later to discuss the failures and trapping of this training."

Magda stiffens nearby. The deep grooves between her eyes form three ridges as her face hardens into an angry mask. I can't be the only one who thinks Mother's new leadership role is only in place for her and Dieter to spend more time together.

I make a move to pick up the snake and Dieter steps on it. "I'll keep that."

I understand his caution with the venom. It's a neurotoxin and Dieter was a soldier in the Gulf War, just like that guy, Thane. I've heard others talking about what happened to the men and women stationed with him, how they were exposed to toxic chemicals and given experimental drugs meant to protect them from exposure.

Supposedly, that's one of the many reasons he doesn't believe our government will keep everyone safe when the SHTF. Logically, there's no way to promise safety on such a large scale. And a world with rule of law will inevitably lead to the sacrifice of some to protect the many. Pandemonium will be inescapable. But we should feel safe now, among the group of people sworn to protect us.

TOBYISMS FOR ACTION
4
I DON'T BELIEVE YOU

THE TOUCH OF Mom's hand between my shoulder blades wakes me from a deep sleep. I must have dozed off in front of my laptop. The screen is dark, but the photos of my sisters are spread like a hand of cards below my dried-out bowl of macaroni and cheese.

"Where did you find these?" Mom picks up the age-progression photos, her mouth downturned more in sorrow than in anger.

I lean into my shoulder, wiping the sleep-drool from the corner of my mouth. "They fell out of a sketchbook you left under the pillows on the couch. Where did *you* get them?"

"Blake had them made. For my art. That's why I hid them. I didn't want you to think—"

"I don't believe you." When you go through hell with someone, you can tell when they're lying.

"I showed you the start of my new painting."

"And I saw the progress you've made on it since."

She wrings her slender hands like they're suddenly ice-cold. She's lucid for the moment, but I can tell she wants to slip away to her studio or with the news on TV by the way her eyes are losing focus. Her bedroom door squeaks and I turn my head, expecting to see Banquo, but it's Jonesy. Dressed for work in a black suit, but in need of a shave.

I snatch the age-progression photos out of Mom's hand and wave them at him. "Why now?"

He's slower to answer, shifting eyes to Mom that suggest regret. "I thought I had a lead, but I got it wrong. And before you go jumping down my throat for not telling you earlier, let me say I needed to check my sources before presenting something that might not pan out. Regardless, you should leave detective work to detectives."

"Why? *She's* not," I tell him. "You think she's painting fields of sunflowers in that studio or something?"

"What your mom does in her art studio is her business. That's her private space and I respect that. What you're doing on social media is different. It's dangerous, Toby. You could end up spooking someone into further hiding, or prompt them to do something that puts your sisters in more danger. The case *is* cold, but we are still working on it."

A familiar weight plummeted into my stomach when he said he had a lead but got it wrong, gutting me. You might think that news gets easier to take over time. I'm here to tell you it doesn't.

"And still you guys have nothing," I rage. "Mom and I have all our chips stacked on the table, but my sisters are the ones paying the price, so don't ask me to stop looking, Jonesy, because I can't. I won't. Not until your last lead has you on your hands and knees digging up their bones."

Mom walks out and heads for her studio like the whole conversation makes her feel *more sinned against than sinning*, as King Lear would say.

Jonesy hangs his head. He knows I'm right.

The stench of cigarettes enters the space around us. "She's smoking again?"

Jonesy shrugs as if to say he can't stop her. "She says it carries her back to a particular place in time while she's painting."

"I could do the same thing for her by popping out the fuses and taking them with me for the day." I twist out of my seat so I don't have to see his reaction to that truth. "I have to take a long hot shower and get to work. My spine is trashed from sleeping hunched over on the table. You gonna be around for dinner?"

That's my way of apologizing to Jonesy.

He shakes his head. "Not tonight. I have some bad guys to catch, remember?"

I remember. The marrow in my bones remembers.

I'm halfway to the bathroom when he says, "Toby." His tone asking for another second.

I spin, closing my eyes for a beat before shaking my head in that shallow way that says *no* but asks *what?* simultaneously.

"I just wanted to say I'm not gonna stop looking, either."

The Nikko's lunch crowd is dying down. I'm glad because I need to change the bandage on my arm. It aches a ton today, but I still have a second shift to get through before I can go back to my missing persons search. I do a quick walk-through of my section to check if anyone is looking for their check or a refill on a drink. There's one table finishing up that I ask Brooke to keep an eye on.

"Do I get to keep the tip?" Her plum-stained mouth curves into a smile.

"Here's a tip. The dad is here all the time. You won't get more than five bucks out of him. But if you bus the table, it's all yours." I hand her their check.

I make a beeline for the kitchen, where we keep the first aid supplies. I grab the white plastic case off a wire shelf and knock down a pair of the elbow-length, heavy-duty gloves that make the dishwashers look more like falconers. I shove them back onto the shelf and head for the employee bathroom. I'm examining the shitty job I did patching myself up at home when Stavros fills the doorway.

"How you did this? Not here?"

"No, not here. I was climbing a fence."

A gleam of satisfaction brightens his eyes. "You almost got caught, didn' you?"

"You jinxed me."

"Greeks don' jinx. We curse or we give the *Mati*. Jinx *eínai malakó*. It's soft. It's for people who aren't sure of themselves."

I forgot about the *Mati*. "I'll be sure to act with confidence next time one of your customers needs the evil eye."

"Ha!" That's the way Stavros laughs. He just says the word *ha* with force.

He grabs my arm at the wrist and peels off the butterfly stitches without warning.

"It's just a cut."

He tugs my arm over the bathroom sink, simultaneously grabbing the blue wound wash with his free hand. He squirts it over my wound and the brain-zapping sting makes me suck saliva-filled air through my clenched teeth.

"All right. I won't give your customers the *Mati*. Stop torturing me."

"Some people deserve it." He opens the cabinet above the toilet and pats my arm with a clean towel then brings my arm closer to his face to examine the cut again. "You could have had one, maybe two stitches, but it's okay. *Eínai entáxei*."

Stavros takes out a new set of butterfly stitches and does a much better job than I did with one hand. He wraps the whole thing in the sticky gauze they use at the doctor's office after they take your blood.

"Thank you. I mean, *efharistó*."

"Very good. You welcome. *Parakaló*."

When I return to the floor, Brooke tells me I have a new party at table six. "And that guy gave us five bucks, just like you said."

"Far be it for me to say I told you so."

Four guys in their thirties, dressed head to toe in camouflage, are seated at table six. That's not unusual for San Diego. This is a military city with bases for the marines and the navy. Only these guys are giving me a civilian vibe. Their clothes are a little stiff, and they're too old to be fresh recruits.

"How are you today? I'm Toby. I'll be your server. Can I get you anything to drink? Maybe a starter? The dolmades and the flaming saganaki are excellent choices."

"Flaming," one guy says, laughing the same way as Stavros, only on him it comes across rude. "He must be talking to you, Greg. But what do I know? It's all Greek to me."

Oh, fucking shoot me now with this shit. I'm trying so hard not to roll my eyes.

"I'll have a Coke," the one named Greg says.

The passive-aggressive homophobe—whom I'm going to call *Bob,* for all intents and purposes, because I don't care what his name is—asks for a pint of beer, and the other two follow-along guys order the same.

"Are you in the military?" I ask. "The owner gives fifteen percent off for active duty."

Bob looks momentarily confused then a light bulb goes off behind his eyes. "Oh, because of our *clothes.* No, man. We're going hunting."

"In *San Diego?*"

This I have to hear. We're more of a harvest-mussels-and-spiny-lobsters town. The only thing people around here are hunting down is the best California burrito or craft beer.

"We're heading east to the Inland Empire. There's a place up there where you can book a guided tour to hunt deer, coyote, hogs. It's gonna be epic. We figure, the way things are going with our government, it's only a matter of time before the shit hits the fan and it's the end of the world as we know it. We want to make sure we can feed our families off the land. Before people start resorting to cannibalism."

"Hunt or be hunted," one of the follow-along guys says.

"Right. The zombie apocalypse. Seems inevitable," I tell them. "Probable, even. I'll be right back with your drinks."

I walk away to get their order, wondering if there's something in the water making everyone act crazy.

Brooke hands me the two waters for the follow-along guys. "Did that guy just admit to going hunting in preparation for the zombie apocalypse?"

"Yep. Fear the Walking Dead."

"We need to fear more pressing shit than that if those idiots are walking around with guns."

Truer words have never been spoken.

✣IFAK✣

INDIVIDUAL FIRST AID KIT

THE NEWS ISN'T playing inside our house for the first time in weeks. This is what it will be like when the end of the world as we know it comes, times a million. We have a few solar lanterns in the kitchen, but real power won't be back on for another seven hours. That's fine by me. I could use some time in semidarkness to think before I venture out to meet Ansel.

I can't assume he won't be there based on his assignment to bug out. One of the rules of being in the coalition is if we make plans to meet somewhere, we assume the other party will show unless—after a reasonable amount of time has passed— they don't. Then assume the worst and act accordingly.

I dig inside the oak cabinet where we keep commercialized medicine, looking for the ibuprofen bottle with the nearest expiration date. I don't know if it's the rush of what went down in the woods with Annalise, the loss of blood, or hunger, but I have a monstrous headache. I swallow two round tablets dry before opening the refrigerator to see what we have to drink. Goat's milk, fresh-pressed apple juice, chicken stock. I pour myself some goat's milk and chug it down to coat the pills in my stomach, wishing I had something stronger to combat the pain in my arm.

My stomach growls, nagging me that it's past time to eat. Trust me, I don't need the nudge. I'm figuratively starving right now. I start the fire in the wood-burning stove so we can get water boiling for the MREs, but it's going to take time for the logs to burn and bring the cast iron up to heat. I could easily devour all the ready-to-eat Chili Mac meals myself, but I'll have to make do with one and whatever we have in the fridge that will spoil after not having electricity for twelve hours.

The skin on my scalp prickles, letting me know Mother is watching my every move, trying to dissect what she thinks happened. "Take two more of those," she says dully. "Eight hundred milligrams is the prescription dosage."

I go back to the cabinet and do as directed, waiting for her to finish removing her mud-covered boots so she can examine my arm.

"Annalise shot Honey in the arm on purpose," Birdie blurts as she pulls a few battery-operated lanterns out from under our galvanized farm sink. "Blue saw her."

My eyes dash to my middle sister. She tucks one side of her dark hair behind her ear, tapping her temple with her index finger on the sly twice so I catch on she means *saw her* in the Blue way.

"I noticed your quick-thinking bandage," Mother says. "Did you move into her sight line?"

I shake my head. "I think it was meant as a warning shot, but she got too close."

Mother's body stiffens. "*Warning shot?* For something you did, or for Dieter's announcement yesterday?"

"Mostly Dieter's announcement." Removing Rémy from the equation isn't about me being nice. It's an act of self-preservation.

"How bad is it?" Mother asks.

I'm not woozy anymore so hopefully it's not too bad. I unwrap the fabric covering the wound and it starts bleeding freely. "I need stitches."

Mother throws me a clean kitchen towel, her face a quick-changing mask between Reactive anger and Responsible concern. The missing third R worries me most since I'm unsure what Mother is ready or willing to do about it. She goes to a cabinet to sort through her jars for supplies without saying another word about Annalise. She gets like this during conflict, debating whether creating an uproar would be worth the results, with us, with other people, strangers. I felt like that in the woods with Annalise. When I chose to bide my time and get my facts straight before giving up what I knew versus what I didn't.

Mother turns to me with her IFAK and suture kit in hand. "Ready?"

Not really, but I uncover my arm so she can make her assessment.

"Birdie, bring one of the stronger lanterns over here. I want you to do some of the stitches."

"No!" I protest.

"I'll be watching her. She can do it. Get some gloves on, Birdie."

"But it's on part of my arm that will show in the summer. If I wanted a tattoo, I'd have Birdie handle that needle, no problem, but I'd rather wait for Blue to do this. Needle and thread are her thing."

"A blunt needle," Birdie says. "What are you so afraid of, Honey? It's not like I would stitch the word *MOM* on your arm in all caps or anything. I mean, I could if you wanted. Then you'd really look the part of a high school outcast, even when you buy their castoffs to dress just like them."

I stab her with my best sarcastic sneer. Having *MOM* on my arm is the least of my worries. Birdie would definitely stitch something far worse and think it was hilarious.

Blue rushes inside a few seconds later, letting the screen door slam behind her as she pushes back her hood. "I brought in some blue potatoes from the root cellar and the chicken eggs you asked me to put aside for Dieter. You might have to take the ones I collected earlier to have enough. I thought we could wrap the potatoes in aluminum foil and tuck them in beside the burning logs to have with the MREs, but I wouldn't mind if we had popcorn."

"I could eat my body weight in popcorn right now," I tell her.

We have blue popcorn seeds just for her. We can't grow blue corn in Washington, but Mother bartered for it in town for Blue's last birthday. Good thinking on the potatoes, though. I should throw a few russets for Ansel's black eye in my EDC before I leave.

Mother stops what she's doing and stares at us. Her deeply hooded hazel eyes are as blank as those of someone peering into the hadal zone, observing creatures she's never seen before.

"What's wrong?" I ask.

Her focus returns. "You girls have grown up so fast. You're old enough now to fend for yourselves if I wasn't around."

She pulls on latex gloves and lays out a curved needle, suture thread, needle holder, forceps, chlorhexidine solution, liquid lidocaine, and a hypodermic needle on a metal tray layered with clean paper towels.

She's waiting for us to protest and say we'll always need her. The truth is, if we had to, my sisters and I could take care of everything on this homestead ourselves.

After a few seconds without a reaction from us, she says, "I don't think bringing this accident to Dieter's attention will help. The best course of action is to keep doing what's needed to ensure our safety and survival, which means keeping peace in The Nest so we can stay on here."

I don't say I'm not sure Magda and Annalise want us to stay, so I just say, "Okay."

"Tell me about the rattlesnake you brought back from your hunt."

"It was the only thing available."

"Annalise told her to shoot it," Blue says.

"No, she didn't."

"Yes," Blue says. "She did."

"That's not how I remember it, but even if she did, it doesn't matter. We were running out of time. I needed to bring back something as my kill."

"Oh, you don't *remember it* like that?" Birdie quips.

I know what she's implying, but it's not the same. I was losing blood and daylight. I did what I needed to do.

"But *you* decided to throw the snake at Dieter's feet yourself?" Mother asks.

"My arm was throbbing. Dieter was reprimanding us. So, yeah. I guess so. I was mad. It happened kind of fast."

I lock eyes with Birdie as that last sentence travels from my brain out my mouth. Her eyebrows go up, but it's not the same. Everything happens fast in training. That's the point. I'm not lying.

Mother rearranges her supplies with pursed lips, trying to understand my behavior. She's become more secretive in the past few months, holding her cards closer to her chest. I have to believe it's because of her increasing closeness to Dieter Ackerman.

"Maybe you should step down from your leadership role if it's already causing backlash for us," Birdie squawks at Mother.

"It's not a bad idea," I admit. "Magda and Annalise might back off if they think they're in a position of power."

"Nepotism never benefits the greater good. Look at what's become of our country. The greed. The recklessness with people's lives. Things are not going to get better. We need to think about the group as a whole. Our survival is paramount, and that includes documenting and creating emergency medical practices for all situations when prescription and over-the-counter medicines aren't available. There's more to what we're trying to ensure than you girls understand."

Birdie's mouth slants as she shoots me a side-eyed I-told-you-Mother-is-banging-the-leader-of-The-Burrow look, and

I'm starting to believe it's true. Apparently, love makes you do stupid things at any age. But maybe it makes you do more desperate things as you get older, when your options become limited.

Sometimes I listen to what she's saying and think she can't possibly be our mother. She doesn't have a creative bone in her body. All she thinks and obsesses about is this place. Her utopia.

But when she takes a seat at our big oak farm table and pats the bench beside her, I sit. Letting her press the kitchen towel on my arm for a few minutes before peeling it back for a less bloody look. The cut is three inches long and a half inch wide, revealing the scarlet tissue beneath my skin. Mother pinches the wound shut to gauge the gap. Then she takes my free hand and puts it over the kitchen towel so she can fill the hypodermic needle with lidocaine. I know from experience the lidocaine injections will hurt more than the actual sutures.

"Come over here, girls," Mother orders. My sisters approach the table with rapt curiosity. The same way they'd observe the butchering of a chicken. "What kind of stitches do you think would work to lessen the chance of a scar?"

It's a trick question. I know the answer, but let my sisters answer.

Mother removes the towel and injects the first dose of lidocaine. I probably only need six total, one for every inch, three on each side. I squeeze my eyes shut with each sting, fighting the urge to curse and pull my arm away.

"Simple uninterrupted," Blue says. "Maybe a mattress stitch in the middle where it's deepest."

Birdie nods. "Continuous would work, too."

"Yes, but it's not the stitch that matters when it comes to scarring. It's how tight you pull the sutures that puts the skin at risk of puckering," Blue reasons. "Same with needlepoint and fabric."

"Correct," Mother says. "Bring me a mug of that hot water

and the chlorhexidine solution I left on the counter so we can put that knowledge into practice."

By the time they have everything ready, the lidocaine is working. My chest relaxes where I was holding the muscles of my upper body tight. I end up with more stitches than I wanted, because of the combination of techniques, but I don't feel anything more than a tugging sensation. And thanks to Blue, the stitches look nice and even.

"Can I do one?" Birdie asks.

"She needs two more."

Mother and Birdie look at me, waiting for me to give my okay. I nod, but not without comment. "Don't pull."

"I won't."

Birdie slips on a pair of latex gloves and takes the needle holder and forceps from Mother, finishing the last two stitches with her tongue poking through the right side of her mouth. Her stitches are neat and even, matching the ones Mother put in place.

"See. Perfect," Birdie says. Ever the one to pay herself a compliment.

I'm choking down the last bland bite of my watery Chili Mac meal, without the egg I wanted on top, when Mother announces she's going to The Burrow to bring Dieter the eggs he needs. *Needs* is a curious way to say that, almost subservient. I don't like it.

"Why doesn't Magda bring Dieter *her* eggs?" Birdie gripes. She tosses the empty trilaminate pouch from her MRE in the trash.

"She may have. He needs several dozen. I should be home in an hour or two. Don't stay up too late."

It will be a miracle if I can stay up to meet Ansel, never mind too late. I watch Mother collect the eggs and a few test tubes from different medications she's been formulating. She checks her face and hair in the round mirror next to the door before walking out. If she isn't interested, and nothing is going on, why would she check her reflection?

The second she's out the door, Birdie says, "*Several dozen eggs?* What are they making over there, quiches?"

"Who knows."

"I'm making popcorn," Blue says, pulling out a mason jar full of dark blue seeds and shaking it like a maraca.

"If you're making it, Blue, I'm eating it."

"Same." Birdie takes a repurposed glass milk jug full of juice from the fridge and drinks straight from the bottle.

"Mother will kill you if she sees you doing that."

"Mother isn't here, my dear eldest one." She takes another swig before passing it to me.

She's right, I'm thirsty, and for now the juice is still cold. We're on our own for a least an hour or two. Consequences be damned.

Blue climbs a step stool and pulls down our hand-cranked, aluminum popper. "Go sit down. I can do this."

The ibuprofen and lidocaine have taken my pain down several notches. Enough for me to feel the pull of exhaustion. I need coffee. Preferably from an IV drip, but I'll make do with what we have. "Blue will you take out one of those instant coffee packets for me?"

"Are you sure? You'll be up all night."

"I'm sure. I still have some homework to finish." And a few hours to kill before I leave to meet Ansel in the woods.

"Not me," Birdie says. "But I'm so here for this popcorn session. It will be like old-timey TV. Radio hour interview or whatever. Starting with Honey."

"*Me?*"

"Yes, you. We saw you with that boy from school in the woods."

The popcorn seeds sounds like rapid-fire ammunition as Blue pours them into the aluminum popper. I can't tell if this is an attack, yet.

"We walked away to give you some space." Birdie adds another log to the wood-burning stove and takes a seat on our worn, beige couch, folding her legs to the side as she pulls a crocheted afghan across her lap. "In retrospect, we probably should have interrupted, since our absence gave Annalise an open to ambush you. But that was Rémy Lamar, wasn't it? Soccer team? The one who was trying to take our picture outside the school? His scrawny friend with the big ears is always smiling at me in the hallways like he's amused, even when I'm not doing anything out of the ordinary."

"Yes, all the boys love Birdie. You two better make some room for me on the couch when I'm done," Blue says, placing the popper on the wood-burning stove.

"I know the friend you mean. His name is Brian Sharazi. I see him staring at you in the cafeteria sometimes. But yes, that was Rémy Lamar. He's in my chemistry and art classes." I sit beside Birdie and pull half the afghan over my legs. "He told me Mr. Whitlock gave him a map to the abandoned treehouse so Rémy could take pictures of it for a photo competition or something. I was trying to get him out of the woods."

"Not right away," Blue chimes in over the kernels popping like the balloons at school. "You *like* him."

"No, I don't. He's in some of my classes. We talk sometimes. It's not my fault he was out there taking photos."

"Maybe it is, though," Birdie says. "Not your *fault* exactly, but why would Mr. Whitlock send Rémy Lamar to the treehouse near our property? What if Whitlock sent him to scope out our property so they can come for our supplies when the shit hits the fan? Lines will blur. You know it, and I know it."

"Rémy Lamar is not going to come for our supplies, but I wondered about Whitlock, too."

"The truth will catch up to all of us."

That statement is in alignment with Blue's extreme weirdness, but I don't doubt it's true. Lines have already blurred.

Blue dumps the fresh popcorn in a huge bowl and hands

it to Birdie before going back to the kitchen for something. She returns with a mug of weak but much appreciated coffee, sweetened with sugar and goat's milk to the color of caramel, a confection I would kill someone for right now. I read the lapis-blue words embroidered on the front of Blue's black T-shirt right above her heart. *All Of This Is Temporary.*

Truer words have never been stitched.

"I like your shirt, Blue." I grin at her, and she squeezes her way between us, being extra careful not to bump my arm.

"I stitched it last night while Birdie was crying over Daniel Dobbs."

"You'd cry, too."

"He'll be back in a few days. He's a pro at this stuff," I say. "It's . . . temporary."

"Yeah," Birdie says, then, "yeah," again. A tentative word steeped in so much uncertainly she had to say it twice.

I know why. It's the word Mother uses whenever we move someplace new. *Don't settle in too much. This job, house, town might be temporary.* She didn't say that when we came to The Nest, and so far it doesn't seem like we'll be leaving any time soon.

❖ SNAFU ❖

SITUATION NORMAL
ALL FUCKED UP

THE MYSTERIOUS, ABANDONED treehouse sits at the farthest edge of the compound property on The Nest side. A fixer-upper that members of the coalition have restored little by little over time, long before we ever got here. Its existence is an unspoken thing. The adults don't know about it. We don't think. But the rest of us know it's there if we need a place to go that's even more understated than our houses or barns. What anyone uses it for is their prerogative, but it's first come, first serve. I think most people use it to drink or make out. That's my guess based on the bottle caps and, well, let's just say we've seen the occasional condom wrapper. I suspect some people use the trailer-style homes on Overcast Road for the same purpose.

Blue and Birdie don't know I'm on my way to meet Ansel, but I taped a note written in cipher to the window in case one of them wakes up.

Went to get Birdie's bag. Be back soon.

It takes roughly thirty minutes to get there in the dark, and I'm two-thirds of the way. ETA: late. I was hesitant to leave before Mother got home. Fearful of being caught either halfway down the trellis or jogging across the property to get to the trees.

But time was running out. I promised Ansel I'd be there at midnight and it's 12:07 now.

The moon is full, high above the trees, softly illuminating the muted blue-green forest. I'm dressed the same way I scolded Rémy for earlier, all dark colors. Purposely, though, to blend into the darkness and avoid being seen. Only I'm wearing a headlamp, which I use to search the perimeter for glowing eyes. Predatory animals live in these woods. Mountain lions and black bears—oh my—but attacks are rare and usually springtime seasonal. Regardless, I packed my EDC as it should be, plus the addition of a russet potato, a small jar of dried arnica flowers, and a personal screech alarm because the night is full of potential pitfalls. Like the tree root I just came close to tripping over.

The air around me smells dank and earthy and peppered with the occasional hoot of an owl. I read a book of African myths once that said if you hear an owl hoot at night it means someone is going to die. Let's hope it's not me. I touch the rough, crackled bark of trees as I pass by, thinking about Rémy's reference to the color of my eyes. Two seconds later, a pine cone clonks me on the head. I pick it up and tuck it inside my pocket to remind myself that Mother Nature tried to knock some sense into me. My sisters saw me with Rémy, but what did they see? Just a girl talking to a boy in the woods. Birdie likes to think she knows everything about having a boyfriend because she was the first. That's the problem with having siblings that are only a year apart.

A branch snaps in the dead of night and I freeze, reining in my wandering thoughts to focus on the present.

"Ansel?"

No answer.

I keep walking, looking and listening more closely. I'm almost there. Maybe the crack was him climbing up the ladder, a rung come loose. I weave through the last dozen pine trees and see the beam from Ansel's flashlight waving across the forest floor, searching for my arrival.

I slink around four more ancient trunks and look up. Ansel is standing on the small deck, leaning on the one-by-four safety railing, twenty feet in the air.

"Sorry I'm late."

"I thought you might be when I saw my dad leaving with your mother. I was worried they were going to your place."

"They didn't. I don't think."

I spot Ansel's mountain bike before I climb the ladder rungs nailed to the tree's trunk. Smart thinking for getting here faster. Dirt bikes or ATVs would have been quicker but much louder. We're trying to avoid detection. Ansel extends a hand to me. I have to stretch my left hand awkwardly across my body to take it because my right deltoid is injured. Thanks to you-know-who.

"I thought you might get stuck bugging out and not make it."

"We built a shelter and I told them I'd be right back. They didn't question me."

Right. Because even if Ansel *is* on the verge of a demotion like Annalise said, he's still Dieter's son. There's been a general understanding that if anything were to happen to Dieter when the SHTF, Ansel would take his place as The Burrow's leader.

He hoists me into the one-room treehouse. One wall has a retrofitted circular window that makes the treehouse look like a birdhouse, which my sisters love. Over the years, random cushions and nonperishable food have been added and left behind. Tonight, someone left a quarter bottle of whiskey. I wouldn't mind taking a shot before I ask Ansel the heavy question weighing on me. The one based on his behavior around mother during his supply pickups.

"Do you think it's true about my mother and Dieter . . . *are they?*"

"That's what people are saying." He runs a hand through the front of his hair and pats the top twice.

"Mother says it's a lie."

"Then maybe it's a lie. I'm starting to learn other people's love lives aren't my business." He shrugs and steps away in a long stretching motion to grab Birdie's EDC. "Your sister's bag," he says. "As promised."

"Thank you. You're a lifesaver."

He tugs his earlobe and his mouth twitches uncomfortably. "Not exactly."

"Don't be so modest, Ansel. You have no idea how much trouble we'd get in if we didn't get our phone back."

"It's not that," he says. "I couldn't keep her bag at The Burrow, anyway. I hope you don't mind, but I took the liberty of going through it for anything that might get us in trouble."

"Like flash-bang grenades. Why was Birdie even with you guys? I tried to stop you in the air shaft. I swear you looked right at me. You were holding bolt cutters. What were you guys getting for Dieter anyway?"

Ansel pulls his chin back. "I don't know why Birdie was with Daniel. She shouldn't have been. To tell you the truth, I don't remember seeing you. Everything happened way too fast. Just do me a favor and don't tell me anything else about where you were or what you saw. The less I know about your involvement the better."

"I have *no* involvement other than following protocol. But Birdie is claiming she doesn't remember everything, so if this was some secret squirrel operation for your father nobody can tell me about, just say that."

"We were there to get sodium," he says quickly. Maybe too quickly. "Our normal distributor got busted, and we knew the school had a bunch locked up in the chem labs. That's why I needed bolt cutters. It was supposed to be easy. Create a distraction that forces everyone outside, get what we need, get out. But when Annalise saw your sister there, whether Birdie was officially invited or not, she egged her into throwing the first flash-bang grenade before we were ready, and everything went sideways from there."

"You thought stealing from the school would be *easy?* During *the day?* I may not have been invited either, but it doesn't take a genius to know that might cause a SNAFU."

"Okay. You run the next civilian interaction training mission."

"Sorry. I was too busy keeping Birdie from doing anything stupid that day. But with Situation Normal All Fucked Up, why didn't you just tell your father Annalise was the one that went off command and save Daniel from being sent out solo? He wouldn't send *her* out alone, would he?"

"The way she's been acting lately, he might. The truth is if we blamed Annalise, we would have had to say Birdie was there, too."

Ansel touches the skin beneath his black eye like he's wiping away a loose eyelash. It's a reflex, but it speaks volumes.

"So you and Daniel lied to keep Birdie out of it."

He nods once with a slight tip of his head. "That's the deal I made with Annalise."

"Thank you. I know your sister can be abrasive. I just didn't know she could be so vindictive until I had my own run-in with her today."

"Listen, Annalise isn't happy about a lot of stuff, and she's looking for weak links. She's on a mission to convince our father to let her join The Burrow. Insisting on her rights for equality, saying she doesn't see a reason to stay in The Nest. She took charge of the mission without his consent. And when it failed, she acted like she came in at the last minute to fix everything. She's trying to prove I don't have the stomach for leadership."

"Because you'd be a different kind of leader or because he made our mother leader of The Nest?"

"Both."

"You guys are twins. Technically she wouldn't actually be taking any rights away from you as the oldest. I'm not saying what she did is right, but the whole women over here, men over there setup does set everyone in The Nest back decades."

Ansel sighs. "That's not the intention. And it's not that simple. You know separation is for safety. If we lose The Burrow,
we still have The Nest and vice versa."

"Fine. That doesn't matter right now. I'm just glad to have
Birdie's EDC back. I brought you something, too."

I take off my EDC, kneel down to unzip it, and hand him
the potato.

"A raw potato. Gee, thanks. Is this some prepper equivalent of making a guy cookies? 'Please accept this raw food item
I grew as my thanks, but you still have to cook it yourself.'"
He grins and, just like with Birdie, I realize I haven't seen it
in days. Maybe weeks. "I guess I could wire it up and turn it
into a battery."

"It's for your eye. Raw slices will help with the bruising.
And so will this." I hand him the small mason jar full of arnica flowers. "Steep two teaspoons of dried flowers in one cup
of hot water for ten minutes and let it cool. Wet a clean cloth
with the solution and apply it to the area around your eye as
many times a day as you can. It works best if you do it right
away, but it will still help."

"Ah." He nods his understanding. "I think everyone's seen
my shiner and made their assumptions. What about you? Why
are you favoring your left arm?"

"Ask your sister."

Ansel leans against one of the rough, cedar-planked walls.
"Do I want to know?"

"An Outsider from school was in the woods. Annalise saw
me talking to him and assumed I told him where we lived. Her
arrow *accidently* skimmed my arm."

"That sounds like my sister. Shoot first, ask questions later.
Was it over anyone special?"

I hesitate in giving him that answer because there's an un-
derlying insinuation in his question. Pausing only makes it
seem like I'm hiding something, so I glance up at him from
my crouched position and say, "Rémy Lamar."

No big deal.

The battery-operated lanterns are casting feathery shadows across his eyelids. If he weren't studying me so inquisitively, the shadowy fringe of his eyelashes would hit his brows, making him cartoon-sinister. As it is, he looks more dejected than angry.

"Oh. Him." His expression dulls further. "What was he doing out here?"

"He said he was taking photos." I zip my EDC and search through Birdie's bag.

"Of?"

"Stuff in the woods." I stand and toss a bruised apple through the circular window for some lucky animal to find.

"You were in the woods," he says. "My mom and sister were in the woods. I was on my way to bug out with some of the Burrow Boys in the woods."

I stop riffling through my sister's EDC pockets. "What are you saying? Rémy Lamar, soccer player and yearbook staff photographer, was purposely in the woods to spy on us? For what?"

"I didn't say that, you did. You're the one who talks to him."

"It was just a coincidence."

"Okay. But maybe Daniel and Birdie aren't the only ones acting like Romeo and Juliet."

"That's ridiculous. Of course I talk to him. He's in my classes."

Rémy *is* an Outsider who happens to be in my classes, just like anyone else. Twenty minutes ago Ansel claimed he was starting to realize other people's love lives weren't his business, so who is he to press the issue? The truth is Rémy has asked me out, sort of, not really, and I've mostly declined. The only reason Ansel would press me on him is if someone—namely Annalise—filled his ears with tales of me and Rémy long before seeing us in the woods. That's the thing about the compound. It's like a smaller town inside a small town when it comes to gossip.

I pull out our family's shared cellphone. I'm immediately relieved the screen isn't cracked, because it's one less thing to worry about when it comes to Mother. I press the Power button to fire it up, but the battery's dead. You win some, you lose some.

"You have everything you need?" He rubs his temples.

"Yeah. I just need to charge this when I get home. You okay?"

"I've had a headache since I went to bug out. I just need to head back and get some sleep."

Ansel starts turning off lanterns.

"Wait."

He stands slowly from his crouched position, curiosity narrowing his familial blue eyes.

"I don't know if you can tell me this, but I'm curious about Daniel's parents. How they died."

"He never told Birdie?"

"It didn't seem like he had last night when he was telling us about Thane being the only guy he knew of that your dad sent on a solo mission." I sling my EDC across my back, hoping he'll tell me more.

"Those two things are related." He extinguishes all but one light. "Daniel's dad was a combat medic in the military. Different branch than my father. I guess you can say your mom filled that position on the compound after he died. Alice knows much more about medicine and pharmacology than Daniel's father ever did, but he could treat wounds. Thane was a different story. A loose cannon, always wanting to change things, or be named as co-leader. He didn't think leaving me in charge if something should happen to my father was a good idea, so he started pulling rank, initiating middle-of-the-night trainings, claiming my father asked him to set up simulated raids. Stuff like that. During one of those simulations, Thane got hurt. The Burrowers who were raided didn't know it was a drill, and he got stabbed."

"By who? Daniel's dad?"

"No. David Dobbs was in the wound *healing* business. Long story short, my father told Thane if he wanted to stay he had to follow rules that were already in place. He sent him to bug out so Thane could decide whether or not he wanted to be part of our coalition or take his chances alone when the shit hits the fan. Speculation was spreading that Thane might be talking to the feds. Telling them about our stockpiles, guns, ammo. Wrong radar stuff. But they were friends once upon a time, military brothers, and because he was injured my dad was more lenient. He asked Daniel's father to follow him. See how Thane was doing, decide if he was gonna play by the rules or go rogue. Thane didn't trust military doctors after the Gulf War, but since he let Daniel's father treat his injuries on the garrison, my dad figured it would go okay. They found David Dobbs's body in the woods with his throat cut, and Thane was nowhere to be found. Nobody has the full story since none of us were there. But Daniel's mother wasn't the same afterward. She didn't trust any of us, and a few months later she took her own life."

My stomach sinks to point of nausea. "That's terrible. How could she do that when she still had a son that needed her?"

Ansel hangs his head. "I don't know. She was distraught and depressed. My father was named as Daniel's next legal guardian in their will."

"Wait. He sent Daniel out alone after what happened to his dad? I'm sorry, Ansel. I know he's your father, but that seems callous."

Ansel takes the deepest breath, and the shadow on the wall moves with him in unison like a grim puppet. "Daniel is well trained for survival, Honey. He knows the rules. Never tell anyone the location of the compound or bunkers. Keep prepping to yourself. Be alert of what others are saying. When the SHTF it's us against them. Stay below the radar." He counts them off with his fingers and I bristle.

"You don't have to recite them to me. I know. But he's just a kid that got caught doing something he shouldn't have been asked to do in the first place. To be fair, your sister is the one who jumped in and took over the mission, sort of like Thane."

"I don't disagree. Trying to go undetected among Outsiders was a risk. We thought we had it covered. We did until Annalise showed up. Daniel only got caught because he ate up time trying to get Birdie out of there. The only thing the rest of us can do now is stay vigilant about what happened and pretend like he acted rashly, alone. So if I don't talk to you at school, it's not personal. It's because I'm not sure this is over yet."

"I thought your dad took care of everything?"

"He did. He is. Just, try to keep clear of whatever shakes out from all this if you can."

"You know I can't do that when it comes to my sisters."

"Try," Ansel says. "For your own sake, and theirs."

I take both EDCs and make my way down the ladder. I got more information out of Ansel than I expected, but I'm mad everyone is still keeping secrets. If this thing isn't actually over then it's my job to make sure Birdie doesn't stir the pot. Daniel said he trusted Ansel. I have to trust him, too.

Ansel offers me a ride on his bike, giving me the seat while he stands and pedals through the trees. We bounce around and over rocks. Me, holding tight to his jacket without wrapping my arms around his waist. I bite back the pain a few jarring obstacles send into my shoulder. Ansel turns off the six-hundred-lumen flashlight strapped to his handlebars as we approach the edge of our property, so much faster than I would have made it here on foot.

I jump off the seat, but immediately dig my fingers into his forearm when I spot Mother walking up the path to our front door.

"Back up," I whisper. "Into the trees."

Ansel walks his bike backward out of sight then presses the illumination button on his watch to check the time. "It's almost one A.M. You think she's just getting back from being with my dad?"

Before I can tell him I don't know, I spot the beam from another flashlight switch off. "Did you see that?"

"What?"

"Over there." I point to the trees in the direction Mother would take to get to The Burrow. If she walked. It's far enough that driving would make more sense, especially with eggs and test tubes in tow. "I thought I saw another flashlight turn off. Do you think it's your dad?"

"I'll take the woods," Ansel says. "If I get caught, I'll just say ... I don't know what I'll say. I'll think of something on the ride. You all right to go inside?"

"I'm taking the trellis."

"Don't get caught."

"I won't. But if I do, I'll blame you. Tell Mother we're madly in love."

"You might try to sound more convincing."

He sounds disappointed again. The truth is I never even considered it, him, Ansel. Unless Birdie's ribbing me about him. The best I can do is smile, blowing off the awkwardness. "Thanks for the lift. Wish me luck."

"You don't need luck. You're more than capable of getting inside undetected. In fact, I think you're capable of almost anything."

Ansel turns his bike around and disappears through the trees before I can say he gives me too much credit.

I slink across the yard in a wide arc, hunching to remain unseen past the windows. I make it around the house to the cucumber trellis and strap one EDC on my back, the other to my front. It's much harder to climb with Birdie's bag catching on the wood. I make it onto the roof and turn to look for the flashlight I saw earlier. The trees are dark. Maybe my eyes were playing tricks on me. I lift the window sash slowly and wriggle inside. I only take one step inside when I hear a creak on the stairs. Then another, and a third. I stand as still as a statue.

I will not get caught and profess false love for Ansel Ackerman. I don't move an inch for what seems like ten minutes but in reality is probably thirty seconds. The creaks are followed by Mother's footsteps moving across the floor downstairs this time. I exhale and tiptoe to my bed, carefully unlacing my boots and sliding them off. My sisters are still asleep. The room looks undisturbed. Mission accomplished.

I lower myself onto my mattress and mull over everything Ansel told me.

Birdie is lying on her side with the comic she's been drawing next to her head, along with a yellow origami bird. I didn't know she could make those. I watch her for a minute, wondering if I should wake her up and tell her what I learned about Daniel's parents, or keep it to myself for now. She's stressed enough. I'll let her think things are okay until they're not. Knowing more about the night Thane got sent away won't ease her anxiety over Daniel.

I know I should go straight to bed, but I've broken through exhaustion and could stay up for another hour or so, although I'll pay for it in the morning. I grab my notebook and plug our phone into the outlet near my bed so it'll start charging when the power comes back on. Just a few more minutes, twenty tops, and I'll rack out. Right after I write a quick letter to Bucky.

Dear Bucky,

When we first moved here, I swore not to make any friends. I wasn't even willing to try. Now, I feel protective of Rémy Lamar. The guy who's always got his camera pointed at me. He was in the woods today where he shouldn't have been, within the compound boundaries. He was looking for the same treehouse where I met Ansel tonight to get Birdie's EDC. I lied and told Rémy the treehouse didn't exist. It's better if he thinks it's some urban legend. A hidden Podunk, Washington myth made to keep people wandering around the woods in search of another Bigfoot. Only he had a map, marked with a red line by Mr. Whitlock that was clearly pointing him toward the compound. If Birdie's right, why would Mr. Whitlock give that to him? Maybe that's why he asked Rémy to stay after class yesterday? I thought for sure he'd ask the same of me, but nope. Honestly, I don't know what it is about Rémy Lamar that makes people like and trust him so much. He made a joke in the woods tonight about wanting to be our D'Artagnan, and my first thought was that position is already taken. By you, of course. If he's lucky, maybe he'll earn my trust before TEOTWAWKI. Not that any of us will be lucky when the SHTF. But especially not Outsiders. I'm almost done painting a self-portrait at school. Rémy helped me with my eyes by calling them sugar-pine bark. A real romantic, this guy. I hope you know that's a joke. He and my art teacher, Ms. Everitt, want me to enter it in a national self-portrait scholarship. They have no idea Mother thinks making art is a waste of time. She makes sure we keep up with our schoolwork, though, and have good grades. She's nothing if not an enigma. The good news is I got Birdie's EDC back from Ansel and I'm charging our phone. Everyone has been acting weird since they set off the flash-bang grenades at school. Weird, even for us. Ansel told me to stay clear of the whole thing until it blows over. I thought it had. But you know I can't do that when it comes to Birdie. I will tell you this, though. If one more person says they don't remember something that happened around the whole flash-bang grenade thing, I might lose it. The only forgiving theory I can think of is there might be something toxic in our soil, making people forgetful. I saw a news story once about a guy that died after inhaling mold spores in his garden compost. And when we lived in New England and studied the Salem Witch Trials, we learned the ergot fungus found in the rye they grew was attributed by some scholars to the accused villagers' bizarre behavior. Ergot is the same fungus used to make LSD. All of which begs me to question whether our dirt or compost could be contaminated. How else do you explain lapses in memory? If I've learned anything while living here, it's to pay attention to my gut instincts and how people behave. And lately, I'm seeing a big uptick in nervousness, rash decisions, and forgetfulness. I had my own memory blip today, but I'm not sure it's related. I'll mention it to Mother. Chemistry is a big hitter in her wheelhouse.

I'll keep you posted. Wish you were here for real.

Love,

Honey

✦ EOD ✦

END OF DAYS

I BOLT UPRIGHT like a corpse shocked by a defibrillator and reanimated. After getting roughly four hours of sleep, I feel close to dead. But if I don't want to raise suspicion from Mother, it's chores and business as usual. Sometimes it helps to remind myself that if we were in a post-apocalyptic situation, this would be normal. My sisters and I would have to do our part to keep things running, even on little sleep. But the tired is deep down in my bones today, making me shaky. An exhaustion on par with running a high fever in a body that does not want to obey and for which there is no medicine other than caffeine. It's nice Ansel thinks I'm capable of *almost* anything. We'll see if he's right.

I swing my bare legs to the floor and toss my pillow at Birdie, hitting her peaceful face.

She moans and pulls her comforter up to her chin, knocking her hand-drawn comic onto the floor. "Five more minutes. Every teenager this side of the world gets to sleep in."

"That's factually inaccurate," Blue tells her. Our youngest sister is already sitting up, rubbing the inner corner of her right eye. She's still dressed in the *All Of This Is Temporary* shirt she was wearing yesterday. Let's hope that irony extends to what happened at school and it is actually over, despite what Ansel implied.

"If I didn't get four hours of sleep because I was out getting our phone and your EDC back, I might take your weak complaints more seriously."

"You did?" She fights her way out from under her covers, all limbs punching and kicking. "Did Ansel say anything about Daniel? He should be back in two days." Birdie's version of *sorry you had to break curfew to cover my ass.*

I struggle to process her questions with my exhausted brain. Yes, I got it. Yes, he did. Stay out of it.

Birdie lunges for the phone.

"I doubt it's charged all the way. The power's only been on for an hour."

"It's at eighty-five percent," she announces.

"I saw your note," Blue tells me. "How's your shoulder?"

"It feels like I got grazed with an arrow going two hundred feet per second at close range."

"Now *that's* factually accurate." Blue grins at me. "Ansel is so much nicer than his sister. It's amazing they came out of the same womb."

"On the same day," I add. Ansel didn't say, but I bet Annalise was born a minute later and resents her brother for being first on that, too.

"You want me to take a look at your stitches?"

I shake my head. "I'll take care of it when I shower. Right now I need coffee. A milking bucket full of coffee."

"Me, too. Just not as desperately as you."

"Oh," Birdie chirps. "That's how he did it?"

Blue shakes her head at me with a tiny eye roll, acknowledging Birdie's tendency to focus on herself and whatever she has on her mind.

"That's how who did what?" I ask.

"Daniel. He left an origami chicken in the pocket of his

jacket. The instructions on how to fold it were still open in the search window of our phone."

"I thought *you* made that bird. Let me see."

Birdie hands over the phone and I accidently swipe away the open screen with my thumb. Underneath the open search window there's a text message from Daniel that says, *A little birdie will tell you what you need to know.*

A little birdie will tell you. A little birdie will tell you. A little birdie will tell you.

"Can I see it?"

"What?" Birdie gawks at me like I'm dumb for not remembering I just asked for the phone.

"The origami chicken."

"Get your own boyfriend to make you one."

"First off, Rémy Lamar is not my boyfriend, despite what you or anyone else thinks they saw in the woods. Second, didn't you read your text from Daniel?"

"Yeah. It said, *A little birdie will tell you what you need to know.* He made a paper bird for me to tell me how he feels, just in case I feel sad."

"Oh my god, you're such a Birdie brain sometimes. Let me see the damn thing."

Birdie huffs and hands over the origami chicken. I flip it over, peel apart sections of pinched paper, and there, underneath its body, is a blue line from a ballpoint pen. I start to unfold it and Birdie jumps up.

"What are you doing? Stop."

"He left you the instructions on how to fold it up on purpose. I think there's a note inside."

I manage to get it unfolded without ripping her paper bird. And I'm right. There is a note, written in our cipher. I decrypt it in my head—*Dirtierdevilbread 928836.* It doesn't make any sense and presents two problems.

"You taught Daniel our cipher?"

"Oh boy," Blue says.

"I was *starting* to teach him." Birdie takes the creased square of paper from me and studies the encrypted message.

"Why would you do that, Birdie? We might need that some-day to communicate with each other. Just us."

"Drop the dagger eyes. This isn't an End Of Days com-munication method. Daniel isn't going to come back and start giving the Burrow Boys lessons on how to use our ci-pher. He's dyslexic and was struggling to get the hang of it himself."

"Okay. Then what does it mean? Maybe it is an EOD mes-sage."

"Give me a second. I think he was trying to say *Dirtier Devil Bread* or *Dirty Devil Bread*. We used to work on it and laugh over how he'd screw up words. Being able to laugh about it made him feel better about his disability. We ate devil's food cake in the barn once and he dropped his, frosting side down, and ate it anyway. He probably just wanted to remind me of something funny."

"What about the numbers?" Blue asks.

"I don't know what the numbers mean. Maybe he was try-ing to do more letters and got confused." Birdie starts search-ing through her EDC like there might be a live animal inside that needs rescuing.

"There's nothing in there that's not normal stuff," I tell her. "But Ansel said he doesn't think this is over, so don't take your normal gear with you today. How'd you do it, by the way?"

Birdie looks at me doe-eyed. "What?"

"The flash-bang grenades. What did you use?"

"A soda can, sugar, potassium nitrate. Basic stuff we have around the compound."

"You remember that, but not what happened?"

"I told you, I don't. You can ask me as many times as you want. I'm not lying."

It's still hard to believe, but I don't press her on it this time since there was some confusion around my shooting the snake and bringing it to Dieter, and my theory about our soil might hold the answer.

"Fine," I tell Birdie. "But you should fold that up and hide it inside your pillowcase until Daniel gets back, just in case. We have to start our chores."

"Yes, ma'am. Is there anything else I should or shouldn't do, or is it okay for me to go pee?"

"Honestly, Birdie. If I didn't love you so much, I'd strangle you."

Don't tell Birdie what to do. That's something Blue and I have known our whole lives. If one of us says something like *Birdie, you should grow your hair out,* her response would be to take scissors and cut it shorter the next day. It's always been like this. I pull on the pajama pants I was too tired to slide into last night, throw my hair into a bun, and head to the bathroom right behind Birdie for a peek at my arm.

"Do you mind?" Birdie says, paused in the middle of squatting to sit on the toilet.

"You're just peeing. What's the big deal? Here, I'll run the water."

She huffs her annoyance. Now, *that's* typical.

I wriggle my arm out of my shirtsleeve and pull it above my shoulder. The stitches look the same as yesterday, no redness or signs of infection. It's bruised from the impact, but the stitches aren't puckering in the least. The scar should be mostly nonexistent. My knee, on the other, hand feels itchy and tight where I cut it on the sheet metal. I put my foot on the basin and pull my pajama leg up.

The toilet flushes behind me. Birdie bumps me with her hip to get in front of the sink to wash her hands. "Thank you for getting my EDC. But if you think the conversation about Rémy Lamar is over, you're wrong. You can't lie to us or yourself forever."

"You should worry about the words Daniel left for you

instead of thinking about what I'm doing or not doing with Rémy. And brush your teeth. Your breath stinks."

Birdie huffs her dragon breath in my face.

"Sometimes the truth has to hit a person like a hammer," Blue says, squeezing past us to use the toilet.

Nothing like having two nagging little sisters who think they can see right through you. To tell the truth, I like the picture Rémy took of me, and the way he talks to me like I'm not *weird*. He's cute. I like the way he smiles and his cheek dimples. I don't know. Now that I shooed him out of the woods, I'm not sure keeping his questions at arm's length will be as easy.

I find Mother examining mold-filled petri dishes in the bay window when I get downstairs. The news is chattering in the background, keeping her company. More doom and gloom and foolishness from our Commander in Chief. Mother has gone the traditional route of growing mold on homemade bread, but there's also a jar of lemons with mold developing on their yellow rinds. The kitchen smells like hot toast and the one thing that will keep me alive today. Coffee. I lift the percolator and find it mercifully full.

"I opened a new jar of jam," she says. "Blackberry."

I watch Mother poke at her new specimens before I whip up the nerve to ask about the potential of the mold infecting our soil. "Do you compost moldy bread or food?"

"Never. And certainly not this blue-green mold. Why do you ask? Is Mr. Whitlock teaching you about mold in chemistry?"

It's early in the year. Too early for progress reports, so I'm not sure how Mother knew my chemistry teacher's name, unless she overheard me talking to my sisters about the new teacher at school. "That's more of a middle school experiment. I just read a story about a man who breathed in a bunch of mold spores from his garden compost and died."

"I read that story, too," Mother says. "People new to sustainability think composting is simple, but you have to educate yourself about what is and isn't viable."

"I think he bought his commercially."

"The government's lack of inspections can be blamed for that, I guess."

Most people don't give much thought to compost. They buy it in bags based on cubic feet they don't understand and buy their food at Safeway by the pound, tossing their scraps in the trash. They have no idea how much of what they're discarding can be regrown from the scraps they send to the landfill. Stuff like green onions and lettuce and celery love to regenerate.

Blue bounds downstairs. "Yes. Coffee. Please. And thank you. Is one of those mugs for me?"

I nod and hand her a mug. "Where's Birdie?"

I imagine her staring at the unfolded origami chicken and its message, hugging it to her chest as she pines for her temporarily dispatched lover boy.

"Back in the bathroom," Blue says. "She's dealing with the female curse."

"Better her than me." I grab a serrated knife from the magnetic stripe next to the stove and carve two thick slices of homemade bread, holding one up for Blue with raised brows.

"Yes, please."

I pop them into the toaster and breathe a sigh of relief out of my youngest sister's view. I worry about Birdie getting pregnant when she flies out at night to meet Daniel. We had the talk. God knows Mother never did. But Birdie does what Birdie wants in the heat of most moments. Case in point with this whole flash-bang grenade debacle. But maybe she actually listened to me when I told her not to get pregnant. She didn't deny having sex, which was rough for me to accept. But if she's going to do it, at least do it safely.

I take another sip of piping hot coffee, letting the steam open my nostrils. Birdie comes into the kitchen with a bunch of white toothpaste blobs dotting her face.

"Sheesh," Blue says. "You sure you don't want to just cover your whole face with that stuff?"

"That's funny, coming from someone who was born with a sac over her head."

My eyes dart to Mother. It's a joke about Blue's birth she doesn't like. Our youngest sister was born with a caul, a piece of amniotic sac covering her face. I remember Mother telling me the story about her being born blue, trying to not tell me too much about the cesarean section, but wanting me to know how Blue howled when they cut the sac away and she took her first breath, the color rushing back to her tiny face. There's a bunch of myths surrounding people born with a caul having psychic powers. Maybe she was born with a caul, maybe it's make-believe. Blue is weird. We just accept it.

"That sac made me who I am," Blue says.

Birdie's version of a comeback is to take Blue's piece of toast as it pops up warm and crusty, and put it in her mouth. "I licked it so it's mine."

I spread my piece with butter and jam and give it to Blue. "That's yours."

"I'll just eat a slice without toasting it. We have work to do."

Mother stops tending to her mold and tinctures to give us some direction, knowing we'll screw around until she kicks us out. "The goats have been milked and Blue collected the eggs last night, so you girls can rotate jars and cans and weed the garden in between your homework. I'm going to keep working on this antibiotic. One of the biggest threats to us is infection, especially staph infections, which can be antibiotic resistant."

I remind myself to take a sample of dirt from the garden. Maybe Mr. Whitlock can test it for mold. That will give me an opening to ask why he sent Rémy into the woods with a map that led him right to our compound.

❖ BOHICA ❖

BEND OVER, HERE IT COMES AGAIN

MR. WHITLOCK HAS me paired with Rémy for today's lab experiment. Chemical bonding. I glance at my last lab partner and see Shawna paired with Brian Sharazi this time. It's hard not to wonder if my prepper-slash-map-giving chemistry teacher is messing with me or if that's just today's lesson. He does jump around the textbook rather than following the chapters in order. I'm either thinking about it too hard, or the paranoia surrounding everyone on the compound is becoming a contagion.

The prelab was part of our homework, defining terms and answering a few questions on ionic and covalent compounds. My weekend was packed with making up chores, so I had to finish the assignment in the parking lot this morning before school. It's what we have to do sometimes. Usually when Dieter Ackerman shows up in the morning to "talk" to Mother, and we want to get out of the house before it gets uncomfortable. This morning Birdie had that stubborn look, ripe to ask him about Daniel. I rushed her out the door to avoid any potential meltdowns that might have come from his answers. Apparently, preventing Birdie from incriminating herself is now my biggest responsibility.

Brian beans Rémy in the head with a crumbled piece of

paper. I'm astounded by how dumb that is, considering we're dealing with open flames.

"Is he trying to start a fire?" I ask.

Rémy opens the paper, but it's blank. "It might take the chill out of the room."

I'm not sure what that's supposed to mean.

The six beakers on our table contain small amounts of different chemical compounds: sugar, salt, oxalic acid, cobalt (II) sulfate, nickel (II) sulfate, and starch. I use a Sharpie to mark the pie tin we're using with the numbers one through six, clockwise, to keep track of the chemicals left to right. I scan the lab sheet and read the procedure for *Part I: Melting Point*. Easy. We just have to place a small amount of each compound on the pie tin. I pick up the metal scoop and get to work.

Rémy leans closer to examine the lab sheet and bumps my injured shoulder. "Looks pretty straightforward."

"Yep. Pretty simple."

"Doesn't seem like there's any undisclosed information."

"Shouldn't be. We just have to follow the steps."

He's crowding my personal space, pressing against my arm with his shoulder. It takes all of my willpower to not react. I casually lean away and place the small sectioned aluminum pie tin on an iron ring positioned above our Bunsen burner.

"Do you want to light it?"

"Sure."

Rémy claps me on the deltoid and squeezes, the way you would with a buddy. Only this time, I wince. My breath catches in my throat and he looks me dead in the eye and tips his head, but I give nothing away.

I don't know why everyone is acting like there's some prize being awarded to whoever can outweird the *weirds* this week. I put it out of my mind and watch Rémy twist the ring at the bottom of the Bunsen stand. I twist the gas valve on the table, releasing a stinky, rotten-egg puff of sulfur with the first leak of methane gas, and hand him a safety match that he strikes away from us before lighting the burner. A big yellow flame shoots up. Too big. We don't want to fry the compounds. He turns the ring again until the yellow part is out of the flame, but still tall enough to brush the bottom of the pie tin once we put it in place.

"There you go," he says. "No hidden surprises in sight and nobody got hurt."

Nothing undisclosed. No hidden surprises. Nobody got hurt. I'm trained to read people and situations, and Rémy is tossing around more loaded implications than necessary.

When he picks up the pie tin for the next step, I clamp my hand over his and squeeze. "Stop."

Rémy flips his hand over so we're palm to palm and interlaces our fingers with a sly grin. "If you want to hold my hand, you could have just said so."

I'd be lying if I told you I didn't feel what can only be described as a covalent bond, the electrostatic charge of two atoms attracting. Instead of letting that reality settle into my thoughts, I big R React—negatively, I should add—picking up his hand in mine and banging it on the table. The knock is louder than I anticipated. I shift my gaze around the room at prying eyes before whispering, "What's gotten into you? If you want to talk about the woods, maybe *you* should just say so."

I release Rémy's hand and lean away, cuffing the hand he was just holding over my injury, closing off my body language.

Rémy scooches his stool closer with a bumping scrape across the floor and leans in.

"I saw Annalise Ackerman shoot you in the arm with an arrow," he whispers. "I was leaving like you said, but then I remembered I should have asked you about getting that coffee again when I had the chance. I turned around and you were standing there, watching the path, looking...like you always do, protective, and ready for whatever's coming, so I picked up my camera to take your picture and that's when I spotted Annalise slinking up behind you. She shot her arrow before I could warn you. Honestly, I wasn't sure she wouldn't shoot me, too, so I left, like you told me to, because I value living. In retrospect that was shitty, because you could have been really hurt."

I'm staring at him, completely mute. When we first came to The Nest, Mother put the word *survival* as an acronym on the refrigerator.

Size up the situation
Use all your senses
Remember where you are
Vanquish panic and fear
Improvise
Value living
Act swiftly in your best interest
Learn basic skills

Value living. He's right. He sized up the situation and acted in his best interest. I know I should say something, but what? I can defend Annalise's actions, but I need to know exactly what he saw first.

"It was an accident," I tell him.

"No," Rémy says. "It wasn't. And I have photos to prove it."

Shit. Shit. Shit.

"She was hunting with me and my sisters. I moved into her sight line."

"You didn't, Honey. I saw her shoot the same tree as you. Is there something I should know, because she's been mad dogging me in the hallways all day. I knew you were friends with her brother. I see him sitting with you at lunch sometimes, but I never see you talking to his sister at school."

"Annalise is more closed off than Ansel. She's the shy twin."

"*Shy?*" Rémy laughs loud enough to draw attention. "Annalise is in my government class. She is the opposite of shy."

"Okay, well, not shy, but sort of a lone wolf."

"And she lives on Overcast Road, too."

The implication is that he already knows, and I'm taken aback. "She does. But how would you know that?"

"I was feeling guilty about leaving you in the woods after what I saw, so I drove over there on Sunday to check in and see if you were okay."

Not good. Not good. Not good.

I need to think. I take over putting the pie tin above the flame before we use up all the gas in the tank talking to each other. The compounds start melting immediately and I make a quick note of which ones went first, and in which order, along with the ones that didn't react with heat. But I have to say something, because I'm the one who told him about Overcast Road in the first place.

"I never told you which house was mine."

"I know. But that old station wagon you drive would be hard to miss, so I thought it was worth a shot."

I raise one eyebrow at his use of *shot*.

Rémy rubs one temple. "Try. It was worth *a try*."

Mr. Whitlock clears his throat loudly, grabbing our attention. He triple taps the tip of a pencil on his desk. The standard get-back-to-work gesture of all teachers.

"We have to document the reactions," I tell Rémy.

"Yeah. We do," he says, keeping on point, "because when Annalise spotted me driving ten miles per hour up and down your street, she walked into the middle of the road to make me stop."

It's not unusual for any of us to be at the storage trailers, picking up or dropping stuff off. But it is a private road. Anyone driving by at that speed would draw suspicion.

"What did she say?"

"She asked if I was lost, so I asked if she knew which house was yours."

Good god. He has no idea how much that must have bugged her. Especially after seeing us in the woods.

Please say she didn't tell you. Please say she didn't tell you. Please say she didn't tell you.

If Annalise decides to knock me down a peg because she sees me as a threat to her position in The Nest, telling Dieter an Outsider showed up at our bogus houses looking for me would work perfectly in tandem with catching me and Rémy in the woods.

"She told me to hold on and went to talk to the two guys dressed like G.I. Joes that were moving boxes into her house. When she came back out, she leaned into my window. Kind of intimidating, actually. I've never been less than a desk away from her. Anyway, she pointed to one of the houses and said you weren't home."

"I wasn't," I tell him. "I was at the library. We need to do the soluble part before the end of class."

My lie feels as liquid as the next step in this lab. The potential reaction and ramifications just as unpredictable. Inside, I'm roiling. Everyone interacting with Annalise lately is acting strange, and something about it doesn't add up. *Size up the situation.* That's something I know how to do, but it's difficult when there's so much secrecy. I get that Annalise is a force to be reckoned with. Hell, I'm glad she'll be on our side when the SHTF. But she's not in charge of everything, regardless of her ambition. I put a small amount of each powdery compound in a tray that looks like a plastic egg holder. I top them with plain water and wait to see how they'll dissolve.

"So we're just gonna gloss over the part where she shot you in the arm?" Rémy asks.

"I told you. She was out hunting with us in a greater group."

"Right. I got that. But, I spent the whole night thinking about what I saw and . . . Have you ever watched that TV show *Doomsday Preppers?*"

"I'm familiar with it, but I've never watched."

"I've only seen it a few times with my granddad, but your whole aesthetic. The vibe of you and your sisters . . ."

Bend Over, Here It Comes Again. The BOHICA moment.

"Yes," I answer before he can ask.

"You're a prepper." Rémy's eyes globe before he blinks several times, letting it sink in as he connects dots. "And so is Annalise."

No question. Fact. If I say yes, maybe he'll stop showing up places unannounced.

"That would be the thing that bonds Annalise and I together."

I'm grateful he's whispering. Discretion is everything, but I have a sinking suspicion Rémy isn't the type to accept an answer and let it go. I keep documenting the solubility of each compound, anticipating the volubility of words destined to flow from Rémy's mouth. It's my own fault. I violated the first rule of prep club.

"The whole thing? Doomsday, grenades, rocket launchers, fear of an impending zombie apocalypse, Stephen King's *The Stand*?"

"Can you stop judging me through whatever lens you saw on TV for a second?"

"*The Stand* is a book."

I've read it, but flip him an exasperated huff anyway. "Through the pages of a book, then."

"Sorry. Those are my only frames of reference."

I put my pencil down, take a breath, and try to think of a local disaster. Some correlation that will make prepping more logical for him. "Has your family always lived in Washington?"

"In different parts. My grandparents used to live in the foothills of the Cascade Mountains."

"When Mt. St. Helens erupted?"

Rémy nods. "They lost their home and moved to Seattle. Eventually, we all migrated back here."

"That volcano's eruption is a good example of why we're preppers. Horrible things happen all over the country, the world, all the time. Shootings, terrorist attacks, bombings, natural disasters. There's a shelter under the U.S. Treasury in Washington, DC, built for Franklin Delano Roosevelt. Supposedly, it was temporary and they built something more permanent later. The bottom line is, our government knows things could turn for the worst on any given day. A nuclear bomb could be fired at us. The economy could collapse, causing people to revolt. Preppers take steps and measures to ensure we have provisions and shelter in place, so we can defend ourselves and our belongings if necessary. Not all preppers are like the ones you see on TV."

"That's good, because this one guy had a pregnant girlfriend and he was trying to teach himself how to do a C-section, and all I could think was *that he's going to kill her* and *the baby*."

"This is why preppers despise that show. Anybody serious about preparing for the end of the world wouldn't dare make a spectacle by appearing on TV. We have all the spectacle we need watching our POTUS. Luckily, our mother is a nurse practitioner, and so far nobody's gotten pregnant."

"I still don't get why Annalise shot you in the arm. It doesn't really scream, *Hey, we're on the same side*."

No. It doesn't. He's right about that, and having to ignore and excuse her actions is beginning to make my prepper psyche crumble. I don't know if I owe him an explanation. That's not my usual tack, but I'm going to tell him the truth. Consequences be damned. He's in too deep now.

"Her father, Dieter Ackerman, is the leader of our whole group. When she saw you and I talking in the woods, she thought I invited you there."

I don't explain the distinctions between The Nest and The Burrow or Mother's new role. I've already told him too much.

"She thought you invited *me* hunting?" He suppresses a laugh. "My mom is the town librarian. The only thing I'm hunting down is the next book in the series I'm reading."

"Fair enough. One of the rules of our coalition, our prepper group, is to not get too close to Outsiders or tell them about our lifestyle. Annalise saw what she saw and made assumptions about us. I'm breaking a bunch of rules by telling you anything, which I wouldn't if you weren't so persistent all the time. If I were you, I'd just forget what you saw."

"That's kind of hard to do."

"Try. Nothing good will come from you trying to get close to me."

"You can't know that. It's like saying you won't like a new flavor of ice cream without ever trying it, or you won't go on a roller coaster because you're afraid to get hurt."

He tries to take my hand again. I pull it away and tuck it between my thighs.

"Rémy, I'm not ice cream and roller coasters. I'm not made of sugar and spice, or prom and yearbook photo ops, or cheering for cute soccer players from the sidelines. That's what you're used to dealing with in your crowd. I can't change who I am. Being with me would either squash your spirit or your heart."

"You called me cute, so maybe I'd squash yours."

"Nobody can squash mine, Rémy. Not even you."

The bell shrills, mercifully ending our conversation until I have to see him again in art next period. "Shit. We're not done with this."

"You're right. We're not."

Rémy studies me like I'm a Rubik's Cube with three sides completed. I understand he's not talking about the lab, but don't react this time, even though I know I'm lying to him about more than Annalise. I knew the first time he looked at me with that misplaced dimple drawn to its deepest depth.

"I'll tell you what," he says. "I'll finish this lab and turn it in for both of us, but I get to ask a few more questions."

Outsider tested, Mother disapproved.

He's gone before I can object, and I'm left to deal with a separate but related issue with Mr. Whitlock.

TOBYISMS FOR ACTION
5
LIVING YOUR BEST LIFE

A STRANGE THUMPING sound is coming from Mom's studio, louder than Banquo's tail and more varied. I crack open the door and see my mom slithering in a circle on top of a massive sheet of paper, smearing black paint. She gets on her knees and pretends to dig through the center of a giant bird's nest. I can tell she was dressed in bike shorts and a white T-shirt before she started, but she's transformed herself into one of the distressed ravens from my last piece.

Anyone who didn't grow up with an artist would be thinking about calling a psychiatrist right now. Convinced their only living parent had finally lost her mind completely. When I size up this situation, I see a woman working out the grief of a near empty nest after seeing new photos of her grown daughters.

A paper tube is lying askew near my feet after being flung frantically across the room. She uses the Baroque music playing in the background to determine her moves, like a contemporary dancer wanting to leave a visually arresting record of every chord. It would be fantastic if she did this live, but then she'd have to talk about her inspiration, what drew her to this new method of working, stirring up old gossip about what happened to her kids.

She's completely oblivious to my presence in the doorway. I could clang two frying pans together next to her head and she wouldn't flinch. Not when she's tranced out and working. As I crouch to pick up the empty paper tube, my eyes land on her new painting. She's added a woodland scene to the back of Cassandra's nylon bomber jacket. Tall swirling trees with birds circling above and a sew-on circular patch added to the sleeve with a beaver in the middle. My youngest sister always wanted to dress in Mom's clothes the most. Even at four years old, she'd try to stitch things to the fabrics, pricking her fingers without care. Mom's bond with Cassandra went beyond the rest of us. If they were together, Cassandra was attached to her hip. Even before Cassandra could speak, it seemed like they could communicate with their minds. Our mom knowing what Cassandra needed before she ever pointed her chubby little finger.

I know the beaver Mom added symbolizes the nickname my sisters gave me when I still had buckteeth, and it makes my stomach hurt.

I close the door quietly and take a seat on the couch, crossing one ankle on my opposite knee and tapping the paper tube on the edge of my sneaker. Banquo sighs at my feet like he remembers us rolling and wrestling, using the empty tubes from Mom's art paper as weapons. He was just a puppy then, barking and jumping on us, joining in the fun. I can see it so clearly my eyes sting.

I had just nailed Katherina with a particularly well-placed death blow and was sitting on her chest in victory.

"You're going to hurt one of them," Mom scolded.

I asked my sister if she wanted a tap-out word and she nodded.

"How about *beaver?*" I chucked and chopped my buckteeth in her face, knowing she'd squeal.

"That's a rude word to use with girls," Mom told me. "Pick something else."

I didn't understand what she meant at the time. I was only seven, and she didn't bother to explain because she was on commission and had to get a painting done.

"Bucky *Beaver*," I argued. "I think it's good."

Katherina pushed me off her chest and clapped. "Yes. Because of your ginormous teeth."

Our baby sister, Cassandra, said, "I wuv it, Toby. You're our beavey beave." Then she did a flying jump onto my back right as Imogen bopped me on the head with her tube and said, "Get up, Bucky Beaverman. I want to show you how to fight like a girl. Whap, whap." Imogen's blows always came hard and swift.

I'd let her beat me black and blue with a baseball bat if it meant they were still here. Only, I fucked up. Big. Eleven years ago when I was a little kid. Too little to be put in charge of three weird little sisters until our neighbor could come help. I left them alone and skated to Bash's house, just for a few minutes, so he could show me his new Xbox.

"Don't weave, Bucky," Cassandra whined. "We'll get kidnapped."

"Good," I told them. "No more sisters bugging me all the time."

"But you said," Katherina started through emerging tears, "we have to stick together no matter what."

I didn't intend to stay and play until Bash bet me his new skateboard he could beat me at *Monster Mayhem: Battle for Suburbia*. I don't remember how long I was there before the lights blinked out all over San Diego. And then it rained and rained and rained.

That was the last time I saw my sisters. At seven years old, I had a limited concept of time. Now, I'm painfully aware of every passing day.

�★ SOL ☆

SHIT OUT OF LUCK

MR. WHITLOCK IS leaning back in his chair with his index finger and thumb bracing his jaw as he reads something on a tablet. I don't have to wait long for the classroom to empty. But when it does, I walk past him and close the door, locking it before approaching his desk. When he hears the click of the bolt, he rights himself in his mint-green vinyl seat. It squeaks like it's from the Reagan administration era.

"Ms. Juniper. To what do I owe this conference?" He puts the tablet on his desk.

I put a plastic baggie of dirt from our garden next to it. "I was wondering if you could examine this for me and see if it's infested with mold."

Mr. Whitlock picks it up, turning it over. "I don't see any. Is this a trick question, or is there a method to your madness?"

"Madness. Yes, exactly, like the mold they found in the grains during the Salem Witch Trials. I was hoping you could examine this dirt to see if there are any toxic mold spores."

Mr. Whitlock gives me a smile full of curiosity. "This wasn't extra credit, so you'll have to be more specific."

If I didn't need to rule this out as a cause to everyone's behavior, I'd be tempted to take the baggie and leave. The best way to handle this is with a half lie.

"Everyone in my family has been acting strange since we got this new compost. Forgetting stuff they've done, having headaches and stomachaches. We have extensive gardens and grow most of our own food, which I'm sure isn't a shock, but I read somewhere that a man got sick from his compost and died."

"Forgetting stuff they've done?" He arches a quizzical brow.

"Just forgetting stuff."

I get his skepticism. How can a person not know what they did, right? But what if Birdie wasn't lying? We're all questioning things we've done. Birdie throwing the flash-bang grenade, Ansel's behavior in the supply closet, my own behavior with the snake. All of those situations involve Annalise as the common denominator. As much as I'd love to blame her, it makes more sense that it's our crop soil, because Annalise is one of us.

"I don't mean to sound so suspicious," he says after a long pause. "There have been a few reports of robberies in the surrounding area, and eyewitnesses are telling authorities they've seen cashiers open registers and hand over cash and supplies willingly, but the people in question say they don't remember being robbed."

"That wouldn't be related to the soil from our garden, though. We don't sell soil in town."

"I'll tell you what, I'll see what I can find out about your garden soil over the weekend if you give me a good reason why you'd discuss your coalition's prepper business with Rémy Lamar."

I know I was whispering. Rémy was, too. There would have to be listening devices under the tables for Whitlock to have heard our discussion.

"I can read lips," he says, sensing my apprehension. "It's actually a great skill for a prepper to have."

I bet it is. Better than our cipher, since it can be used more often.

He jabs his tablet with his index finger so I'll look down and read the headline.

DOOMSDAY PREPPER IN CALIFORNIA ARRESTED ON
ILLEGAL WEAPONS CHARGES

"Do you know why stuff like this happens?"

"*Doomsday Preppers* on TV?" If he read my lips, there's no harm keeping on topic.

"Yes. Sometimes. Other times, trust is given to a person who shouldn't be made privy to certain things. Under the right amount of pressure, even a loyal person will crack and reveal what they know."

He's not wrong, but he's not right, either, and that helps me get my bearings. "I'll tell you why I confided in Rémy if you tell me why you sent him into the woods with a map that didn't lead to the abandoned treehouse."

"It didn't? That's the map that was given to me, but I understood from your conversation with Rémy that you ran into each other in the woods."

"I was hunting and he showed up in the wrong place at the wrong time, which didn't leave me with a lot of options. Who gave you that map?"

"Principal Weaver. I'm a yearbook faculty advisor for the ASB club, so I asked him about local points of interest. Something to beef up the yearbook. When Rémy and I were looking through photos of what and who interests him in this town, I gave him the map. We had a nice conversation about you, actually, after he told me about the Scholarship for the Arts America. Winning something like that could be your meal ticket out of your situation. A way out of a town like this for someone like you."

"It's not that simple," I tell him.

"Because of your sisters or because someone in your group thinks you're blabbing?"

"You read my lips, you tell me."

"That's the prepper spirit." He sits up straighter in his chair. "If I were you, though, I'd dissuade Rémy from getting tangled up in whatever dynamics are eroding your coalition."

"Our dynamics are fine."

He clocks my offense. "I didn't mean to strike a nerve. I'm just looking out for both of you. You can talk to me about anything. That offer stands and the invitation is always open. Before you're SOL."

"Thanks. I have to get to my next class. Let me know what you find out about that garden soil."

"It's the least I can do," he says.

I leave his classroom with my trepidations about his prepper status turning into agitation. I should have asked him if he was part of a prepper group instead of getting defensive. Because what he said about the newspaper article might mean he's looking to join a new group. Not that Dieter would approve. We don't recruit from our everyday life, so he'd be the one shit out of luck. And honestly, I'm still a little confused about why Principal Weaver would have a map that leads to our compound. Unless it was marked up as an empty set of parcels for sale before Dieter bought the land. The potential site for a new high school or something. It's the only thing that makes sense.

I startle when I see Rémy waiting outside Whitlock's classroom, hands shoved in the pockets of his jeans.

"Seriously? You don't quit, do you?" I hurry to the art room with Rémy keeping quick pace at my side.

"Can you quit something that hasn't really started?"

Hasn't it, though? I hate to admit it, but Blue was right. I like being around him. Rémy treats me like I'm no different from anybody else. And maybe I like the pictures he took of me, too. The problem is Mr. Whitlock was also right. I probably shouldn't encourage him.

"I see. The direct approach didn't work so you're going with aloof, is that it? Playing it cool. I don't think I've had enough caffeine today to go back-to-back classes with you."

"You say these things, but I don't think you're as impersonal as you pretend to be," he counters.

"Or, and I'm just speaking off the cuff, maybe you're just not as charming as *you* pretend to be?"

"Was I pretending?" He gives me a crooked grin, and damn if that smile with the high dimple doesn't make me feel something.

There's a pack of girls converged in front of the auditorium doors. He could pester any of them. I'm sure they'd love it.

"Oh. My. Gawd! I want to be Katherina so bad," one of them squeals, complete with a vocal fry that puts a temporary hitch in my step. Case in point.

She means Katherina from *The Taming of the Shrew,* our school's fall production. A character who is the exact opposite of girls that purposely sound like they're gargling olive oil when they speak just to fit in with everyone they see on reality TV. One more baahing sheep in the herd of mainstream popularity, even in Podunk, Washington.

I pick up my pace, glancing at Rémy out of the corner of my eye. He's tagging along, step for step, grinning over whatever expression he caught on my face. "You want to audition?" he asks. "I think we'd be shoo-ins for the leads."

"You mean—if the shrew fits?"

He does a jiggly thing with his head and blinks. "Wow. I honestly don't know how to handle the number of jokes rolling off you lately. To be fair, I was thinking I could make something more decent of Petruchio, and you could work your way up to perfecting the acerbic wit of Katherina."

"A real stretch, I'm sure. Does this mean you've given up on becoming D'Artagnan to the Juniper sisters? Moved on to greener pastures?"

He leans up against a locker outside the art classroom. "Not necessarily. What can I say? I appreciate a confident victor."

"That was more Finnick Odair than Petruchio."

"You would know." He mimes shooting an arrow while making a single cluck with his tongue.

It's hard not to grin when I know what Rémy's doing. Turning my tendency to push him away back on me. "I get why you think no one in this school could embody the role of Kate Minola better than me. I don't disagree with you. But I don't have wiggle room in my schedule for twelve weeks of play rehearsals." I yawn, reminding him I'm caffeine deprived.

He opens the locker he was leaning on and throws his chemistry book inside. "How about just letting me buy you that cup of coffee, then?"

"Now, *that* is something Petruchio would never offer a hell-kite like me." I slip into the art room to avoid giving him an answer.

I'm ready to finish my painting, despite feeling like today is the longest Monday in my personal history. I even dressed for the occasion, wearing my favorite studio jeans, the lightest denim with paint swatches crosshatched on the thighs where I've wiped hundreds of brushes. They're loose and worn to silky soft, and I chose them because I wanted to be comfortable and unencumbered enough to finish the part I've been avoiding. This past week showed me exactly what I want to say with my eyes.

I stare into the rectangular mirror clamped to my easel and see my truth, just like Ms. Everitt said. A girl who is independent and self-willed, unexpected and free-spirited, impersonal and unpredictable, stares back at me and I recognize her fully. The problem I had was trying to choose one facet of myself, but they're all me. Maybe that's why my eyes always seem too big for my face. They have a lot of facets to hold. Thankfully, this is a good mirror day. I choose a paintbrush with an extra-long handle and wind my tousled chocolate-brown hair around it and push it through to make a topknot.

I relax, mixing the paint for my sugar-pine-bark irises,

building all the variations of umber and sienna from dark to light. Keeping my sore arm up for an extended period distracts me from what I'm doing, so I rest my foot on the easel's crossbar, bracing my elbow on my knee for support. I work feverishly and with more concentration than I have the past week. Thirty minutes pass before I stand back and scrutinize my work. Something about Birdie is off, an imbalance in the way her leg is stepped out toward the viewer like she has someplace to go and is ready to walk away. I'm still letting everyone think they're all me, but that's one hundred percent Birdie. I've had to wrangle her back for as long as I can remember. But my dissatisfaction with this section of the painting is about more than Birdie's leg. It's the idea that I feel at odds with my sister. That I got mad she taught the cipher to Daniel when it doesn't really matter if anybody knows the code. I pick up my skinniest paintbrush and load it with indigo-blue paint, mixing in plenty of medium to get it fluid. I want to add something decidedly Birdie that nobody else will understand. An artistic olive branch. Her leg is at the perfect angle for decoration. I tempt fate, inscribing the words *Home Sweet Home* down the length of her leg like an inky tattoo, along with the topographic coordinates of our house. I sign the painting the same way, in cipher. When I'm finished, I stand and walk backward a few paces to take in the whole piece from a proper viewing distance. It might be the best thing I've ever done. Ms. Everitt is probably right about the national self-portrait scholarship competition. I don't want to leave my sisters, but I can't help wondering if I'd actually have a chance at winning.

I'm standing there, nodding at my own work when I hear the click-double-click of Rémy's camera shutter. I was so engrossed, I didn't sense him lurking over my shoulder.

"You know Pigpen cipher?" he asks, like he's eager for us to bond over our mutual love of encrypted messages.

The hairs on the back of my neck turn into acupuncture needles. "You can read that?"

"*Home Sweet Home.* I sent away for a secret decoder ring when I was little. I never learned the extended version with the numbers, assuming that's what the rest of your message is."

Everything I believed about the secrecy of our cipher crumbles, along with the lining of my gut. I felt the same way when I learned the tooth fairy wasn't real. I understand what Rémy is telling me. I'm just having a hard time believing it.

"Pigpen cipher? That's what it's called?"

Rémy nods. "You didn't know?"

I shake my head. "Is it . . . do a lot of people know it?"

I get straight to mixing skin-tone paint, big R Ready to cover the message on Birdie's leg in reaction to Rémy's revelation.

"I doubt it. It's pretty hard-core nerd. I learned about it from an old comic book."

I accidently knock a tube of titanium-white paint off the edge of my palette, and several brushes clatter to the floor along with it.

"Why are you so jumpy?" Rémy asks. "*Home Sweet Home.* I think that's pretty cool, considering the subject matter."

"It's just, I thought it was something I made up. Something I've always believed only my sisters and I could read."

"It's not something most people *can* read, if that makes you feel better, especially the numbers."

Ms. Everitt comes over to my easel. "The eyes are perfect. You look caring and capable and ready to take on the world, just like the Honey Juniper that shows up to my class every day. I love that you're letting the world see you for who you are. That kind of honesty, exposed through art, is a much-needed act of rebellion in a world that wants to quiet you. All of us, actually. I'm so glad you took the time to consider what you could do with this painting, especially because of what it might mean for you and your future self."

"Thanks. I'm pretty happy with how it turned out."

I don't tell her exposure and rebellion might be part of the problem.

"Ms. Everitt," Rémy starts, "can you read the text on the leg?"

Our art teacher fiddles with her silver starfish necklace and shakes her head. "No. Is it a secret language? I thought it was just the pattern on her tights."

"It's Vulcan," Rémy says. "But don't tell anyone or they'll take away Honey's nerd card."

Ms. Everitt raises her hand, palm forward and thumb extended. She parts her fingers between the middle and ring finger in a wide V. "Your secret is safe with me. Peace and long life."

"Live long and prosper," Rémy replies as she walks away. His eyes widen like someone just handed him tickets to a comic convention. "Can you believe Ms. Everitt is a Trekkie?"

Strangely, no. Because I don't have a nerd card. That doesn't stop me from wondering whether I can vaporize his enthusiasm with laser eyes. "Why are you always doing that?" I ask.

"Doing what?"

"Treating me like I'm the same as everyone else and not one of the *weirds*."

"I just told you I understand Pigpen cipher, wore a decoder ring I ordered from the back of a comic book, and watch *Star Trek* regularly. What makes you think you three are the only weird ones?"

"*You're* weird? That's why you're trying so hard to be my friend?"

"Is that what I'm doing? I thought I was sending out a different vibe."

We stare at each other, too long and intense for two people anybody would consider just friends. I look around, remembering how Annalise ambushed us in the woods. Wondering if anybody is watching us now. But everyone is focused on their own artwork.

"Let me try a more direct approach," Rémy says. "I was hoping you'd want to give being my girlfriend a try."

"*Why?* There are easily twenty girls in this school who would want to go out with you. I'm out of place here."

"There are twenty carbon copies of the same girl I could go out with, maybe. I like *you,* the way you do your own thing, even when it seems a little out of place. Like when the moon shows up during the day."

"Whoa. Okay, Petruchio. Pump your brakes."

Rémy throws his head back, mouth open in a silent laugh. "See. That's what I'm talking about. You keep it real."

"Then tell me something, since we're on the subject of keeping it real. Why did you try to follow me into the air shaft the other day? I heard Mr. Whitlock stop you."

"I don't know. I didn't really have a plan. I just knew whatever you were doing, wherever you were going, seemed a hell of a lot safer than cowering in a classroom."

"Actually, it was full of spiderwebs and mouse poop."

A commotion kicks up in the hallway outside the classroom, stopping the conversation I've been waiting to have for days.

Rémy says, "Hold that thought," and heads to the door.

He should know by now I won't sit here and hold anything. I grab my EDC and rush to the door right behind him. Responsible, Reactive, and Ready. Hoping for a fistfight, or a fire sprinkler that's sprung a leak and has people trying to save their belongings. The art room is the closest equidistant point from all our classes. If it's anything worse, my sisters will be waiting outside the door.

"Hey, can they do that?" I hear someone ask.

I tap Rémy's shoulder. "Do *what?* I can't see."

"A locker search."

The answer is no, they can't. Not without probable cause.

Remain calm. Size up the situation.

I push past a few people to get into the hallway. A two-person SWAT team is opening lockers and sifting through personal belongings, assisted by Principal Weaver. There's not much to see: sweatshirts, water bottles, gym bags. I scan the hallway for my sisters. Birdie is making her way through a small cluster of students craning their necks. When we lock eyes, she points, and I spot Blue's hair a few paces behind her. The one constant I can always count on is my sisters, even when they're doing things that drive me nuts. Strike that. Even when Birdie is doing things that drive us nuts.

"Whose locker is this?" the SWAT officer asks.

"The fuck?" Rémy mutters under his breath. It's the first time I've heard him swear. He clears his throat "That's, uh, that's mine." He holds up his arm, index finger pointed.

"Yours?" Principal Weaver says, and his tone of disbelief expresses what we all feel. What *I know* has to be some sort of mistake.

THREAT ASSESSMENT CORRECTION:
RÉMY LAMAR | 5'11" AVERAGE-STRONG BUILD |
~~CLOSED~~ OPEN SOCIAL GROUP | TRUSTING
MOST LIKELY TO: ~~marry a ridiculous trophy wife.~~ Use his own judgement.
LEAST LIKELY TO: ~~seduce me with his charms during art class.~~ have anything dangerous in his locker.

Mr. Whitlock pushes through a throng of students and stands beside Rémy. "What's this about?"

The SWAT officer holds up a soda can that's been intentionally sawed in half. "We got an anonymous tip about another flash-bang grenade being put inside a locker along this corridor. Considering the recent incident, we decided it was necessary to investigate. Outside, the smoke from one of these will dissipate and is less noxious. Released inside, we'd have a different problem."

"That's not mine," Rémy says. "That's my locker. But that . . . whatever that is, doesn't belong to me. I don't even drink soda."

"You'll have to come with us anyway for questioning," the officer tells Rémy.

The personal intel on Rémy's beverage consumption is the least of his problems when everyone can see the unlit fuse hanging from the can. I want to jump in and shout, *That's not his*. But I'm in the same awkward position of having to protect Birdie, just like Ansel. My eyes shoot to my sister. She's shrugging, shaking her head as she reaches my side. I rip away the notebook and pen Birdie's clinging to and write, *Is that one of yours?* in our cipher.

She pulls her lips into a tight line and nods.

Blue shows up a minute later. "What's going on?"

"We're not sure yet."

Rémy stares straight at me and says, "That's fine. I'll come with you. But I seriously don't know how that got inside my locker."

I nod so he knows I believe him. I hope that's enough for him to understand I'll make some inquiries. Mr. Whitlock, on the other hand, shrivels me with the harshest I-told-you-so look I've ever seen, and the only thing I can do is look away.

That's when I spot Annalise, leaning on a corner where this corridor connects to another. Watching me without a sliver of emotion in her icy eyes. Ansel was right. This wasn't over. She casually rolls into the adjacent hallway with a mission-accomplished confidence that pisses me off. Whatever she's up to, I've had enough of it.

✝ BOV ✝

BUG-OUT VEHICLE

I STORM THROUGH the parking lot with my sisters, looking for the Ackermans' BOV. The black Ford monster truck towers above the other cars like it's ready to crush them for scrap metal, making it easy to spot. If they're so desperate to stay incognito they should reconsider the cap on their pickup truck's bed because the camouflage paint job screams *Bug-Out Vehicle*.

Annalise and Ansel are climbing inside the cabin when I shove her hard from behind. "What the hell do you think you're doing?"

Ansel comes around to the driver's side of the truck when he hears my voice. I don't remember seeing him at school today. The bruise under his eye is turning putrid shades of ochre and violet oxide, but it's the dullness in his eyes themselves that give him a newly haunted vibe.

"This isn't the place to have this discussion," he says.

"No. Let's," Annalise says. "Come on, Juniper. What's on your mind?"

She pushes my shoulder where she clipped me with her arrow. I muster all the strength I have to not flinch because my arm already hurts like fiery hell after holding it up in art class. I scan the parking lot to make sure there aren't any Outsiders listening.

"Swatting. That's your power play. I know you put that flash-bang grenade in Rémy's locker. How? He wouldn't have given you his combination."

"Your boyfriend isn't the only one with a high-powered zoom lens."

My fists clench. "He's not my... You know what? Think what you want. Rémy Lamar is the nicest guy at this school."

Ansel blinks, taking offense. In all fairness, Ansel has been a good friend to me until he got all secretive. If he has ideas about us being something more, he only mentioned them vaguely in passing. I'm not a mind *or* a heart reader. With Rémy, I don't have to guess.

"We needed somebody to take the heat off of us," Annalise says.

"What *heat?*" Birdie asks. "Nobody has said anything to us at school."

"Ask Daniel? Oh wait, you can't. Because that's what happens to snitches. They get stitches." Annalise looks at my arm pointedly. "I guess Blue isn't the only prophetic one."

I touch the outside of my arm reflexively where the stiff ends of my stitches are poking through my sleeve. "I didn't snitch. I haven't said a word to anyone. Rémy doesn't know anything about us."

It's the first time I've lied to anyone in the coalition since becoming a prepper. I didn't say a word to Rémy until today. Mr. Whitlock had already made his assumptions. Correct assumptions, but not with intel from me. Is that why they smoked his car?

"You guys could have hurt someone with the flash-bang grenades," I add. "Mr. Whitlock could have been inside his car."

Annalise rolls her eyes. "They're loud, but mostly used for smoke and distraction. But don't tell me, let me guess." She taps her naturally swollen pout with her index finger. "Your problem is you think *Mr. Whitlock* can be trusted. Elkwood High's new teacher of the year."

"I don't know *what* I think of him. But having my sister target his car was stupid. It was also *your* idea, Annalise. So what's your next move? Are you gonna keep ratcheting things up around Outsiders? Because eventually, someone will get hurt and it'll point back to you."

She stares at me hard. "You don't *get* what we're doing, do you? Food storage and milking goats aren't the keys to survival. We're trying to figure out ways to survive when complete chaos hits, without hurting anyone, because they'll do it to themselves. But we will take bigger action if needed. The world is populated with zombies willing to execute on whatever someone else tells them. We're the ones who have to *think*." Annalise taps her temple. "And *act*. There can't be any weak links. Especially among ourselves."

It's unnerving sometimes that blond, freckle-faced Annalise, looking like someone straight out of a commercial for a pure and natural facial cleanser, can be so power hungry and vindictive.

"We will all fall together," Blue interjects.

All for one and one for all. That's when a spark of truth hits me. "The light I saw in the woods. Did you follow your brother to the treehouse last night?"

"I don't need to spy on Ansel. He's the most predictable person I know." She stands taller, thinking I'll back down.

"So it's *me* you're keeping tabs on. *Why?* I wasn't even part of the stupid flash-bang grenade mission."

"I don't think we can trust you. *Any* of you." Annalise swipes her index finger at us, and I can't help thinking she's implicating Mother at the same time.

I don't mention that I've never broken a single compound-wide rule until Ansel asked me to meet him at the treehouse. One, because I don't need to justify myself to Annalise. And two, because I don't know what Ansel has told her.

"Is this really about your dad making our Mother the leader of The Nest? I didn't say anything to him about you shooting me with an arrow, but I could have."

"*Our* dad," Annalise says. "Correct. None of you know your place. But go ahead, run to our father with your complaints. I dare you. You have no idea who my father is, but it's not like you can run to your own dad for answers."

That would be hitting below the belt for most people. But considering we don't remember our father, I'm unfazed.

"You sound like a six-year-old, Annalise. Nobody wants to take your daddy away, especially not me or my sisters. And not that it's any of your business, but you're right. We don't know much about our dad, so it's impossible to have him in our lives. If that's okay with us, why should you care? You don't need to know anything about us beyond our ability to train and prep and be ready for whatever comes. Trust, in that context, is implied."

"I know more about *all of you* than you think, *Honey Juniper*."

That's virtually the same thing Mr. Whitlock said when he told us to get our EDCs and go home.

Ansel tugs his sister's arm. "That's enough. Let's go."

His gaze flits to the school and mine follows. Sure enough, Mr. Whitlock is holding one of the doors open, watching us. I'm curious how much of our conversation he read on our lips. Maybe we're too far away.

Annalise gives me a sardonic smile. "My brother's right. Get into that sardine can you call a car and get back to the compound or you'll be next. This conversation is over."

On that point, Annalise is dead wrong. This conversation is far from over. She doesn't know me at all if she thinks I'm intimidated by scare tactics. My sisters and I hold our ground while they climb into their truck and pull away, watching Ansel stare back at us through the sideview mirror. Maybe we're closer to something than we appear, as the mirror decal implies. Something that *is* eroding our coalition.

"You want me to drive?" Birdie says. "You look like you want to punch something."

"No. I'm fine. I could rip her head off with my bare hands, but I'm fine. Let's go."

"You want me to kill her?" Blue asks on the way to our car. She points above the breast pocket of her T-shirt where she stitched the words *Cute, But Psycho, But Cute* in bright blue thread. "Just saying. I think she underestimates me."

"At times, I think we all do," I tell her. "But thanks for the offer. I'll remember that if I change my mind."

We pile into the station wagon with Birdie calling, "Shotgun."

I should take us straight home. I should. But I'm still white-knuckled over Annalise using Rémy to get whatever *heat* off the rest of us. I can't face Mother right now, not without laying into her, too. I can barely face Birdie for getting us embroiled in something that's trickling down to other people.

I take the turn to Main Street.

"Where are you going?" Birdie asks.

I fish inside my EDC for our cellphone and toss it into her lap. "Call Mother and tell her we're going to AMVETS to look for a new pair of jeans for me."

"Why?"

"Because I ripped them crawling through the air shaft to get to you," I snap.

"Sheesh. I just wanted to get home and see if Daniel got back early." She wraps herself in his coat. "Jeans with ripped knees are what everyone wears anyway. You should know that since you're the one who always wants to dress on trend."

"Can you just go along with me for once?" I know it's not entirely Birdie's fault, but I need her to stop asking questions for the time being.

"I could use some new T-shirts to embroider," Blue says. "Do you have money?"

"I have the emergency fifty I keep in my EDC, and I don't care if I spend it."

Blue meets my eyes in the mirror. "Our attachments will one day reveal the cause of all our suffering."

She's on a roll today, to be sure, but what Blue said shouldn't be taken at face value. Our attachments to one another challenge what other people consider a normal life. Going to college, entering an art competition, going to a coffee shop after school with someone who isn't related to me. That one was oddly specific, I know. But I am worried I'll face more consequences over my relationship with Rémy. However that's defined.

The AMVETS thrift store in Elkwood is a concrete eyesore. It's only a few steps away from the colorful row of the Main Street shops gentrified by yuppie newcomers. This kind of refurbishment only used to happen in cities. Now, even the smallest towns are falling victim to commercialized coffee shops and overpriced handmade goods. All because of a pervasive need for areas of urban escape without the loss of luxury and convenience. Most people don't realize that urge to escape is their gut instinct warning them of the likelihood of urban collapse. They feel the tug, but they're not paying close enough attention, so they wrap it up in getaways designed to help them unplug, turning offline into their new luxury. It's a blatant catch-22. We take their money. They take other people's money. The only ones truly winning are the banks, with added "interest."

I pull into the parking lot and we head inside, ready to scan the clothing racks that occupy the center of the room. The whole place smells like a mothball stew, steeped in discarded memories and buyers' remorse. Shelves with discarded small appliances, tacky holiday decorations, and cheap glass vases line one wall behind mismatched furniture and rear projection TVs that weigh hundreds of pounds and could survive an atomic blast. The shoe racks are one thing I always avoid and can't bring myself to buy secondhand. Clothing can be washed, altered, stitched with sayings by Blue. But shoes have a personal history mashed into the soles. I don't want to step into someone else's shoes unless I'm in a situation where I have no choice.

I'm hoping to find a decent pair of jeans for around ten dollars, telling myself that having the right skinny jeans is part of my personal camouflage for surviving high school. I scrape hangers to one side and discover Birdie is right. Most of the women's jeans are distressed or ripped on purpose. The best ones still have the threads across the openings. I sling a promising pair over my shoulder. They're twelve dollars, a decent brand that's nicely faded, and most important, the right length. I spotted a small dot of red nail polish near the seam on the left hip, but most of my shirts will cover it.

I make my way over to Blue. She shows me a couple of white button-downs and a black T-shirt. "I was thinking about embroidering the collars on these. What do you think?"

"I like that idea. You can tie them at the waist and stitch something on the collars or the sleeves."

"Yeah, like . . . *Not* on one collar and *Yours* on the other."

"*Buzz* and *Off* would be funny if you add little flowers or bees or something."

Blue nods with a grin and keeps flipping through the shirts on the rack. I turn to the rack behind her and search through the men's shirts, trying to picture Rémy Lamar in something used. My hand stops on a pigment-washed, Prussian-blue Henley shirt. Not because I can see it on Rémy, but because I've seen something similar on Daniel.

I twist the tag inside out and find the initials *DD* written in Sharpie. It's something Dieter suggested we do so our clothes don't get mixed up when the day comes for us to spend an extended period of time in the bunkers. My sisters and I are okay with sharing, so we just write *Juniper*. Nesters don't hoard clothes, and sharing helps us expand our options. It's the same with the Burrow Boys. Limited wardrobes means less to pack and move when the SHTF. *Limited* being the operative word, which is why it's hard to picture Daniel donating clothes. I take the shirt off the hanger, unsure whether to show Birdie or hide it from her.

"What's wrong?" Blue asks. "Why do you look shell-shocked?"

"I think this shirt belonged to Daniel." I keep sifting through the rack, trying to remember what Daniel was wearing all those times he showed up outside our window, or on the field for training. I come across a navy-blue and hunter-green flannel that makes my breath hitch when I examine the tag. I scan the store for Birdie. She's fiddling with an old console-style record player, completely unaware her boyfriend's clothes are selling for three dollars apiece.

Blue takes the shirts out of my hands and examines the matching tags. "Do you think making Daniel go with less was part of his punishment? Not on his solo mission, but in general."

"That seems unlikely. Clothes can be used for bartering. They're not worth as much as alcohol or cigarettes in trade, but people will need clothes, especially if the power grid blows. Maybe it was just those two shirts and he didn't want them anymore. Should we look for anything else of his?"

"A net that will enmesh us all."

That's the least crazy thing she's ever said. We stand there staring at Birdie, who's moved on to the artwork people have donated. Velvet paintings of droopy-eared dogs, a couple of paint-by-numbers. She holds up a gold-framed oil painting of a woman with her same fringed haircut. Birdie and the subject of the painting are both staring at us over their shoulders with dark eyes, our middle sister mocking the expression of her doppelgänger until our delayed reaction strips the amusement from Birdie's eyes and replaces it with curiosity. One eyebrow arches and disappears beneath her curtain of bangs.

I unfreeze, go around the other side of the clothing rack, and search through the men's pants and jeans while Blue keeps sifting through the shirts. I'm flicking past dad jeans and corduroys, looking for the cargos Daniel always wears, when Birdie makes her way over to us.

"Did you *see* that painting? What are you two doing looking at men's pants?"

"We found something," I tell her.

"Me, too. I might have to dip into my own emergency money for that piece of Dorian Gray magic."

Blue and I keep swishing hangers right to left and left to right, respectively.

"You should. She looks just like you," Blue says, but there's little to no enthusiasm in her voice. She drops one of Daniel's shirts and crouches to pick it up fast, shoving it under her armpit to keep it concealed.

"What are you holding?" Birdie circles the rack to Blue. "Let me see what you found."

Blue's eyes shift to mine. I don't know what to say. Birdie uses my hesitation to rip Daniel's flannel shirt out of Blue's grasp. When she sees it, she sucks in a breath so hard it creates a vacuum effect around us. Neither Blue nor I say a word when she rips the Henley away from her, too. Birdie stares at the shirts like she's seeing ghosts then buries her face in the fabric and inhales. I guess I'd probably smell them, too.

"I was flicking through the rack and saw them," I tell her. "I thought I recognized Daniel's Henley, so I checked the tags and kept looking to see if it was a one-off before calling you over."

"They're his. I'd know without seeing his initials."

Birdie riffles through the men's shirts, sliding hangers at light speed. She finds another shirt and curses under her breath before coming back around to the pants section to whip hangers aside. She finds a pair of Daniel's cargo pants and a ferocity crosses her face I've never seen before. "What the hell is going on here?"

I shrug. I've been asking myself the same question. I don't tell her *here* is not the place we have to worry about, but that's what I'm thinking. Something is off about Dieter sending Daniel out alone and Annalise suddenly having her claws in everything.

Birdie takes Daniel's clothes to the register and I try to stop her. "What are you doing? You're not gonna *buy* those?"

"Five times three for the shirts and ten for the pants. Yep. That's exactly what I'm gonna do." She plucks the jeans I was planning to buy off my shoulder and adds them to her pile on the glass checkout counter before removing the emergency fifty she keeps in her own EDC. When the cashier hands her thirteen dollars change, Birdie turns to us and says, "There's no way Daniel would sell that flannel shirt. It belonged to his father."

"But the initials were DD," Blue says.

"For David Dobbs." She tosses me the skinny jeans. "Sorry about the pair that got ripped." Then she marches out of the store to the car, leaving me no choice but to follow. Once Birdie has her mind set on something, there's no stopping her.

Birdie nods once at the blond-bearded homeless man sitting against the building. He's wrapped in a fringed plaid blanket, holding a cardboard sign asking for money for food or a ride to San Diego. "Did you serve?" she asks him.

"Yes, ma'am. Three tours. Lost full use of my left arm, but not my marbles."

"I'm sorry that happened to you." She hands him five dollars. Then she digs a protein bar, a water bottle, and her dogeared paperback copy of Cormac McCarthy's *The Road* out of her EDC and hands them to him. "I hope these make your weekend better."

Everything she handed over is easily replaceable or I'd object. There will be so many people just like him on the outskirts of society when the SHTF, and we're not being trained to hand out supplies. But today, in the land of plenty, if that's what makes Birdie feel better, who am I to stop her?

"Thank you. God bless you, ladies." The man looks at us with eyes so clear and blue they reflect the clouds. The kind of skies I hope he'll find in San Diego. A sick feeling swells in my stomach as the military-style Bivy sack Achilles brought us pops into my head. A blanket meant to keep someone like this homeless man dry and insulated from inclement weather. Ochre brown, so it must belong to someone from The Burrow. We should have opened it up and looked at the initials inside before giving it to Dieter.

☆ JIT ☆

JUST IN TIME

BIRDIE TOSSES ME my jeans and gets to work rolling Daniel's clothes up into tight bundles that she shoves into her EDC. The pants are thick, but only make her bag bulge a little more than normal. Giving away some things to the homeless man made extra room for Daniel's clothes, which leads me to believe my sister was working on a plan before we got into the wagon to drive home.

"Don't say a word about the clothes to Mother until we know if Daniel is back," she says.

I put my hand on her arm, stopping her from fleeing too quickly. "I wouldn't. I won't. What are you thinking, Birdie?"

"The truth is something to be found not believed," Blue answers.

I keep my hold on Birdie and turn to look at the weirdest Juniper in the back seat. "Meaning?"

Blue shrugs. "I don't know. That's what came to me."

"She's right, though," Birdie says. "Somehow, she's always right. And if Daniel isn't back, I'm gonna find out why."

"Okay. But not alone. Never alone. We stick together no matter what."

Mother is lowering mason jars into a pressure cooker. Judging by the disarray of the bay window where she keeps her supplies for research into medicinal extractions, I'd say canning applesauce wasn't Mother's top priority today. Especially when I spot a rattlesnake head in a closed jar next to her microscope.

"You're home. Good. Just in time. I need to tell you girls something before you go out to do your chores."

"Did you extract venom from the rattlesnake I shot?" I ask, without letting her finish. My eyes flick to Blue. She told me to give the snake to Mother. She looks at me blankly. No need to say *I told you so*.

"Yes. But that's not what I wanted to say. I had to give Dieter one of our goats for research into antivenom. Apparently, there's a shortage, and if we can create a supply, we can circulate it among ourselves for use as needed, use it as a weapon in extreme cases by putting it on arrows or bullets, as well as selling or bartering opportunities when the SHTF. A single vial of antivenom is worth thousands of dollars."

Mother always says the letters in the acronym, like saying *shit* in front of us is wrong. It's the motivation of our entire existence. I don't see why it's a big deal. "When *the shit* hits the fan, Mother. Just say it. If you're going to talk about the potentiality of using rattlesnake venom as a deadly weapon, surely you can say the word *shit* in its relationship to hitting the fan."

"You mean *if*," Blue says loudly, full of conjecture. "Which one of our goats was worth the price of potential profit?"

We all turn our eyes on her. She's holding the shirts that will soon be stitched with sayings full of as much inference. My sisters and I have all thought it, but none of us has dared to say *if* the shit hits the fan out loud until now. Blue has always been best at remaining expressionless in tense situations, but the storm behind her eyes right now is unmistakable. I know it doesn't help, but I tried to warn her the goats weren't pets.

"June," Mother answers. "She was our lowest milk producer."

I won't lie. I was silently praying she wouldn't say Maggie or Milkshake.

"I need to go feed the others and take Achilles hunting," Blue says. That's it. No further comment on the goat Mother gave to Dieter. She pulls on the Bog boots she left by the door and walks out.

"Blue, wait!"

She turns. "What's done is done. Let it go."

"There are things we have to do for the greater good," Mother says. "It's my job to protect our group and help ensure long-term survival. We can breed another goat or barter for someone else's."

"What exactly about sending a sixteen-year-old into the woods to bug out alone was done for the greater good?" Birdie chirps.

"That was disciplinary. My understanding is Daniel got caught and wasn't as close-lipped as he should have been."

"I don't believe that," Birdie snaps, and I'm inclined to agree. "The people who live on this compound, especially the Ackermans, are all Daniel has left. Nobody from The Burrow was with him when he went to speak with Principal Weaver."

"Honey's chemistry teacher was there," Mother says. "So were the police and a federal agent."

Honey's chemistry teacher. I'm starting to suspect everything I do, anyone I talk to, is being watched and reported on by the same people I'm supposed to trust most.

"To be fair, isn't what happened to Daniel Dieter's fault?" I say, coming to Birdie's aid. "He's the one that sent them on a civilian interaction training mission."

"Sneak in. Sneak out," Mother says. "Whose idea was it to use flash-bang grenades?"

"I don't know," Birdie tells her. "But I would bet my life it wasn't Daniel."

"I know he's your friend—" Mother starts.

"You *don't* know," Birdie pipes, her face flame red. She's

about to go off like a Roman candle. "You don't know any-thing. You just—*do* whatever Dieter wants like the rest of his robots. Take a goat, give him one of our chickens, all our eggs, run off in the middle of the night doing god knows what, walk miles home from town. Have you lost free will or is the sex with him so mind blowing your brain got mangled?"

Mother marches up to Birdie and slaps her across the face. My sister's jaw drops with the loud crack and her hand goes to her cheek, but she doesn't back down. "That's what I thought," Birdie says.

It's the first time Mother has laid a finger on any of us. I rush to my sister's side, but Birdie waves me away. "I'm fine."

"Birdie."

"I said I'm fine."

She might be. Birdie is as strong and stubborn as a ram. But I'm not fine. Everything Mother said implies that she knows why Daniel was punished so harshly. I know my sister was pressing every button. She's the empress of saying things that get the biggest rise out of someone, and in a battle of wits, my middle will most certainly win. But when it comes to laying hands on Birdie or Blue, no one, not even our mother, has that right.

Mother's face crumbles into a mask of regret. She takes a tentative step toward Birdie, and I step in front of her. "Leave her alone."

"I'm sorry," Mother coos, ignoring me. "My little lost Birdie, I shouldn't have."

"I'm not little anymore, Mother. And I'm not lost or afraid. I'm right here, fully aware of what's happening and glad to know where your allegiance lies. If I'm wrong, maybe you'll at least think about it next time Dieter is telling you what to do or filling your head with lies." Birdie picks up her EDC and slings it across her chest. "I'm gonna go help Blue with the animals."

The screen door slaps against the frame as Birdie leaves, making Mother flinch.

"Honey, you know I would never do anything to hurt you girls. You're my whole world. Your happiness is the thing that's fueled every decision I've made. I've always only wanted to keep you girls safe from harm."

"You turned us into doomsday soldiers," I tell her. "Bringing us here. Teaching us how to survive against all odds. Well, the lessons certainly seeped in, Mother, so believe me when I say this. If you ever raise a hand to one of my sisters again, we'll use everything we've learned about staying safe from harm to get away from you. Three against one for infinity. Then you can have your precious Nest and everything that comes with it when it's empty. I know Birdie was out of line. She has the ability to turn any saint into a sinner. But no one, not even you, gets to abuse their power to hurt us."

I walk away. Alice Juniper's third daughter to leave her standing in the kitchen to contemplate what she's done, the decisions that led us here, and how quickly listening to your heart instead of your head can spoil a potentially good situation. And yet, as I make my way across the yard, my hypocritical thoughts go to Rémy, wondering what happened after he got pulled into Weaver's office. Just like Daniel.

I find Birdie by the chicken coop, pressing Daniel's shirt to her face. When she lowers it, I see the cherry-red sting on her cheek. "Are you really okay?"

"I will be. Blue went into the open field with Achy. She's pretty mad about June, so I don't think we should tell her one of our non-laying hens is missing. What happened with Mother after I left?"

"You may have tipped your hand on the Daniel thing," I tell her. "But don't worry. I told her I would fuck her up if she ever raised a hand to either of you again."

Birdie feathers her bangs with the tips of her fingers to hide her amusement. "No, you didn't."

"You're right. I didn't. At least not in those words. But you're my middle. Nobody gets to inflict bodily harm on you. Except me." I sweep my leg behind Birdie's and take her down while she's not expecting it. Before she can retaliate, I push her down flat and sit on her stomach. She flails and tries to wriggle free like a flipped-over beetle, but I have her pegged.

"Get off."

"Nope. I need to know you accept being taken down by your one true protector."

Birdie groans and squirms again. She doesn't give up for another minute and neither do I. Not until she pats the ground next to my boot and says, "Fine. *Beaver.*" Ceding to me with our childhood tap-out word.

I spring up, pumping my fists in victory before helping her off the ground.

"Horse," she says, dusting off her backside.

"Wimp."

Birdie shakes her head. I'm glad she's grinning and not raging or, worse, crying.

"What are you gonna do when we go back inside?"

"Nothing. She made her own bed. Let her lie in it." She saunters into the coop and scoops up some fresh feed. "I'm more concerned with finding Daniel's clothes at AMVETS. I'll give him until end of day to show up, but then I'm going to The Burrow to ask about him."

"You can't. If Dieter figures out you were involved, he might decide to send you away, too. Especially if they think Daniel snitched about our group. He told you to play dumb and DTA to protect you."

My sister huffs dismissively. Ever the impatient one.

"I'm not denying something is going on, Birdie. Not after Annalise used Rémy to *take the heat off us* or whatever. I'm just asking you to give it a few more days. Daniel may have overestimated his ability to complete his tasks alone."

"Maybe," Birdie says. Only, she's got the same determination in her eyes she had at the thrift store. The one that warns me to stay vigilant tonight.

Dear Bucky,

You won't believe how much has happened since I last wrote. I need sleep like a fish needs water, but I have to get a million things off my chest. I'm worried about Birdie. We found her boyfriend's clothes at the local AMVETS, which left us all unsettled. Do you remember being on a seesaw and holding the other kid in the air until they panicked and contemplated jumping? They'd get you back after the next few up and downs, a teeter-totter battle for control. That's how I've always felt about my relationship with Birdie. Lately, she's always on the verge of jumping something, to conclusions, into action, but never safety. I'm trying to understand why everyone is acting so secretive so I can make things right for Birdie and Daniel, apologize for the flash-bang grenade Annalise Ackerman planted on Rémy, and heal my failing friendship with Ansel. But I need help. The only person I felt like I could trust with my questions was Mr. Whitlock, my prepper-slash-chemistry teacher. I understand the tight corner that backs me into, but it was a risk I had to take. He already knew more than I told him because he can read lips. There's a threat I never anticipated. Worse, I learned Rémy can read the cipher we've been using to pass secret notes. Apparently it's not a secret. It's called *Pigpen cipher* and lots of people know it. I'll let you know how it all shakes out. Stick with me.

Love,

Honey

☀ NVD ☀

NIGHT VISION DEVICE

A DULL THUD outside rouses me out of sleep and my first thought is Daniel must be back. I illuminate the face on my watch. It's one A.M. Tuesday—not Monday, as promised—but Birdie will still be happy to know he kept his word.

My eyes adjust to the dimness of the room, and unless I'm mistaken, the haphazard blankets heaped on Birdie's bed means she's already flown the coop. I tiptoe to the window, where the sash is open a half inch. I don't see my sister or Daniel making a getaway, but they couldn't have gotten far. Believe me when I say these two lovebirds are going to be the death of us unless I strangle them for their reckless stupidity first. Not literally, of course, but Birdie is definitely testing my boundaries for compassion. She knows the curfew is still in place, and I'm getting tired of being the one who has to worry about covering for her recklessness.

I tug on jeans and a zippered hoodie as quietly as possible. Birdie has never gotten caught, but there's always a first time. Blue is mumbling in her sleep when I approach her bunk. I lean closer to listen.

"She should have stayed home," she mutters. "Bucky should have stayed home, too."

I think she's subconsciously confused and means Birdie,

but I couldn't agree more. I shake her shoulder and hold a finger over my lips as her eyes open and focus.

"Birdie isn't here," I whisper. "Did she say anything to you?"

She shakes her head.

I crouch down and push Birdie's blanket around, lift her pillow, hoping she was smart enough to leave us a note, but no. Birdie, as always, does what she wants without thinking. If I know my sister, there's a good chance she and Daniel are making out in the barn. No amount of preparedness will save her when I catch up to them. She can deal with the embarrassment of being physically dragged home by her older sister.

"Listen, I'm gonna go after her," I tell Blue. "If Daniel's back, she didn't go far."

"Maybe it's time for you to listen for once."

"What's that supposed to mean? I always listen to you, Blue."

"Our end will bring our beginning to light."

Now *that* grabs the brass ring for weird. I used to wonder if Blue was one of those people who can sleep with their eyes open. Even now, I contemplate waving my hand in front of her face. I looked it up on the internet once to make sure she didn't have some rare form of narcolepsy and learned sleeping with your eyes open is called *nocturnal lagophthalmos*. I dug deeper and found something called *confusion arousal* in kids who talk with their eyes open while asleep. But Blue is always awake when she says these things.

She crawls down from her bunk and pulls on a pair of jeans. "You went out the other night and were lucky you weren't caught. This time, I'm coming with you." She taps the back of her arm where we have our tattoos. "One branch, three berries. We stick together no matter what."

I can't argue with that and don't disagree.

"Hurry up. Grab your EDC. We need to find Birdie and bring her straight home before she gets us all in trouble again."

I double-check my own EDC to make sure I put my night

vision device inside when I reloaded it for its intended use. I have my headlamp, too, but an obvious light source could get us seen by anyone stationed in the lookout towers.

"Ready," Blue says.

I open the window wide, and we crawl onto the roof and scurry down the trellis. It's cold enough to see our breath tonight, but not so cold that frost took hold of the ground. If it had, we'd be able to track Birdie's footprints. I tug Blue's sleeve and pull her into the inky dark night toward the barn.

The goats stir but don't bray as we enter, and we're met with the kind of stillness and quiet Birdie is incapable of maintaining. A prickling sensation rises on my scalp as I realize I may have been wrong. If Daniel didn't come back, Birdie may have gone to The Burrow.

The determination in Birdie's eyes flashes across my mind as I stare down the path to the training area. *Damn her.*

"What do you think? Should we split up? It's not optimal, but I can go to The Burrow and see if Birdie was dumb enough to go over there looking for Daniel. And you could go home in case she went back, and we missed her."

"She's not home. Plus, I said what I said."

"Okay. Let's go."

She's right. We should stick together. Taking the normal path isn't an option past curfew. I lead Blue back into the dark, dank woods with the moon laying a lattice of light for us. The snap of twigs and crunch of leaves between the trees sends a flutter of unseen birds to flight, but nothing that might alert anyone to our presence. We keep skittering along the edge of the woods to the Ackerman house. The *male* Ackerman house, on The Burrow side of the property. The yellow lighting from their garrison extends to the trees.

I put an arm out to stop Blue and study the new construction taking place on the property. There's always been a bunker for the Ackermans directly behind their house in what most people would call a backyard—if ten acres counts as a yard—but now it's marked with a yellow-and-black biohazard symbol. Several concrete boxy buildings with steel doors pepper the acreage between mounds of dirt and sod that will ensure the new bunkers appear as hillocks from above. I don't remember any compound-wide disclosures about expanding membership in the coalition, but it makes me revisit Mr. Whitlock's motives for helping us.

Tonight, two Burrow Boys are delivering supplies to the bunker. I pump my hand so Blue will follow my lead and get low to the ground. Inch by inch, I pull the night vision device from my EDC to get a closer look. Both boys are wearing gas masks, wheeling in combustible tanks and metal boxes under the cover of night. I hand the NVD scope over to Blue, but so far, there's no sign of Birdie.

A few seconds after they've wheeled everything inside, someone else comes out from behind the bunker, pulling another person toward the woods like they're about to commit murder. I tug on Blue's sleeve and we move away from the Ackermans' bunker, backing deeper into the woods. I can almost make out the face of the taller figure pushing the other one up against a tree. I extend my hand for the NVD, but Blue doesn't pass it over. The taller one takes a knee to the balls, and his groan echoes through the trees. I crouch and weave from one tree to another, trying to size up the full scope of the situation. The one that's buckled over from the strike below the belt managed to keep his hand pressed on the other Burrow Boy's chest, pinning him in place.

"I'm trying to keep you safe." I recognize Ansel's voice. The other boy could be Daniel, but then where is Birdie? I weave strategically, two more places forward like a living queen in a game of chess, waiting for Ansel to make his next move before I let him know I'm out here.

"Like you kept Daniel safe? He said he'd be back on Monday. He's never lied to me or not been where he said, so I have to assume the worst."

Birdie.

My breath catches in my throat. I look over my shoulder for Blue, and her shadowy figure peeks out from behind a tree. She didn't pass me the NVD because she never followed me forward. She holds her index finger to her lips and brush-waves her hand, gesturing for me to get Birdie while she waits.

"Hey!" I whisper-yell and step out of hiding. "You can stop pressing her against that tree now."

"You heard her," Birdie says.

"Last time I did that, she ran. In the wrong direction," Ansel says, completely unsurprised to see me.

"She's not gonna run anywhere this time."

The directive is for Birdie. Ansel must not trust her enough, since he doesn't ease up. Pulling rank with me serves no purpose. Ansel knows I'm first-in-command when it comes to me and my sisters. I don't know why he's posturing.

"Are you wearing Daniel's clothes?" I push Ansel's locked arm off my sister's breastbone.

"So?" Birdie's version of *challenge me.* She's shaking her arms out like a boxer preparing to do damage in the ring. There is no flight with Birdie. Only fight. I put my hand on her arm, and she paces back and forth to settle down.

Birdie *is* dressed in Daniel's clothes. His cargos, Henley, and the flannel shirt she said was his dad's. Her hair is tucked into a black beanie with the bangs sticking out and brushed sideways. From a distance, I'd believe she was Daniel Dobbs.

"Why *are you* wearing Daniel's clothes?" Ansel asks.

"I'd be interested in hearing that answer myself." Annalise's voice rings from the trees before she inserts herself into the mix. Lurking. Ever the observant one.

My eyes flick to Ansel, but he looks equally startled to see his sister.

"They were at AMVETS," Birdie squawks. "So *I'd* be interested in hearing how they got there in the first place."

"You really are hell-bent on digging your own graves, aren't you?" Annalise says.

"I'll dig one for you while I'm at it," Birdie snaps. "But first, I want to know why people are walking in and out of your bunker. Is Daniel in there? He told me he'd be back by end of day today, the latest." Birdie does a double take when she catches Ansel shaking his head in our peripheries.

"He *told* you?" Annalise's voice drips with derision. "When?"

Ansel drops his head, and my pulse clicks into a fast metronomic beat for him. He brought Daniel to our house against orders.

Don't snitch, Birdie. Don't snitch, Birdie. Don't snitch, Birdie.

"He left me a note."

Ansel shifts his eyes to mine, and a sense of relief passes between us. I've got to hand it to Birdie. She didn't even blink. When it comes to covering her ass, my middle has the grace of an award-winning actress.

"A note, huh?" Annalise bends on one knee to fix the cuff of her pants, or maybe her sock. It's hard to tell. "What else did this *note* tell you? Did it say where he went? Because he wasn't at the bug-out location."

"If I knew where he was do you think I'd be here instead of there?"

"I don't know. Let's find out." Annalise is holding something in her open hand. Something she took out of her sock or shoe.

"Annalise, don't!" Ansel jumps in front of me and Birdie, arms wide, and the gust of a flowery breeze wafts across our faces.

I lift my head off my pillow and find Blue and Birdie sitting side by side on the bottom bunk, waiting for me to wake up. I don't remember going to bed or leaving the woods or anything past Annalise showing up after we found Birdie being dragged away from The Burrow by Ansel. I fight the throbbing in my head and swing my legs to the floor. A clump of dirt drops off my filthy clothes and lands next to my boots. I think it's safe to assume we got back late since I'm still so tired I can't put all the scenes from last night in order. My lower back aches like it belongs to someone who's sixty instead of sixteen. I press the heel of my hand against my forehead to alleviate the thumping in my skull.

"She did something to you," Blue says.

"Who did? What time is it?"

My sisters are dressed for school. I don't understand why they didn't wake me.

"Annalise. She blew something in your faces and told all three of you to follow her to their truck. And you did. I could only follow you until she loaded you up and drove away. I tried to stay awake. I waited hours for you to get home, but I dozed off."

"I don't remember getting into Annalise's truck."

Birdie raises both eyebrows. "Maybe you'll believe me *now*."

It takes me a minute to register what she means. "What exactly did you see, Blue?"

"Annalise was being her normal aggressive self, but then she bent down to get something, and when she stood up, she blew it into your faces. A powder of some kind."

"Was it dirt?" My brain is still stuck on the soil I gave Mr. Whitlock.

"No. Not dirt. It flew like baby powder. What's the last thing you remember?"

I close my eyes and bring myself back to the woods. "Ansel. He jumped in front of Birdie and me and yelled *don't*."

"I still think Daniel is in that bunker," Birdie says. "But something else is going on over there."

"There's a biohazard sign on the door. They could be using that bunker to mix chemicals for perimeter deterrents, but that wouldn't be secret. Whatever happened feels specific to Annalise."

"And Ansel," Birdie says. "I remember the exact same thing as you. Then nothing. My clothes are just as dirty, and look—" She lifts her boyfriend's flannel shirt off the floor and examines every seam. "White powder. Inside the pocket."

I examine the arctic-white dust. It could be any number of substances that might make a person conk out. Crushed sleeping pills, Rohypnol, even antihistamines in large enough doses. I take off my hoodie and search every centimeter of it for the same powder. I find it inside the pointiest part of the hood and look at my sisters, at Birdie specifically. "But *why?*"

"You tell me. You're the nonbeliever."

I deserve the flippant response. I didn't believe her when she claimed she couldn't remember what happened with the flash-bang grenades. Annalise was there, too, and Birdie said... Holy crap, Birdie said Annalise grabbed her chin and blew on her face. But what if she was blowing something *in* her face?

If I didn't know for sure something was up with Annalise's behavior, I know it now.

"You were acting out of character when we were hunting, too," Blue says.

"I know. You said that. You guys have a different recollection of me shooting the rattlesnake and bringing it to Dieter, but I didn't lose track of everything that happened. Not like this."

"Should we tell Mother?" Blue asks.

"No," Birdie and I answer together. But for different reasons.

"Mother said she wanted us to keep the peace. I'll bring our clothes to Mr. Whitlock and ask what he thinks of the powder without giving away too much. Until then, keep your distance from Annalise."

✥ JIC ✥

JUST IN CASE

I DIDN'T TELL my sisters to steer clear of Ansel, but he's back to avoiding me at every turn. To be fair, he's a sorry sight, as zombified as I am. And judging by the looks I've received in the hallways today, I'd say I resemble the level of *weird* everybody's been waiting to see crawl to the surface. It was just a matter of time. I'm projecting their thoughts, but I do feel like I crawled my way out of a grave. Birdie and I took a nap in our station wagon during lunch and fell asleep so hard Blue had to splash water on our faces to rouse us.

Normally, I wouldn't take kindly to waterboarding, but I needed to be alert to talk to Mr. Whitlock. The one person who I should, by all accounts, avoid. Not only based on his prepper status, but the way he's inserted himself in the peripheries of everything going on with the Burrowers and Nesters. It's normal for most preppers to use discretion when dealing with someone outside of a group. Which is exactly how Mr. Whitlock went from being my favorite teacher, to someone I had to wonder if I could trust, to the best person to ask about the residue on our clothes. Trust, unlike chemistry, is not an exact science.

Brian Sharazi and Shawna take seats at the same lab table as me. I give them a tentative smile and look over my shoulder. "Where's Rémy?"

"Suspended," Brian says. "And benched."

In an instant I know how Birdie felt when she looked at Daniel and asked, *Because of me?* "Did they say how long?"

"Three days. Anybody with a working brain in their noggin knows there's no way Rémy made a flash-bang grenade out of a soda can. Never mind being stupid enough to keep it in his locker. Obviously, it was a plant. I just hope it wasn't somebody on our team." Brian shakes his head, lips quirked disapprovingly. "Rémy's mom came in threatening to lawyer up, or hire a private investigator, and Principal Weaver backed off his original plan to suspend him for eleven days."

"It pays to have a squeaky-clean school record," Shawna says.

Her eyes do a spontaneous dance over me on her use of *squeaky* and *clean*. I get it. I look less than my best, which is a stretch for acceptance at this school on a good mirror day. "I know I'm a mess," I tell her. "I had a rough night."

"I wasn't going to say anything."

"I went over to Rémy's last night and he looked worse than Honey. He told me one of the SWAT officers tried to come at him in a racial profiling way and his mom *went off.*" Brian uses an open hand next to his mouth to emphasize the last two words.

"Good for her," Shawna says. "I hope her supersmart librarian vocabulary brought his prejudice straight to the surface."

"So, he'll be back tomorrow?" I ask.

Brian shrugs. "I think so."

"Did he say anything about me?"

"Yes. I almost forgot." Brian leans down into his backpack. I hold my breath, waiting for him to return to a seated position and deliver me the middle finger sent from Rémy. Instead, he flips me a folded piece of notebook paper, taped shut on two sides. "He said to give you this."

"What is this, elementary school?" Shawna says. "I take that back, even those kids have cellphones. Hasn't he heard of text messaging? Snapchat? Did his mom revoke *all* his privileges?"

"Would yours?" Brian asks.

"Of course, but surely he's smart enough to use the old I-need-the-internet-for-homework excuse?"

"It's not him. It's me," I tell them. "I don't have my own phone. He does have my email address."

Shawna's eyes go cupcake round. "Okay. I don't mean to be judgy, but I don't understand that, like, at all."

"I have a cellphone, but I share it with my sisters."

"Oh. He probably didn't want them snooping in on what he needs to say. The note is a quicker delivery method than an email you might not even check, because who does?" She winds her coppery ponytail around her fingers several times, creating a spiral she lets swing and hit her shoulders. Sometimes, I enjoy watching Shawna translate an opinion she's already voiced. If I weren't tired as a dying dog, I might even laugh.

"What's it say?" Brian asks.

"He taped it closed," Shawna says.

"I know. But considering the circumstances . . ."

"This is why you're single," Shawna tells him. "You don't get subtlety."

"Well, so are you. Unless you don't want to be." Brian waggles his eyebrows.

"No, thanks. Maybe. I don't know," Shawna says, backsliding on her whole point.

I ignore the rest of their standard-issue mating ritual to focus on the incomplete square with the bottom line missing Rémy drew on the outside of the folded note. The letter H in Pigpen cipher. I slice through the Scotch tape with the tip of a sharp pencil and find the whole note written that way.

"That explains everything," Brian says, spying.

"What do you mean? Can you read this?"

"No. But if *you* can, I know why everyone thinks you're weird. Plus it explains why Rémy—who tends to run away from the pack——can't stop talking about you. That wasn't a metaphor for how he is on the soccer field. When we're playing, he doesn't run in the opposite direction of the ball or anything," he clarifies.

"Don't stop there," Shawna says. "Please keep rambling. Honey and I would love to hear more of your Sharazi-wisdom."

"Okay. So my man Rémy obviously thinks Honey is a space alien. He loves all that government conspiracy–slash–cover-up stuff. So he wrote her a note in alien hieroglyphics. It's a test, see? If Honey can read that . . . Bam! Space alien status confirmed."

"Oh, that's kind of cute. Like on *Roswell*. Except Honey and her sisters would be the aliens instead of the superhot boys."

I stare at Shawna like she's the being from outer space, since I have no idea what she's talking about.

"I own the box set," she says as a form of explanation.

My eyes flick to Mr. Whitlock to see if he was reading lips when Brian said *government conspiracy–slash–cover-up*. He shrugs in a way that's borderline amused while suggesting I run with Brian's line of thinking.

"You got me, Brian. That's my big secret. I was sent here to study the strange ways of earthling teenagers. My time on planet Earth is running out. Soon, I'll have to take my observations back to my home planet to prepare for the interrogation. That's why I'm so tired. I don't know how much longer I'll be able to breathe this inferior air."

"Well, you can't beam up or leave or whatever you nerds do until we complete the new prelab," Shawna says. She turns her head and covertly pops the corner of a chocolate chip blondie between her pink-frosted lips. She pushes the baggie of treats to me. "Have some of this. Maybe our Earth sugar will revive you long enough to decode Rémy's alien love letter later."

I grin and take a blondie, hiding it on my lap away from Mr. Whitlock's prying eyes.

Ever since I explained why I crawled through the air shaft, Shawna and Brian have treated me like I'm one of them. I don't usually trust people who fit into the high school social scene, and I know I promised myself I wouldn't make friends at this school, but Rémy changed all that when he wouldn't take my continuous brush-offs for an answer. I fold up Rémy's note and put it in my front pocket. I don't need to wait to decode it. I already read the whole thing. It said:

I'll be back Wednesday. I have a bunch of photos to show you regarding turkey sandwiches for lunch.

I take that to mean the photos he took in the woods when he spied Annalise slinking up behind me.

When the class ends, Mr. Whitlock stations himself by the door and ushers students out, claiming he's got papers to grade. I'm pretty sure the real reason he's trying to empty the room is because he knows we have some unfinished business around what happened to Rémy and cracking the case of the moldy garden soil.

I stand in front of his desk, gathering some courage while I wait for the last few students to leave. I ignore the sidelong glances and think about Mother saying she didn't know I had an added interest in chemistry. I didn't then, but I suppose I do now.

"We have to stop meeting like this," Whitlock says. "Behind locked classroom doors in ten-minute spurts. Other students and faculty might wrongly assume I lean toward favoritism."

"Did someone say that?"

"Not yet."

"Okay. Good. Maybe we won't have to meet behind closed doors anymore if you found something off about the soil I brought you."

"Sorry to disappoint you, but it's garden variety. No mold. Nothing unusual." He takes a seat at his desk.

The soil was a stab in the dark, but the powder ... I bite the inside of my cheek. "I have something else. I can't tell you much about it because I'm not sure if my, um, hypotheses are correct, but—" I reach into my EDC for the Ziploc bags holding our clothes. "I found some white powder on these. They're

Birdie's and mine. I don't know what it is or how it got there. Could you ... Would you mind looking at this, too?"

Mr. Whitlock holds out his hand and I pass him the bags. "I'd be remiss if I didn't voice my concern over the things you keep bringing me."

"I understand, but you said there was nothing wrong with the dirt, so maybe this is the same. Flour, baking soda, some kind of white powdery mildew."

"Lye. Arsenic. Anthrax, or anything else that would prompt you to bring it to me."

"I doubt it's arsenic or anthrax," I tell him.

"So do I, considering you look a little dead on your feet but relatively healthy. Can you at least tell me what the circumstances were around your discovery?"

"I'd rather not say, if you don't mind, until I know what it is."

"Fair enough. I asked you to trust me. The least I can do is offer you the same until we know something." He puts the Ziploc bags in a desk drawer. "Can we talk about what happened with Rémy Lamar yesterday? Off the record."

I knew that was coming. I shrug one shoulder and pick at the corner of a stack of papers on his desk. "What about him?"

"My warning about not getting him wrapped up in your group's dynamics didn't stick. We both know Rémy isn't to blame for producing flash-bang grenades, which means he was a scapegoat for someone else."

It's getting harder for me to keep what I know a secret when I keep asking for favors. "I can't talk about that."

"You don't have to. I'm an observant person. It wasn't hard for me to figure out who else might be part of your doomsday coalition, besides Daniel Dobbs. If I'm not mistaken, the Ackermans fit the profile."

"Maybe you should ask them about it."

He lets out an amused snort. "I get the impression the Ackerman twins would sooner have their fingernails ripped out with pliers than speak to anyone about their family's initiatives."

"I can't help you, either. I met up with Ansel in the treehouse to ask, but he didn't know much. It could have been any number of people."

"The same treehouse you told Rémy didn't exist?"

Shit. He got me. I said too much. I stay poker-faced, waiting for him to fill the silence with his own conclusion.

"I took a stroll in those woods myself yesterday," he says. "Following the same map I gave Rémy. Do you know where it led me?"

"Not the treehouse."

"Correct. Not the treehouse, but to a bunch of houses on a section of land that isn't part of any Elkwood residential maps. I did some exploring and found another path through the woods that brought me to the edge of a clearing, or should I say, proving ground. Several men were doing some shooting. Nothing too out of the ordinary if it weren't for the type of weapons they were using. Any idea who lives on that property?"

"Nope. We live on Overcast Road."

"Along with Daniel Dobbs, the Ackermans, and some former students who graduated in the last few years."

"Is that unusual? It's a small town. Lots of students that go to school here live on the same streets."

"That's true. Regardless, if you or any other kids that are part of your group were leaning toward actions that could get you and your sisters into bigger trouble, it might help to have an Outsider you could go to for advice, or protection. Prepper to prepper."

Trusting him is becoming more twisted than a juniper tree. He's wending his way into dangerous territory, and it's making my pulse tap like a woodpecker's warning.

He knows something. He knows something. He knows something.

Rémy told me he had photos to prove it when it came to

Annalise. The turkey sandwich photos from his note. He's probably taken dozens more, even out on Overcast Road. If he used those photos to get himself out of trouble... I stop my unfounded suspicions from spiraling when I catch myself moving my hand to cover the arrow wound on my deltoid. We're talking about Rémy. The direct approach is best. "What did Rémy tell you, exactly?"

"About you specifically?" He shrugs. "Nothing I hadn't figured out on my own. He was more concerned his suspension would interrupt his ability to act as student liaison for the art competition. Makes sense. National attention is something colleges like to see on applications. Naturally, I spoke to Ms. Everitt on his behalf and got everything squared away."

I can't stop my eyes from narrowing. I can usually spot a lie, but his face gives away nothing, a prepper trained in the art of impassivity.

"That disturbs you. Would you have preferred it if Rémy had told me something you can't?"

I shake my head. What's disturbing me is his interest in our group. But asking may bring an irrefutable truth to the surface. The dynamics in our coalition are *not* fine, like I told him. And I'm not a hundred percent sure we *are* safe. At least, not from Annalise. At the same time, his interest in our group can't go on without question forever.

"I have to ask... are you looking to join a prepper group? Is that why you're so interested in what we're doing?"

"Let's just say I wouldn't mind meeting the person in charge. Is that something you might be able to arrange?"

"Introductions aren't really how it works. My mom found the group through some secret online prepper network. She had to apply, offering up her specific skill set, and wait for an invitation to join."

"Could I speak with her? Or maybe *you* know how she found the secret prepper network?"

"I never asked. You'd have better luck with Ansel or Annalise if you want to go the informal route."

"Ah," he says, catching on. "Their father is the man in charge. Do you know much about him?"

I shake my head again. The truth is I don't know much about Dieter Ackerman. I never felt a need to dig deeper. Our life as Nesters has always been about prepping and training and staying safe. Questioning Dieter's motives never occurred to me because I accepted that they were fueled by a potential power grid failure, extreme weather, economic collapse, viral pandemics.

"It's just us," Whitlock says, being as observant as he claimed. "Honey, I have to ask if you think the white powder on your clothes may have come from someone inside your group. You don't have to say who."

A shadowy blur obscures the edges of my peripheral vision. I glance at the door and see the students in his next class gathering outside.

It was Annalise. It was Annalise. It was Annalise.

I keep my expression numb to the accusation screaming inside my head, because it's just a guess. A theoretical finger-pointing based on what we know and what Blue saw. I look straight into Whitlock's concerned blue eyes and nod. Just once. And the bell trills above the door like I tripped a listening device that was hidden there all along, waiting to alert the masses of my betrayal. Confiding in Mr. Whitlock was the right thing to do if I want answers. But to what end? I haven't thought that far ahead.

"Thank you for trusting me," he says. "I'll write you a late pass for Ms. Everitt."

Mr. Whitlock writes a quick note saying he kept me behind after class. He scribbles his cellphone number on a separate late pass and hands it to me. "Just in case you need it. I'll look into what you gave me right away and get back to you. Do you have a cellphone?"

I shake my head for the last time, knowing it's a lie.

"I'll find a way to get in touch with you if it's urgent. I trust you'll do the same."

I take the note and his JIC number and leave, questioning and replaying everything I told him. Just In Case. I don't know what happens to someone who betrays The Nest or The Burrow. *Snitches get stitches.* That's what Annalise said, but what if the consequences are worse?

TOBYISMS FOR ACTION
6
SUSPECT YOUR ALLIES

BUSTED. FOR THE first time in three years. Mom is waiting for me wrapped in the bloodred Lady Macbeth robe Jonesy got her for Christmas. Not that her dagger eyes are helping.

"You better have a good reason for sneaking in at this hour." She points her cigarette at me and lifts it to her lips, taking a deep drag.

"You know those things will kill you if you keep it up, right?"

She squints and sniffs the air between us. "What's that smell?"

"Nicotine, formaldehyde, arsenic. Nobody smokes anymore. It's not chic or whatever." This is my way of avoiding the fact that I came home at two A.M.

"No." She steps closer and sniffs my jacket. "What smells like dry cleaning chemicals? And what's that white powder on your shirt?"

I stuff my paint-stained hands in my pockets and look down at my chest. The white powder in question is powdered sugar. From some donuts Bash got for free from Holey Donuts because they were about to close. I ate three blackberry jelly ones, but don't have time to explain, because she's firing more questions at me.

"Were you with Bash? What are you two doing this time of night? Where is he? Your eyes are red. Are you boys doing drugs? You can tell me." She's inches from my face.

"*Drugs?* Are you serious? I'm not the one that was rolling around on the floor covered in black paint. Are you sure *you* aren't on something?"

"No. I never." She shakes her head. "I don't. I didn't know you saw me making that piece."

"You were in a deep trance. I didn't want to interrupt you."

She drifts into the kitchen to run her cigarette under the faucet. Something catches her eye outside the kitchen window, making her dip and bob her head like she's watching a kite. Only it's pitch-black outside.

"What are you staring at?"

"A military drone." She tosses her extinguished butt into the trash can and faces me. "There was a story on the news earlier about some teenagers that got arrested for smuggling drugs across the border."

"You think that's something I would do?" My eyes pop out of their sockets. "Suddenly, I'm El Chapo or something?"

"It's just, I did some stupid things when I was your age, and I got worried when I saw you weren't home. You know how my mind operates."

I do and I don't. I've just gotten good at guessing.

"This is powdered sugar. From some serious crack-like blackberry donuts, to be fair. Bash went home, to answer your other question, where he's probably riding out his sugar high with a game controller in hand."

She opens the fridge and pulls out a jar of blackberry jelly. "I had the same thing, except on toast." She licks her middle finger, touches a spot on my shirt, and licks the sugar off. "I'm sorry I accused you."

"Just so we're clear, though, I'm not doing drugs. I don't need them to make art. I guess I'm like you in that way, only a lot less cool."

"You mean less experienced," Mom corrects me. "You're plenty cool, Toby, and you have lots of talent. But to go to the next level you have to be ready to show your art to the world. Not because you think it's good, but because it means exposing yourself to people who will pry, whether they love your work or hate it. Looking for everything they can find to justify their opinions one way or another. The trouble is they find the shiny stuff, as well as tarnished bits. It's probably worse now that everything is online."

She's not talking about me, but I bite. "Street art is automatically out there for everyone to see. They don't always know who made it, but I follow a bunch of different hashtags online and have seen pictures of my work. People seem to like it."

Mom stares like she's seeing me clearly for the first time in years. "When did you get so grown up?"

I shrug one shoulder. "I never really allowed myself a childhood, to be honest."

She averts her eyes. That one struck home. "Sometimes I forget your sisters aren't the only things we lost that night. I owe you an apology for that, amongst my other failings as a mother."

"It's fine."

"No, it's not, Toby. And the other day, when you accused Jonesy of not working hard enough to find your sisters, I knew it was time to tell you the reason he hasn't stopped looking."

"He said the case is still open. I was just saying there hasn't been much progress."

"Yes, and it's still open because of me. Because I would know if my girls were dead. And the reason I would know is because of something I did a long time ago when I was a college student who needed money."

I get the sense she's about to tell me something huge. I take a seat opposite her at the kitchen table. She flips her pack of smokes over and over without removing one from the box.

"When I was a college student, I volunteered to be part of a study that was trying to prove the validity of ESP. More specifically, the pursuit of whether or not a person could perceive something that hadn't happened yet. Distance was an important factor to the visiting professor in charge. He only took students that excelled in their areas of study or extracurriculars, claiming they had more expansive minds. He was trialing an LSD-based drug of his own design, taking his cue from the CIA's MK-Ultra experiments."

"That happens in that Stephen King book. *Firestarter*. The daughter ends up a pyrogenetic."

"Yes. It wasn't a mere fabrication of the author's imagination. Those kinds of experiments have been going on since the sixties."

"So, you took hallucinogens?"

"In a highly controlled academic environment. Your father also participated."

My eyes shift to a shoebox of old photos on the end of the table. I haven't gone through them in years. I was ten when my father died. I remember writing *Bad Memories Do Not Open* on the cover in black Sharpie because we had lost everyone, and the memories inside those boxes made us cry. Mom pulls the shoebox closer, takes out a photo, and slides it across the table. It's of her and Dad, sitting on the lawn of a university with a bottle of wine. I see the similarities in our features and builds now that I'm older.

"Seventy-five students participated. For your dad, it wasn't a pleasant experience. He was an engineer, grounded by logic and reason. For me, as an art student, it opened up doors in my mind I could only dream of accessing. I didn't notice anything different about myself until you kids were born. Little things, like being able to anticipate your wants before you said anything. I chalked it up to mother's intuition. But then Cassandra came, born with a caul, as they say. I saw the embryonic sac covering her face when they cut her out of me, and felt like I was suffocating, too, before they snipped it away and her skin pinked up from terrifying blue. I don't mean that sympathetically."

"You and Cassandra always seemed to have a special bond and a secret way of communicating."

She nods. "Yes. That's true. With you and the other girls, it was always little things. I buy blackberry jam on a whim, you come home and tell me you ate blackberry donuts. Once the girls disappeared, though, it started manifesting in my artwork. I draw strange things because I feel viscerally driven to it in a way that's transcendent. Is that because of your sisters? I don't know. I didn't have them long enough to delve into that mystery. But early on, I told Jonesy about it. I wanted him to see if he might have better luck tracking down information about the study.

"Unfortunately, we were both told a fire destroyed the research and Dr. Maddox, the professor in charge, was long gone. The university didn't even have a list of the students that participated. But I know enough to believe this: if your sisters were no longer with us, I'd feel it as acutely as my own death."

I feel the same way, but——My heart jackrabbits for a few beats. "Are you saying your drawings are a way of *seeing* them?" The idea of them being in some hellscape is worse than thinking the trauma made her lose her mind.

"I can't be sure. The images that come to me haven't been entirely clear until the last year. Tight spaces, soldiers crawling, smoke bombs. But not a single image of a place I can pinpoint."

She takes a cigarette out of her pack, taps it on the table a few times, and returns it to the box. "A gallery contacted me about doing a retrospective of my work. But only if I'm willing to show three new pieces at the reception so everyone can see what I've been doing since I stopped working on *The Bard's Mistress* series."

"Are you gonna do it?"

"My new drawings are more personal, but I'm willing to talk to them about the idea. It would mean leaving you home for a week or so, and I'm a little uncomfortable with that idea. Jonesy said he'd go with me, even though he's voiced his concern over the publicity's impact on the case. On one hand, your sisters could see it, and it might trigger their memory—although the likelihood is slim, considering how young they were. On the other hand, it might spook their captor into doing something rash. Either way, it could lay bare every secret we keep. But like you, I'm willing to take that chance."

For the first time in eleven years, I'm lightened by a sense of hope.

"I'll be okay alone. I can stay and watch Banquo." My dog thumps his tail under the table when I say his name. "Have you given any thought to what you'd call the new series?"

"*The Juniper Sisters.*"

A lump lodges in my throat when she uses the name of our street. The last place they were seen, which looks nothing like her drawings.

⁕ SIP ⁕

SHELTER IN PLACE

BIRDIE IS COMPLAINING about having to wait for Daniel again. I'm only half listening because I'm scouring the internet for two things pecking away at my brain. The Ackerman family history, for one. Driving home, I made a connection between Whitlock asking if I knew much about the leader of The Burrow and Annalise saying she knows more about us than we think. I don't know what Annalise knows, other than we don't have a dad and moved around a lot. But I do know this. The past can inform the present when it comes to their family, too.

So far, though, all I found was a German chemist named Emil Ackerman, a Nazi scientist recruited by the United States government to develop biological and chemical weapons for Operation Paperclip, a secret program carried out by the Army Counter Intelligence Corps after WWII to help with the Cold War. They didn't list his children, but Dieter was a soldier in the Gulf War and became a scientist. Maybe following in his father's footsteps. I don't want to assume, but it would further explain his distrust of government, a preoccupation with impending doom, and the combustible tanks going into the bunker. Until I decide if it's better to ask Ansel or Mother for confirmation, I've abandoned that search to comb through teen prepper forums, looking for posts about anyone being sent away from a group. The one consistent opinion is whenever someone leaves a prepper group, they're rarely welcomed back, especially if they were kicked out for breaking major rules. If that happens, a few forum members said they make sure that person is *neutralized, depending on the severity of the infraction.*

"It's been *forever,*" Birdie twitters, pacing by the window. "What if Daniel came back and Dieter told him to stay inside that bunker until his suspension was over? Ansel could have lied."

"I don't know, Birdie. I have a lot of the same questions." I close all the tabs and lean back in the wooden chair.

"What were you doing over there?"

"Nothing. It doesn't matter." I wish I could say, *Something to put your mind at ease.* Only it won't. *Neutralized* leaves too much to the imagination.

"You're making that keep-Birdie-in-the-dark face."

She marches over and checks my search history before I can protest. "*What happens to preppers asked to leave a group?* So you *have* been listening to me. What did it say?"

"Nothing, or I would have told you." I snatch the mouse out of her hand before she sees the stuff about Emil Ackerman and jumps to conclusions. "What's with you two? Blue said the same thing to me the other night. I always listen to both of you."

"Our eyes don't always see what our hearts know," Blue says.

"What do *eyes* have to do with listening?" Birdie huffs.

That one grabs top grades for obscurity. Blue gives me a slight shake of her head like she doesn't get it, either. It's just another thing that popped into her mind.

"Girls!" Our mother's gravelly voice strains its way upstairs.

"What now?" Birdie gripes.

"Girls, come down here!" she hollers again when none of us answers fast enough.

"Coming!" I take the mouse from Birdie and clear my search history.

Mother is surveying the sky through the kitchen window when we march downstairs. I flick my gaze to the television in case there's some weather coming we didn't know about. A quick intake of the story reveals a record day for the POTUS on social media. The oh-my-god-did-you-see-what-he-just-tweeted coverage of his behavior has become our new normal. But today he outdid himself, sending more than thirty antagonistic tweets into the world in under twelve hours, inciting multiple Twitterstorms.

"What is it?" Blue asks Mother. "Is it Achilles?" She starts pulling on her boots, ready to flee.

"No. Achilles is fine. I think they might be drones."

I rush to the huge bay window as Mother takes out the navy-blue tablecloth she stores in a drawer beneath the sill and covers her petri dishes and microscope. Squares of neon-violet lights are moving through the inky sky around our property like a spaceship looking for a place to land, the Juniperions come to take me home.

The question is: How did they find us?

The CB radio crackles to life with Dieter's voice. "Juniper 4321, this is Ackerman1. Turn off and remove all batteries from cellphones. Stat. U.S. government UAV surveillance drones spotted above compound. Code 3. Employ SOP for SIP. Over."

Unmanned Aerial Vehicles. Standard Operating Procedure. Shelter In Place.

Click. Pop. The power is cut, plunging the house into darkness. We can't use lanterns this time. Code 3 means secure the location against Outsider infiltration by sheltering in place. Cutting power makes the compound difficult to see, but the drones have spotlights. We can't go full dark unless we're underground, and we can't head for the bunkers.

It make sense that Mother covered her stuff in the window before she ever got the call. She's nothing if not calm and efficient in an emergency. I don't know if that's from her training as a nurse or a prepper. Probably both.

"Go get your phone," Mother says calmly, reaching for her own.

"I'll go," Birdie says, rushing for the stairs.

"They can see inside our house," Blue says. It's not a question. I'm not sure if it's one of her Blue-isms or she's being rhetorical.

"Put on a balaclava and close all the curtains, too," Mother yells to Birdie. She rushes to her bedroom and brings out two face masks for me and Blue. "Put these on and close the downstairs blinds."

Balaclavas are not standard operating procedure for Code 3 situations, but we do as directed.

"You think they're trying to spy on us?" I close the blinds behind our couch before removing my mask.

"Us. Them. Everyone," Mother says. "The director of the FBI admitted to using drones for domestic surveillance, border patrol, investigations, the protection of key personnel on the ground during classified operations. It's been going on for years, which proves some people weren't as paranoid as others claimed. The issue at hand is how our compound got on their radar in the first place."

My skin goes cold as Whitlock's face flashes in my mind. His questions about our coalition, the map he gave Rémy. Mother strikes a match and lights a candle on our coffee table. Her face cast by deep shadows that mirror her concern. Mother said she heard Daniel wasn't as close-lipped as he should have been, and we refused to listen. But what if we were both wrong? What if Whitlock talked to someone after talking to me?

Birdie rushes down the stairs to rejoin us, thick bangs poking up as she peels off her mask. "What do we do now?"

It's the question of the hour, the month, maybe our whole lives. "There's nothing left to do but wait," Mother says.

Birdie flops aggressively into an easy chair. *Wait* is not in her vocabulary. To be honest, it's not in mine anymore, either.

LISTENING POST

THERE'S A SUBSTITUTE teacher standing behind Mr. Whitlock's
desk when I walk into chemistry. I'm not entirely surprised
since we spotted another unmarked car parked outside the
school this morning. Still, his absence makes me stop short.
Birdie actually spotted the car first and threw her head against
the seat moaning, "What now?" It's become her standard response. But I kept my suspicions to myself and looked for Mr.
Whitlock's car. I didn't spot his Subaru in the faculty lot and
thought he might be having it detailed on the school's bill.
Now, I'm not sure what to think.

The reality of how reliant I've become on Mr. Whitlock
hits me like ice down my back. Maybe I told him too much.
Maybe the feds are following up about Rémy. He's not here,
so I can't ask. And I don't think I should call Whitlock on his
cellphone to ask if he snitched, whether he gave me his number or not.

The dry-erase marker squeaks across the whiteboard behind Whitlock's desk as the sub writes her name in giant swirly
letters. She nods a greeting to me before announcing we'll
be using this class time to catch up on anything we've been
working on that isn't lab related. Translation: Mrs. Amanda
Abbott doesn't know anything about chemistry and is only

here to hand out bathroom passes and make sure nobody sets the room on fire. My initial assessment is confirmed when she pulls out a notebook and a Jane Austen novel, flipping to her last marked page. A lithe, modern embodiment of Elizabeth Bennet herself.

THREAT ASSESSMENT:
AMANDA ABBOTT | 5'6" WEAK TO AVERAGE BUILD |
UNKNOWN SOCIAL GROUP | TRUSTING
MOST LIKELY TO: attempt to write the next great American novel.
LEAST LIKELY TO: pay attention to the hours and years passing before her eyes.
10/10 WOULD IMPEDE GROUP SURVIVAL IN EMERGENCY SITUATION.
CASUALTY POTENTIAL: high

I head to the table where Brian, Shawna, and Rémy are huddled, practically touching foreheads. When I slide onto a stool, they bloom apart like a human flower. "Was it something I said or something you heard?"

"Hi, Honey." Rémy tips his head to one side and rubs his thumb under his chin.

It's the first time I've heard my name sound like a term of endearment and didn't cringe. He looks good for someone who was wrongfully suspended. But I can't get a read on him, which is another first for me. I know Annalise is the reason he got suspended, but blurting that out in front of Brian and Shawna is out of the question.

"We were just talking about your alien language," Brian says.

I blink despite my best efforts to retain a neutral expression. "Oh yeah. What's the verdict?"

"Apparently, unless you have a decoder ring from Dieterack, the ruler of your planet, you're not allowed the knowledge of the—" He furrows his brow at Rémy. "What did you call them?"

Now Rémy smiles at me. "The Juniperions."

"Right," Brian says. "The Juniperions."

Dieterack. The Juniperions. Clever. I need this kind of levity today.

Rémy shrugs one shoulder. "The language is secret, but I did tell them why you're really here on Earth."

"Oh yeah, why is that?" I lean in to listen.

"To escape your home planet, of course, after you learned you were initiated into a group led by a leader hell-bent on starting a rebellion." He schools his voice so I pick up on what he's really trying to say.

"Seriously," Shawna drawls in what can only be described as a vocal eye-roll. "Am I at a nerd convention or is this how all people without cellphones and Snapchat behave?"

"Hey! I have email, remember?"

"Email. Right." Shawna shakes her head disapprovingly and pulls out a baggie of snow-white meringues. "Here, have some—puffy space cookies."

The three of us descend upon that baggie like we haven't eaten in days. They're so melt-in-your-mouth delicious, dissolving on the tongue right as the vanilla hits, that I say if meringues be the food of space, bake on.

Rémy is watching me devour another cookie. His tawny eyes searching mine with an intense seriousness that makes my throat constrict. I'm not paying attention to the pause in the four-way conversation, because I'm suddenly dying to get him alone. And yes, I know how that sounds, but it's not entirely what I mean.

"Maybe Brian and I should move down and leave you two alone for a while. You're fogging up the beakers."

"No. Don't," Rémy says sharply. "We need you to stay here."

We?

The beakers are clear and free of fog, incidentally, but the comment from Shawna is enough to break our focus on each other. She darts her eyes from me to Rémy, equally perplexed as I am. The only difference is Shawna hasn't been trained to keep the emotion from showing on her face.

I write, *Everything okay?* in my notebook using cipher and turn it toward Rémy.

He writes, *Not exactly.* I didn't spot the decoder ring on his left hand until he started to write his reply. Learning my sisters and I aren't the only ones who know Pigpen cipher is one thing. Seeing Rémy's stainless steel childhood decoder ring takes it to the next level.

He writes, *Wait 5 minutes. Fake sick. Get pass for nurse.* Then he gets up and walks to Whitlock's desk to talk to the sub.

"What's it say?" Brian asks. And just like last time his question earns him a "Tsk" from Shawna.

"Sorry. No Dieterack decoder ring. No translation."

I keep one eye on my watch while we make small talk. Brushing the occasional meringue crumb off my sweater until the minute hand ticks its fifth mark. I slide off my stool and clutch my stomach with a moan.

"Oh no," Shawna says. "There aren't a lot of allergens in those meringues. Just egg whites, sugar..."

"It's not your baking," I tell her with a wink.

I grab my EDC and trudge to Mrs. Abbott's temporary desk like some character in a play about sexual awakening.

Starring Honey Juniper: Unexpected Girl Next Door.

She looks stricken by my pained expression. "What's wrong? Do I need to call someone for help?"

"No. This happens to me every few months or so, but never this bad. I think I need to go see the nurse. She may have to call my mother to pick me up."

Her face blooms with the kind of understanding only women know, and she writes me a pass to the nurse without hesitation. "Take care."

"Thanks."

I shuffle out and find Rémy leaning against a row of sky-blue lockers, examining his camera's viewfinder. I scan the hallway to make sure nobody's watching and head toward him. My chest tightens, knowing what Annalise did to him. When he hears the soft pad of my lace-up boots, he looks up and smiles. Not in his usual effortless way. This is the tentative smile of somebody about to deliver bad news.

"I'm so sorry." That's the first thing I say. "I know you didn't have anything to do with the—"

Rémy shakes his head, raising his index finger to his lips, stopping me from saying *flash-bang grenade*. "Let's go to the library and work on *that project*."

He's acting like there's a listening post nearby. Every single person in my life, except Blue, has been on a paranoia streak. Rémy hasn't given me a reason to distrust him, but holding my questions while we walk silently through the hallways is a legitimate struggle.

Elkwood High has the smallest library I've ever seen. Four tall stacks and a row of shelves along the back wall might be a decent-sized school library for a town with under five thousand residents, but compared to those in the other towns and schools I've been to, it seems miniscule. Rémy walks through the room completely at ease, the town librarian's son, nodding to a few people sitting on sky-blue plastic chairs at circular tables. He makes a right turn between the stacks farthest from the door, leading me all the way to the back corner. I'm ashamed to admit that I've never been inside the town library, where his mom works, so I don't.

When we're alone, in the quietest place in the school, he asks, "How'd you get out of class?"

I guess we need an icebreaker. "Female problems. You?"

"I paid a sophomore on the soccer team to text me from a burner phone pretending to be my mom. He did it from outside Whitlock's class so I could get it back and give it you. The only number in the contacts is mine."

"Burner phone? What are you, a spy?" I wrap my concern in a thin blanket of humor.

His chest visibly rises and falls. It's not a sigh, exactly, but it levels the same anxious vibration that keeps me thinking there's a paranoia contagion loose in Elkwood. And then, he hands me the phone. A burner that's a million times nicer than the phone my sisters and I share. "It's not who *I am* you have to worry about," Rémy says quietly. "It's who Mr. Whitlock might be."

"What do you mean?" I narrow my eyes, stomach clenching for real this time.

"I take a lot of photos, as you know. I take them of people doing everyday things; sometimes I take them of nature or try to capture weather. Up close, from far away, different perspectives. I've taken hundreds in the last month alone, and half of them are of you and your sisters."

"You're always pointing your camera at me—*us*—when you think we aren't looking. What's that got to do with Whitlock?"

"I weeded through my photos while I was suspended, putting them in folders by the date they were taken, subject matter. Take a guess who else shows up the most in the photos of you and your sisters."

"Annalise Ackerman?"

"She's lurking in a few. But Whitlock is in a ton."

My thoughts rush to Mr. Whitlock saying he was observant, that he had figured out who else was part of our coalition.

"He asked a lot of questions when they tried to pin that soda can smoke bomb thing on me."

"Rémy, I—"

"It's okay. I know when I'm being framed. My dad was a cop in Seattle."

"Your dad's *a cop*?" My heart stalls for a beat. That must be why Annalise warned me to stay away from him.

"He *was* a cop," Rémy clarifies. "He got shot by a heroin addict and died in the line of duty."

"Oh. Sorry. I've never lost anyone like that. I don't know what to say."

"It's okay. It was a long time ago. We don't need to talk about it. Whitlock, on the other hand, said some stuff we definitely need to discuss."

"About the flash-bang grenade, or me specifically?"

"Both." Rémy pulls his laptop out of his backpack and takes a seat on the floor, long legs extended and crossed at the ankle. I sit beside him, shoulder to shoulder, thigh pressing against thigh, letting the warmth from his body take the chill from my thoughts.

He double-clicks a folder called *Honey* and pulls up every photo from the last two months. He clicks through them one by one, and I see my sisters and me through Rémy's eye. Birdie, sitting on the table in the cafeteria looking ingénue gorgeous. The Birdie that makes Brian Sharazi stare. Blue, pressing a lapis-blue pencil to her cheek during an assembly. A petite cobalt-haired pixie, shouldering *weird* like a badge of honor. And me, twisting my hair into a bun to get down to business, climbing into the air shaft, looking like Katniss Everdeen in the woods. Responsible, Reactive, and Ready. And then I see Annalise in the background of a shot from the woods, stalking me. Rémy clicks to the next photo and I spot Magda watching us through the trees.

Click, click, click. Whitlock is in the assembly two rows behind me, staring. In the back of the student cafeteria, eyes glued to my sisters and me. He's hovering in nearly every photo of us. Rémy keeps going, moving through time backward. He pauses on a photo from the day they threw the flash-bang grenades, before my sisters and I got outside. It's of Whitlock, shaking hands with a man dressed in a black suit in front of an unmarked car.

Rémy speaks first. Good thing, because my thoughts are screaming *traitor*, making it hard to form words.

"He asked if I'd help him get information about where you live. I didn't understand. I thought he meant the house on Overcast Road until he said *the compound.* That's when he explained why he gave me a map to your real house. The one that put you and me in the same woods and ultimately got you shot in the arm by Annalise."

I throw every keep-quiet rule to the wayside once again, because I need a sounding board for my suspicion. Someone I can trust. "Do you think Whitlock's been talking to the feds about us like some neighborhood watchdog this whole time?"

"Or he *is* a fed."

"No. He's a prepper like us. Annalise targeted him to keep him away from our group. He was trying to get me to talk to him about our group. He said—" For a moment I lose the ability to speak. The hum from Rémy's laptop turns to howling in my ears. *He said he wouldn't mind meeting the person in charge.* "He gave me his private cellphone number and asked if I could arrange a meeting for him with Dieter Ackerman."

"Is your coalition doing something that could get you in trouble? I mean real danger, Honey, not minor stuff that can get you suspended from school."

What's in that bunker? What's in that bunker? What's in that bunker?

Daniel's pensive expression flashes in my mind. *He sent this guy named Thane out once.* Later Ansel told me, *Speculation was spreading that Thane might be talking to the feds.*

Thane never came back. Now Daniel is gone. The reality that Daniel snitched to Whitlock before me—that *Whitlock is a fed*—hits like an overarching ballistic missile to my psyche.

I missed all the subtle clues, but they were there. Ansel telling me Daniel knew the rules. Whitlock giving Rémy the map. Annalise insinuating Birdie can't talk to Daniel because snitches get stitches. I thought she meant me, because of Rémy, but I was wrong.

"I have to go," I tell Rémy, jumping to my feet. "I need to find my sisters."

"Honey, wait! You can't just pull them out of their classes."

"Watch me."

⁝ GOOD ⁝
GET OUT OF DODGE

BLUE IS IN geometry, sitting alone near the windows, tucking a strand of cobalt hair behind her ear as she works on corresponding angles or whatever they have going on today. I'm working on correlations of my own, but I need my sisters to help me. I wave Rémy away so he'll move down the hall before I knock on the classroom door. When I pull it open, Blue looks up like she's been waiting for me.

"Sorry to interrupt, but I need to talk to my sister."

Her teacher looks from Blue to me. "Is it urgent?"

"Oh no," Blue laments. "Is it Banjo?" My little sister is playing the part of young girl stricken with worry for her beloved pet. A complete sham I'm beginning to recognize as a family trait. Showing for one day only.

Starring Blue Juniper: Lead Weird Sister.

I nod, forcing my eyes to water before I make a show of hanging my head.

"It's our dog," Blue explains. "He's been really sick, Ms. Jennings. Can I have a pass to go with my sister?"

"Do *you* have a pass?" her teacher asks me.

I dig inside my pocket and show her my pink slip for the nurse's office. Ms. Jennings comes closer and squints at the pass. "Why the nurse?"

"I had a substitute," I tell her. "She wasn't sure how to handle the situation when it came to a dying pet."

"Okay. Go ahead, Blue. Work on those quadrilaterals at home if you can, or find a way to let me know if you need more time."

"I will. Thank you, Ms. Jennings."

Blue follows me into the hallway. She's wearing one of the white shirts she bought at AMVETS, knotted at the waist. One word is embroidered on each collar in thread that matches her hair. When read left to right it says *Weird Sister*.

"What's going on? Where's Birdie?" Blue spots Rémy waiting a few feet nearby. "Why do I get the feeling you keep showing up places you shouldn't?"

"Sometimes, but not always," he says. "Just think of me as D'Artagnan."

Blue blinks wide eyes, asking for my interpretation.

"He means well," I tell her. "Birdie is still in PE with Pennick."

I look all around, thinking of a plan on the fly, aware Blue's eyes are glued to me.

"You didn't answer the real question. What's going on?"

"I'd rather tell you and Birdie together. Maybe you should go into the locker room alone. Pennick might not notice if it's just you. Get Birdie then meet me at the ADA elevator and I'll explain."

"She won't come easily without a solid reason up front."

"Tell her we think Whitlock is a fed," Rémy says.

"Your *chemistry teacher*?" Her eyes bulge. "So he's not actually a prepper."

"I'm not sure what he is right now. Just tell Birdie that when Daniel said DTA, he was right, and that I think I know why."

"That'll work. She'll come along just at the mention of Daniel." Blue juts her chin at Rémy. "Is he coming, too?"

"Maybe. I didn't think that far ahead."

I'm the biggest enforcer of sticking together. But lately, I've had to let go of the idea that if we're not all together, someone will get hurt. Don't get me wrong. Normally, I wouldn't consider splitting up if I thought my sisters might be in imminent danger. Not with this new information on Whitlock. But getting from the locker room to the elevator shouldn't pose a threat. If that spot was good enough for Ansel, it should be a safe bet for us, too.

"I'm coming," Rémy announces, before I have a second to decide whether I should integrate or dispatch him. "I can show your sisters the photos. Plus, skipping doesn't feel like a big deal, considering I haven't been here for the last three days."

"Which is probably why you should go. Ms. Everitt will question why you didn't show up. Plus, if what you showed me is accurate, you'd be wise to steer clear of the whole situation. Mr. Whitlock was pretty adamant about me dissuading you from getting tangled up in things."

"Mr. Whitlock is a hypocrite," Rémy says.

"Fair enough."

"Maybe you should one-up him and go to the cops yourself. Circumvent Whitlock's whole MO by telling them your side of things."

Under the right amount of pressure, even a loyal person can crack and reveal what they know.

A new suspicion bolts through me, electrifying the little hairs on the back of my neck. Could Whitlock have turned Rémy into an informant? What if his mom made a deal with Whitlock that if Rémy agreed to get information about The Nest and The Burrow, his suspension would be minimal? I grab Rémy by the shoulders and spin him against a wall, shoving my hand up the front of his shirt to check for a wire before he can even put together what's happening.

"Whoa." Rémy raises both hands in surrender and I let him go. He's clean. "What was that all about?" He straightens his shirt and adjusts the wireless headphones around his neck, gaping like I've lost my mind.

"Sorry. I had to see if Whitlock's play for you to get information on us worked."

"You thought I was wearing *a wire?* Are you nuts?" He looks amused for half a second, but it's quickly replaced with concern. "You haven't actually told me anything incriminating, by the way. But now I'm starting to worry for real."

"I understand why you would, and I appreciate the blind trust, Rémy, I really do. But I've broken a lot of rules for you, and I have no idea what that means for either of us in the long run."

"What rules?"

I glance at the ceiling and blow out a breath. "Before we moved here, my family was already prepping solo. Canning and stockpiling food, water, medical supplies to have on hand in the event of an emergency. But ever since we joined The Nest—that's what we call one part of our coalition—we've added loads to our skill set. Hunting, trapping, shooting, shelter building. You name it. We'll be ready for The End Of The World As We Know It. But one of the rules for living within this group is we don't date anyone who could expose our setup. That means only dating within the coalition or not at all. Every secret we keep is meant to protect us."

"So no Outsiders," he says.

"Right. My sisters and I never make friends with other people. Not in the traditional sense. It's too hard to navigate when you don't do what everyone else is doing. Even at our other schools, we weren't allowed to participate in clubs, or play organized sports, or do anything outside of our art or what we were doing at home. Our mother is a nurse practitioner who runs paranoid when it comes to Western medicine. We grew up with a strict understanding that we wouldn't be allowed to participate in any activities that required a physical examination. She doesn't trust hospitals or doctors and gave us all our vaccinations herself, at home. So this thing with you and me, this friendship or whatever, it's not prepper approved."

"Can we focus on the *or whatever* part for a second?"

Rémy is nothing if not consistent.

"It's not possible," I tell him. "Or at least not probable."

"It's already happening."

He's right. I know he's right. "But it's a bad idea. If the feds are looking into our group, it's because there's something bigger going on. Sure, we have guns and ammo and self-defense systems set up, but that's not a crime."

"Not being with me could be considered criminal." Rémy takes a step closer. "The whole point of being with someone is you can let your guard down and tell them everything going on inside your head without fear of being judged."

"I wouldn't know."

He tilts his head. "I find that hard to believe."

"It's true. None of the boys in our group have ever interested me. And before that, let's just say I was always considered one of the *weirds*. Completely closed off from approach, so it didn't matter."

He takes another step, purposely bridging the gap between us. "So, you're weird. That's what makes you interesting. You're also an amazing artist. Smart. Quick-witted. Fierce. Free-spirited. Protective."

I flip my hair. "You forgot beautiful."

"*Beautiful* is too basic a word to describe you. And *weird* is not an insult."

"Tell that to the student bodies of the six schools I've attended." The bell rings, rightfully shifting my thoughts back to my sisters. "Come on. We have to go."

The hallways are filling up with students, making it easier, and in some ways harder, for Rémy and me to blend into the fold. Any minute now, Birdie will be entering the locker room where Blue is waiting. I scan the hallways for Ansel and Annalise, but they're nowhere to be seen. We turn down the hallway that leads to our art class to get to the ADA elevator. A fever rises over me when I spot Ms. Everitt hanging our self-portraits on the wall opposite our classroom. I can make an excuse for myself, but not Rémy. I'm trying to think of something to say when I notice my painting hung center stage, probably because it's the biggest and gives the wall some balance.

Ms. Everitt's face lights up when she sees us approaching. "I'm so glad to see you, Honey!"

I don't get why her enthusiasm extends to me alone, but I play along.

"I'm glad to see you, too, but I might not be able to stay for class today. I'm not feeling great."

"Oh no. I'm sorry to hear that. Is it a flu? Your stomach? Because if you can hang on for a little, just until the news team arrives to interview you."

"*Me?*"

"Yes, you. Your painting. You won, silly. Out of every high school artist in the country. I'm so glad you had a change of heart."

Only, I didn't.

"I'm sorry, Ms. Everitt, do you mean the scholarship competition?"

"Yes!" She clutches my upper arms energetically, cheeks flushed with pride. "This is so exciting."

Heat rises to my face, burning with suspicion and resentment. "Can you excuse me for a minute, Ms. Everitt? I'd like to collect my thoughts."

"Of course. Use the classroom. It's empty."

Empty because everybody is in the hallway, wearing faces that fail to hide their disappointment. I pull Rémy inside the art room and unleash the fire of my temper.

"Did *you* do this? I told you I couldn't enter this thing. Now I have to talk to reporters? If Dieter Ackerman sees me on Channel Seven news, I'll be eighty-sixed. I thought I could trust you."

"First of all, I didn't do this. Once the administration found out that there was real money attached to the scholarship, they handed over the logistics to the faculty advisors. Second, everyone whose art was submitted received an email with the details. I got mine while I was suspended."

"I didn't." My eyes go as wide as a brass gong being hit by a hammer when what he says strikes home. "Whitlock." I grit my teeth so hard they might crack. "That two-faced, sneaky—"

"Federal agent looking out for his own interests while taking advantage of a teenager," Rémy finishes. "I'll accept that as your apology."

I rest a hand on his shoulder briefly before placing it over my heart, forcibly exhaling a tense breath. "I'm sorry. But I can't go out there. I need to leave."

I dart to the windows, seeing if there's a way to make an escape, but they only crank open inward at a sixty-degree angle. Enough to put a leg through, but not enough for a distraught student to jump. Safety first. I raise my eyes to the air shaft, hands on my hips as a proverbial lightbulb sparks.

I can feel Rémy watching me as I grab the stool next to my empty easel and put it on top of Ms. Everitt's desk. Big R Reactive.

"Oh, *come on*. Really? The air shaft?"

"Yes. Really. I need to get out of Dodge. You don't understand."

The only problem is the art room stools aren't as tall as the ones in chemistry. Neither are the desks. The lab tables are set to standing height. I'm at a complete loss, feeling more and more trapped by the second, my heart pounding hard enough to break out of my chest. I need a milk crate or a wooden wine box to raise the stool.

"Honey."

Rémy says my name calmly, trying to instill some reason, but I'm too busy searching the room for things sturdy enough to stack.

"Honey," Rémy says again, with more emphasis.

I stop rummaging around the low cabinets lining the back of the room to whip around. "*What?*"

Ms. Everitt is watching me from the open doorway. She doesn't question what I'm doing, but her eyes shift to her desk where I left the stool. It wouldn't take much to conclude I wasn't thinking about changing out the fluorescent lighting tubes.

"They're ready for you."

I stand and pull myself together, letting my eyes linger impossibly long on Rémy as I make my way to her desk and pick up my EDC. I'm not Ready. Not in the big R way. I take a minute to go over to the easel I've been using and examine myself in the mirror. I run my hands over my thick brown hair, taming flyaways. I'm dressed decently enough in skinny jeans, a heather-gray V-neck T-shirt, and a long, pine-green cardigan. From the outside, to them, I'm the same girl who made the painting given center stage in the hallway. We see what we want to see, like Blue's shirt said. Because for me, this is a bad mirror day. From every angle imaginable.

✣ DTA ✣

DON'T TRUST ANYONE

MS. EVERITT ESCORTS me into the hallway, where a reporter and camera crew are waiting in front of my painting. The slender reporter, a hair-sprayed blonde in her early thirties, dressed sharply in a pencil skirt, lavender blouse, and pointy heels, is chatting with a group of students until her cameraman alerts her to my presence. She turns with the kind of plastic smile and posture that cost thousands of dollars in tuition fees to perfect. But here she is, interviewing the teen about to be handed a full ride to the art school of her choice. Lucky me.

I spot my sisters standing side by side. The circles under their eyes darken with dread as they watch this one-ring media circus unfold before their eyes. If Daniel, who never appeared on camera, was sent away alone, what will Dieter choose for my punishment?

Mother's warbled voice sings in my head like a distressed bird trying to protect its young. *Run. Run. Run.* But it's no use. Any moment now, I'll be turned into the coalition's betrayer, soon to be flung from The Nest.

"I have your winner right here," Ms. Everitt says happily.

But when she looks at me, her sea-glass-green eyes swim with concern, anchored by the stool she saw on her desk.

"Wonderful. Let's get started."

The reporter's voice floats to me in a way that's oddly sooth-
ing. The familiar voices devoid of any quirks or colloquialisms
that continuously play on the television in our house, delivering news and weather.

She explains she'll introduce herself and the news station
before asking me a few questions. I'm nodding, or shaking my
head, in answer to her questions—*Are you nervous? Would you
like a drink of water before we begin? Have you ever been on television?* Yes. No. No.

The whole time I'm searching for Ansel, hoping he'll fling
a paracord lasso around my neck and strangle me before this
goes further. It takes a few scans around the assembled students before I spot him, looking downright miserable because
he knows my potential fate. I watch his twin by birth alone
march up and grab his arm, whispering through clenched
teeth, pointing like I'm a witch accused of heresy—Goody
Juniper on the stand—and she is my accuser. Being able to
read lips like Whitlock would come in handy right now. Ansel
wrenches out of his sister's grasp, and she casts her angry gaze
at me, eyes fiery enough to burn me at the stake.

"Here's the teen of the hour," the reporter says, and I snap
my attention to what's happening whether I like it or not.
"Honey, right? That's sweet. No pun intended." She stares into
the camera, laughing effortlessly at her own joke.

My eyes lock with Rémy's as she says, "How does it feel
to be the recipient of the Scholarship for the Arts America?"

I blink back. "Honestly, it's the biggest shock of my life. I was
just telling Rémy Lamar, the student liaison for the competition,
that never in a million years did I think this would happen."

Rémy nods once, his smile encouraging me to keep it simple so I can get the hell away from this whole mess. I agree,
but then what?

"I have to say your art speaks volumes about what's going on in America right now. The concerns many people have

for our safety and welfare during tumultuous and uncertain times. When you painted this, were you leaning toward any one side of the political fence?"

"Well, Miss—?"

"Fielding," she says, through lips lacquered so red she looks like she drinks blood.

"Miss Fielding. I'm not old enough to vote yet. And my mother taught me it wasn't polite to talk about politics or religion, but I'm happy to discuss my process if you'd like."

"Sounds like your mother taught you how to stay out of harm's way."

Lady, you have no idea.

"Can you tell us why you chose to paint three versions of yourself for your self-portrait titled *Whiskey Tango Foxtrot?*"

Oh, because my life is one huge WTF right now.

"They're meant to represent my past, present, and future," I answer. "None of which have ever fully escaped our present-day prejudices and impending doom, as you pointed out. But if something catastrophic does happen, I hope those of us who survive will remember to keep the arts alive."

I don't explain that it's a painting of my sisters and me, because it's easier to flip her a lie that follows the rules of the competition.

"That's quite a sophisticated and self-aware view, making perfect sense for your beautiful and evocative piece of art. I'm sure all of our viewers can see why the judges, some of the top art critics writing today, chose your painting out of the thousands of entries. Are there any other thoughts you'd like to share with our viewers about your work before we sign off?"

I'm screwed no matter what I say, so I turn to the camera and smile. "Rules breed rebels. I think it's important to think for yourself when making art. That way you're leaving a mark as uniquely yours as your own fingerprints. We've all been taught that the black sheep is a deviation from acceptable standards and something to be avoided. Still, when you see it among a herd, its lack of conformity is what steals your breath and captures your attention."

"As you will continue to capture that of the art world, no doubt. You heard it here first, from up-and-coming young artist Honey Juniper in Elkwood, Washington. *This* is Bridget Fielding for News Seven."

When all the niceties have been handed out and the news team is packing up to leave, I scour the hallway for Ansel. He's nowhere to be seen, and I don't know what to make of his absence. Despite everything that's happened, I still consider him my friend. I know there's a zero percent chance his father won't see or hear about this segment for *Channel Seven at Seven. News Beyond the Headlines.*

"You were great," Rémy says. "Totally at ease."

"You might as well say your goodbyes now," Birdie tells him. "She's screwed."

She doesn't know yet that the proverbial screwing doesn't only apply to me. "We have to go," I tell Rémy. "I need to fill them in away from prying eyes."

"You want me to come with you?"

"You can't. I'll text you if anything comes up that we can't handle alone."

"Fill us in on what?" Birdie says. "Blue said you found out something about Daniel."

Don't say Daniel snitched. Don't say Daniel snitched. Don't say Daniel snitched.

My eyes flick to Rémy. "I did. And Whitlock. It's more complicated than we thought. I'll tell you everything on the drive home."

If I tell Birdie my theory now, she'll go off the rails. I need to be one hundred percent sure, with proof.

"You'll text me?" Rémy says to confirm.

I nod. "You're one of the only people I can trust beside my sisters."

"Like D'Artagnan."

Provisional D'Artagnan. The DTA rule doesn't apply.

The bay window in our kitchen is nearly empty, all of Mother's equipment and experiments gone with only the hanging plants left in place. Not a great sign. She left us a note saying she went into town to sell more of our products, along with a list of things she expects us to do. Milk the goats, feed the chickens, rotate the cans, pull up anything in the root cellar that needs to be eaten before it goes bad. None of it matters right now, because we're trying to decide how to deal with the inevitable backlash of me appearing on the news tonight. Not to mention wrapping our heads around whether or not Whitlock is a federal agent.

"What if we break the TV?" Birdie suggests. "Open the back panel and remove parts so it doesn't power on." She polishes an apple on her shirt and takes the loud, juicy bite that cuts into my nerves.

"That would only stop Mother from seeing the news. Not everyone else."

"A wave of inevitable truths that was set in motion long ago," Blue says.

Every time I think our little sister can't out-weird herself, she earns another gold star.

"Whitlock had an agenda all along. I know better than to trust somebody just because they say they're a prepper. I only let my guard down because I thought he could get us answers about the white powder. But now..."

"He got caught," Blue says.

"Who got caught? Whitlock?"

She shrugs. "That's just what came to me."

Daniel got caught. Whitlock got caught. I'm gonna get caught. Only one of those truths is verifiably in motion. "Can you get me our cellphone?" Blue goes to the kitchen to dig through her EDC and I get a better idea. "Never mind. I don't want to call him from our phone if he's a fed." I fish the burner Rémy gave me out of my bag. Then dig through all my pockets for the late slip Whitlock gave me with his cellphone number on it.

"Where did you get that phone?" Birdie asks.

"Rémy wanted me to have a burner in case ours got taken away or is being bugged."

I catch the what-the-fuck look that passes between Birdie and Blue right before I punch in Whitlock's phone number. My heart skips a beat the first time it rings, and my brain runs through everything I might say. *Help. I think I got myself into a world of shit. Are you a federal agent?* But then it kicks over to voicemail and further considerations add to the adrenaline coursing through my veins. Am I willing to give up Dieter Ackerman to save my own hide? If what Blue said *is* true, Whitlock may have gotten caught. The only question is by who? And when? He said he'd find a way to get in touch with me about the white powder if it was urgent. Since I never gave him our cellphone number, the only way to get in touch with me would be through email.

I make a mad dash for the stairs without explanation, my sisters hot on my heels.

Our computer is older, and it takes forever for the operating system to sync up all the systems and applications that haven't been updated to standard in years.

"What's going on?" Birdie asks.

I hold up my index finger, open Suremail, and log in, but there aren't any new emails in my in-box. Not from the school about the national self-portrait scholarship competition, and not from Mr. Whitlock. "Rémy said everyone who was entered in the art competition received an email. I should have received one, too. Especially if I won. Whitlock told me he'd figure out a way to get in touch with me about the white powder on our clothes. Since he took over coordinating the competition, I thought maybe..."

"Did you check the junk folder?" Blue says.

"No. Good thinking." I double-click the folder and right there in black and white are two emails misfiled as junk. One from the EHS art department and one from Pryce Whitlock, aka pwhittyteach@suremail.com. "Come look at this."

Honey,

I analyzed the white powder on your clothes and discovered it has the same chemical makeup as cocaine, only the molecules are rearranged into a drug known as scopolamine. Street name: Devil's Breath. It is often blown into the faces of unexpecting victims, causing a loss of self-control and rendering them incapable of forming memories during the time they are under the drug's influence. In essence, the victims are like zombies. At high doses, it's lethal. Please, trust me. You and your sisters are in danger. Call my cellphone or meet me after school in my classroom so I can help you.

P. Whitlock

I can't breathe.

Devil's Breath. Devil's Breath. Devil's Breath.

"Annalise drugged us," Birdie says. "Blue was right. What do you think we did that night we came home filthy?"

"I don't know. Ansel doesn't know, either. But Daniel had to know something. Why else would he say *Don't Trust Anyone?* Everything has to be connected. The white powder, the way so many of us forgot where we were or what we did, Mr. Whitlock."

I tread lightly, hoping my sister will link Daniel to Whitlock herself, because I need her to stick with me.

"Oh my god, what if he doesn't come back?" she says.

I swivel and gape at Birdie. "What if *I* don't come back? I've been so focused on your safety, I disregarded my own." The letters for Devil's Breath swim in front of my eyes and I make the missing connection. "Where's that origami bird Daniel gave you?"

Birdie rushes out of the room and flies back, handing it over. I unfold the origami chicken with shaky hands. *Dirtierdevilbread 928836.* I see our oversight immediately. "It doesn't say *Dirtier Devil Bread.* Daniel was trying to tell you *Dieter Devil's Breath.*"

Birdie's gasp is loud enough to suck the air from the room.

"Before Ansel dragged you away from the bunker the other night, did you notice if there was a lock on the door?"

"There's a keypad."

"928836." I hand her the unfolded yellow square of paper. "I bet it's the passcode."

"Does this mean we're going back?"

"I think we have to. I want to know what's in that bunker just as much as you do."

"What about the news story airing tonight?" Blue asks.

"We could cut the power to the whole compound," Birdie says. "I think there's a transformer box mounted on the pole near the road."

"Dieter would flip on the generators if he thought the power outage extended past The Nest and The Burrow," Blue says.

"She's right."

My temples pound out my imminent sentence.

You're a goner. You're a goner. You're a goner.

The reality of that makes my temples thump like drums. Annalise may have already informed her father. I need to be Responsible, Reactive, and Ready. All three big Rs. "First things first, what do we know? Dieter will most likely call another meeting, right? What if we go over to the bunker and use Daniel's passcode while everyone else is gathering in the training area?"

Birdie writes the numbers from the yellow paper onto her palm with a Sharpie. "I'm in. I told you something strange is going on over there, and I still think Daniel might be inside."

To be honest, I'm more worried he's not.

"What about Mother?" she asks. "She should be home soon."

"We'll leave her a note saying we'll come back for her once things with Dieter cool down."

"They won't," Blue says. And her tone is so free of doubt it gives me the chills.

TOBYISMS FOR ACTION
7
HOPE IS ALIVE

BASH WALKS INTO Nikko's at the end of my lunch shift and takes a seat at the counter. He knows Stavros hates when our friends hang around. He must be in a mood to tempt fate. I finish taking my last order and punch everything into the POS system before bringing Bash a menu.

"I still have forty-five minutes."

"I know. I got off early and needed some feta fries."

"I have to go straight home today and take care of Banquo. My mom's out of town, talking to some people at a gallery about doing a retrospective of her work. I think they want to help jump-start her career."

"No shit," Bash says. "That's great. I was worried about you when I left, but . . . Wait. We should have a party."

"And invite who? You, me, and Brooke?"

"I'm not down," Brooke says from the soda fountain. "You nerds just like to play video games."

"Told you. You still want those fries now that she emasculated you?"

"Yep. And a Coke. Brooke will be sorry when I have enough money saved to go to the Art Institute, where I'll learn to design video games and become rich and famous."

"I'll be the first to say I knew you when," Brooke says. "You want me to ring him up for you, Toby?"

"Please."

"*Thank you, Hookie*," Bash says.

"Call me *Hookie* again and see what kind of feta you get on those fries."

Brooke got caught skipping school when we were juniors. Her dad laced into her in a big way outside the principal's office, humiliating her in front of half the school. I don't think she ever skipped again, but people called her Hookie all the way through graduation.

"Let me take care of this table and we can bounce," I tell Bash. "I want to grab a sub from Sandwich Slayers. I need a break from Greek and fried chicken."

"Who needs a break from Greek?" Stavros asks, walking in on the conversation.

"No one," all three of us say simultaneously.

"Good. Because the Mediterranean diet is the most healthiest. You could eat Greek food every day and be like Adonis."

Brooke is smiling and blinking her eyes at me, trying like hell not to laugh as she walks away to check on her tables.

"Who invited fried chicken boy to the restaurant?" Stavros asks.

"No one," Bash says. "I just wanted to eat some delicious feta fries because I, too, would like to look like Adonis."

"Ha! Good luck for you with this." Stavros pats my arm. "No discounts for friends."

"I know. One more table and I'll get him out of here."

An hour later, I'm tearing into a turkey sub, recounting the conversation I had with my mom between bites while Bash drives to my house. His fingers are wrist deep in a bag of salt and vinegar chips when I get to the part where she thought the powdered sugar on my shirt was cocaine or something.

He balks and wipes his salt-covered fingers on his work pants. "Man, has she got you wrong. Although we could smoke some weed inside the house since she's gone."

"You got any?"

"No."

"Me, either. But Jonesy left a few beers in the fridge."

The first thing I do when we pull up is let Banquo outside. Then I check my phone for messages from Mom. It's the first time we've been apart overnight since my sisters vanished, but she must be doing okay since Jonesy's with her. The light from the TV is flickering through the windows into the backyard. I left it on for Banquo while I was at work since he's used to it always being on. He runs inside and barks for a treat, trained to know that not shitting in the house earns him a biscuit. I toss it in the air before searching the fridge for Jonesy's beer. He may or may not remember leaving them here. Guess we'll see if he's a good enough detective to uncover the case of the missing IPAs.

"Check this out," Bash says from the couch. His eyes stay glued to a human interest story when I hand him a beer. "We never had reporters come to our art classes."

"Here's the teen of the hour," the reporter says as a tall brunette walks into the frame. "Honey, right? That's sweet. No pun intended."

She announces they're at Elkwood High School in Washington, ready to interview the lucky young artist who won a full ride to the art school of her choice.

"The chick who won is hot in that I'll-kick-your-ass-if-I-need-to sort of way," Bash says.

"Whoa! What the . . ."

"Relax, man. She's not *that* hot."

The girl has her brown eyes fixed on someone in the crowd when the reporter asks, "How does it feel to be the recipient of the Scholarship for the Arts America?"

I grab the remote and move closer to the TV, blinking to make sure what I'm seeing is real.

"Honestly, it's the biggest shock of my life," the girl says. "I was just telling Rémy Lamar, the student liaison for the competition, that never in a million years did I think this would happen."

I hit Pause and toss the remote onto the couch so I can grab my phone from the kitchen table and write down *Rémy Lamar, student liaison art competition.* I pull up the photos I took of the new age-progressions for my sisters.

"What's up?" Bash asks. "You forget to text your mom or something?"

"Come here and look at this."

Bash saunters over and I hand him my phone. He looks between my phone and the TV screen. "Ohh, *shit.* You don't think—"

"I don't know. She's around the same age."

The TV resumes play when Banquo jumps on the couch and hits the remote.

"I have to say your art speaks volumes about what's going on in America right now," the reporter says. "The concerns many people have for our safety and welfare during tumultuous and uncertain times. When you painted this, were you leaning toward any one side of the political fence?"

The camera pans to the winning girl's painting and my heart thumps a million beats per minute. It's a triple self-portrait, two of the faces partially covered, but the one in the middle is strikingly similar to the girl centered in Mom's painting, the same girl in the age-progression photo on the phone in my hand. The gas masks and balaclava on the other two shock me less now that Mom told me about being drawn to certain subject matter in her art. But what does hit me like a gut punch are the symbols written down the leg of the figure on the right, because it's the Pigpen cipher Bash and I once used.

"Well, Miss—?" The girl asks. I can't bring myself to believe it's her. Not yet. We've been wrong before. Jonesy has been wrong.

"Fielding," the reporter clarifies.

I grab the remote from under Banquo's butt, rewind, and pause it on the painting. "Look at the writing on her leg."

Bash's eyes balloon. "No fucking way!"

I make a mad dash for my bedroom and fling open my desk drawers, throwing everything aside, on the floor, I don't give a shit because I'm looking for one thing. The stainless steel spinning decoder ring our dad gave me before he died. I find it in the top drawer, tucked inside an old Yu-Gi-Oh! trading card tin. *Yes* fucking way.

I race back to the TV. It only takes me a few seconds to spin the ring and decode the message. *Home sweet home.* The rest is two sets of numbers, the first followed by an N, the second a W.

"Bash, the numbers on her leg, are those coordinates?"

"Oh fuck. You think they've been looking for you all this time and she thought to use the cipher?"

My thoughts exactly. I grab the remote and press Play. There's a two-second delay before the interview resumes and the girl says, "Miss Fielding. I'm not old enough to vote yet. And my mother taught me it wasn't polite to talk about politics or religion, but I'm happy to discuss my process if you'd like."

That sure as shit sounds like Katherina. Even at age six she was a stickler for rules.

"Sounds like your mother taught you how to stay out of harm's way."

My stomach clenches. Whoever she's talking about isn't our mother.

"Can you tell us why you chose to paint three versions of yourself for your self-portrait titled *Whiskey Tango Foxtrot?*"

"...to represent my past, present, and future. None of which have ever fully escaped our present-day prejudices and impending doom, as you pointed out. But if something catastrophic does happen, I hope those of us who survive will remember to keep the arts alive."

She's lying. She shook her head in that tiny way she always did before she dropped a fib. I'd bet my life the other two masked figures in the painting are Imogen and Cassandra. My head is humming with disbelief. I tune out the reporter to watch Katherina closely. When she finally looks at the camera, I see her eyes. Really see them and recognize them as my own. They're our mother's eyes.

"Rules breed rebels," she tells the reporter and I whisk back into focus. "I think it's important to think for yourself when making art. That way you're leaving a mark as uniquely yours as your own fingerprints. We've all been taught that the black sheep is a deviation from acceptable standards and something to be avoided. Still, when you see it among a herd, its lack of conformity is what steals your breath and captures your attention."

"As you will continue to capture that of the art world, no doubt. You heard it here first, from up-and-coming young artist Honey Juniper in Elkwood, Washington. *This* is Bridget Fielding for News Seven."

"Honey *Juniper*. Elkwood, Washington. What the actual fuck?" I pause the picture before the clip ends in case I want to rewind it again.

"It's her. It has to be her," Bash says. "What are you gonna do?"

My adrenaline is through the roof, making me nauseous. It's the same time in Washington. I can't call the school. Jonesy is with Mom. If I call them and freak her out, she might lose her opportunity for a show. Plus, it's not like I can show them the clip. But if I'm wrong—*fuck*—if I'm wrong it could send Mom into another spiral where she disappears into herself for months, maybe years. Lots of people are making political art based on everything happening with our current POTUS, *an overweening rogue*, as my namesake Sir Toby Belch would say.

But if I'm right, *it will have blood; they say, blood will have blood.*

Nobody understands my anger and despair like Lady Macbeth.

Mom and Jonesy are supposed to be back in two days. Maybe I can get a jump on this and see if it's a wild-goose chase without them ever knowing I was gone. But if something happens to me, if I disappeared, too, they wouldn't know where to look.

Shit. Shit. Shit.

I have to do this.

"Toby!" Bash says, snapping me out of my head.

"I have to drive up to Washington."

"*Now?*"

"Not *right* now, but yes. I don't have a car. They took my mom's Prius."

"I'd give you mine, but I don't think it would make it. Can you rent one?"

"Too expensive. No credit card."

But then a possible solution to my problem hits me. "Can you drive me back to Nikko's?"

:INCH:

I'M NEVER COMING HOME

WE CAN'T LEAVE for The Burrow until Blue goes to Achilles's mew, puts on his hood to keep him calm, and tethers him to his jess. There's no way we'd be able to come back for him, but their bond is such that once Achy has the hood on, he won't screech. She brought the carrier with the handle on top that she built out of wood to transport him when necessary. Not that it's ever been necessary.

Birdie takes the origami chicken from Daniel. I grab a pen, the notebook I use to write letters to Bucky, and a few granola bars. Blue said she had everything she needed. We exit our house through the kitchen door shouldering I'm Never Coming Home bags, just like Daniel. Our INCH bags are also geared to the hilt with snares, medical supplies, slingshots, fishing line and compact poles, a bow, and hatchet, knives, folding saws, fire starters, compasses, a small shovel, tarps, Bivy sacks, duct tape, and the best of our clothes for outdoor survival. This may not be a natural or man-made disaster, but situationally, the logic applies.

Both phones are tucked in my pockets. I contemplate turning them off to save battery life, but set them to Vibrate until we know for sure what's going on. As the screen door slaps behind me, I realize Birdie was right. We wouldn't actually know what a home looks like long-term. Blue was right, too. Maybe Bucky can't save us in the physical world, but he will be with us wherever we go. And that peculiarity, completely unique to us *weirds,* gives me some comfort.

"I can take Achy's carrier for you," Birdie tells Blue. "It's the least I can do, considering you wouldn't have that vicious bird if it weren't for me." She bumps into Blue to let her know she's joking, and Achilles flaps his massive wings, forcing Birdie to lean out of the way. "Traitor," she tells him. But it's me that word clings to like a prickly bramble.

We take the surrounding woods to The Burrow, watching and listening for anyone making their way to the training area. I didn't give much thought to Mr. Whitlock calling the clearing a proving ground, but I can't deny the low booms we've heard over the last year. The Burrowers use this spot to test their homemade explosives and hand-forged, knee-high cannons. Stuff they'll use in the future to deter intruders.

The rain hasn't started yet, but the smell of ozone is building in the forest air along with the rise in humidity, exaggerating the pine scent and earthiness. A squirrel runs scatter-footed across the path when he hears us coming, making Achilles flap his wings again. He doesn't screech because he hunts by sight and the leather hood helps keep him from taking off after prey. My sisters and I keep as quiet as possible. Voices carry through these woods like an errant pinball bouncing from tree to tree. When we're a quarter mile from the Ackerman house, we cut to the right. I lead them in a wide arc, approaching the bunker from an angle. It takes longer but keeps us from skittering along the edge of the woods, where we'd be easier to spot.

We're about thirty feet away when I tell my sisters to leave Achilles's carrier at the base of a moss-covered western hemlock.

Birdie nocks an arrow on her bow, ready to defend us should we be seen.

"Do you want to put Achy inside?" I whisper.

Blue shakes her head. "If I need to, I'll let him fly."

My sisters are nothing if not a complex study in fight or flight.

We move as one unit to the spot where Ansel was dragging Birdie away from the bunker. I pump my hand to let my sisters know I'm going to drop behind a massive cedar tree, perfect for keeping all three of us out of sight.

I take the night vision device out of my EDC in time to spot Dieter exiting the bunker with Connor. The lens turns everything as acid green as the sickness gripping my gut. I'd bet anything Connor Clarke is one of the burly G.I. Joes Rémy spotted with Annalise on Overcast Road. He's one of Dieter's most unwavering robots, and I finally understand why. From what I can tell, Dieter is leaving him behind to guard the bunker while he takes care of business. Presumably, the meeting where yours truly is supposed to be the unwelcomed guest of dishonor. The biggest issue for us is the rifle Connor is carrying. Military issued and designed to kill quickly, making it obvious that precious cargo is stored inside that bunker.

Birdie pecks at my arm before taking the NVD. The adjustable scope only requires single-handed operation, making it advantageous if you want to grab the arm of the person with you and squeeze like you're checking their blood pressure. Which is exactly what Birdie does when she sees Connor for herself.

I whip out our shared cellphone and text Ansel:

I need your help ASAP. *At the bunker behind your house. Connor Clarke is armed and guarding and I need to get inside. I've got my* INCH. *I know . . . a lot.*

I show Birdie the screen on our cellphone then hold my breath and wait.

Please respond. Please respond. Please respond.

Birdie pulls my head close and whispers, "Do you trust Ansel? I mean really trust him? Or should we ambush Connor and take him out?"

She must have forgotten Daniel said he trusted Ansel with

his life. I don't know the proper way to sign my answer. We have hand signals for hunting, but sometimes we have to make stuff up as we go. I point to myself (*I*), crisscross my wrists in front of my chest and actively close my fists (*trust*), then point at Ansel (*him*). That feels right to me. Even if it's wrong, my sisters nod like they understand my meaning.

I search the ground for a stone heavy enough to throw long distance and lob it as far as I can. When it hits the ground, I take the NVD from Birdie and watch Connor walk around the concrete building housing the bunker's staircase. He's alone, but doesn't shoulder his rifle like I would expect. That doesn't mean he's any less of a menace. Getting him out of the way won't be easy. Not without Ansel's help.

I draw my Gerber folding knife from its holder on the side of my EDC, heart pounding since I'm not sure how this might go. One way or another, we're getting in that bunker to see for ourselves what Whitlock was after, even if that means taking Connor down. Three against one.

I never truly understood the phrase *I can't believe my eyes* until I see Ansel come out of the bunker and blow a handful of white powder in Connor Clarke's face. I thought for sure he'd be at the meeting with everyone else, impatiently awaiting the prepper witch trials, if you will. I know for sure Annalise is all too ready to point her accusatory finger at me. And Magda would back up whatever her daughter says, even though the trick Ansel just pulled is the Ackermans' own form of witchcraft. Does that make him an accomplice, or has he simply wised up to his sister's maneuvers?

Birdie is tapping my arm again for the scope, but I'm watching Connor willingly hand over his rifle. I gasp when Ansel butts Connor in the head with the stock, hard enough to stun him, then puts him in a sleeper hold. Connor doesn't fight back because he's temporarily lost all free will, a zombie, just like Whitlock said in his email.

I hand Birdie the scope and lean against the trunk of the

giant tree next to Blue, trying to fathom what just happened. What *my friend* just did to someone else from The Burrow.

Our cellphone vibrates in my pocket. I pull it out and see a text from Ansel that says, *You're clear.*

Friend or foe, I text back.

Friend. Always.

I grab my sisters and we march out of the woods like a three-girl army, minus the gas mask and balaclava from my painting, but primed for anything just the same. We must look something fierce because Ansel adjusts his grip on the rifle, prompting Birdie to raise her bow.

"I'm not your enemy, Birdie. Lower the bow." His voice holds all the authority granted him by his last name, but my middle sister isn't easily intimidated.

"I will," she says. "But first, I want to ask you something. One last time. Is Daniel inside that bunker?"

I keep my own thoughts about Daniel as closed off as my expression.

"I've already told you he isn't," Ansel says. "I have no reason to lie to you."

"You have *every* reason," she snaps. "Your last name is Ackerman, isn't it?"

"I didn't get a say in that any more than you three did." Ansel throws up a hand, asking me for help.

I push Birdie's bow down. "We don't have that much time."

"You're right," Ansel says. "My dad is on a tear about you being on the news. Annalise has gone completely rogue. Running her own missions like Thane. She has him convinced you talked. That you knew Whitlock was a fed. You're not safe here. I'm not sure any of us are safe here anymore," he says.

"We know about the Devil's Breath," I tell him. "Annalise used it on us, just like you used it on Connor, didn't she? What did she have us do the night we all came back exhausted and filthy?"

"I still don't know," he says. "We may never know. She's on a power trip."

"What about our mother? If she's second-in-command—"

"Your *mother*." Ansel mocks me with a carping laugh. "She and my father are as tangled up as everyone suspected, and more. Do you know how Devil's Breath is made? From the seeds of trees that produce datura flowers. They emptied Alice's greenhouses this morning. She's no less complicit than my own mother or Annalise."

Birdie gasps and her eyes snap to mine, swirling dark. A maelstrom of disbelief, fury, and heartbreak. My own heart becomes a wildling, veins twisting and tightening around its bony cage, threatening to tear itself out. Mother was more of a pacifist before we joined The Nest. Worried about climate change and natural disaster. Accepting she had a hand in making Devil's Breath is insane. It begs me to question whether she was truly a willing accomplice or under the influence of Devil's Breath herself all along.

"What else are they making? I want to see for myself," I snap at Ansel. "Mr. Whitlock—"

"What do you know about *Whitlock*?" Ansel's face hardens.

"Everything," I lie. Then guilt forces me to honesty. "And nothing. I found out too late he was a fed."

"Better late than never, I guess."

He may be right about that, but what if he's wrong? We still haven't heard from Daniel. "If we're not safe here, we need some leverage. I can't take anyone at their word. I need to see it with my own eyes. You don't have to stay here, either. You can come with us."

Ansel's face is pure conflict. "I'm sick of Annalise's constant manipulation. Tired of trying to find ways to circumvent my father's decisions. But you're asking me to help you take my family down."

"I'm not. I'm asking you to help me save mine."

"You know that doesn't include Alice."

I nod. "I know. Especially if what you said is true."

"It's so much more than that, Honey. I don't want you to leave, but there are things you deserve to know." He looks over his shoulder and checks his field watch. "They're gonna start looking for you once they realize you're not showing up for the meeting. You probably only have about ten minutes."

"Ten minutes is all we need."

His lips are a tight line as he inhales and nods. "Be quick."

We storm the door together, and Ansel puts an arm out to stop Blue. "You can't bring your falcon down there. The air . . . it's not safe. There are respirator masks next to the door. You should put them on, just in case."

My eyes go round as moons. "Splitting up isn't optional."

We stick together no matter what.

"It's okay," Blue says, sensing my distress. "He's not lying. I'll stay out here with Achilles."

Ansel stares at the ground, his shoulders curled inward. That's when I know he's gutted over his family being mixed up in something dangerous. And powerless to do anything about it, because he's tied by blood to the whole coalition. In coming here, I've cleaved his allegiance in two. And yet still he's helping us, because . . . because he has feelings for me.

"Ansel—" His name seeps from my mouth with gratitude.

"Don't thank me, Honey. I can't handle it right now. And please don't ask any more questions. Just go."

He pets Achilles without fear, watching the falcon's head turn in clicks to his touch, avoiding my eyes like he's the one wearing the leather hood.

Birdie beats me to the keypad and punches in the numbers. I set an eight-minute timer on my watch, giving us two full minutes to get out. The staircase into this bunker is the same as all the others. Concrete and dimly lit by motion-detecting, solar-powered lights whose batteries are mounted outside the overall structure. Respirators hang by the door for us to put on.

"You ready?"

Birdie nods, and we pull the protective masks on and open the door. These quarters are nothing like the ones designed for living below the ground. No makeshift kitchen or bunk beds built tight to the ground. No shelving units filled with canned and dried foods. This is a lab fixed inside an oversized bunker. And Daniel, as expected, is nowhere to be seen.

I move around the room and take in the cabinets and table, microscopes, Erlenmeyer flasks, and Bunsen burners, test tubes, a centrifuge, and stainless steel sink. Several notebooks and clipboards are scattered around the stainless steel table. I flip through the pages and witness a plan for how to access the Pacific Northwest water systems. They point to a drawing for a chemical compound in Mother's handwriting, her initials signing the corner.

For a second, my naïveté tries to convince me this is something to ensure our access to clean water. The good mirror view of the prepper in me hoping for the best. But then I spot several jars containing the heads of rattlesnakes. Above them, rows of amber glass bottles line wall-mounted shelves, each plastered with the same biohazard label we saw on the tanks being rolled inside. They're labeled with their chemical compound.

I pull the periodic table to the forefront of my memory. Benzene. Sodium. Potassium nitrate. Cadmium. Uranium. My heart skips a beat. Hydrogen cyanide. The danger of these chemicals trips all my alarms. Every one volatile, explosive. One label reads *Tabun*. A word I've read somewhere before. I rack my brain trying to remember the article about Emil Ackerman and the nerve agents he helped develop for Operation Paperclip. Tabun, *one drop on a rabbit would kill it within minutes.*

I look for Birdie when I hear the clinking of glass, forgetting for a moment she's in the bunker with me. "Don't touch anything," I scold.

She startles at the terseness in my muffled voice and turns fast, nearly dropping a test tube full of Prussian-blue liquid. I hold my breath as she returns it to its holder, careful not to spill a drop.

"We don't know how these compounds behave. Come here. Stay close."

My sister backs away from the corner and comes to my side, looking at the notes over my shoulder.

I always believed Dieter put preparedness and self-preservation above all else. But his notes paint a different picture. His documentation talks about initiating widespread proliferation of potentially deadly toxins to be used in what he decides are emergency situations. The goal being to decrease the size of the surviving population.

The idea of our mother leaning toward anarchism as a means of survival makes my stomach twist with disgust and betrayal. I understand some of the chemistry, but most of it goes beyond the high school lab. These are the notes of a person who can only be described as a homegrown terrorist. Someone paranoid and secretive, but methodical. This plan is deranged and it makes my chest hurt to think that under our noses was a man ready to cause the shit hitting the fan for a lot of people if he felt it was warranted. And then what, use his fledglings from The Nest like a baby-making farm to rebuild society among his hand-chosen members? Isn't that the definition of a god complex? I've never had any intention of procreating with any of the Burrow Boys, including Ansel. Not even if the fate of the world depended on it and we were the last girls on this compound. Hell, even if we were the last girls on earth. My body, my rules. I'd take my chances against their poison first.

I don't know how many times we've heard Dieter say, *When the shit hits the fan it will be us against them.* Coming back for Mother isn't a reality. It's too consequential. Because right now, it's *us* against *them*. Ansel was right. We aren't safe. Maybe nobody is safe here anymore.

I clock the frightened look in Birdie's eyes as I pull out the burner phone. I need to take as many photos as possible for Mr. Whitlock. FBI agent or not, making myself a snitch or not, because this goes beyond the scope of normal.

Sweat runs down my back as I can a few photos. There's not enough time to text Whitlock everything I'm seeing, but if I call him again, he might answer. I pull up my call history and hit the green phone icon. It rings within seconds. Birdie and I gape at each other with mirrored perplexity because the echo of the ring is coming from inside one of the cabinets.

Birdie reaches for the door handle and I swallow a lump, hoping Mr. Whitlock isn't inside. Because if he is, I doubt he'd be unharmed. The cabinet is stocked with rubber lab aprons and hazmat suits. Boxes labeled with supplies line the bottom. The phone is still ringing, but the sound is dampened and distant, like it's coming from an adjoining room or maybe inside one of several boxes. It stops, and I dial again, listening, searching through boxes while Birdie pats down the suits and aprons. We can't find it anywhere.

The timer on my phone beeps and our eyes meet fearfully. We're out of time.

"We have to go."

I push Birdie toward the exit and grab one of Dieter's lab notebooks, shoving it inside the back of my shirt, securing it with the waistband of my cargo pants as we rush to ground level. We rip the masks off and drop them without care before bursting back outside.

Blue is gone.

I spin in a panic. "Where's Blue? Connor. Did he take her? You were supposed to be watching out for her," I say to Ansel.

"I dragged Connor out of view. Blue is in the woods waiting for you. I *was* watching out for her."

Of course he was, because Ansel is the Ackerman anomaly.

"And Whitlock? Does Dieter have him? Is that why he wasn't in school?"

"There are some things you're better off not knowing."

That's as much of a confirmation as I need. There's only one person left I can trust outside the coalition. I don't tell Ansel I have Whitlock's number or that I tried to call him from inside the bunker. Whitlock can't help us now.

Ansel hands me a topographic map. "This will take you to a bug-out location where you can pick up some supplies if you need them." His eyes flick to Birdie. "It's the same place I sent Daniel to keep him safe."

"You knew where he was this whole time? Why didn't you tell me?"

"Because you don't have a reputation for keeping your thoughts and emotions under wraps. Daniel's safety was my top priority."

Birdie doesn't argue and Ansel doesn't say safe from who, because we all know. Snitches get stitches, or worse. They get neutralized.

"You'll find the map for your next location inside a buried cache near Lake Dowie. Draw the lines for the second leg of the trip on the map I gave you. It'll show you how to get to the Gemini Caves. Pick up what you need at the first stop and move out ASAP. You have your phone, right? I'll text you what I know as things develop."

A deep groan comes from the side of the bunker. Ansel hustles over there to check on Connor. I snap a quick photo of the topographic map with the burner phone and send it to Rémy with a text telling him where we're headed. First location Lake Dowie, then on to the Gemini Caves. I send him a few photos of the lab just in case something happens to us. JIC. It's best to have somebody beside Ansel know where we're headed, even if Rémy is an Outsider.

"What's that?" Ansel's blue eyes darken like storm clouds. "That's not your phone."

"It's a burner. I got it from Rémy."

"Are you trying to get him killed? What did you send him?"

"*Killed? What the hell, Ansel?* He doesn't know anything. Your father could be the cause of the Shit Hitting The Fan in a big way. Trust me, Rémy is the least of your problems. And besides, somebody other than *you* needs to know where we're going. Somebody else *I trust.* Unless you're willing to come with us to talk to the right people."

Conflict wrings his face; Ansel's torn between knowing I'm right but needing to stay loyal and see this through. "We wouldn't even make it into town."

He rips the burner out of my hand and throws it on the ground, smashing it with the heel of his combat boot.

"What are you *doing?* I need that."

"So do I. That phone will make it seem like we got into it and you got away." He hands me the rifle. "Hit me in the cheek. Hard enough to make it bleed."

"No. Are you crazy? I'm not gonna hit you."

"I will." Birdie snatches the rifle and butts Ansel in the cheek hard enough to leave a gash. "I feel like you deserve that."

Ansel pitches forward from the strike and presses the heel of his palm to his cheek. But then he bolts upright, perking his ears up like an animal in the woods. I pick up the faint murmur of Dieter's gritty voice and go into flight mode, grabbing Birdie's arm, pulling her away from the bunker.

"I'll do my best to keep them off your trail," Ansel says.

"How?"

"The same way I got Connor to hand me his gun." He digs inside his pocket to retrieve a small plastic bag filled halfway with white powder.

"Are you sure? You can still come with us."

The downhearted way he stares at me, like there's nothing

he'd rather do, confirms every teasing thing Birdie ever said about him. "I can't. You have to go. *Now*. Before it's too late."

Birdie and I sprint for the woods. I carry my heart like a lead weight, knowing Ansel always meant for us to be more than friends—much more than my EOTWBFL—and now he's putting himself on the line for me.

We find Blue behind the cedar tree, removing Achilles's hood and untying his jess. She pumps her arm once and lets him fly when she sees us coming. "We'll be faster if he follows from the air."

"Where's Ansel sending us?" Blue asks.

I open the map. "Along the Lewis River up to the edge of the national forest through a place called Misty Woods that will take us to Lake Dowie, and then the Gemini Caves."

"What? No," Birdie says. "We can't. Nobody hikes near Misty Woods."

"Maybe that's the point."

"That's not what I mean. Daniel told me people die or get lost out there forever. Some people claim it's an urban legend, but the land is supposedly cursed with blood and ill-fated or something."

"It's where people meet their beginning and their end," Blue says. "The dead are just waiting to be found."

"That doesn't help at all," Birdie gripes.

That Blue-ism may or may not be true. If nothing else, our little sister consistently ups the ante on weird.

☆BOL☆
BUG-OUT LOCATION

THERE'S NO WAY for us to know what's happening, or if Rémy got the text messages and pictures I sent before Ansel smashed the burner. I check our shared phone for messages and see we're getting low on power. Rémy hasn't replied and soon we'll be out of range for cell service, completely on our own. I take a chance and turn the phone off to preserve its battery life in case we hit a spot in range closer to the lake.

We've been backpacking northeast for six hours to get to the first bug-out location near Lake Dowie. Based on the map's scale, we've traveled sixteen miles. There were a few state-supported trails free of detritus that made it easier to hike for parts of the trip, and we hauled ass through those sections. We haven't run into anyone. Most people know better than to hike at night in woods known for cougars and other predators. We didn't have much choice.

"You think they'll find us?" Blue asks.

"Not if Ansel can help it."

We cross over a tributary, holding hands because we're too lazy to take out trekking poles. I jump to the bank ahead of my sisters and pull them over one at a time. It doesn't take long for the trees to break open and show us the lake. Quiet and contemplative and full of its own secrets.

"We made it," Blue says, wriggling out of her pack.

She let Achilles fly along the way, keeping his bell on to keep track of him if he went out of sight, but she calls him down now and puts him inside his carrier for the night. You might not think holding a falcon weighing 2.2 pounds on your arm would be tiresome, but you'd be dead wrong. I dare anyone to keep their arm raised for five and a half hours without a falcon and see how long they last. Sixteen miles hiking through the woods and Blue didn't complain once. She never does.

The peaty smell of algae adds to the murkiness of the trees rotting along the lake's perimeter. Find water. That's the first rule. Ansel sent us straight to a site where we could wash up and get a drink. I use my flashlight to find a flat spot on the ground, free of rocks and sticks.

"We'll make camp here and dig up supplies in the morning."

"Are you kidding?" Birdie says. "I'm starving. Let's dig it up now. There has to be MREs in there, or some hardtack, at least."

"Hardtack? You're so hangry you'd dig holes at midnight to eat that sawdust?"

"It's better than nothing."

Not really. Hardtack is a thick, flavorless cracker made from flour, water, and salt. Baked. That's it. And like its name implies, it's hard as a freaking tack. I'm hungry, too. Don't get me wrong. We ate granola bars for dinner hours ago, but they don't sustain you on a big hike for long.

"No way am I digging holes and boiling water at midnight, Birdie. I'm just gonna drink my fill with my LifeStraw at the edge of the lake, take my Bivy out, and get some sleep."

"Me, too," Blue says. "I'm hungry, but I'd rather gulp down water and sleep for a few hours."

"Fine," Birdie gripes. She ransacks her own bag like messing up her gear is going to irk me. But I'm not the one who has to redistribute her pack's weight in the morning.

I pull out an anodized aluminum mug that can be used for food or coffee. It fits over the bottom of my widemouthed water bottle to save space, but I have to take everything apart and dump out a handful of small supplies tucked inside to get to my LifeStraw, which is the thing I need most. Every inch of an INCH gets used.

Camping near water is a smart way to get distance from predators. Plus, it makes meal prep and cleaning up easier. I put my headlamp on, and Blue and I trek to the edge of the lake. The smell of salmon rises off the water like a powerful cologne. Two varieties make their home here: kokanee and chinook. We don't have proper bait to catch one for breakfast, and I'm not about to look for maggots or fish eggs. There's an excellent chance a dead animal is decomposing in these woods, full of squirming white fly larvae, but chances are also high that animal didn't die of natural causes. Fish eggs are usually carried by sportsmen, not survivalists trying to make a quick escape. If there was a can of roe in my bag, I'd eat it. Maybe with some hardtack to keep it real, but the denial prepper nature prevails with my exhaustion.

Blue clings to the back of my all-weather jacket while I fill my water bottle, keeping me from slipping into the lake. I take an extra minute to splash some water on my grimy face before she pulls me back. We take turns like that, using the LifeStraw to slurp up filtered water, collecting some for Birdie. The syringe-style filter is a game changer and worth stockpiling since nobody wants to get sick from the ever-present bacteria in lakes. Streams are a little safer because they're moving and being naturally filtered. Even then, we don't drink from them without some kind of filtration or purifying tablets.

Blue puts her Bivy next to mine when we get back to Birdie, then places Achy's carrier above her head. I think she likes knowing I'm right beside her. To be honest, I take some comfort in that, too. That's what happens when you share a room with your sisters your entire life. Birdie drinks the water we brought her then sets up her Bivy ten feet away. I stomp over and pull it right up against mine on the opposite side.

"Four or five hours," I tell her, "then we'll get up and dig into the cache, okay? This *is* a survival situation. You can do this, yeah?"

"Yeah. Okay."

She doesn't look happy, but Birdie usually listens to reason when it matters. It's not like I expect a merit badge for successfully managing the first leg of the trip, but I did nail all three big Rs. Responsible, Reactive, and Ready, getting us here in one piece using only a topo map and a compass. I can sleep soundly on that. I hope she can, too.

Our INCH bags weigh in at around forty pounds each, so we don't carry tents. We have tarps, and our Bivy sacks are one-person mini tents that zip all the way around once you're inside them. And since we don't have any food animals might smell, I'm all for hunkering down in the open. We slide into our Bivys and zip up. It takes twenty minutes for my body heat to fill the space and make it cozy, but I still can't sleep. I'm as comfortable as a person can be on the ground, but all I can think about is the potential horrors inside the notebook I took from Dieter's lab. Birdie is already snoring. For someone who was so hungry she didn't want to sleep, she dropped like a fly. I would love to write a letter to Bucky, but I'm spent. My bones and muscles achy and weak. I'm about to close my eyes when the unzipping sound of Blue's Bivy catches my attention.

"Bucky wants us to come home," she says.

It's not the weirdest thing she's ever said.

"We are," I whisper. "We will."

"I know." She turns on her side and zips herself back into her cocoon.

Safe from harm for now.

LONG-TERM FOOD STORAGE

BLUE IS SHAKING me awake. My Bivy sack is unzipped, exposing my head and shoulders to the crisp morning air. I was dreaming about Bucky. He was walking through the woods with us yesterday, saying everything would be fine. *But the end is drawing near,* I told him. He looked me dead in the eye and said, *Yes. Finally.*

But what does that mean?

I slither out of the worm-like cocoon and quickly layer up. Birdie is on her knees digging up soft dirt with the mini shovel from her INCH. She's cursing under her breath, just under the threshold of flipping out.

"What's wrong?"

"*Wrong?*" she seethes. "There's nothing here. Ansel sent us to a spot with no supplies. No long-term food storage. Nothing."

"Maybe another hiker found it and thought it was left by a Trail Angel. Are you sure you're digging in the right spot?"

Birdie points sharply to a tree blazed with BB for *Burrow Boys,* only the first letter is flipped to resemble a butterfly, making it less obvious. It's a symbol I've seen on the stocks of rifles, ammo bags, tents. Caches are usually buried forty-five paces from a blaze. I'm eyeballing the distance, but it seems like the right spot.

"Did the ground look dug up and put back together?"

Birdie gives me a dirty look. Blue shakes her head, actually giving me an answer. I'm moved to take the shovel from Birdie and dig myself when her next stab hits pay dirt. She digs faster and unearths a cylindrical, speckle-gray plastic container with an X-marked screw top. The commercial tub is made for holding and preserving fifty-pound bags of dog food, but it's sturdy enough to keep in-ground for extended periods of time. For a second, I'm impressed with the ingenuity. I've seen caches made from PVC pipe, food storage buckets, and military-grade metal, but that's not the point. The point is the cache *is* here, as promised.

"You should give Ansel more credit," I say.

Birdie ignores me. Ever the one to think and do what she wants.

She unscrews the lid and sighs with relief. Out of the corner of my eye, I see Blue kiss Achilles's head before releasing him to hunt. The map is on top of a couple of MREs, also as promised. Underneath those we find three pull-tab cans of baked beans, a heavy-duty trash bag that can be used for shelter from the rain in a pinch, a hand-crank flashlight, a small folding knife, cordage, a cheap compass, a mini first aid kit, and matches in a waterproof container. We already have everything except the food, so that's all we should take, and only as much as we need to get us to the next location.

"Let's eat the beans and leave the rest. We know how to hunt and fish, we don't need to take the MREs. Plus, the beans can be eaten out of the cans fast without having to make a fire."

"Let's take *one*," Birdie says.

I don't argue such a small point. If having dehydrated egg scramble on hand makes Birdie feel better, I'll allow it. I pull it out and hand it over. Habit makes me look for the stockpile list so I can cross off what we took, despite knowing we aren't going back to The Nest.

I find a small field notebook at the bottom of the tub. Everything inside is listed. And I mean everything. Nothing has been crossed off, which means one of two things. Either Daniel never used this cache to stop and eat, opting to go straight to the second location, or he never made it here at all. I dig a pen out of my INCH and copy the lines from this map onto the one Ansel gave us. I return everything we don't need, screw the lid on, and lower it back into the hole, keeping my observations about the ground and LTFS to myself until we know for sure.

"Are you gonna eat?" Birdie is already halfway through her can of syrupy beans.

"In a minute." I bury the cache and stomp the dirt down with my boots. There's no denying the ground was disturbed this time. It will take weeks for it to tamp down and blend into the surrounding ground. Not days. *Weeks.*

I scarf down the sticky beans to catch up to my sisters. They're actually not bad cold, or maybe we're just too hungry to care. We pack the empty cans into our bags, following the leave-no-trace rule, and head out for the Gemini Caves.

Each of us carries something different in our INCH for hunting and making camp. I have a bow and folding saw, Blue has a slingshot and Achilles, and Birdie brought a bow and a machete. She's leading the way. Ten miles into the hike, we start ascending through an overgrown thicket. Birdie has to use her machete to bushwhack our way uphill. We have to stop periodically for her to hack away at brush or branches, which slows us down. After the third or fourth time, I can't help but pay attention to the water calling my name from inside my pack. "Hey! Let's stop for a few minutes. I need a drink."

"Fine," Blue says. "But only for a little while because the trees are too dense for me to call Achilles down."

Something must catch Birdie's eye down the embankment on our right because she drops her pack and scurries down the hill without her usual announcement. Slipping and sliding, grasping at thin tree trunks and branches.

"You're gonna break your neck!"

"What is it?" Blue hollers.

Birdie clambers sideways to get her footing and holds up a skivvy roll. It's how we pack our clothes to keep them compact, layering and rolling multiple items into tight bundles the size of homegrown eggplants.

She wastes no time untangling the bundle, and even from up on the hill we can see her chest heaving. "It's Daniel's."

"Stay here," I tell Blue, dropping my pack against a tree. I dig around its pockets for a long length of utility rope then tie a bowline knot around the thickest nearby tree trunk. I rappel down the embankment beside Birdie. There's more than just a skivvy roll. Birdie also found a slingshot and water bottle marked with the initials DD scattered among the forest rubble.

"Is this blood?" she screeches, thrusting the skivvy roll at me.

There are rust-colored smears on his clothes. Plants with clusters of bloodred berries are growing all over the surrounding terrain. It could be blood or could be from the plants. I don't want to completely dismiss her fear.

"Should we go all the way down?" she asks when I don't say anything.

She's really asking if I think Daniel slipped and fell and is hurt, or worse. She can't say it, and neither can I.

"I don't see anything else. Not his pack or a hat or a shoe or anything he would have been wearing. Maybe he was camped out and he had to leave fast because of a predatory animal. If he got hurt, his INCH would be here. Even if he got scraped up he could make it to the second location, don't you think?"

Birdie gives me a hesitant nod.

"We're almost there," I reassure her.

We use the rope to climb and Birdie does her best to cram Daniel's stuff into her pack. I don't care how much we've trained. Hiking thirty miles in twenty-four hours is hard as hell. It gives you plenty of time to think about the zombie apocalypse everyone believes is coming from watching TV, and how you've witnessed some real-life crazy shit, but also how hard it would be to decapitate zombies with a machete if you needed to stay alive. The only undead present at the moment are me, Birdie, and Blue.

Thirty minutes later, we're at the entrance to what Ansel called Misty Woods. We have another mile or so to go before we set up camp, and the farther in we go, the mistier it becomes, true to the place's name. I don't know if the land is truly ill-fated or cursed, but we do come upon a tree whose bark has grown around a rusty old bicycle, lifting it ten feet in the air with a tire poking out of each side of the trunk. I push away thoughts of what happened to its owner.

We walk a few more miles and it gets harder to deny something weird is going on out here. Two trees have yellow cordage wound between them like a game of Cat's Cradle. Eyes are painted on several trunks in white. Whatever Daniel told Birdie about this part of the forest could just as easily be a series of pranks by locals over the years to keep the urban legend alive. Rémy would love it so much more than our abandoned treehouse.

I take out our phone and see a text from Ansel that says, *Incoming.*

It was sent hours ago, making me think he replied back at the bunker and it got delayed by patchy cell reception. Now, I've got zero bars and can't message him back. That lack of connectivity makes Misty Woods more foreboding than anything man-made and strung between the trees.

TOBYISMS FOR ACTION
8
RIDING A THIN LINE

STAVROS LENT ME the Nikko's catering van once I explained my situation and promised I wouldn't let anyone else drive. Since Bash couldn't get out of his shifts at The Chicken Coop it's just me and Banquo. His golden-brown head is sticking out of the half-open window, tongue dangling like he's living his best life. That might have more to do with the cooler of food Stavros gave me. I forgot Banquo's kibble, so I've been feeding him chicken and lettuce from a couple of undressed Greek salads.

We've been driving north on I-5 for sixteen hours with only a couple of gas and bathroom breaks, but made it to Washington State physically unscathed. Emotionally, I'm a wreck. I learned you can haul ass in an empty van, but sixteen hours is still a shitload of time to think and invent scenarios. Like, how might things turn out, or what you might want to say to someone you haven't seen for eleven years, knowing you left them alone.

I never allowed myself to think my sisters were dead, because my bone-deep belief was so much stronger than my fear. And now I know why, even if I still need proof.

I don't know exactly where I'm going, but I'm not lost, either. I called Elkwood High this morning and tried to talk to the student liaison for the art competition my sister mentioned on the news. Rémy Lamar. They wouldn't bring him to the phone, but they did give him my message because he got in touch within a few hours.

One of the weirdest conversations of my life.

Imagine telling someone, "Hey, my name is Toby Ellis. I wanted to ask you about Honey Juniper, the girl who won the art competition. Yeah, I think she's one of my sisters who went missing eleven years ago. Her name is actually Katherina."

Then having that guy say, "Like the chick from *The Taming of the Shrew*?" And you have no idea how the fuck he'd know that, or why he's laughing because, yeah, that's exactly who she's named after, only you don't have time to ask for clarity because time has never been on your side.

It didn't take long for either of us to explain ourselves. Which included me telling Rémy to visit my social media pages for everything I've posted about the missing persons case. And him saying he's worried Honey and her chemistry teacher—who's probably FBI—might be mixed up in something dangerous.

My sisters are living with a bunch of doomsday preppers was the big takeaway and explains so much about our mom's drawings my head might explode. Rémy had tons of theories, but none substantiated by facts, so I left out anything having to do with Jonesy. The conversation ended with me telling him I was driving to up to Washington from San Diego, and him saying Honey and her sisters haven't come back to school since the news story aired, but he knows where they live.

Honey *and her sisters*.

Long story short, I'm about to meet a guy I don't know, but who has a vested interest in my sister, and we're going to pay her a visit together, because that might be less weird than me showing up alone.

Bash has strict instructions to give my projected whereabouts to Mom and Jonesy if I'm not back before them, or he gets an SOS text saying I ran into trouble with the van or something. After what Rémy told me, I'm more worried about *or something.*

I pull up in front of a coffee shop in Elkwood. The *only* coffee shop, sitting among other small businesses boasting handmade, locally sourced products. I was able to get some dog food for Banquo in the general store, which he's refusing to eat now that he's been spoiled with grilled chicken.

The guy walking up to the Nikko's catering van with a look of recognition is not how I pictured Rémy Lamar. After driving along winding country roads, I thought he'd be more backwoods or pro-gun-looking. Like the guy who sold me the dog food wearing a red T-shirt with white letters that read THE RIGHT OF THE PEOPLE TO KEEP AND BEAR ARMS SHALL NOT BE INFRINGED. Okay. Technically, that's accurate. We had a huge discussion about the intent of that amendment and how it got skewed when I took government in high school. Still, when I saw the shotgun mounted on the wall behind him, I thought it best to keep my liberal opinion to myself.

Rémy is dressed like something straight out of an REI cataloge. Beats by Dre slung around his neck, backpack, stainless steel water bottle attached to his belt by a carabiner, puffy vest, and thick flannel. He's carrying two large take-out coffees and a lot of confidence.

I roll down the driver's side window. "Are you Rémy?" The doubt in my voice is more obvious than I intended.

"Not what you were expecting?"

"I guess not."

"Because I'm black or because I'm so good-looking for these parts?" He smiles, and I notice he has a dimple high on his right cheek.

"A little of both," I answer honestly. "This area doesn't seem real diverse."

"Come on now, Washington State boasts a whopping three-point-six percent black demographic. The town I live in, point-twenty-eight percent. That's basically my family and two strangers."

I squint, trying to gauge his seriousness.

"I'm messing with you, man. My family's not that big."

Sarcasm is something I understand fluently—thanks to Bash—and can definitely appreciate for the rest of this road trip, because I'm pretty tired and more than a little tense. Rémy comes around to the passenger side of the van and puts the coffees on the roof. The minute he opens the door, Banquo is all over him, sniffing him out to decide if he's friend or foe before licking his chin.

Friend it is.

"Aww, hey buddy. He must smell my dog on me."

"What kind?"

"Pitbull. You know, keeping with the stereotype."

I don't say anything.

"I'm still messing with you," he says. Completely amused with himself. "We have a husky-beagle mix. She might be some other kind of hound. We don't know. She's tricolored with blue eyes and likes to bark at the microwave."

That makes me laugh, and I think this riding with a complete stranger thing might be okay. Rémy hands me a take-out cup before getting into the passenger seat. "I didn't know how you take your coffee, so I got it the same as mine. Cream and two sugars."

"That's perfect. I appreciate it."

"I have your sister's painting in my mom's minivan. I didn't know if you had room to bring it to her."

I look over my shoulder. "Tons of room."

"Okay. Cool. I'll go grab it."

He's back in minutes, carrying a large painting wrapped in brown paper. I unlock the doors and he slides it between the wall of the van and some stacked, hard-rubber catering

containers. Banquo nudges his hand to be petted as soon as
Rémy gets in the passenger seat.

"Do my sisters like dogs?" I figure after the warm-up, I can
lean into my purpose for being here.

"That's a good question. We didn't get that far. They have
a lot of animals. Chickens, goats. Honey's youngest sister has
a peregrine falcon. But she never talked about the farm animals like they were pets. I think it's the whole prepper thing.
They raise animals for food." He pulls a DSLR camera from
his backpack and fast-forwards through a bunch of pictures.

I'm still tripping over Cassandra having a pet falcon when
he hands the camera to me.

"Go forward."

The next picture is of Katherina, *Honey*, sitting on a stool
in front of an easel. The light is streaming across her back
from the windows and her expression matches the contented
look our mother gets while working. All worries fading to the
background as she moves brush against canvas. I click forward
and stop on a photo of a girl with chin-length hair and thick
bangs. She's staring across a crowded cafeteria with a look that
rides the line between aloof and ready for battle.

"Who's this?" I turn the camera to Rémy for confirmation,
even though I'm pretty sure I know.

"That's Birdie. She's the middle sister."

"Imogen," I tell him. "She was always a little ass-kicker."

Each click forward makes the lump in my throat expand.

"And this? Is this Cassandra?" I show Rémy the profile shot of
a girl with cobalt-blue hair, pressing a colored pencil to her cheek.

"Blue," he says.

"Her hair, yes. But what's her name?"

"Blue," he repeats emphatically.

I swallow the lump. Honey, Birdie, and Blue. "They have no
idea who they are," I tell Rémy.

"I beg to differ. Your sisters know exactly who they are. You
can trust me on that. You ready to start this rescue mission?"

"As soon as you tell me where to go."

"Right. Slight change of plans. While you were driving here, Honey texted me the photo of a map of where they're going. Plus some random pics of lab stuff. I tried to text her back but it went straight to voicemail, which makes me think they ran into some trouble."

"With the chemistry teacher who might be an FBI agent?"

"Or other people in her prepper group."

"So we're *not* going to their house?"

"Correct." Rémy pulls a paper map out of his bag. "We're going to the Gemini Caves. She said that's where they're bugging out. I bought the same map Honey sent me and marked up the fastest route."

"What's bugging out?"

"It's like camping for preppers, but also hiding. From someone or something. She didn't give me any details. She just wrote, *Bugging out then JIC.* I had to look that up. It's a prepper acronym that means *Just In Case.* I didn't take that to mean anything good."

"Okay. Where to?"

"Take a left out of the parking lot until you see the signs for 503 North. We take that for about an hour then hike in for about another hour or two tops, depending on terrain, so maybe three or four miles."

I drive out of the parking lot and hang a left, trying to make sense of things like bugging out and prepper acronyms.

"I wouldn't have a clue how to read that map," I tell Rémy. Making small talk keeps the lump from forming in my throat again. "The only reason I know which direction is west is because I can usually spot the coast."

"My grandfather was a park ranger. We did a lot of camping, hiking, fishing."

I hear the shutter of his camera and realize he just took a pic of my profile. That's the least of my concerns, so I let it go.

"We have the ocean and beaches in San Diego. People camp

there, but for woods like this we'd have to drive pretty far north."

"That's gonna be culture shock for your sisters."

All this time, I never thought how they might take the news. He goes into a story about seeing my sister get shot with an arrow by someone named Annalise and all I can think is who the hell took them and how did they end up in Elkwood, Washington? We've been right under their noses this whole time. Why couldn't Jonesy find them?

I have more questions than answers by the time he tells me to pull off on the side of a long, winding road without much of a shoulder. By now, Rémy knows the whole story about their real mom and what happened the night they vanished into thin air.

He's gone through the stack of photos I took from the shoebox at home and compared them to the age-progression photos, and had his mind blown, just like me. Believing my sisters' lives revolve around preparing for the end of the world as we know it, the zombie apocalypse or whatever, like those guys that came into Nikko's, is a serious kick in the teeth.

I pop the gear shift into Park. "What do we do now?"

"We hike. I think you should leave your dog in the van. Once we find them, we can come back for him."

"Okay. I'll let him out to go to the bathroom. He can usually hold it for about seven hours if I'm at work."

We get out and I open the back for Banquo. He leaps into the grass to do his business right away.

"You're wearing Vans." Rémy looks me over. "And a hoodie."

"It's the official uniform of San Diegans. I didn't know we'd be hiking."

He unwinds the plaid scarf around his neck. "Take this. It'll help keep you warm and stop mosquitos. Your sisters will undoubtedly have extra clothes and supplies. Prepared is kind of their thing."

Banquo walks up to me, tail wagging. I load him back into

the van, check that he has food and water accessible, and pat his head. "You stay, boy."

It's chilly enough to see our breath when we exit the van. I wrap Rémy's dark green plaid scarf around my neck and tuck the ends inside my sweatshirt. I'm grateful for his company and knowledge, because these woods are deep and dense. I'd be lost inside of an hour without him.

Rémy tips his head toward the tops of trees when we hear the screech of a falcon. A raptor is soaring in circles. A few miles away if I had to guess.

"That's a good sign." Rémy scans the map then the sky. "He could be Blue's. He's definitely in the right spot. You ready?"

I follow him into the woods, between tall trees. "I've been waiting years for this."

✢ SFWF ✢

SHELTER, FIRE, WATER, FOOD

WE FOLLOW THE new set of coordinates to the bug-out location on Ansel's map. We don't have to home in on the exact spot, because Daniel's belongings are scattered all over the campsite.

Birdie's face lights up like a Roman candle. "He's still here. You were right, Honey. All of this is Daniel's."

She's so happy, she's failing to assess the situation. SFWF. Daniel's gear doesn't look like it's been touched in days. His tarp is hung for shelter, and there's a fire ring made of large stones, but I'd say he made one or two fires tops unless he was shoveling out ash every morning. I pick through his belongings while Birdie calls his name through the trees. There's no clues to the food he's been eating. No small fish or bird bones, no seeds, just a pile of dried greens. Something he may have foraged. I don't spot his bow, knife, or rifle, either. Nothing Daniel would use to hunt. I guess it's conceivable that he used traps and snares, but I remember seeing his bow attached to his INCH bag.

"Daniel!" Birdie calls again. Her voice boomerangs back from the trees. "I bet he went down to the river for water. We could drop our stuff and go find him, but maybe we should wait. We don't want to sneak up on him and freak him out."

"He's not here," Blue says.

"Why would you say that?" Birdie squawks.

Blue doesn't answer. But I know why.

Every inch of this camp feels abandoned, and Blue is usually right. I take off my pack and set it under Daniel's tarp in case it rains. There are bears in these woods, and hundred-pound cougars that will eat a human if they're hungry enough. The area is called Gemini Caves, so I'm assuming there's at least two. I look around, pick up my bow, and sling the quiver across my back.

"Fine," Birdie huffs loudly. "We can just set up and wait for him to get back." She drags her INCH bag next to mine under Daniel's tarp.

"Stop talking," I tell her. "I think that's the mouth of a cave." I nock an arrow on my bow and use it to point fifty feet past Daniel's campsite. I push fear aside and amble toward the five-foot opening. It sits at the bottom of a massive stone ledge, the moss-covered exterior, surrounded by piles of deadfall fighting to regenerate itself back into existence. My sisters rush behind me.

"Why are you moving so slow?" Birdie whispers. "You're freaking me out."

"Shh. Predators." I look at Birdie sideways and see she's holding her bow.

My first fear is that a cougar or bear made its home in this cave and Daniel didn't see it when he made camp. It's dusk. A bear would have come out when it heard noises. A cougar would wait until nightfall. That's my second fear. A predator still inside the cave, lying in wait. I scan the ground for tracks. Something was dragged over here but all the footprints look human, made by hiking boots of various sizes and tread. Enter my third and worst fear. The coalition caught up to Daniel.

Don't be inside. Don't be inside. Don't be inside.

We move in formation to the mouth of the cave. My heart is pounding so hard I can hear the blood rushing through my veins above the background of our heavy breathing. This is the type of situation we've been trained to face. And yet, when presented with the unknown, my body reacts with free will.

Blue tugs my arm, pulling me closer, "I have a flashlight," into my ear.

"Come around to the side and shine your light into the opening." I whisper back. "Try your best to stay out of the way in case a cougar or bear charges us."

Blue shines three hundred lumens into the cave and I see him first. Sitting lifeless against a jagged, metamorphic wall, his head and upper body tipped to one side. Daniel's entire belly is soaked in dark crimson blood. A handful of two-foot spears are scattered around him, like he spent his last hours whittling weapons to defend himself.

When I hang my head and lower my bow, Birdie rips the flashlight out of Blue's hand and rushes past us into the cave.

My whole body goes numb when she screams, "No!"

"He's dead," Blue says quietly. "Here, but not here."

I nod and sobs build at the back of my throat as I listen to Birdie cry his name then, "No, no, no," over and over. Hoping her denial might turn back time. She lets out a scream filled with so much anguish the cave walls may start to shake and weep alongside her.

I hold my breath and count to ten, twenty, sixty, before I dare to enter the cave. Birdie is kneeling on the cold ground, rocking back and forth, alternating between groaning and weeping. Her outpouring of grief slices through me, tearing out my heart with vicious teeth. I lean forward and put a hand on her shoulder.

"Don't touch me!" she seethes, her face nearly unrecognizable. "Didn't I say we should look for him?"

I deserve the accusation she's leveling. "You did. But Ansel—"

"*Ansel?* Ansel sent him here and now he's dead."

"Tell me what you want to do. Whatever it is, Birdie. I'm so sorry."

I'm at a loss. Our training prepared us for how to behave in emergency situations, but not this. Not the death of a friend.

"We can build a stretcher and carry him out," Blue offers. "If we use the map to find the main road maybe we can thumb a ride into town and get help."

My ears perk up with the roar of a dirt bike. "Someone's coming."

Whoever it is, they're coming in fast. Maybe help was already on the way. I peek out and see Ansel coming to a sideways stop.

Birdie steps out of the cave and sails an arrow right past his head.

Ansel raises his hands. "Hold your fire. I'm here to help."

"Daniel is *dead!*" she shoots back. "Did you double-cross him? You were the only family he had left. He trusted you with his *life*. That's what he told us."

His face screws up in disbelief, despite my sister's distraught appearance. "What are you talking about? I switched out the maps for this location so he'd be safe, so nobody could find him."

"He's not *safe*," she spits. "He's not even breathing."

Ansel stares at me, confused and blinking.

"It's true," I tell him.

He walks past us to the cave, and I put an arm out to stop Birdie from following. She stomps away, sits on a felled tree, and folds her tearstained face into her lap. I'm so glad Blue follows and sits on the log beside her, because I can't. I'm not finished with what's inside that cave. But I watch Blue put an arm around her shoulders and see Birdie start to shake and sob again until Blue says, "Let's make a fire. It's getting dark. Daniel would want us to, don't you think?"

I wait until Birdie nods before I walk my deflated heart back inside the cave. I'm trying to be strong, but when I see Ansel sitting against the wall next to his best friend, legs straight out in front, my whole body shakes. I've seen them sit side by side like this dozens of times around the compound, during lunch at school. Only this time Ansel is racked with grief. He wipes under his nose as my shadow passes over him, and I fight back stinging tears.

"He's wearing my watch," he says, "but I never gave it to him. I thought I lost it in the woods when I was dragging your sister away from the bunker."

"The same night Birdie and I came home covered in dirt?"

He looks up, long lashes soaking wet, before he swipes a hand across his face. He picks up one of the spears next to Daniel. "These are for Punji traps. The tips are usually coated with venom or poison."

There's a long beat. Ansel's face goes blank.

I know the look. I've seen it on my own face on bad mirror days. "Do you remember anything else from that night?"

"Nothing. Jesus Christ. Did *I* do this?" He covers his mouth in horror.

"You weren't alone," I tell him. "Blue saw Annalise use Devil's Breath on all of us. She told us to get in your truck and we did. I remember you jumping in front of Birdie and me, but then nothing afterward."

He shakes his head in denial.

I have to ask the unthinkable. The thing that will wreck him the most. "What if Annalise asked you where to find Daniel that night?"

"I don't know. I can't remember." His shoulders shake from holding back the anguish he feels, knowing, suspecting he may have had a hand in Daniel's death. And the worst conclusion of all. We may have been here once before. Ansel, Birdie, and me.

"It's okay." I crouch and put a hand on his leg. "We'll figure it out. What *do* you remember?"

"Nothing from that night." He glances at Daniel and puts his head against the cave wall, closing his eyes for a long beat. "Our assignment during the SERE training was to ambush

Daniel on his hike and make it harder for him to get to his bug-out location. The problem was I had already given him a different map. The two locales aren't that far off. The original bug-out location is on the other side of the river. Connor was getting agitated when we couldn't find him and decided to track Daniel through the woods. When we caught up to him, I stayed farther back, watching. Letting Mateo and Connor mess with him a little, knowing I'd intervene if needed." He goes quiet and the temperature drops ten degrees while I wait for a confession.

"Did it go too far?"

"No. We took some of his stuff. I made a big show of pushing Daniel down an embankment so I could tell him to bolt once I . . ." He pushes his cheek with his fingertips and gnaws the skin inside. "Once I used Devil's Breath to get them to make camp. It worked. Daniel got away, and I was able to get back to meet you at the treehouse."

"You knew about the Devil's Breath this whole time."

I hold my temper, stem the flow of conclusions. Because he needs to tell me the truth as much as I need to hear it. No matter how much that pains either of us.

"I knew they were making it, but I didn't figure out Annalise used it during the civilian interaction training mission until you said I looked right at you. I don't remember seeing you. I remember more than Birdie, but I never . . . I only carried Devil's Breath on me that one time because I knew I'd need it to help Daniel get away if we caught up to him. There's something to be said about the size of the dose."

"Two times," I correct him. "You used it on Connor at the bunker. It's deadly in large doses, isn't it?"

His eyes go to Daniel's belly. "That wound isn't from poisoned spears. That was a gunshot or a knife."

"Does it make a difference? It doesn't change the outcome."

"A gun is business. A knife is personal."

"We have to tell someone, Ansel. This is murder."

"We have a bigger problem," he says. "Annalise is on her way here."

To kill us. To kill us. To kill us.

My blood runs cold. I stand and look past the mouth of the cave. "Do you think she'll come alone?"

"Depends on the directive. She could be with our mother, at the very least. Connor and Mateo, at worst. Daniel narced about our stockpiles of ammunition and weapons to Whitlock and look what happened."

"Where *is* Whitlock? Your father had his phone in the lab. I called and it rang inside the bunker, but we couldn't find it." If we're dealing in confessions, I have to fess up on my end, too.

"What you really mean is you couldn't find *Whitlock*. It's not as easy to dispatch of a federal officer."

"He's *dead?*" A cold shiver passes over me.

"He wasn't last time I checked."

"We have to tell my sisters."

"Tell us what?" We didn't notice Birdie until a sketchbook lands on the ground between us with a thud. "Daniel left a note. We found that inside his INCH. It's written in cipher."

I swoop down and pick up the sketchbook before Ansel can grab it. The note is on a random page between sketches of the treehouse and barn, written in Daniel's crooked handwriting. The lines are shakier than his origami note, like he was struggling to get his thoughts down before... I can't think it. I explain our cipher to Ansel without going into detail then read the note out loud.

It's not your fault.
You didn't know what you were doing.

It was Annalise. She made you dig your own graves.
Tell Birdie I love her.
Then tell her to run.

"The Devil's Breath," Blue says. "Annalise must have dragged you out here to dig your own graves, like Daniel said. Maybe you literally did that, and Daniel was here, and she . . ."

She doesn't finish her assessment. None of us do. It's unspeakable.

But the reality is if I had shown up to the last meeting, I may have met the same fate.

⁺⁺ WROL ⁺⁺

WITHOUT
RULE OF LAW

ANSEL STANDS AND hoists his bug-out bag onto his shoulder. "Daniel's right. We need to get you out of here."

"I'm not leaving him here." Birdie points at Daniel without looking at his lifeless body. "If Annalise is coming here looking for a fight, we'll give her one."

"She's right, too," I tell Ansel. "We have no idea where they are, but we have to get out of these woods one way or another. Preferably alive. Grab your best weapon. Blue, slingshot. Birdie, bow."

Blue's eyes shoot to the sky in search of Achilles. I see him soaring in a circle. Safe. That makes one of us for now. "I also have a monkey fist," Blue says.

"That'll work." The heavy knotted ball of paracord can deliver a powerful blow, if needed.

"I brought this." Ansel lifts the side of his jacket and pulls out a 9mm tactical pistol. The Burrow's standard-issue six-round Glock 43.

"You are *not* gonna kill someone. Nobody else is dying because of Annalise."

"If you had to, Honey. If your life depended on it. You

or one of them. Would you take the shot?" he asks me. "Because whoever walks out of here tells the story of what happened."

Our training. The drills. Hand-to-hand combat. Everything that brought us to this moment, and the thing my memory resurrects is the moment I asked Rémy if he would kill an animal if he needed to eat. But deer and wild turkey are different than human life.

"I don't know," I answer honestly. "Not if there was another option. Death doesn't feel like a suitable punishment."

"Then I'll need to be extra confident about my aim." Ansel looks at me, unblinking, and I know he'll do his best to defend us, even if that means taking someone else's life. My heart hurts over what Dieter might have turned his son into, given enough time. A mindless robot in direct opposition to the person Ansel is at his core. Someone loyal to what's right in the end, sensitive, and true to his word.

We step outside the cave with only the light from the fire to guide us back to the camp Daniel made.

"It's gonna be okay," I tell them. "We'll stick together."

"No matter what," Birdie adds.

The first arrow comes out of nowhere within seconds. Sailing right past my face into oblivion. I yell, "Scatter." My survival instincts taking charge.

Big R Reactive.

We disperse in opposite directions, grabbing our bags as we bolt for the trees to take cover. My heart is swelling in my chest, making it hard to breathe.

Together but separated. Together but separated. Together but separated.

"Come out of hiding," Annalise shouts. "We just want to talk about what happened."

I make my first threat assessments to get a handle on the situation and keep count of how many people we're up against.

THREAT ASSESSMENT:
ANNALISE ACKERMAN | 5'8" STRONG BUILD |
NONEXISTENT SOCIAL GROUP | UNTRUSTING
MOST LIKELY TO: pierce anyone who crosses her in the
heart with an arrow.
LEAST LIKELY TO: feel remorse after same said assault.
1/10 WOULD IMPEDE GROUP SURVIVAL IN AN
EMERGENCY SITUATION.
CASUALTY POTENTIAL: low

I nock one of my arrows and pull it tight, aiming for Annalise's voice in the dark. I'll shoot her if I need to protect myself or anyone else.

"Like you talked to Daniel?" Birdie replies, fifty feet from
my left.

I hear the whoosh of an arrow.

"You bitch," Annalise seethes and steps out of hiding. I can
see her in the light from the fire, her bow primed. "You're as
dead as Daniel."

Connor runs out from the woods behind Annalise and
heads for the trees where Birdie is hiding, and I don't know
where to point my arrow.

I hear the unmistakable shock of Ansel pulling back the
slide on his Glock. He's somewhere in the trees on my right. I
know he'll shoot. I've seen Ansel in training. He never misses.
He fires a warning shot at the ground by Connor's feet, making him rear up.

Connor turns to seek Annalise's instruction, and I wonder
if he's being manipulated by Devil's Breath or simply brain-
washed.

THREAT ASSESSMENT:
CONNOR CLARKE | 6'1" STRONG BUILD |
NONEXISTENT SOCIAL GROUP | TRUSTING

MOST LIKELY TO: follow orders due to need to please authority.
LEAST LIKELY TO: think and make judgement calls for himself.
3/10 WOULD IMPEDE GROUP SURVIVAL IN AN EMERGENCY SITUATION.
CASUALTY POTENTIAL: low

"Guns. That's how you want to do this." Magda makes her presence known. "If I'm not mistaken, Ansel, you're on the wrong side of things."

THREAT ASSESSMENT:
MAGDA ACKERMAN | 5'8" STRONG BUILD |
NONEXISTENT SOCIAL GROUP | UNTRUSTING
MOST LIKELY TO: fool you with initial kindness.
LEAST LIKELY TO: reserve loyalty for anyone outside her immediate family.
1/10 WOULD IMPEDE GROUP SURVIVAL IN AN EMERGENCY SITUATION.
CASUALTY POTENTIAL: low

Ansel steps out from the trees and points the Glock at his mother.

I use their conflict to get closer to Annalise, watching all points for who's at my three, six, and nine. Annalise is at my twelve. A clean shoulder shot would be enough to slow her down, if not stop her completely.

"You're an Ackerman," Magda berates her son.

"I'm a survivalist," he counters. "And you're behaving within our own coalition without rule of law. Drop your weapon."

Magda gives a calculated grin and juts her chin. Two seconds later, Ansel is tackled from the side by Connor and pinned. "You're not in charge yet, son."

Connor holds him down with one hand and punches him hard in the face. Ansel grunts and rolls Connor so they're scuffling in the dirt, each trying to get the other in a sleeper hold. Ansel flips Connor onto his back and delivers a blinding headbutt to his face. Connor's nose gushes blood, but Ansel doesn't give him a second to recover before slamming him in the side of the head with his gun. Connor moans, holding his ear, and Ansel stands and shoots him in the knee. Point-blank. His scream of pain fills the air and echoes through the trees in time with Ansel swinging the gun long-arm at his mother, delivering the same shot before she has a chance to pierce him with an arrow. Magda drops, face contorted by pain, but crawls for her bow. Annalise's war cry rings with pure rage. I'm about to let my own arrow fly to stop her from killing her brother when Blue jets out from hiding, swinging the monkey fist like a lasso. She lands a hard strike to the back of Annalise's head before fleeing behind another tree.

This is the shit hitting the fan.

Annalise grunts and brings her hand to the back of her head, spinning to find her attacker. She recovers and lets another arrow fly in Blue's direction. Missing, or we'd hear Blue's involuntary cry of pain. I take my shot, piercing Annalise's shoulder. When she folds forward, Birdie rushes from the woods and delivers a fierce sidekick that knocks her down. She pounces on her and starts throwing punches that land hard with snapping thuds. Magda crawls forward to rip Birdie off her daughter. Out of nowhere, she's pegged in the face with an egg-sized rock that could have only come from Blue's slingshot. Magda reels and Blue pegs her again. Blood spurts out of Magda's mouth and runs down her chin. The look in her eyes is murderous as she advances in the direction of her attacker, bow drawn. I let loose another arrow, piercing her leg above her wounded knee. Two down.

Someone sneaks up behind me. A fourth Burrower lying in wait. I land a hard elbow strike, spin, and pin them to the ground before doing a double take. I've never seen this person before. He's in a hoodie and jeans and definitely *not* one of the Burrow Boys.

"I wasn't trying to sneak up on you," he says, choking and wriggling. "Let me go. I don't understand what's happening."

"Who the hell are *you?*"

"It's me. Bucky."

"What the fuck did you say?" I ease up just enough to slam him back down again, my adrenaline going haywire.

"I said it's me. Bucky. Your brother."

Ansel rushes over and grabs a fistful of my jacket, pulling me to my feet. "Get up. Get off him. Move. Rémy Lamar showed up and said that guy's your brother."

"*What?*" I'm a live wire, wriggling out of Ansel's grasp. "We don't have a brother."

I use the light of the full moon to stare at the guy Rémy brought with him. He looks so much like the imaginary Bucky from my mind, only older and without buckteeth.

"Honey! Snap out of it," Ansel shouts.

A new awareness strikes me like a stick across my back. Rémy *is here? Now?*

The guy claiming to be Bucky stands and Ansel grabs him by the shirt and pushes him toward thicker forest. "Run behind those trees with Rémy and stay there. Don't move."

He listens without question, making a mad dash to safety only to drop into a hole with a surprised yelp. He lets out an anguished groan that tells me he got injured in the fall.

I start to run toward him, and Ansel catches me by the arm. "Leave him. He's safer out of sight. Find some rope. I'll cover you at your six and nine."

"Go ahead." Annalise's smug voice comes through clenched teeth.

I freeze and look back. Birdie has Annalise's arms pinned under her knees. Gerber knife hovering, ready to plunge it into Annalise's chest.

"Do it," she says to Birdie. "Then live the rest of your life knowing you watched me kill your boyfriend while you stood there like a zombie, powerless to do anything to help."

Birdie roars in rage and lifts the knife higher, her hand shaking.

"Fuck!" Ansel runs hard and dives sideways, knocking my sister off Annalise. Birdie scurries to her feet and charges forward again. Ansel catches her and holds her back by her arms. "Stop. You're not a murderer, Birdie."

"I might be. I want to kill her. I hate her," Birdie yells, inconsolably.

"Look at me," Ansel says. She refuses and he shakes her shoulder. "Birdie, look at me. Please." Her chest is heaving. Her breaths coming hard and fast through her nose. "You are *not* a murderer."

My sister whimpers, fists still balled in outrage; she must be feeling the loss of Daniel all over again. There's a slip of silence before Ansel says, "*You,* on the other hand."

"Shoot me then," Annalise spits back.

"Don't tempt me."

I race to my INCH to get the rope while Ansel handles Birdie and his sister. I trust him. I've always trusted him. Blue bolts past me before I reach my bag, bringing Ansel her cordage. That's when I see Connor, facedown, wrists and ankles trussed, and I know what Ansel has in mind.

It doesn't take us long to tie all three of them against separate trees, stripping them of weapons. They're bleeding and wounded, but not fatally.

"Are we gonna leave them out here for animals to find?" Birdie says.

"They are the animals," I tell her.

"Can I come out now?" I'd know that strident voice anywhere.

"Yes. Come out."

I wait for him to show himself outside the cover of trees,

and lace into him. Just not exactly in the way he's expecting. "What the hell are you doing out here?" I grab him by his puffy vest and throw my arms around him in a hug. "You could have been hurt."

"Killed, actually," Birdie says.

"Your brother saw you on TV and called the school and left a message for me. We followed the map you sent from the burner. I thought you'd be glad to see us. I wasn't expecting the melee."

My eyes flick to Ansel when Rémy mentions the burner.

"*Our brother?*" Birdie guffaws. "Did Blue hit you in the head with her monkey fist or something?"

"Who did you bring out here with you?" I ask. "We don't have a brother."

"I think you do, actually."

I stare at him blankly, taking in his flashlight and headlamp. Ever the prepared one. "No. That's not possible."

"Then who's inside this hole?" Blue asks from somewhere in the near distance.

I search for her cobalt hair in the darkness and find her at the edge of the trees. We rush to the hole that swallowed Bucky during the fight.

"It was covered with brush," Blue says, pulling up long conifer branches. "It could have been any one of us."

"It should be all of you," Annalise says. "Thanks for shooting that rattlesnake, by the way. The venom came in handy."

I raise my bow and sink an arrow into the tree an inch above her head. Rémy shines his flashlight in the hole, and I peer down at the boy calling himself Bucky. The first thing I see is the Punji spear piercing his thigh. "Are you okay? Can you talk?"

He looks up at me wide-eyed and nods, but he has the woozy look of someone on the brink of passing out from pain or shock.

Birdie shakes my arm. "Did you hear what Annalise said?

What if Daniel was whittling the spears *clean* before he died and missed one?"

My heart leaps into my throat. "Ansel, he'll die. The venom."

Without thinking, Bucky does the dumbest thing imaginable. He grits his teeth and pulls the spear out of his leg with a groan, never considering whether it hit a major artery.

My yelp of "No!" comes too late.

Ansel jumps into the hole and lifts Bucky up so we can grab him under the shoulders and pull him out and onto his back. Blood is seeping through the leg of his jeans.

"Keep his head above the wound in case she isn't lying about the venom."

"Use the scarf to tie it off," Rémy says.

Ansel climbs out of the hole. "It's too thick." He peels off his jacket, removes both his shirts, and tears the fabric of his cotton undershirt into strips. He wraps Bucky's leg, trying not to make a tourniquet. Tight is the usual impulse, but preppers know if the spear was tainted with venom that's the wrong move.

"Oh my god," Birdie says. "*Look* at him."

I understand her meaning instantly. Even with his cheeks scraped from the fall and smeared with dirt, I see it. Saw it early when I had him pinned to the ground. He has our same nose with the flattened bump, our big brown eyes, and puffy lips. I shake my head to stay focused on the immediate threat to his life, but my heart is fluttering like a butterfly trapped in a box.

Bucky is real. Bucky is real. Bucky is real.

"Rémy, how far is the road?" I ask. "Can I run for help?"

"No." Bucky grabs my forearm. "We have to stick together. No matter what."

My gasp is echoed by Birdie and Blue. The skin on my arm rises in goose bumps from Bucky's hand all the way to my scalp.

"How?" I whisper. A one-word question weighed down by a million more.

"The antivenom is on the compound," Magda says snidely behind us, taking away Bucky's chance to answer me. "You'll never make it in time."

"She's right. It's thirty miles away," Birdie says. "We'll never hike there fast enough, even if we make a stretcher."

"Phran," Bucky gasps.

"You have a plan? You can barely move."

"He drove us here in a catering *van*," Rémy says. "It's three miles west."

"That's our best bet," Ansel says, buttoning his flannel. "I can carry him, but it would be easier if we still had some rope to strap him onto my back."

"I brought rope," Rémy says. "I didn't know what the hike out here might be like, so I brought some rappelling gear."

To be honest, the Boy Scout answer wasn't what I was expecting, but I'm glad he came prepared. All my assessments of Rémy Lamar have been wrong.

"We can't leave Daniel here," Birdie wails. The thought has her verging on hysterics.

"Where is he?" Rémy asks. "I can go get him."

"He's in the cave." I shake my head, eyes downcast.

"Oh." His eyes bulge then flick to Annalise with "Oh" again. Understanding what could have happened to me in the woods when Annalise let her arrow fly, grazing my arm when she could have pierced my heart. Rémy looks at my middle sister. "Birdie, I know you don't know me. But my dad was a cop. You guys shouldn't move the body. It's better if we send someone back for him."

"What about us?" Annalise says. "You can't just leave us here."

"We'll send someone for you, too," I say. "Maybe not who you want, but someone."

Rémy takes Ansel's bug-out bag and his own backpack by the top handle. My sisters and I wrap the rope under Bucky's butt and over Ansel's shoulders like a backpack. Then we gather our INCH bags and hike out of the woods, fast as humanly possible.

It takes us an hour to get to the catering van, but feels like ten when nobody knows what to say. Not me to Bucky, who seems like he's losing the fight with pain. Not my sisters, who are as confused as me. Not Rémy, who just saw enough to explain who I am apart from what everyone assumes at school. More than what they assume, if not worse.

A tan dog with a black muzzle starts barking wildly from the passenger seat of the van when we reach the road. My eyes shoot to Blue, because he's the dog of her dreams, and I finally understand how prophetic her *opinions* have been all along.

"I always wanted a dog," she says.

"You have one," Bucky chokes out.

"Banjo."

"Banquo," Bucky says. "Close enough."

Blue smiles and calls down her falcon. Achilles sails and descends, landing on her gloveless arm more gently than I thought capable.

Bucky is hanging on through the pain, looking wide-eyed at Blue's falcon and a little worse for wear. He asks Rémy to help him get his phone and keys.

"I'll drive," I tell them.

Rémy hands me the keys without question and takes the passenger seat without contest from Birdie, who's helping Ansel make a soft place for Bucky with the Bivy sacks in the back of the van. Blue climbs inside with her falcon and raises her arm to a stack of rubberized containers. Once Achilles finds a secure place for himself, I pull onto the road and take off, driving way over the speed limit and trying not to swerve. For Bucky, and for Achy, who should be in a carrier.

"You know," Rémy starts, "if someone told me I'd be speeding down a winding road someday in a catering van with the Juniper sisters, a trained falcon, a dog named after a Shakespeare character, the son of a prepper cult gone rogue, and the long-lost Juniper brother that got infected with rattlesnake venom, I would have laughed in their face and said they were on drugs."

"And then you got to know me?" I offer.

"*Know* is a weak way to put it," he says.

I give him a sideways glance, because that's true for me, too.

"Our last name is Ellis," Bucky says.

Ellis. I repeat it a few times in my head before tuning in to the one-sided conversation Bucky is having on the phone.

"I found them," he says. "Yes. All three of them." There's obvious strain in his voice. He's getting worse.

There's a long pause.

"They're fine. I don't really know. A lot happened. What do you mean you already knew?"

Another pause.

"You're *in Washington State? With Mom?* Who's Tom Lockey?"

I glance over my shoulder when Bucky says *with Mom.*

Our real mom.

Ansel says, "That's Whitlock's real name."

I go completely bug-eyed, even though that wasn't the thing that initially tripped me up. "Who is he talking to?"

Bucky puts the phone to his chest and answers, "Jonesy. Detective Blake Jones. He's been looking for you for years. He's on his way. Another agent named Tom Lockey called him after he figured out the cases were connected." His voice grows weaker with each word. "He's already on his way to your compound."

I swerve the van and Rémy grabs the wheel from the passenger seat.

"Just focus on driving. Your sisters and Ansel can handle what's happening in the back."

"Okay. Everything is gonna be fine," I say, glancing at myself in the rearview.

I listen in on Bucky telling Detective Blake Jones about the Punji spear, that we're on our way, and to send an ambulance.

"Tell him to send two," Birdie says. She meets my eyes in the rearview and I recognize her fierce look. She's out for blood.

I speed south on route 503, listening to Rémy tell us how they followed the map I sent. When they saw Blue's falcon, they took it as a sign. It's so strange to hear him tell me that Bucky, who isn't our imaginary friend at all but our brother, Toby, reached out to him after he saw the news coverage of the art competition. The same story that was going to get us thrown out of The Nest is what reunited us. Bucky chimes in, telling us about false leads, letting Rémy fill in blanks whenever the pain becomes too much. Bucky is fighting more discomfort with every mile, but hell-bent on showing us age-progression photos. The roads are winding, and I need to watch where I'm going or we'll crash and never get there.

THREAT ASSESSMENT:
TOBY ELLIS | 5'10" AVERAGE BUILD | OPEN SOCIAL
GROUP | UNTRUSTING
MOST LIKELY TO: fight for what he believes is the truth.
LEAST LIKELY TO: give up after being told no.
8/10 WOULD IMPEDE GROUP SURVIVAL IN AN
EMERGENCY SITUATION.
CASUALTY POTENTIAL: medium

"Katherina," he says weakly. "That's your real name. Katherina Ellis. Birdie is Imogen and Blue is Cassandra."

"Those are Shakespearean names," I say.

"Yes. Our mom used to paint modern Shakespearean scenes."

I swerve the van again. "You don't mean *Evie* Ellis, the painter?"

I adjust the rearview and see him clutching his leg, nodding, and my heart goes berserk and pumps out truths.

This is why we're artists. This is why we're artists. This is why we're artists.

And then Bucky says something to my sisters about living on Juniper Road in San Diego, and the big twisted trees in front of our house, tripping a memory I always believed was nothing more than a vivid dream.

The familiar brown station wagon with wooden panels pulls up and I worry we're in trouble for not following directions.

"What are you doing out here alone, honey? You'll catch your death dressed like that. Your sister looks like a little lost bird walking about without proper shoes, and you," she addresses our youngest sister directly, "your lips are turning blue. Get in and I'll take you home and make you all some hot chocolate to warm you up."

It is wet and cold as a bathtub filled with ice outside. Colder than a Popsicle straight from the freezer that sticks to your tongue because you can't wait for a lick. I didn't know what else to do when the electricity blinked out on us. I urge my sisters to pile into the warm back seat and we huddle together, wet and tired from walking. And, to tell the truth, a little lost because the heavy rain changed the way everything looks.

Hanging from the rearview mirror straight ahead is a green paper tree, cut out of thick cardboard. I am old enough at six to sound out the white letters printed across the front. J-U-N-I-P-E-R. A pretty word that fills the car with a rose-like woodsy scent when the heat starts blasting, a smell that is much stronger than the two big trees we left behind. This is better. Much better, I think, and close my eyes and inhale.

Alice.

Alice *Juniper?*

✦✦ TEOTWAWKI ✦✦

THE END OF THE WORLD AS WE KNOW IT

I SPEED DOWN the dirt road to our homestead, growing anxious as I steal glances at Rémy. He would have found The Nest if he kept following the map. I'm not sure what I'm expecting, but his face isn't registering shock or surprise. I suppose, to the Outsider, it might seem like the land of milk and honey. A small family farm in a place full of family farms. But he knows it's more than that and still he's not judging us. Ever the open-minded one. The Burrow, on the other hand, would probably bowl an extra pin like him over with its obstacle courses, shooting targets, and bunkers.

"Stay in the van," I tell him once we're parked. "I don't know what we're walking into and everyone here has guns."

"My dad was a cop."

"They're not cops," Ansel says, backing me up. "Honey's right. Stay here."

Beads of sweat are peppering Bucky's upper lip as he hands Rémy his phone. "In case Jonesy calls. Use the GPS to give him our exact location if needed."

"What do I do with the falcon?" Rémy asks.

Blue opens the back of the van. "Nothing. He knows what to do."

Achilles flutters to the open van doors and takes for the sky.

Rémy's face is pure amazement, but there's no time for us to stare in awe. We need to get Bucky inside fast.

Ansel and I take him under his shoulders and help him toward the house. We catch snippets of an argument between Alice and Dieter inside. Random words stick out in the heated conversation. *Fate. Rogue behavior. Annalise. Magda. Missing. Feds. Prison.* I pause and Ansel pulls me forward. There's no time to hesitate from fear of Dieter's wrath.

When Alice sees us bursting into the kitchen she sucks in a breath. "You're alive. My god, I thought—"

The shock in her voice so clear there's no denying the truth. We were never meant to return to The Nest, for *Mother* or anyone else. Not that she's spared any blame. Annalise and Magda meant to kill us, either on Dieter's orders or their own volition.

"You thought *what?*" I snarl. "That we'd be dead? You trained us to be soldiers, to protect what's ours, and that's exactly what we did. Blue, clear the table."

Dieter turns hard eyes on Ansel. "What is this? Where's your sister?"

"Tied to a tree in the woods like the animal you turned her into. Mother and Connor are there, too."

"You left them defenseless?"

"*Defenseless?* They tried to kill us. They're lucky we didn't return the favor."

Blue sweeps jars and mugs to the floor, letting them crash and shatter.

Ansel and I hoist Bucky onto the table. He leans back on his elbows, trying to gauge the full situation, but his arms are trembling like they might give out. "You have to help him. The spike he pulled out of his leg was coated with rattlesnake venom."

Alice is in a state of near shock. "Who is this?" she asks, staring at Bucky's face, even though every syllable is tainted with knowing.

I want to torture her, let her puzzle it out, but there's no time.

"He's our brother. Bucky."

She shakes her head in denial.

"Yes. Toby Ellis. Remember *him?*"

"Toby," she whispers. "How?"

"Forget him. He's an Outsider," Dieter barks and stomps forward, wrenching his son's arm. "Where exactly did you leave them?"

"I don't remember," Ansel says. "There seems to be a lot of that going around."

Dieter delivers a sharp backhand to Ansel's nearly healed face that makes me cringe. Ansel shakes it off and squares his shoulders, looking past his father. Past me. Tipping his chin at something in the next room.

I don't understand until I hear a gun click and Birdie steps beside me. "She said *help him.*"

I didn't clock my middle sister's whereabouts while we were helping Bucky onto the table. And now, she's aiming the gun Alice keeps behind the painting in her bedroom right at her.

Dieter reaches for his Glock, and my sister turns the gun on him without blinking. "Don't even think about it."

"You've never shot anything bigger than a wild turkey in your life."

"You underestimated me. That's good." Birdie's words match her ice-cold eyes.

Dieter reaches for the Citizens Band Radio against better judgement and Birdie shoots the wall next to him, missing by a couple of inches. The deafening explosion makes everyone duck. My ears are ringing when I stand back up, my pride giving way to fear when I realize Birdie might be angry enough over Daniel's death to kill him.

"Next time I won't miss," she says.

"Birdie," Ansel says her name like a plea.

"Don't *Birdie* me," she says. "That's not even my name."

My eyes flick reflexively to Alice, and she dips her head.

"Easy does it," Dieter says, with his hands up. He reaches slowly for his pocket and pulls out a vial of white powder. "If I drop this, we're all dead, so put the gun down."

Birdie narrows her eyes. "That could be anything. I'll take my chances. For Daniel."

I yell, "Don't!" right as Blue pushes Birdie's arm down from the opposite side. Stopping our sister from pulling the trigger on something she'll regret forever. The bullet meant for Dieter's head hits him in the ribs. Alice leaps forward as he loses his grip on the vial, catching it in a closed fist before it hits the ground.

"You're bigger than a turkey," Birdie says. "Shall we go for round two and see who bags the biggest prize *this* time?"

Dieter is moaning, teeth clenched tight as he reaches for his gun again. Blood pooling between the fingers of his left hand.

"Birdie," I plead. "Give me the gun. I won't lose you over this asshole."

Her sight is locked on Dieter. I'm so terrified she'll take a kill shot, I try a different tactic.

"Ansel, take your father's gun and get him a towel from under the sink to hold against the wound until the authorities get here."

He moves in for Dieter's Glock, and his father clamps a hand around his arm. "I'm your father."

"You're my father and everything you're doing is wrong." Ansel pries himself free of Dieter's grasp in more ways than one.

"I never meant to hurt you girls," Alice says nervously. "I saved you. There was a blackout. You were walking down the street in the rain alone. You could have been killed, hit by a car like my own husband and daughter. Your mother was so selfish. Always asking me to help out. Give you girls rides. Make sure you had a neighbor to go to if you needed. I even put the stitches in your brother's lip. *He* left you alone. You were so precious, and Evie was always working on her ridiculous paintings. She didn't deserve you."

"So you *stole* us?" The biting accusation leaks out of me like acid. "You had *no right*. Our lives were not yours to take and control." My voice and hands are shaking now. "You knew we had a brother we called Bucky, and denied it when we made him into our imaginary friend."

Alice looks at Blue first, then Birdie, but not me. She won't dare look at me.

"Her real name is Allison Murphy not Alice. A lice. A lie. Malice," Bucky whispers before sinking limply into the table.

"The poison," Blue yells. "Help him. Please."

Alice sifts through cabinets for supplies and brings out a small vial and syringe. "We can't know if this antidote was made from the same species that poisoned him, but we'll try."

Alice cuts off the bandages tied around Bucky's leg with scissors then slices his jeans open around the wound. Blood pools from the puncture, dark and ominous, filling the hole left by the spear. Alice douses it with wound wash and Bucky hisses, arching his back with the sting. I grit my teeth and watch.

"It didn't hit an artery. He'll be okay. Do you feel nauseous? Is your face or leg numb?" She grabs his wrist and takes his pulse.

"Maybe a little. I can't tell. Everything is sort of numb right now."

"He might just be in traumatic shock," Alice says to me.

"We all are," I snap back. "But we can't take any chances."

She takes a deep breath, letting go of what her training is telling her to do. Trusting me without the benefit of being able to pull labs and wait for results, like they would in a hospital emergency room. She picks up the syringe and administers the antivenom via push injection into his thigh. "That's all I have in the house. He'll need several more if it was in fact coated with venom."

She injects his leg with lidocaine and keeps working, cleaning and bandaging the wound. "This could have been much worse," she tells him.

"I'm not sure it could," he says, voice cracking. "The last eleven years were pretty rough. I'd say this is the easiest part."

Alice hangs her head and says, "I'm sorry," so quietly I almost miss it.

"The feds are here," Blue announces, interrupting whatever clemency Alice was hoping to get from Bucky.

I whip my head toward the window where Blue is letting the curtain fall.

The authorities waste no time barging into the house, armed and covering for each other. Ansel moves fast and takes the gun from Birdie, slipping it into a kitchen drawer, before somebody sees it in her hand. A look of understanding passes between us, but I'm worried that his father's actions won't bode well for him.

An officer asks us to step outside while they talk to Alice and Dieter. Bucky is up now, limping but able to walk on his own. I look back at the woman we've been calling Mother for eleven years, knowing she probably saved his life. Emotions rush through me in an unexpected flood of contradictions. Gratitude and resentment. Satisfaction and regret. Love and hate.

"Farewell, bastard!" Blue says to Dieter as we walk through the door.

There's a hitch in Bucky's unsteady step. "That's from *Troilus and Cressida*. You're named for Cassandra in that play."

"The things we don't know will become the things we knew all along."

Now *that's* the most accurate thing the littlest *weird* has ever said.

"Spoken like your namesake," Bucky tells her.

They must have found Mr. Whitlock in a bunker because they're putting him into an ambulance when we get outside.

Even from this distance I can see the bloody lip and black eye he got from one or more of Dieter's conscripted ruffians. I yell his undercover name before the EMTs can whisk him away, and he turns toward my voice. I place one hand on my chest, trying to say thank you with all my heart. He nods back with his familiar knowing grin, and my eyes prick at the corners against my will. I don't know if I'll ever speak to him again, but I'll try. He deserves my thanks and apologies.

A tall, dark-haired agent with graying temples rushes up to us.

"Jonesy." Our brother breathes with palpable relief.

He hugs Bucky tight, and I step back to give them space. "You should have waited for us," Jonesy reprimands.

"Is that your way of saying I was right?"

"I guess it is."

"Well, tell it to my sisters. I don't think their day-to-day protocol lines up with wait for help." Bucky pulls each of us forward. "This is Honey." He takes a few steps to the left. "And Birdie."

"And I'm Blue." She smiles at Jonesy. "I have a pet falcon. If he can't come, I'm not going, either."

"I think we can make arrangements to ensure he's delivered to San Diego. Can you get him into a carrier?"

"Yes, only I don't have it anymore. It's in the woods somewhere. But I can call him down to his mew. That's secure."

"Perfect. I can't wait to meet him. But right now, there's someone I'd like to reacquaint you with," Jonesy says.

I hold my breath as he opens a car door. A woman who looks like a version of my future self steps out and steals the air from my lungs. Evie Ellis, the artist whose work I was inexplicably drawn to during a slide show at school.

"That's our mom," Bucky says, as if we wouldn't recognize ourselves in her eyes.

When Evie Ellis lays those same familial eyes on *us*, her

knees buckle like she might faint, and Jonesy takes her hand. Her steps are cautious, shoulders hunching as she pulls her cardigan tighter. She starts shaking more with each step.

Blue runs forward and throws herself into the arms of a woman I barely remember, making her break into sobs. "Your hair," she says, laughing through her tears. "It's cobalt blue."

"Is there any color better than blue?" our youngest sister asks.

"No. Not really."

"I'm Honey," I tell her and shrug. "I guess . . . Katherina."

"I know," she says. "I'd recognize you anywhere. You've always had the same protective look in your eyes."

I grin but swallow hard, knowing her recognition of me is the good mirror version. There's so much we need to catch up on about each other.

Birdie is holding back, chewing her nails and fighting tears. Her heart has broken so many times in the last twenty-four hours, it's a miracle she's still standing.

Blue takes our mom, our real mom, by the hand and leads her forward. "This is Birdie. Bucky said you named her Imogen, after someone in *Cymbeline*. She's had a really rough day."

"Hi Birdie," our mom says. "I've been looking for you for a long time."

Birdie does something I never thought I'd see in a million years. She flings herself into our real mom's arms and sobs and sobs and sobs.

"It's okay, honey," she tells her. The term of affection makes her shift her eyes to mine again. A gentle smile plays on her lips, knowing *I'm Honey,* or I was. And suddenly we're all blubbering messes trying to understand how we came to be in this place.

Finally, she hugs Bucky so tight I think she might break his spine.

"*So foul and fair a day I have not seen,*" he tells her.

If I remember correctly from my English class, that's a line from *Macbeth*. His wife was power hungry and together they tried to take down anyone who threatened their power. Wife, daughter, either way it sounds about right.

"Do you girls want to get your things while I talk to your friend Ansel?" Jonesy asks.

I wipe my eyes with the back of a bloody, dirt-covered hand and look for my EOTWBFL. Ansel is leaning up against an unmarked car, talking to a federal agent.

"He helped save us," I tell Jonesy. "Ansel is a good person. He deserves leniency and help. He's not like his family."

"I'll do everything I can," he says. "I promise."

Bucky said Jonesy never gave up looking for us, so his promise warrants my trust.

My sisters and I head inside to our bedroom and retrieve the physical things we want to take away from this life. Birdie's comics, Blue's needlepoint. Mentally, everything about The Nest will always be with us.

I hand them their bug-out bags. "I don't know what else to take."

"Anything and nothing," Birdie says. "Most of it's a lie."

"Most, but not all," I say, gathering the notebooks that hold all the letters I've written to Bucky over the years.

Birdie smiles. I haven't seen her do that in a long time. "Are you gonna let him read those?"

"Maybe. Are you gonna let him see your comics?"

"Of course. I made him a cape-wearing hero." She turns and lays her hand on Blue's shoulder, stopping our little from collecting her needlepoint supplies momentarily. "You were right. Bucky didn't save us, but he *was* there."

"I know," Blue says. "I told Honey he wanted us to come home."

She did. In the woods before we fell asleep. The wonders of Blue never cease.

We look around the room one last time. Birdie sighs and goes to the window, searching the trees for the freckled boy who will never visit her in the middle of the night again, except in dreams.

"It's time," I tell them. "We never belonged here."

"That is factually correct," Blue says.

We walk down the creaky steps, past the living room, where Birdie threw cushions around looking for the EDC that kickstarted this whole ordeal. We march through the wooden screen door, letting it slap behind us like a gavel issuing freedom.

"What are those?" our real mom asks.

"Some of our art." Blue shows her the needlepoint she's been working on and Birdie's comics.

Starring Bucky Beaverman: Lead Anti-Hero.

"What about *your* art, Honey?" she asks.

"I don't have anything here. My last painting is at the school."

"The one that was on the news?" Bucky asks.

I nod and kick at the dirt with the toe of my boot, wishing I'd taken the painting with me.

"Rémy brought it. It's wrapped up in the back of the catering van."

Bucky limps to the van and opens the double doors. At the same time, Rémy steps out of the passenger seat, lifts his camera, and takes my picture.

"Have I ever mentioned you're relentless with that thing?"

"Damn straight, I'm relentless." He shows me the photo in the viewfinder.

I'm filthy, a cut on my forehead is crusting over, but I look strong. Resolute.

"I'm surprised you're still here. Most people would have cut and run."

"I'm not most people."

No, he isn't. He never was. "Thank you," I tell him, and mean it so much my chest aches.

"You don't have to thank me, Honey. It sounds too much like goodbye."

"You deserve my thanks, Rémy, so be quiet for once and let me get this out. Thank you for following your own suspicions and looking into what was happening. And for taking all those photos of my sisters and me and seeing what I couldn't. And most of all, thank you for wanting to be my friend and sticking around even when I tried to push you away."

"Still in the friend zone, huh? After all that?"

"Boyfriend, I guess. If the world as we knew it didn't just end."

"Does that mean I can finally kiss you?"

"Do your worst, Petruchio."

Rémy slips a hand behind my head. I didn't know how much I wanted this to happen until his lips press down on mine. I'm clinging to him, returning his kiss like I may never see him again. I don't want to let him go.

We pull apart, and he touches my cheek so softly I can't help but lean into his hand. "This doesn't have to be goodbye."

"It's not," I tell him. "I'll write to you."

"Okay. But we can also text and video message. You have friends here. Brian. Shawna. I bet they'd love to hear from you. And let's not forget email. That old faithful form of communication."

"I know, but I'm still gonna write you letters, on paper, because that's what I do."

"A Dear John letter?"

"No. Never. That would mean a true goodbye, and I'll never forget everything you've done for us."

He looks away, which is un-Rémy-like, and I follow his eyes.

Dieter and Allison Murphy are being taken into custody. She stares back at us, face sagging with hurt. All I feel is numb. This place she made us call home was all a lie, like every other town or city. Lies piled on top of lies. Now we know why we were always moving. Not to find the safest place, but because we were running. Hiding until Alice's paranoia grew and she made us part of The Nest, thinking they would protect us.

Strangely, in the end, we were perfectly prepared for own survival. And nothing that happens going forward will ever refute the fact that for a long time we *were* the Juniper sisters.

⁑ YOYO ⁑

YOU'RE ON YOUR OWN

JONESY AND OUR real mother let us walk away from The Nest on foot at my request. I want to walk out of this life the same way we came into it, on foot, with nothing more than the clothes on our backs. Only this time, we're not on our own.

We only get a mile before it starts sprinkling. Within minutes, it's raining harder, but not soaking us through. Jonesy pulls up and asks if we want to hop into the back seat of his car, or maybe the catering van Rémy is driving, following us out of this place. I think Jonesy's pressing concern is more for Bucky than us. My sisters and I could walk to San Diego if needed, but he's injured and limping.

To my surprise, Bucky shakes his head. "Not yet."

"I'll pick you up in another mile," Jonesy says. "Before you hit the main road."

"Stick together," our real mom says from the passenger seat, making tears form in my eyes that are camouflaged by the rain on my cheeks.

For a brief moment, I can't help wonder if we should have taken the ride. Not from Jonesy, but way back when Allison Murphy pulled up alongside us, familiar and safe, and changed the course of our lives forever.

"Do you think we'll be able to keep the names we have?" Blue asks, pulling a swatch of cobalt hair between her lips.

"I think if that's what you want, sure. As long as she lets me legally change my name to Bucky."

"If she hasn't yet, I doubt it's gonna happen," Blue says.

"Hold on," I say and freeze, tugging on Bucky's arm to stop him. "This means I'm not the oldest. I'm a middle child."

"Welcome to invisible world," Birdie says. "I'm not sure how I feel about the name Imogen. I'll have to look it up."

"At least you're not named after a literal *shrew*," I say.

"*Hey*, our mom loves that play," Bucky says, "Katherina is a badass. And Imogen is mentioned in a lot of stories, not just Shakespeare."

"I'm still the baby. No matter what my name is," Blue says.

"We know, Blue. We know."

"If it makes you three feel better, Sir Toby Belch was a drunk in *Twelfth Night*," Bucky tells us.

I dig around my bug-out bag for the hundred milliliter whiskey bottle I keep inside to help start fires, clean wounds, or trade in an out-of-supplies emergency. "Here. You earned this."

"I could have used this a few hours ago." He doesn't hesitate to take a swig.

I know he means the drink, but I should have thought to use the alcohol to wash his wound. It only goes to prove that maybe I'm not always big R Ready, even though I tried.

"I wonder what it will be like to have normal lives," Birdie says.

"I don't know about *normal*," Bucky tells her. "We're all artists."

"I think she means we won't be the weird sisters anymore."

"Well, you were born a renegade, Imogen Birdie. And you, Cassandra Blue, a soothsayer, and you, Katherina Honey, a protective peacemaker. Weird is good. It's in your DNA."

"Since I'm not the oldest anymore, I won't have to worry about everyone all the time. I can pass that torch to you."

"I'm happy to take it. I've been searching for the light from that beacon for a long time."

"I just hope you live up to the Bucky you planted in our heads," Birdie says. "It's a pretty tall order."

"I promise to spend the rest of my life trying. Until the crack of doom."

A look passes between my sisters and me that Bucky can't fully understand. But I think he will, in time.

Dear Rémy,

This may come as a shock, but I miss the sound of your camera shutter. San Diego is full of smiling tourists taking sunny photos. I must turn my head a hundred times a week to the whirring click, thinking you'll be behind the lens. I'm sure you're grinning right now. Normally, I'd tell you to stop, but I'll allow it since there's only one you. I'm not sure anyone else will ever view me the same way. Through a glass lens or otherwise. But rest assured, we're still the weird ones. The missing sisters who were found by fluke and circumstance years later thanks to two boys who didn't know how to give up. I don't know all the details of what happened once we left the compound, but Dieter was on the FBI's wanted list for amassing weapons. He's being investigated as a domestic terrorist, because of what they found in his lab. Ansel made a bargain and is working toward becoming an emancipated minor. Once that goes through, we can reach out and offer him a landing pad. I guess that makes three boys that didn't know how to give up. His sister and mother were charged with the murder of Daniel Dobbs. I haven't asked for all the details. I will, soon, but right now everybody is insisting we take it easy. They still don't understand what it was like for us to train as preppers and survivalists. Maybe they never will. All I know for now is that we haven't fully adjusted to the San Diego chill vibe. We still carry EDCs full of supplies for TEOTWAWKI, only we call them backpacks now like everyone else. Bucky is slowly reading every letter I wrote him when I thought he was just our imaginary friend from childhood. I still look at him and can't believe he's real. Especially when he takes us out at night and shows us the street art messages he painted on our behalf, railing at the police for not finding us. To be fair, Jonesy is amazing, and our mom, our real mom, is the greatest artist ever. Alice used to tell us making art was the work of dilettantes. That it served no purpose. She was wrong about a lot of things. Making art is never a frivolity. For us, it was lifesaving. I hope you look at the painting I left with you and remember everything about me and my sisters without regret. I can't wait for you to visit this summer. Before you ask, yes, that means you can kiss me. You better. The world could end at any moment. More soon.

Love,

Honey

ACKNOWLEDGMENTS

The idea for this story came from my own paranoia about the fate of the world we currently live in, and what might come to pass if we don't stand together against erroneous political extremism and greed. With that said, enormous thanks to everyone at Tor Teen for believing in this book, especially my whip-smart editor, Bess Cozby (lover of all things doomsday prepper), who worked tirelessly on this book from day one. We made it all the way to publication by sticking together, no matter what.

THREAT ASSESSMENT:
BESS COZBY | 5'7" AVERAGE—STRONG BUILD | CLOSED
SOCIAL GROUP | TRUSTING
MOST LIKELY TO: fight for a story she loves until it stands proudly on a shelf.
LEAST LIKELY TO: overlook even the smallest of plot holes.
0/10 WOULD IMPEDE (PUBLISHING) SURVIVAL.
CASUALTY POTENTIAL: low

Dana Lédlová (aka @myokard_) is the superstar illustrator responsible for the incredible cover artwork. It is everything I could have hoped for and more. Lesley Worrell, jacket designer,

Peter Lutjen, art director, and Nicola Ferguson, designer, for Tor Teen deserve so many thanks, in addition to gold medals, for accepting my feedback on the cover and interior pages. You smashed it. I'm head over heels for the design of this book.

Huge, heartfelt thanks to my agents, Suzie Townsend and Devin Ross, for believing in me and this story. I'm doubly lucky to be represented by such strong, intelligent women. Believe me when I say, you're the stuff (publishing) survival teams are made from.

THREAT ASSESSMENT:
SUZIE TOWNSEND | 5'3" PETITE—STRONG BUILD | CLOSED SOCIAL GROUP | TRUSTING
MOST LIKELY TO: take an author and show them dreams can come true.
LEAST LIKELY TO: let me sit on my laurels when there are words to be written.
0/10 WOULD IMPEDE (PUBLISHING) SURVIVAL.
CASUALTY POTENTIAL: low

THREAT ASSESSMENT:
DEVIN ROSS | 5'6" AVERAGE—STRONG BUILD | CLOSED SOCIAL GROUP | TRUSTING
MOST LIKELY TO: let me run with an idea until we've exhausted every angle.
LEAST LIKELY TO: focus and stick to the goal, even when the going gets tough.
0/10 WOULD IMPEDE (PUBLISHING) SURVIVAL.
CASUALTY POTENTIAL: low

My deepest gratitude to Mia Roman and Veronica Grijalva at New Leaf Literary & Media for working on foreign rights for this book, and Pouya Shahbazian and Mariah Chappell for working on film rights. Dani Segelbaum, thanks for scheduling all the things and giving me expert London travel tips.

Thank you to my friends, family, and fellow authors for your encouragement, support, humor, and camaraderie. I'm especially grateful to my writing confidants, Robin Reul and Nikki Katz, for always taking my phone calls, texts, and emails, and for clapping enthusiastically for everything large and small. Thank you to my longtime bestie, Holly Maguire, for allowing me the use of her maiden name for the art teacher in this story. Your artistic abilities and innate creativity will forever be an inspiration to me. Much appreciation goes to my sisters, Nia (oldest) and Angie (middle), for unwittingly teaching me everything I needed to know about sister sibling dynamics. I'm still the youngest and the *weirdest.*

I'm eternally grateful to the booksellers, readers, and bloggers who give of their time to share and promote the books they love. I see you. Thanks for making my cover reveal a smashing success and for always supporting me and my books. When the SHTF we will save all the books together. Christy Hayes, your enthusiasm for my books is unparalleled. I can't thank you enough for shouting about my books from every metaphorical rooftop imaginable. You are more than an avid fan; you are a treasured friend. In case you're unaware, the rest of us are expecting you to lead us through the end of days.

Last, but never least, to my husband, Michael, for insisting this prepper idea was a good one. Not a day goes by that you don't encourage and inspire me. Thank you for reading every word of this book and taking long walks with me to discuss the plot. You are my true EOTWBFL.